A QUESTION OF ALLEGIANCE

Peter Vollmer

First published by Endeavour Press Ltd in 2017.

Foreward

Nambia, or South West Africa as it was known before becoming independent in 1989, was initially an Imperial German colony until after the First World War, when it was mandated to South Africa. The South African government ruled the country as if it were a fifth province applying the same rules and treating the inhabitants, both black and white, as if they were citizens of South Africa. The Germans who owned farms from before the First World War all retained ownership and the fact that the government had changed had little impact on the daily lives of the German colonists. Also, there was little or no effort on the part of the South African government to interfere in any way with German traditions, schooling etc. As applied to the country, it allowed the inherent German character to continue without interference, thus most German colonists' children continued their academic studies in Germany as opposed to South Africa.

This is a work of fiction.

However, to some degree, it is based partially on the lives of my grandfather and his children. Members of my family did serve in the German Luftwaffe and Wehrmacht. Their sons and daughters did study in Germany and used a house owned by my grandfather in Kiel, Germany, as the family's base. Nevertheless, South West Africa was always considered to be home. My father bore the scars of many Mensur duels and he was a member of a 'Studentenbund' and as a scholar did attend a naval gymnasium in Kiel. The farm, it a background to part of the story, was managed by my uncle for many years. It was there I spent many of my school holidays. Armed with a Mauser .22 rifle, I would, at the faintest light of dawn, hunt guinea-fowl along the banks of the Lever River that flows through the farm.

While this is a work of fiction, I have embellished many stories based upon the lives of my family. My father and uncle experienced some of the incidents herein and I found them unique thus compelling me to write this novel.

It would like to thank my agent, Thomas Cull, who is a source of continuous encouragement and who has helped promote my books; to my proof editor David Baclaski for his indispensable expertise, and to my close, loyal friend and neighbour, George Carter, who continues to partner me in golf notwithstanding my meager contribution to our scores and who has steadfastly worked his way through my first draft manuscripts, pointing out the abuse to which I subject the English language.

Finally, I'd like to thank Endeavour Press, who have taken a risk of possible financial loss but still print my books.

CHAPTER ONE

My brother had the floor. That he'd already had a good few beers was not that apparent, his bearing still that of confidence and aplomb. He stood amongst those seated around him and glowered at his audience with a hint of disdain.

"Really, you are insane if you think you can launch a Nazi political movement in this country – the country mandated to South Africa. Don't for a moment believe that the South African government wouldn't intervene." He paused as if to allow this tit-bit of information to sink in. He frowned. "Be sensible! This is no longer a German colony! Have you forgotten? We lost the damn war! You also need to realise that Germany is thousands of miles away, and finally, we Germans don't even represent a majority in the country!" He said his voice booming through the beer hall loud enough to be heard over the constant murmur of the crowd.

While my brother had found some support, this was insignificant seen against the reaction from the pro-Nazis that dominated the crowd. Howls of protest followed. My brother waved his arm at the crowd in disgusted dismissal and resumed his seat, his face registering his disappointment at their response.

If I hadn't realised the seriousness of the situation, I would have found it amusing. The atmosphere amongst the guests and patrons in the beer hall had degenerated to a point where it seemed the attendees were losing their decorum. The mood was now ugly and confrontational and I thought an outbreak of violence a distinct possibility. The chairman hammered his wooden gavel on the stout mahogany table on the raised dais where he sat, shouting for order; the two deputies seated on each side of him also lending their voices to his shouts. Most of the crowd ignored them. Their voices rose, confronting those they disagreed with in heated argument, gesticulating with raised fists and accompanied by loud vocal threats of violence. There were a number of reasons for this, one of which was the vast amount of beer that had been consumed since the men had started congregating in this converted gymnasium from about five that afternoon.

This seemed to be another new German development – holding political meetings in beer halls. Originally, this was supposed to have been a two-hour meeting, the idea being that all could get home to supper and their wives and girlfriends at a reasonable hour. The meeting now approached its fourth hour.

In Germany, Adolf Hitler's Nazi party was in control of the country. This was the reason for the heated debate. A few were realists and realised that there was little they could do to influence matters, and being 6,000 miles away there was no role Germany could play in its previous colonies. However, many saw Adolf Hitler as the saviour of Germany who would return it to its previous greatness and assumed the return of the old Imperial German colonies to this new Germany to be a matter of course. A few did not agree. After all, this was South West Africa, administered by the South African government as a mandate, and therefore subject to South African law.

My father remained an ardent supporter of the now defunct era of German imperialism, which had ended nineteen years ago. The walls of the living and dining rooms of our house in the Bismarckstraße in Windhoek were still adorned with portraits of Otto von Bismarck, Hindenburg, Kaiser Wilhem II, and other famous German aristocrats. Similarly, the walls of my father's study were hung with paintings of the German Imperial Navy's battle line; battleships, cruisers, frigates and destroyers which had taken part in WWI's greatest naval battle, the Battle of Jutland. This had rubbed off on his children and we saw Hitler as an opponent to our German way of life, although this did not signify that our love for our home country had waned; at heart, we remained ardent and loyal Germans. None of us supported the Nazis. We saw them as a bunch of opportunists and near renegades. Of course, we had followed our father's thinking on this topic as he had his father's – we remained fervent imperialists.

My father was a man of vision. He considered his children to be citizens of both South Africa and Germany, and insisted that we be able to converse fluently in the languages of both countries and that our education have some South African flavour. To that end, my brother and I were sent as boarders to private schools in South Africa, my brother to Grey College in Bloemfontein and I to Christian Brothers College in Kimberley. We both matriculated speaking fluent English. Of course, we spoke German and were able to converse and write in Afrikaans as well. Subsequent to that, we were still required to obtain the German Hochschule Abitur certificate, the minimum German scholastic qualification, which would ensure our acceptance in German universities.

Over the last few months, my elder brother George and his friends had on occasion visited these recently introduced bi-weekly Nazi gatherings at the Schulabend. Of late, these had become more frequent and presented an opportunity for celebration. The beer was sold at discounted prices to attract the patrons, a ploy which many could not ignore.

As the evening progressed and with beer flowing, my brother and his friends began to heckle the more outspoken of the Nazi-supporting fraternity which mainly seemed to consist of members the blue-collar German populace in the town and its surrounds.

My brother had insisted that I accompany them. At first, this was fun, the exchanges still infused with some banter, but when the topic changed to that of the Jewish question, and the Nazi sympathizers now even adorning the beerhall's walls with swastika flags and even singing the Nazi Party anthem song, the Horst-Wessel-Lied, in defiance of the South African government, the scene rapidly became ugly.

My father owned a number of farms and invested heavily in the karakul industry. He had a contract with a karakul-pelt buyer, a foremost member of the local Jewish community and with whom he had done business for many years. Actually, the man was considered a member of my father's small circle of best friends. The man had been a German infantry soldier during the First World War, leaving Germany with his family for South West Africa immediately thereafter. The fact that the man was Jewish was never an issue – he was considered, first and foremost, to be a German.

In time, my father also purchased vast quantities of appliances, machinery, wholesale goods, and haberdashery to stock his general dealer stores from the Jewish merchants in the town as well as importing these from specific Jewish businesses in Germany.

Many Jews in the country had become house friends of German families, some often visiting each other at home. Their children even attended the same German schools as had the Lutheran and Catholic children of the German families. These were not visits of convenience intended to boost business relationships but rather that of true friendship.

This custom went back to before World War I. Some of their children had become friends of my brother and me.

My brother was not about to allow these Nazi upstarts, as he called them, to defame those that our family considered friends for no other reason than that they practised a different religion. Already the odd remark had been heard that we, the Aschenborn family, consorted with the Jews. The Jewish community controlled a few industries: the karakul pelt-buying industry, which was a major industry in the country, numerous wholesale hardware outlets, trade agencies, property development companies, and the printing industry. The Jews in the community were an integral part of the economy.

"Come on, George," I said to my brother taking him by the arm. "It's time to leave. This mob is spoiling for a fight, but no, still you insist on antagonising them!"

My brother jerked his arm away. "I'm not leaving. I'm not about to let a bunch of uneducated arseholes subscribe to me what ideology I should follow and who my friends should be. Fuck them!" he hissed, his eyes ablaze.

I had seen that the elderly in the crowd had begun to make a discreet withdrawal, having determined the mood of the mass of people in the hall and having realised where this was going. Already there were shouts of 'Hang the Jews!' 'Hang the traitors' and 'Hang the Jewish ass-lickers!' Although this was shouted with a laugh and more in jest, still the underlying implications were clear. A feeling of xenophobia tainted the atmosphere.

I then heard a shout: "Let's fuck up the Aschenborns and their Jew-loving friends." This was accompanied by a roar from the crowd and others shouting 'Catch them!'

The Aschenborns – that was us! It definitely was time to leave.

Fortunately we were standing close to the main entrance. I didn't wait, I grabbed my brother and ignoring his protestations and attempts to fight me off, I dragged him outside. Some of his friends followed. They began streaming from the hall. There were howls from my brother and his friends at our rapid departure, but I wasn't waiting. I don't think they were opposed to making a rapid departure as some inside the beer hall already had that crazed look in their eyes. I bundled him into the Studebaker President saloon, my father's pride and joy, switched on the ignition, and depressed the starter button. The straight eight-cylinder engine started and we exited the parking lot, leaving a dust cloud of sand and gravel. A number of his friends clambered aboard. By then, my brother and his friends had perceived the hostile attitude of the Nazi-sympathisers in the hall and we were glad to have left.

"We should have taken them on! Especially that idiot Emersohn. God, he looks stupid in his bloody Nazi uniform and that ridiculous Sam Brown belt. Christ! And those bloody stupid 'Sieg Heil' salutes! I wanted to kick the arsehole in the nuts until they popped out of his ears! Nothing could've given me more pleasure. What a fuckin' arsehole!" He closed his eyes and shook his head as if in disbelief. "He didn't even finish Standard 8 and now he is some big shot in the Nazi movement here, strutting around as if he's God's gift to the German nation." He sighed, "Hell, you should've let me sock him!"

I listened to his tirade with one ear, but I knew he realised that to stay could have only spelt trouble.

Of course, this was one of my brother's less attractive character traits. He loved a fight. Give him brandy and he became an antagonistic bastard. For no reason at all he'd even start a fight with an absolute stranger who happened to be standing next to him pissing in the urinal in a public toilet. This was usually preceded by a 'What the hell are you looking at'. That was often sufficient to start an altercation. I'd seen it happen.

The evening's proceedings, aided by the beer consumed and my brother's unfriendliness towards what he considered riff-raff, had clearly awakened a feeling of distrust and loathing. Most of this was directed at Emersohn, a budding Nazi activist and a man my brother detested and considered beneath him. Emersohn's new-found pompous attitude and a threat that 'I'll get you' directed at my brother at the previous meeting just aggravated the situation. Of course, the other three men in the car agreed with his views. It was clear that the lot of them were spoiling for a fight. I had no intention of getting into a punch-up with a bunch of fanatics. I made sure I just kept going and ignored their calls that I turn round and return to the meeting. I was still seen as the little brother and, while not considered a tag-along, I was never to forget my place.

Eventually, the intensity of their dissonance towards the Nazis gradually subsided. I finally persuaded them that to return to our house and raid my mother's refrigerator was a better option. We knew that my mother usually had at least a dozen quarts of beer reserved in the lowest shelf of the ice-chest, for my father and his friends. They agreed, laughed and began to see the funny side of the meeting. Its political significance finally forgotten. They believed this to be a one-off incident and that the local German community would come to its senses. They agreed that Hitler would only last a few years, as had the previous political aspirants in post-war Germany. Many still believed German politics to be a mess.

*

My brother and I were due to depart by boat for Germany in a week's time. Our father was insistent that we attend university in Germany. My brother was due to start his final year and I my first semester. We both had opted to study mechanical engineering. On our return, we would take up positions in our father's engineering businesses of which he owned three. These had prospered and were expanding. While in Germany, we usually lived in Kiel where the family owned a large house which our father used for his regular visits to the 'home country'. He annually visited the international trade fairs at the Leipziger Messe.

My mother and father returned just before midnight from a dinner at the home of Dr Egger, a prominent local surgeon. He and his wife were close friends of our family. Every winter, the two men, joined by a few others, would depart on an extended hunting trip with personal servants in tow. This was an annual ritual, no more than an excuse for a week-long carousal and an inordinate amount of beer. The sons were never invited.

On arriving home, my brother and his friends related the occurrences of the evening to my father, who found what we experienced rather amusing. He shook his head in dismay and said that he did not understand what a handful of ardent Nazi-backers proposed to achieve in a country allied to the British and run by South Africa. He mentioned that if the local Germans thought that South West Africa were ever to become a German colony again, they'd be relegated to be a bunch of yokels.

"Father, are we going to have to contend with this in Germany? I mean, I understand the SA [the Schutzabteilung] are everywhere: marches, rallies, and everything else you can think of just to garner support and mess the Jews around," I asked knowing that we'd soon leave for Kiel.

"My son, listen to me," he said. When he used that 'My son, listen to me' preamble, you knew that he expected you to pay special attention. "Just stay away from political beer hall gatherings and rallies. If you don't bother them, they shouldn't bother you. Just watch your older brother."

He poured a twenty-year-old brandy into a snifter and looked at George, his first-born, with a smile. "He can be a hothead at times and it is not a good idea to pick a fight with these people, certainly not in Germany. Just ensure that any interaction you may have with any Jews over there is discreet. Those Nazi pricks are up to something with the Jews and be careful you aren't caught up in it. That could be dangerous. I've a got a bad feeling about where this is going."

"But Father, what about the Jews here?" my brother asked, concerned. He had not forgotten the evening's anti-Jewish remarks.

"Nothing will happen here. They wouldn't dare. Alex Stern and Irma were also at the doctor's dinner this evening. Obviously, the shenanigans these Nazis are up to were a topic of conversation. Still, they're not concerned. As Alex said, the South African government will never let this bunch of fascists get out of hand."

He swirled the cognac in his snifter and took another sip.

"Christ, they're supposed to show allegiance to South Africa," added my father, shaking his head in dismay and disbelief.

I always believed my old man knew best. I looked at him, elegant in his dark suit with waistcoat. His pocket-watch chain glinted in the light, thrust forward by his prominent paunch. He was slightly more than six feet in height, his shoulders broad. He wore a subdued maroon silk tie with a matching handkerchief stuck in his breast pocket. His hair had thinned and greyed and he it wore cut short, cropped near-military fashion, his scalp showing. He was overweight, his cheeks beginning to sag. A grey-black, short-clipped moustache adorned his upper lip. His presence exuded a picture of confidence, success, and opulence, but then he was one of the richest men in the country.

My father and mother had arrived from Germany just before the turn of the century. The family in Germany had owned both a brewery and a printing works in Kiel, the harbour city situated in Schleswig-Holstein on the Baltic Sea. My mother was from Leipzig. Actually, she was half-Norwegian. Her father had been the chief harbour pilot of Oslo. When her father died in an accident, her mother had returned to Germany with her daughter. My parents had met at the Leipzig Messe, largest of the annual German trade fairs.

My father made his fortune in the coastal diamond fields in the Namib Desert. He was one of the first prospectors and miners. Using money brought from Germany, as well as that loaned to him by his family, he had rapidly developed his claims. In order to personally oversee the mine's activities, he and my mother endured harsh makeshift living conditions in the Namib Desert. They chose to live in tents and shacks, while others squandered their new-found wealth building opulent mansions in the desert, buying the latest fashions from around the world, acquired at ridiculously high prices, and strutting their nouveau riche wealth at balls and cotillions which were then regular occurrences.

My parents chose to ignore these pastimes. My father, after repaying his debts and accumulating some wealth, established his first engineering business and opened a large general dealer store in the capital. He eventually became a shareholder and the leading consulting engineer for the first brewery to be erected in the country. Thereafter they never looked back; they became established members of the new elite in the colony. My brother was born in 1912, followed two years later by a sister and two years thereafter by myself.

*

Our parents drove us down to Walvis Bay, a small British enclave on the South West African coast, the only real natural harbour the coastline offered. The journey took two days. We stayed overnight at the Kaiserhof Hotel in Karibib, its architecture and décor a throwback to the era of German imperialism. As we entered the harbour town we saw the liner towering above the other ships alongside the quay, its huge single funnel painted red and black sticking out even higher than the cranes on the dock. The ship was due to depart in a few hours' time. The family's large Studebaker sedan swept onto the quay close to the gangplank. A customs official approached, enquiring whether we were boarding. My father explained that only his sons would board. The customs official directed us to a small building where our papers were perused and stamped.

12

We bade our family farewell on the quayside and boarded the *Carnarvon Castle*, a British passenger liner of the Union Castle Line sailing to Southampton in England. While many may have thought it strange that we chose to sail on a British ship, it was at my brother's insistence that passage was booked on the liner. Only later did I realise that my brother, who had made the crossing numerous times as he was now in his third year at university, knew that that the passengers from South Africa included hordes of young women and, as he so crudely put it to me, he proposed to hump his way to Europe.

As we exited the customs offices, my brother closely inspected the line of inquisitive passengers hanging over the railing of the promenade deck who were taking in the new arrivals and the other activities on the dock.

"My God," my brother whispered, "there's enough pussy here to keep me happy for the entire voyage." He held his forearms out from his waist; his palms turned upwards and lifted his eyes to the sky. "Lord, I thank you for this opportunity. Amen."

I ignored the theatricals. I'm the shy type when it comes to women so I took only a surreptitious look at the railing from below my lowered brow. He was right, it was lined with passengers, many young women. To say I did not experience a feeling of excitement and expectation would be a lie. I was nineteen going on twenty in the next month or so and still had to lose my virginity, this to my brother's dismay. However, I realised that if it ever came to that, it would hardly be due to my own initiative, I was just too damn shy when it came to matters of a sexual nature. A few amateurish kisses and half-accidental feels or fumbles was all I could add to my short list of sexual exploits.

My brother was different. He was unable to hold a conversation with a young unattached woman without including a few subtle innuendos and ambiguities. A born flirt and womaniser who was forever drawing my attention to some woman's décolletage orderrière. Let's just say I thrived on the promise of what was still to be.

My father had the foresight to book two separate cabins in tourist class. Although this was not first class, to which we did not aspire, but at lcast it just a class below, giving us access to most of the liner, the evenings' entertainment, and the best dining room. It was only the cabins that did not match the first class cabins.

Soon stewards were carrying our cabin trunks aboard with us following, welcomed by a ship's officer as we stepped off the gangplank onto the deck. Very few new passengers were boarding at Walvis Bay and for a few moments it seemed we were the centre of attraction with at least a score or more of passengers inquisitive to see whom else was boarding.

None of this was lost on my brother. He stepped aboard exuding an air of feigned importance, lifting his homburg to the passengers, the women in particular, and jocularly greeting them.

When still on the quayside with my father, I noticed that he had also not missed the young women. As I recall the incident, my face still burns with embarrassment. He had never spoken to me about a man's need for a woman. He now touched on the subject, making sure my mother was out of earshot.

"Matthias, have you ever been with a woman before?"

Of course, I knew exactly what he was getting at. Coming from my father, the question shocked me.

"Mmm, well ..." I stammered, still aghast, and I must have must have paled at the crude question put to me.

He interrupted me. "Obviously, you haven't. I would suggest you do something about this – soon. Speak to your brother. He should be able to give you a few hints," he said with a humorous smile on his face. He then took my hand and said goodbye, the last words he whispered were, "Be careful over there."

My mother hugged me, kissing both my cheeks, the tears streaming from her eyes. I was not to know that I would not see my parents for another fifteen years. My mother would have died before then.

We waved goodbye to our parents from the upper deck as the tugs assisted the liner from the quayside.

"What were Father's last words to you?" my brother asked.

"He told me to be careful over there," I said.

"Hmm." He paused for a moment. "Christ! Don't catch a case of the clap is what he said to me."

We both laughed uproariously.

I had to concede, my father was truly something!

CHAPTER TWO

We were barely two days at sea when I was already smitten.

Dinner was served in the first-class dining room, black-tie dress being compulsory. If you thought this too much trouble or too formal, then there was always the second dining room, by no means as opulent and enjoyable, although the food was still first-class fare. Normally, the captain joined the diners in first-class for dinner but this evening it was not to be the case.

The chief dining room steward showed us, the newest arrivals, to our table. Imagine my surprise when I was seated between two young and attractive women, my brother on the other side, he too seated between two gorgeous women. He glanced at me, his eyes twinkling, the faintest of smiles on his lips. Of course, I then realised what had happened. Had I been more observant, I would have noticed the senior steward fawning over him. True to form, my brother, a man of a thousand initiatives, had handsomely tipped the steward, so ensuring a happy voyage as he later put it. The steward formally introduced us. There were eight of us seated at the round table: four were women, my brother and I, and lastly, a young man. He looked more timid than I did. The ship's third officer made up the eighth.

Her name was Tippi Shepherd. I never did find out whether Tippi was her name or just a nickname. Of course, it could have been a dimunition of some other name. She was a tall brunette. When I first saw her she was wearing a conservatively cut wine-red evening dress, merely showing a hint of the swell of what I thought an alluring bosom. Her dark hair was parted on one side, cascading to her shoulders, the ends turning up into an outward curl. Her eyes were brown with a hint of green and, when she smiled, a dimple appeared in her left cheek close to the corner of her mouth. Her teeth were white and straight and revealed themselves whenever she smiled, which was often. A plain, thin, silver chain served as a necklace from which a dark polished crystal stone hung. I thought the stone to be tourmaline.

Fortunately, my brother had hardly noticed her. He was in earnest conversation with a rather voluptuous blonde who would occasionally laugh heartily at something amusing he had said and, in so doing, would lean forward, affording him a glimpse of a magnificent pair of breasts seeming ready to pop out of her plunging neckline.

Soon my initial awkwardness disappeared, slowly replaced by an air of relaxed bravado fuelled by how easy it seemed to converse with this woman. A few glasses of wine also assisted. She was relaxed and spoke to me as if we had known each other for years. Usually I was at loss for words in the company of such beauty. She listened to everything I said, appearing to be hanging on every word.

Dinner lasted an hour and a half. During that period I had told her most of my life story, I having gleaned a lot less from her. However, as the meal progressed, she did twice lay a hand on my arm just for a moment of fleeting gesture. I'm sure I felt her leg accidentally touch mine, she not hurriedly removing it.

While dinner was served, a soloist played the piano. He was a master on the keyboard, his choice of music lending the right ambiance. Yet, now that coffee was served, the first cognacs brought to the table, and a few cigars lit, the soloist was replaced by a five-piece band that played the most recent dance tunes interspersed with a few that would suit the older couples on the floor. Most joined their partners on the floor as did we. The band played a Viennese waltz, my brother sweeping past us with the blonde in his arms, she with her head thrown back in classic ballroom posture. They both oozed confidence and we were all very aware of their expert technique. Of course, he was an adept dancer. Women loved to dance with him. Clearly, the blonde already succumbed to his charm.

I, too, had taken dancing lessons but rhythm had not come easy to me. I had been one of Mrs Baumgartner's pupils that were more arduous who required repeated lessons and incessant coaching before she finally considered me a reasonable dancer. Nonetheless, she had ensured that I could step onto the floor with some confidence. A master I would never be, but certainly above average. We joined those on the floor. Tippi stepped into my arms and we immediately whirled away, our movements in synch.

Tippi drew her head back and looked up at me. "You dance well," she said.

"Thank you. I'll take that as a sign that we belong together." I ventured humorously.

She laughed, giving my hand a squeeze.

I held her close aware of the swish of her multiple petticoats as her dress wrapped itself round my right leg, our inner thighs occasionally touching.

We danced numerous dances together but I also danced one or two dances with George's blonde, soon realising that she preferred dancing with him and was merely being polite. For once, my brother behaved like a gentleman, refraining from being too forward and treating the ladies at the table with due deference. The blonde only had eyes for him, they continuously holding hands and he bending down to whisper in her ear.

At three in the morning, we decided to call it a night. My brother and the blonde had long since disappeared and I could only imagine that he had persuaded her to join him in his or her cabin. I had heard that her parents had put her on the ship in Cape Town en route to London to live with her grandparents. I knew that the docking of the liner in Southampton would herald the end of my brother's brief but intense liaison. I could recall him once making the comment that while he had bedded many, love seemed to elude him. I never knew whether he was being boastful or merely sad. His true feelings were always difficult to read.

Tippi and I stood on the promenade deck, she wrapped in my dinner jacket to ward off the early morning cold. She leaned against me, her head resting in the crock of my neck, I aware of a feeling of arousal.

After toying with the idea for a good few minutes, I softly asked, "Would you like to come round to my cabin for a while? It's cold out here." Actually, I never said it. It came out as a croak, causing her to smile mischievously at me.

"While I find you to be wonderful company, I think not tonight. Take me to my cabin," she said. I was aware of the resoluteness in her voice.

I led her down the stairs to her deck and we stopped in front of her cabin door. She then lifted herself on her toes and kissed me softly on the lips, her tongue briefly darting between my lips. It was the briefest of kisses, lasting only a few seconds. She then moved away, opened the door and with a casual wave disappeared into the cabin, closing the door behind her. For a short while, I stood there staring at the closed door, the faint taste of her lipstick in my mouth and the woman-smell of her in my nostrils, my arousal fading.

My brother joined me at a small breakfast table on the deck porch overlooking the promenade. It was after nine in the morning. He got the steward's attention and mimed pouring from a kettle. The steward got the message, came over with a pot and poured the dark steaming liquid into George's cup. While George added milk and sugar, he placed his breakfast order with the steward.

Later, the steward returned with three plates: one with two large, crisp German rolls; the other with three pickled Bismarck herring, and the third with about half-a-dozen slices of pepper salami.

"Christ, is that what you're having for breakfast?" I asked somewhat astounded.

"There's nothing better after a wild, wicked night. The herring clears the head," he replied laughing.

"You better not let your blonde see that. She'll never let you get near her again," I remarked, scowling at the mixture of raw fish, pickles, and cream on his plate.

He laughed. "Don't worry. She's still recovering from last night," he said. "Incidentally, did you lose your virginity last night?" he asked looking up from his plate at me.

I shook my head.

"Well," he continued, "you'd better do something about it. If you continue yanking that thing of yours you'll eventually damage it," he chuckled.

"Just fuck off," I retorted. "It's really none of your damn business."

"I don't know about that. I heard Father speaking to you before we got on the boat."

I picked up my cup without replying. I did not intend to discuss the subject with him. He looked around the porch and promenade deck. "It's a grand day. I think I'll spend the rest of it around the pool soaking up the sun and watch the women strut their stuff," he said, grinning.

I thought it a good idea and murmured in agreement.

About an hour later, I arrived on the pool-deck dressed in my swimming costume, a one-piece affair with trunks and vest sewn into one. This was an unglamorous piece of clothing manufactured from woven cotton, the fit slightly loose and seeming to accentuate every bulge of my body. It was an unglamorous grey with a red panel around

18

the waist. I threw a large bath towel over an unoccupied chaise longue and flopped down on my belly. Fifteen minutes later, Tippi arrived wearing a pair of white, plastic-rimmed sunglasses; and a costume similar to my own but with a short skirt.

"How are you on this bright and sunny day?" she asked with a smile.

"Terrific," I replied giving her my best smile, my eyes travelling the length of her long, well-formed legs. She did not miss that.

She lay down facing me on the neighboring lounger. "God, you are pale. You'd better be careful. We're well into the tropics now. The sun will toast you," she said.

Of course, she was right. Other than my arms and parts of my legs, my skin was a sickly white. I would have to restrict my time out here in the sun if I did not want to take on the hue of a boiled lobster.

"I'll remember that," I said running my eyes over her body noticing that whatever showed was tanned. Clearly, she loved the sun and had to be a frequent visitor of Cape Town's beaches.

I opened my eyes to see George arrive with the blonde-haired woman from the night before. They were clad as we were. We had been introduced but I could not recall her name. Tippi realised this. She leant over towards me.

"Mandy," she whispered from the corner of her mouth.

George had pushed his chaise longue against hers and they were lying down, their bodies touching. I realised that my brother had made rapid progress, the obvious intimacy between them well-advanced. I saw that Tippi had taken note of the libidinal relationship between the two. I decided it was time that I became more forthright and made my intentions apparent. I got up and pushed our deck recliners together and without a word lay down again, our shoulders not quite touching. Tippi merely looked at me. Damn my brother. He had the audacity to give me a wink, a 'well-done' message, as it were. Had Tippi seen it?

After about a half-hour, my skin began to take on a distinct blotchy-red hue. From the paraphernalia contained in a woven-straw beach bag, Tippi removed a bottle of some lotion which she insisted I apply. Taking dollops of it onto my hand, I began to apply it but when she saw that I could not quite cover all areas, she took the bottle from me, pushed me down onto my stomach, and proceeded to rub the lotion into my shoulders. From there, she then started on the back of my legs. At first, I was embarrassed, unable to quite hide that I was aware of her and her soft hands. Of course, I was aroused. I turned to look at her, but remained on my stomach. Was this an attempt to arouse me or was she making fun of the situation? Did I detect a hint of a sexual caress as she applied the cream? Surely, her rhythm had slowed. Did I detect a change in her demeanour?

"Stop," I said. I gestured towards her lounger. "Come on. Lie down next to me." I realised my voice sounded husky.

She did so, bending forward to slide onto the recliner, the front of her costume gaping open revealing the swell of cream-white breasts. She knew what she was doing but seemed not to care. Our shoulders touched. She made no move to separate us. By now, my arousal was rampant and, as if on cue, my brother piped up.

"You've had enough sun on your back. Turnover, tan your front," he said trying to stifle both a laugh and Mandy's giggling. They had been watching.

'Jesus, the bastard,' I thought. I felt the blood rush to my face, my embarrassment so acute. I balled my fists and clenched my teeth. I could've given him a crack right then, but of course I would've had to stand, which now wasn't the thing to do. I merely looked down and studied the weave of the towel I lay on, trying to hide my embarrassment. Tippi moved and purposely bumped my shoulder with her own.

"Don't worry, don't take any notice of him. I'm certainly not," she whispered as if she and I were sharing some secret.

We were then distracted by the steward asking us what we wanted to order from the bar. I ordered a beer as did my brother, the women opting for fruit cocktails.

The previous evening, I'd told her all about myself. Today, she let me into her life. She lived in Cape Town, where she had studied at the University of Cape Town and graduated with a Bachelor of Arts degree, majoring in English Literature. She never revealed her age but I guessed her to be between twenty and twenty-three. I wondered whether she knew that I was only twenty. She told me that she had been deeply involved with a fellow student for a few years but it suddenly ended when she had found out that she was not the only woman in his life. In fact, this other woman was a friend of hers. She admitted that this was one of the reasons for her trip to England. She just wanted to get away from it all and forget the hurt and humiliation she had endured. She would say no more on the matter.

At twelve-thirty, a steward passed pounding a gong informing all that luncheon had commenced.

"I don't think I want to go to lunch," I said.

She laid a hand on my arm.

"Nor do I," she replied, "but I'll tell you what, why don't you come to my cabin and I'll have the steward bring us something light, maybe crayfish salad and rolls. We could have a bottle of wine with it." She added not taking her hand away, waiting for my reply.

I did not miss the significance of the gesture. I smiled and replied that I thought it a brilliant idea.

George and Mandy had already left for lunch. We collected our things and slowly strolled towards the first-class section, which was roped-off, a junior steward controlling access.

"He's with me," she said. The steward unclipped the barrier rope and we passed through.

The appointment of her larger cabin was a good deal more luxurious. A double bed took up most of the cabin. A doorway led to a small but complete bathroom with shower. The furnishings were tasteful and a few paintings even adorned the cabin walls. The sun streamed in through a large porthole that overlooked one of the upper decks.

"Very nice," I said, sweeping an approving eye over the cabin.

There was one armchair. "I'm afraid we'll have to sit on the bed," she said, indicating that the single chair could not accommodate us both.

I promptly sat down. She lifted the large Bakelite telephone from its cradle and asked for room service, ordering the lunch we had discussed plus an ice-cold bottle of Grand Cru. This soon arrived and we immediately got stuck in, finishing the bottle in the process, still dressed in our bathing costumes.

"Stay here. I think I'll take a quick shower," she said.

"Should I come back later?" I asked.

"No, no!" she exclaimed. "Just wait here."

She must have been in the shower for five minutes when she emerged, a large bath towel wrapped around her body, the one end tucked in below her armpit to hold it in place. She sat down and vigorously began to dry her hair with a smaller towel, her head hanging down.

"Why don't you shower?" she asked.

I was rather taken back. I didn't even have a change of clothing with me. I said so.

"Don't worry about that. We'll think of something. Maybe you can put your costume back on."

It was difficult to refuse. It had been hot out on deck and I did need a shower. I was still sticky from the lotion she had applied. I went into the bathroom, removed my costume, and washed myself. Once I'd dried myself and was about to put my costume back on, she suddenly knocked on the bathroom door and said, "Don't put your costume on. Just wrap yourself in a towel."

It was only then that I realised that I was about to be seduced. A couple in a cabin dressed only in towels had to have a significant meaning. This could only go one way. I felt a thrill of expectation pass through me and was aware of an intense feeling of desire.

"Come on!" she called.

I gingerly opened the door and walked out trying not to face her. Tippi immediately giggled.

"Silly man, have you something to hide?" She laughed.

I ignored her and then hunched over, sat down on the bed next to her, the towel all bunched up, hoping that this hid my arousal.

I don't think she missed a thing. She had control of this situation.

The moment I sat, she turned to face me and suddenly pulled me towards her and crushed her lips to mine, her tongue forcing its way between my lips and probing my own. For a moment, I was bewildered by her candour.

She drew her head back but left her hands resting on my shoulders and looked me in the eyes. "I've just realised, you've never done this before, have you?" she sighed. Did I detect disappointment and disbelief? Or was it exasperation? A thought flashed through my mind. George had told me that women were excited when they realised that they were about to be a man's first conquest. Coming from George maybe I should have taken this piece of information lightly.

"Well, I have—"

She interrupted me.

"My goodness! Of course, you haven't! I still don't believe it. Do you want to tell me you've never been with a woman before? Contrary to general belief, some women love to initiate the uninitiated." She hesitated and smiled and then added, "I'm truly honoured."

She leaned forward and kissed me. She took my hand and placed it on her breast. It seemed my brother might have been right.

"You know, you're allowed to loosen my towel," she whispered into my ear. I felt her hand on my thigh just above the knee.

I loosened the towel, and it dropped to her lap. I took her plump breast in the palm of my hand, softly closing my fingers, and then letting my hand slide over the softness of it. God, the feel of it was exquisite! I kissed her eyes and ears and then her neck. My lips slowly slid down until my mouth covered her erect nipple, my tongue rolling over it. This elicited a low moan from her. She arched her back and let her head fall. I felt her hand pull my towel open, it then slid up the inside of my thigh, and she took me in her hand. If I thought I still had inhibitions, they had disappeared. I was so aroused, I snorted through my nostrils. Goodness, talk about a ruttish bull.

Somehow, I lost control of the situation and found myself desperately trying to contain my threatening orgasm. I felt embarrassed. 'God,' I thought, 'were we going to be off to a shotgun start.'

"Don't, don't." I said, my voice hoarse.

"Don't worry," she whispered in my ear, "let it happen."

There was no more holding back. "Oh fuck!" I groaned as I grimaced and my body convulsed. I was mortified.

We spent the remainder of the afternoon in her bed. She had ordered another two bottles of Grand Cru. The wine coupled to my earlier embarrassing but bold and unexpected performance, removed any vestigial inhibitions I may have had. By then, I also came to realise that she had no inhibitions whatsoever. In fact, I had become a keen and dutiful student.

At five, I showered and flaunted my nudity without embarrassment. This really was a very recent development! I dressed again and returned to my cabin. Of course, Fate being what it is, as I got to my cabin door, my brother exited from his next-door cabin already dressed for dinner.

"Why don't you join us for sundowners?" he said. He then stared at me and took in my attire. He arched his eyebrows. "Good God!" he blurted. "You actually did it!"

"What do you mean?" I asked.

"Jesus Christ, man! Just look at yourself. You have an air of accomplishment around you. It's the afterglow Do you think I can't see when a man has had his first fuck? You look like you're still in a bloody trance. What can I say?" He laughed. "Congratulations and well done, brother," he added.

"Please, George. For God's sake don't say anything," I pleaded, knowing that he was capable of making some ambiguous, uncalled-for remark at the most inappropriate moment. I had been a victim of such behaviour before.

"Don't worry. I won't. It's our secret … and hers, of course." He then laughed as if at some private joke.

CHAPTER THREE

A low-pressure ridge had swept in over the United Kingdom bringing the worst of the North Atlantic winter weather with it. As the *Carnarvon Castle* nosed its way into the Southampton harbour approach, gusts of freezing wind accompanied by sleet and rain battered those who had ventured on deck. Low dark clouds scudded across the sky. The sea was grey and dirty, its surface dotted with flotsam which bobbed on an unpleasant chop.

The four of us stood huddled together dressed in our overcoats on the leeward side of the promenade deck, wearing gloves and winter hats. We peered over the railing, staring at the uninviting picture of the Southampton docks as the liner approached its berth. Two tugs had arrived to join the ship and bustled around her spewing black coal-smoke from theirs funnels as they guided and pushed the liner to the quay.

The initial euphoria of the boat trip had long worn off. After the first few days of the voyage, I found that being restricted to the liner was unpleasant. It was difficult to contend with the feeling of being hemmed-in. The restriction was stifling, as was the same daily routine. Of course, the nights and the occasional afternoon spent in Tippi's cabin remained the highpoint of my voyage and solely for that reason I would be sad to leave the ship.

I was smitten, although I doubt that the same applied to her. Somehow, I knew that she did not quite share the same feelings as I. Still, she seemed happy to be with me, was always warm and affectionate, and knew how to make me feel on top of the world. I emerged from this fourteen-day period of libidinous transformation convinced that I was now a schooled lover and thought that other women would find me both suave and irresistible, a man of the world. It was amazing what it can take to change a man. No wonder my father had once remarked that a woman could manipulate a man whenever she put her mind to it.

Soon the liner's hawsers were secured to the harbour bollards, the winches drawing the boat alongside. It was time to disembark and a feeling of melancholy overcame us. We sidled closer to our partners knowing that these would be the last embraces and goodbyes.

Tippi's grandparents were standing on the quay. I pulled her out of sight behind a large van and passionately kissed her, my heart dreading the parting. I insisted that we see each other again and extracted a promise that she would write. She merely smiled sadly and nodded her head. With the back of her hand, she wiped away a tear that rolled down her cheek.

"Darling," she said, "I do know something for sure. I've left my mark on you forever. You'll never forget me, and what's happened between us I will always cherish."

"I know, I'll never forget you," I said, unable to stifle a feeling of foreboding.

I didn't know it then but I was never to see nor hear from her again.

She walked away from me, turned once and again smiled sadly, then gave a final wave and strode towards her grandparents without another backward glance.

The porter had already loaded our luggage onto his trolley and patiently waited for George and me.

"I made enquiries. Our steamer is only a short distance from here. It will dock first at Hamburg and then Kiel," George said to me.

He spoke to the porter and gave him the ship's name. The porter pointed further down the quay. The three of us set off.

"Jesus Christ, don't look so glum. Your situation is no different from mine. Those women are gone. For them we were just a passing dalliance. At least Mandy and I realise this. Forget Tippi. She too will forget you," George said.

I thought him wrong. How was it possible to have a relationship as Tippi and I had and then, without a further thought, walk away from it, and forget?

However, I must admit that for a moment my brother did show some sympathy, which was rather uncharacteristic.

"Matthias, the world is cruel at times. I'm sorry," he said.

The passage to Kiel was awful. My brother and I were forced to share a cabin. The ship stopped over at Hamburg, but only for a few hours where most of the passengers disembarked. The weather was atrocious, the Channel wild. The wind howled out of the northwest and the ship rolled continuously. Most passengers were ill. They hung over the railings oblivious of the weather, some drenched but probably thinking that to suddenly die would be a relief.

After passing through the Kiel Canal, we docked. It took an hour to disembark and pass through German Passport Control. We found a taxi to take us to the family residence on Niemanns Street in one of Kiel's smarter suburbs. During the drive to the house, I observed that there appeared to be more than the usual number of uniformed people on the streets. First were the Customs officers. They were smartly dressed, their greetings curt, and everything was done with a flourish and a show of efficiency. This was very different from when I had previously visited Germany as a child. The same applied to the taxi driver. The Nazi party emblem, the swastika, seemed to be displayed everywhere. He even had one affixed to the dashboard of his car.

In German, the driver asked whether we had just arrived and from where had we come.

George said that we were from South West Africa.

"Wasn't that a German colony before World War One?" he asked.

George declared this to be correct.

"The colony should never have been taken from us. It was the French and British who took it, the swine! They had no right to do so. Don't worry; I'm sure Herr Hitler will see to it that our colonies are returned," he said with an air of absolute conviction.

George just turned to look at me, surprised by the comment.

"The French and the Bolsheviks. They are the curse of the earth," the driver continued.

"Are things better in Germany now that Herr Hitler is in power?" I asked.

"Much better. Nobody is poor. We all have jobs and are living decent lives again. We Nazis have put everybody in their proper place. The Jews no longer have any say. They don't control the country like they used to." The man's vehemence was not to be ignored. It was obvious that he was taken up with the Nazis and sincerely believed they heralded a new Germany.

George jabbed me in the ribs and pointed. We were driving along a main road that consisted of one shop next to the other selling everything imaginable from furniture, hardware, groceries, fabrics and a host of other merchandise. I noticed that certain shop windows were crisscrossed with wide sticky-paper on which was scrawled 'Jude' in large black letters and next to this a Star of David was crudely drawn.

The driver saw what had grabbed our attention.

"That's right. We don't buy from Jews any longer. They're no longer part of the German economy. They can only sell to their own. We no longer want them in the country. We want our country back!" he said forcefully.

I saw that certain shops had uniformed brown-shirts stationed outside the premises. They wore black jodhpurs, khaki-brown shirts, knee-high black boots, and a cap similar to a kepi. A Sam Brown belt completed the picture.

"Why are they guarding those shops?" I asked.

"Those are essential businesses which, unfortunately, are still owned by the Jews. Those troopers are there to ensure that the Jews confine themselves to their business and don't try to become too familiar with their customers. Those guards also control access and make sure that casual shoppers avoid the premises," he said.

Of course, we had heard that there was a movement underway against the Jews, but were appalled to learn to what lengths this had undergone.

"Surely you have read Herr Hitler's *Mein Kampf*?" the driver asked.

"Regrettably, I have not. It is not readily available in South West Africa. The country is governed by South Africa, which is allied to Britain," George replied.

The driver was astounded. He leant over to the passenger seat next to him and then held up a book, which I immediately recognized as a copy of Hitler's *Mein Kampf*, the name emblazoned on the cover.

"Here. Take it," he said, "You must read this. He will save Germany and return us to our previous greatness. Never will we Germans suffer again. To hell with the French and the Bolsheviks – already the Jews are nothing anymore!"

I took the book from him. It was a well-thumbed copy, its cover grimy.

*

The Rechliens were at the house to welcome us. Uncle Willi Rechlien was a portly man in his fifties with a huge paunch. His hair had greyed to a peppery colour. He sported a brush moustache of the same colour. His chin and jowls were flabby and the underside of his eyes had sagged giving him a bloodhound look. He wore gold-rimmed, round spectacles.

What immediately drew my attention was his suit jacket's lapel pin. It was round and ringed with gold. In its centre the swastika flag could be seen.

I had found his wife, Tante Mimmi, to be a withdrawn woman, walking in the shadow of her husband. She was thin, her hair white grey and her face drawn. She had a sharp nose, thin lips, and her complexion bordered on a sickly paleness.

Gustav, whom my father had employed to look after the house in his absence, also served as butler, gardener and chauffeur. He attended to our luggage while Onkel Willi invited us into the parlour and Tante Mimmi busied herself in the kitchen preparing a few snacks.

We brought Willi up-to-date regarding events at home and the present state of our parents' health and general well-being.

"I noticed the book you had in your hand when you arrived," Willi said addressing George.

"Oh, you mean *Mein Kampf?*"

"Yes." Willi thrust out his chest. "As you can see I'm now a Nazi party member. I can tell you that this has certainly opened a few doors for me. My business flourishes and I was able to replace a number of my printing presses at bargain prices. The machines I got previously belong to some Jew in Nürnberg. I just can't keep up with the work the government is giving me. Mein Gott!"

"Those fellows do love paper!" he added, chuckling.

"What's happening to all the Jews?' I asked.

"They're finished!" he said with a wave of his hand, indicating indifference. "They are no longer allowed to work for the government. Mixed marriages are now a criminal offence and they are no longer citizens but are referred to as subjects of the State. We've even given 60,000 of them permission to return to Palestine."

I was unable to hide my dismay.

"Matthias, why so concerned? It had to happen, our Führer had no choice. The Jews controlled the German economy," he said to me, leaning forward in his chair as if to give his statement more credibility.

I noticed that George remained silent. It had to be difficult for him. Henry Stern, with whom he had gone to school and had studied together with at Heidelberg the previous year, was Jewish. He was the son of our father's friend, Alex Stern, the karakul pelt buyer. Because of his hair, everybody called him Ginger.

"I don't think it's right," George said.

Willi looked furtively around the room, his concern evident.

"Don't say things like that. You're wrong. What the Führer is doing is the only way to go. For God's sake, don't let people hear that you support the Jews. That could get you in trouble."

"I don't care, I—"

Willi lifted his arms up high and turned his head away as if not to hear. "Please! I don't want to hear it. Be quiet!" he said and then fled to the kitchen. I was surprised to see the extent of his agitation.

"You've upset the man," I said.

"Christ. They're all crazy here. What is going on in this country? The man was terrified you'd say the wrong thing," my brother replied.

"Please, say no more about the Jews. We'll talk later," I said.

The couple eventually returned, Tante Mimmi bringing the snacks and Gustav carrying the large tray with the coffee and cups.

"Mimmi and I are returning to Leipzig soon. We'll leave Gustav to look after you," Willi said.

I thanked him.

"What are you young men going to do? They have introduced conscription in Germany. All officers and soldiers have to swear an oath of allegiance to the Führer. I've no doubts that were you taken up into the Wehrmacht, you'd find yourselves in the Offizierschule in no time at all. Germany needs men of your background. What could be better?" Willi said.

George was obviously aghast to hear this. "Please, I'm a naturalized South African and therefore exempt from German conscription. Anyway, I'm only staying a year or so to finalise my degree, then I'm returning home," he said.

"What about you, Matthias? You're still German. Your South African citizenship hasn't come through yet."

"Christ, I don't know. If I have to serve, at least I like to have a choice of what I join. I certainly don't want to land up in the army marching all over the bloody place. That's for the plebs, man," I said.

George grinned. "Go for the Air Force. You love flying."

"Yes, George is right," Willi said, "Join one of those gliding clubs. They're more than that, the club is merely a disguise. They train pilots for the Air Force. If they think you've got the makings for a pilot, they send you to some training field in Russia."

"In Russia?" I retorted, surprised at the statement.

"It's true. This has been going on for a while. I heard this from somebody in the Party," he said.

I said I'd think about it. Anyway, there was no rush and I had my studies to consider. I would register with the university within the next few days and if conscripted would wait for the papers. Only then would I do something.

Onkel Willi admonished George for having given up his German citizenship for that of South Africa. George was nonchalant about the matter, arguing that the Aschenborns were of the most successful entrepreneurs in the country and that he had been born there. Besides, he said, he loved the country: the enormous ranches, the deserts and the wildlife and, as he put it, the challenge of the wilds. He further upset Onkel Willi when he said that the only attraction Germany had for him had been its women. My uncle failed to appreciate the comment.

Onkel Willi again countered in a last attempt to secure George's loyalty to his country of origin. He said, "George, the authorities here would consider that you sacrificed your ties with Germany out of expedience, what with the old colony now controlled indirectly by the British and your father needing government approval for the numerous projects and acquisitions with which he is involved, it would be essential that he be a citizen. You could get your German citizenship back within a month. I would see to it!"

"I would need to think about that. Actually, I'm quite happy the way things are," my brother replied.

My brother was a member of a rather famous German Studentenbund and had the duelling scars to prove it. It was without difficulty that he soon made contact with a few of his friends and was invited out for the evening. I chose to spend my first night in Germany at home.

*

It was a few days later when I awoke the one morning to find Gustav shaking me. Concerned, I asked what was wrong.

"It's your brother George." He hesitated. "He's in jail," he said, finding it difficult to pass on the bad news. My brother was the old manservant's favourite person in the family.

"Oh fuck!" I exclaimed throwing off the bedclothes. "What the hell happened?"

"I don't know. I just got a telephone call. He's locked in the Wiesenstrasse gaol. It's not far from here."

"Gustav, I'll quickly get dressed. Get the car out.– We're going now. Christ, the bloody idiot! What could he have possibly done?"

By the time I opened the front door, the BMW four-door sedan was already parked next to the kerb with Gustav behind the wheel. It was an impressive car, with its long bonnet and 3.6-litre engine, its large flared front mudguards, enormous Bosch headlights, and vertical grille. I climbed into the passenger seat and, with a loud growl from the exhaust, we shot off down the street.

The Wiesenstrasse gaol was an imposing building constructed of granite blocks, now weathered to a foreboding dark, dirty grey. Small arched windows, which were barred, overlooked the street. The main gate was huge and of heavy wood and steel construction with large rivets everywhere. It was guarded by two gaolers armed with rifles. The sight of this lent the complex an impregnable presence. The Nazi armbands on the guards added to my concern.

We approached the large desk that dominated the entrance hall and stated the reasons why we were here.

"Aschenborn?" the officer Wachtmeister said, a faint smile forming on his lips. "He will be arraigned this morning. You can see him if you wish."

"Please," I replied.

Loud shouts followed as the name 'Aschenborn' was hollered down corridors accompanied by the rattling of keys and the crashing of steel gates. I was a while before George appeared.

The first sight of him was a shock. He had the appearance of a barfly who had just emerged from a street brawl, looking the worst for wear. He was unkempt. His hair, which he normally wore combed back, hung over his forehead. The shirt under his suit jacket was torn and open to his navel and his clothes were rumpled and soiled.

"Mein lieber Gott!" Gustav exclaimed. "He's still drunk!"

Well, I had to concede that Gustav's description was apt. I also saw that George sported a few bruises, one rather prominent on his chin, swollen and purple. There were also signs of an emerging black eye.

With the warders looking on, I thought it wise to speak English knowing what my good brother was capable of when inebriated.

"What happened? Please, just speak English," I said

He gave me a sheepish grin. For a moment, I thought he would drool, he was still so drunk.

He waved his arm around, nearly losing his balance in the process, to indicate the police officers standing around in the fore office.

"These cunts beat me up!" he exclaimed loudly.

"George! Careful!" I again warned him.

He ignored me, swung round to face one particular officer and walked forward until he stood in the man's face, and said: "You're a cunt!"

The man just stared at him blankly. Thank God, he couldn't speak English. I stepped forward, grabbed him by the arm, and pulled him away from the man. Christ, he was just about standing on the man's toes!

"Jesus! Just shut up!" I hissed.

"Cunts!" he repeated loudly and with more emphasis.

At this rate, we were all going to be locked up. Fortunately, at that moment, Onkel Willi arrived, putting on an officious air. His Nazi party emblem was clearly displayed and he spoke in a voice that implied authority, demanding to know what was happening. The junior officer and my uncle exchanged a few words and then the officer led my uncle to an office, which through the open door appeared quite opulent. It had to be the office of a superior officer. I had to wait a half-hour before my uncle returned. During this period, I saw coffee being brought to the office, which I hoped indicated that whatever was being discussed was in an affable atmosphere.

Finally, Uncle Willi emerged.

"They've released him," Willi said and came to stand closer to me. I could see he was furious.

"I had to promise the man that I would whisper nice things about him to one of his bosses. God! That I had to be reduced to this level. This nephew of mine will be the death of me yet!"

I realised that my uncle would not forget this. There would be a reckoning and we all knew that whatever he chose to do, this would have our father's backing. Of course, there wasn't much anybody could do for George. He was still intoxicated, looking around with that damn foolish leer. He sported a dark shadow on his face. He was dirty and were it not for the cut of his cloth and shoes, he would be taken for a hobo.

Onkel Willi was brought some papers to sign and my brother was then released into our care. Gustav and I took up positions on each side of him and virtually frog-marched him to the huge gate.

I shudder when I think of what happened next. George could not resist turning around at the door and looking at the police officers congregated in the hall. He then loudly exclaimed, "Ihr seid alle Arschlöcher!" *You're all arseholes!* Well, my uncle, paled with anger, came to stand in front of him and slapped him viciously across the face, the loud crack heard by all. His face was etched with the shock of what he had just heard and his lips quivered with fury.

"Der Mann is wahnsinning!" he said to me. *The man is mad!*

Whether my uncle's response to my brother's outburst did the trick I don't know, but we managed to hustle him out of the gaol to the car before anybody came rushing out to re-arrest him. Rest assured, he was not treated deferentially. Gustav threw him into the back of the car where George collapsed in the well, prone on the floor. Gustav slid onto the back seat with his feet on top of him while urging Onkel Willi to drive off.

Only when we were a fair distance from the gaol did I ask Willi why George had been arrested.

"Der Schwein," he said. "You won't believe it. He and his friend stole a whole twenty-five litres of beer, your brother carrying the keg over his shoulder and running down the street to God knows where, with his pal trailing him. Of course, the police apprehended him. Apparently, his friend ran for his life leaving George alone. Please, you can't run away in Germany. I mean there is a damn police officer on every block these days. Still, he had to try and, of course, he was as drunk as a fish."

"Why were the police so severe? After all, it is only beer and he obviously was so drunk he did not know what he was doing. The students are always drunk anyway," I said

"Oh no, but that's not all." Willi shook his head in despair. "When he was told he was under arrest, your brother got such a fright. Is that possible? I mean, is the idiot capable of a fright? Anyway, he dropped the keg, naturally with the sharp end of the rim on the Wachmeister's foot," he added sarcastically. "Of course, the policeman had to be hospitalised. I had to promise to pay compensation."

The old man's expression was a picture of resigned despair.

"God, this was worse than the swimming pool saga," my uncle said.

I had once before heard a remark concerning the so-called 'swimming pool saga' but this was not the time to ask questions. My brother's escapades were notorious.

When we got back to the house, George was taken to his bedroom where Gustav persuaded him that sleep was a good idea. About fifteen minutes later Gustav descended the staircase and entered the parlour.

"And?" Onkel Willi enquired, his eyebrows raised in question.

"He sleeps. I don't think he'll surface before tonight."

"Good, then I shall miss him. My wife and I are leaving for Leipzig at one," Willi said.

I actually was pleased to hear that. If our uncle was still here when George woke there was sure to be a God Almighty row. I wanted to avoid that.

*

At twelve, we set off for the station, leaving Gustav at home in the event that George may wake up. Willi embarked on a near continuous lecture, telling me that my brother could not be trusted and that I should not associate with his friends. The easiest thing was to just agree and assure him that I would do my own thing. Besides, I added, George would soon be leaving for Mittweide in Saxony where he proposed to complete his final two semesters. I would remain in Kiel.

Not having driven on the right-hand side of the road before, my return trip to the house from the station was hair-raising, especially when approaching intersections. A few times I found myself unconsciously straying to the left-hand side of the road, then having to jerk the car back across. It was with profound relief that I stopped the car in the driveway.

It was near five when George step into the parlour. I saw that he must have bathed. He now looked quite respectable, wearing a smoking jacket. The bruise on his chin was still swollen, as was his lower lip, the colour now a distinct blue-black. He now sported a true shiner.

"I fucked up badly, didn't I?"

I nodded, the book I was reading still on my lap.

"Jesus, our Uncle Willi must have being going ape-shit," he said flopping down on the velvet-covered sofa.

Again, I just nodded. "He says he wants one hundred Reichsmark from you for all the trouble you caused and the favours he owes the Wiessenstrasse prison commander. Twenty Pounds Sterling, you should be able to afford that."

"Was it that bad?" he asked.

"Christ! Can't you even fuckin' remember? You called them cunts and arseholes. Tante Mimi nearly fainted when she heard about that. Gustav had to pour her a stiff cognac." I then sniggered. "The pantomime was really amusing, especially Onkel Willi. He was devastated by your behaviour as he put it." I chortled, "Man, I thought he was about to have an apoplectic fit."

"Not funny!" he said.

We then both collapsed in hysterical laughter.

"Rest assured, our father will hear all about this. You're bound to have your allowance at least halved." Again I laughed. "Bloody drunken sod, you deserve what you're going to get." I still wanted to tell him the best bit, but had to guffaw, I hardly able to get the words out "Believe it, you called the Kiel Police Department and the prison wardens a bunch of arseholes and cunts. I don't think they'd ever heard language like that from a gentleman before."

"Oh, my God." he whispered, aghast.

My brother's face was a remarkable sight. He couldn't believe what he had done.

"Cunts, you say? Christ! I don't believe you. No wonder uncle wants 100 marks."

I had to snigger again.

Gustav came in and said that he had prepared supper and that considering George's current sensitive condition he had prepared something special. At seven, we sat down to our meal. Gustav poured us each an ice-cold Riesling and placed plates of pickled Bismarck herring with cream and onions accompanied by boiled potatoes in front of us, proper Baltic Sea fare I thought. Even George ate generously.

During the meal, the doorbell rang and Gustav trotted off to answer it. He returned a few minutes later with an envelope and handed it to my brother.

"That was Herr Heinrich Hübner's second. I should add that I was told to tell you that Herr Hubner is an Oberscharfürher, which is a lieutenant in the SA," Gustav said.

"Is that intended to impress me?" George asked, sliding a knife under the envelope's flap and extracting a sheet of paper. He read it and then silently handed it to me. The letter read that because of a challenge issued the previous night during a meeting of the Studentenbund Gehle when Herr George Aschenborn had, without provocation, insulted Oberscharfürher Hubner and his close family, the Oberscharfürher demanded satisfaction. A challenge was issued which Herr George Aschenborn had formally accepted. The duel was to take place in the afternoon seven days hence. The letter listed the duellers and their seconds and who the appointed umpires and surgeons were to be. The duel was to be fought at some beer hall, which was part of a hotel situated in one of the side streets in the city. Of course, all the bunds in their ridiculous caps would be there. As this was a duel for the purposes of satisfaction, it would be scheduled for a time close to the end of the day's proceedings, this normally taken up by inter-Bund duelling rivalry.

"Stupid bugger!" I said. "How on earth did you get yourself into this bloody mess?"

"I know, I know," George said disgustedly. "It's a pretty bad cock-up, entirely of my own making too. However, I need to add that Oberscharfürher Hübner of the SA is an arsehole of note, a renowned anti-Semite, this only of late. But then, they've all suddenly become anti-Semitic. Unfortunately, he is also the champion Mensur fighter in Schleswig-Holstein. I only found that out afterwards, and as a member of the Studentenbund Hefflingen, which incidentally is made up of the most arrogant of Nazi prigs,that he has loads of support."

He sighed in near-despair, "Don't I choose my opponents well? Many have asked who is this lowly colonialist who has the impertinence to insult a man of his stature. He's a pompous oaf! Now isn't that grand? To be honest, it has had me worried. I remembered the incident when I had sobered up but only recalled my attitude this afternoon. He's not about to forgive me. The bastard could slice my bloody dick off! Of course, you know that I had to have been smashed out of my skull when I told the good fellow from where he and his family emanated and called them those very bad names." He smiled sarcastically displaying a forced nonchalant attitude.

"Bullshit! Console yourself. Your body is protected," I replied doing my best to hide my concern.

George forced a smile. "Yeah well, that's just an expression of speech, my dear little brother, but he is bound to slice up some part of my upper anatomy."

"You're not scared are you?" I asked

He raised his eyebrows, his face expressing mock shock, "Me? Don't be ridiculous."

CHAPTER FOUR

For the next few days, I was kept busy trying to register myself as a student and being admitted to the engineering faculty of the local university. I had planned to move on to another university upon completion of my first semester but staying at home while I acclimatised suited me rather well. It is customary in Germany to move around the universities in the country, spending one semester here and another there, choosing the universities with prudence and spending time at that university known to be particularly well rated for its tuition on any of your major subjects.

Kiel was in the throes of an economic boom. The Deutsche Schiffsbau Werke shipyards were churning out warships as fast as possible, with thousands of shipbuilders employed on these projects. This provided the local economy with tremendous impetus, the unemployment factor now extremely low. The local army garrison was larger than usual as was the police force and the Gestapo. This large contingent of Gestapo officers and men were in the city to ensure that the security surrounding the many naval activities was never compromised.

Germany now openly flouted the conditions of the Treaty of Versailles and virtually thumbed its nose at those who had enforced the draconian conditions. He built warships of every description regardless of the restrictions in terms of tonnage and type. In addition, Kiel was the gateway to the Baltic through the Kiel Canal. The bay and large harbour served as a dock and base for the German Navy, with the German Naval Academy close by in Mürwik.

Originally, my family assumed that my brother would enter the Naval Academy and follow a career as a German naval officer. I believed that my father hoped this would be so.

My mother opposed this. She wanted him to settle in South West Africa. Most of George's schooling, particularly after the junior years, took place at Kiel in a private gymnasium school which was run on lines similar to those of a naval academy: the discipline strict, the demands of honour and trust were of the highest order. The students attended classes dressed in naval uniforms. They all possessed rank and were ordered about in typical military fashion. In fact, the academy was intended to prepare the student for entrance into the Naval Academy. Unfortunately, George never did conform well to authority and, to the delight of our mother, our father was dissuaded from considering such a career for his first-born.

As I understood it, there never had been an intention to send George as a schoolboy to Germany but the infamous 'swimming pool saga' had, as I at that stage understood it, been the deciding factor. I was yet to learn precisely what had occurred and how this came to be seen as one of my brother's less noteworthy achievements. Our sister Inge was still attending a girls' gymnasium in Kiel and would be writing her final examinations, the Abitur, this year. However, she was a boarder and we would see her only once a month. She made no secret that she idolised the Führer and was a staunch supporter of the Nazis. She had joined the BDM, the Bund Deutschen Mädel, which was a segment of the Hitlerjugend, the Hitler Youth, but only for girls. She told the family that she did not intend to return to South West Africa. My remark that I thought she had been brainwashed by the German education scheme and the propaganda that we daily heard, was not taken seriously. Still, I found her over-excessive ardour for the new Germany suspicious. This had alienated her to no small degree from our parents. In fact, Willi and Mimmi Rechlien had assumed the role of parents. While I got on rather well with my sister, my brother did not. There always seemed to be a degree of hostility between the two.

Sorting the paperwork out for my first stint at university took a few days. This was something every freshman had to go through. Eventually a card was issued after payment of a ridiculously low fee. This card permitted the holder to attend lectures and gave access to the other privileges the university offered. It also was used for the purposes of identification. The German government, represented in this case by the Gestapo, would periodically remove students, professors, and lecturers whom they considered politically undesirable from the universities.

Of late, George did not often venture from the house. He was still disturbed by the forthcoming duel with Oberscharführer Hubner. Suddenly and completely out of character, he also shied away from alcohol and spent long hours attending the Mensur training classes honing his skills, no doubt in an attempt to bring his proficiency at least close to that of Hubner.

The day of the duel dawned and as we sat down to breakfast, I was surprised at the confidence my brother now oozed as opposed to the dread he felt on the morning following his arrest and his then sudden recollection of the events that led to the duel.

Using the BMW, we drove to the inn which served as the meeting place for the Studentenbunds where the duel was to take place. On the first floor of the building we found a large hall with a large number of tables with chairs, these were now occupied by students, all wearing their Bund caps, all in various colours; each colour designating the Bund to which they belonged.

The first thing I noticed was that the centre of the floor was strewn with sawdust to soak up the blood which had already been spilled as quite a few duels had taken place during the course of the morning. It was a nauseating sight, but did not stop the students from eating and drinking. Aproned waiters darted between the tables serving steins of beer and plates of steak, schnitzels, frankfurters, and sauerbraten with heaps of potato salad and sauerkraut which they would thump down onto the table in front of the patrons.

George and I approached his Bund's table and he introduced me to the others. I immediately realised that this was a rather solemn affair conducted on rigid lines of custom and etiquette. There was much removing of caps and bowing.

While still eating, the opponents of the next duel prepared, the duellists wearing body padding, their fighting arm bundled up in some type of quilt until it was as thick as a thigh and now rigid from all the wrappings. Their ears were hidden under thick leather straps wound around their heads and they wore goggles over their eyes, the glass-frame protruding similar to that of a chameleon and making them appear myopic. The gloved fighting hand, which held the sword, protruded from the padding. The sword was about three feet long with a large hilt guard to accommodate the padding. The swords were double-edged and razor-sharp, but quite flexible. The points were blunt. The sword not intended to be used as a stabbing weapon but rather to cut, the idea being to flay your opponent with it, slicing him as it were.

The rules were basic. If wounded, you were expected not to flinch or cry out or show any other facial expression. I wondered how you were supposed to do that when your nose was being sliced off. Surely that bordered on the ridiculous! But, I was told that this was a matter of honour. It simply was 'not done'. Also, you were not supposed to step back or bend back and it was considered bad form to avoid your opponent's sword by stepping or bending away. I thought this just another ridiculous rule. However, you were free to advance a step or more. The two umpires would control the fight by keeping their swords crossed between the opponents, standing on each side of them and removing them when the duellists faced each other, indicating that they were to commence fighting. The surgeons or umpires could stop the fight simply by calling out 'Halt!'

This was the first duel I was to witness. Suddenly, the umpires pulled their swords away in unison shouting something, which I presumed must have been 'Start'. I was startled by the sheer aggressiveness and fury with which the duellists went at each other. The swords flashed so fast that these were near- invisible. This was all accompanied by loud metallic strikes and clatter. I saw various strikes to the padding they wore, and while I never saw how it occurred, suddenly blood would appear on the face of one of the duellists. The doctor called 'Stop!' The surgeons then stepped forward to apply some rudimentary first aid and when finished stepped back, allowing the fight to resume. The duellists tired rapidly, the tempo of the fight so fast. It was understood that a fight could last up to fifteen minutes before it was finally halted. Often a fight was terminated well before then because either the doctors had stopped it or the duellists were too exhausted to continue.

Finally, the fight before us was stopped. I would've stopped it earlier. Both combatants had blood pouring from multiple cuts. The one had his cheek sliced cleanly open revealing his teeth, the cut from mouth to ear. Certainly, it was a gory sight. The floor was slick with blood, requiring another covering of sawdust; the blood-soaked bandages, the open wounds and the copious quantities of blood that poured down their faces was a frightening spectacle to see. That my brother considered this a sport was beyond my comprehension.

I leant over towards my brother to speak in his ear, "Brother, you could lose more than your dick here," I murmured in an attempt at humour.

He gave me a dour look. "All I want to do is live through it."

He then pulled a hip flask from his pocket, unscrewed the top and took a generous swig. "Schnapps. Something to steady the nerves," he said and returned the flask to his pocket, not offering to share.

"Hübner and Aschenborn to prepare!" the nominated Bund captain announced.

George rolled his eyes and rose from his chair. "Wish me luck," he said. I did. He disappeared into an adjoining room. The contestants for the next duel entered and I had to watch another display of ferocious duelling and blood spilling.

After the duel, the floor was swept, the sawdust already saturated in blood. This was then replaced with a thin new layer. My brother and Hubner then entered.

I had never seen Hubner before and was surprised to see that he was shorter than George. His hair was blond, but his goggles hid the colour of his eyes. They both formally bowed to the umpires and then took up their fighting stances.

The umpire shouted and the fight commenced with the usual clatter and the flash of steel as the afternoon light reflected off the whirling blades. There was the occasional whack as a sword found either padding or flesh. Already blood streamed from George's forehead. A flat chunk of flesh had fallen to the floor. His face was deathly pale.

A halt was called and the surgeon stepped in to attend to George. The piece of flesh was retrieved with a pair of large medical tweezers and placed in a stainless steel kidney-shaped bowl.

"That will be sewn back," the student next to me said.

'Christ! This is a gory spectacle,' I thought. The bile in my throat threatened to rise.

George's forehead was bandaged, as was a cut that Hubner had sustained to his cheek. I was pleased to see that he had also succumbed to my brother's blade.

"Start!" the umpire shouted. Again, the two men went at each other. By now, they were perspiring profusely, the blades flashing again, the clatter interspersed with the screech of steel upon on steel. Suddenly, George's blade broke, a foot length piece of its end spiralling into the air. The umpire stopped the duel while another sword was brought. Both duellists now sported new cuts. George had a bad cut on the top of his head, the blood poured down the side of his face and dripped onto his padded tunic. The doctors intervened and again attended to the opponents.

The fight was resumed, the tempo much slower as sheer exhaustion crept in and took over, but George still appeared just able to hold his own. The days of practice seemed to have paid off rather well.

"Stop and finish!" the umpire shouted.

George just stood there, he swaying slightly on his feet, his head hanging forward as he gasped for breath, his chest heaving. Blood seeped from under his head bandage and the forehead wound now dripped, forming a steady trickle. I thought he looked as if he were about to die, this impression the result of the copious amount of blood he had lost. Hubner also just stood there. He was also too exhausted to leave his designated spot on the floor and he too appeared drained, his loss of blood seeming to be near-equal to that of my brother.

The surgeons approached them and then led them away to attend to their wounds. The two men went through the ritual of raising their swords in salute to one another and then followed the doctors into the adjoining room. The door had been removed and those in the hall could clearly see the ministrations of the doctors, the blood-soaked bandages and the slow and intricate task of cleaning and stitching the wounds, not that there was any attempt at plastic surgery. These scars were to be proudly displayed.

It was Hubner who first emerged and walked over to his fellow Bund members displaying an attitude of indifference, with three stitched cuts to his cheeks and a gruesome stitched cut on his upper lip, running from the tip of his nose through to his mouth. The sutures could be clearly seen. His lip was already swollen and when he spoke, it was but a mumble, his lips hardly moving.

At no time was any form of anaesthetic or sedative permitted by the surgeons.

Finally, my brother exited the room and walked towards us, certainly not displaying any nonchalance but glad that the ordeal was over. He managed a smile and received congratulatory handshakes and pats on the back from his colleagues.

I took his hand and said: "Thank God, that's over."

He quickly shushed me and then smiled. "I never lost," he said proudly.

"No, you didn't, but you look bloody awful," I added.

"So does he," he retorted looking at Hubner at the other table.

He, too, sported a few nicks and cuts, each with a stitch or two. They had shaved part of his scalp hair and stitched a nasty cut to the crown of his head, but the cut to the forehead was what drew my attention.

"They stitched it back on. The surgeon said that he could not get it to fit properly, but assured me that I would be left with an impressive and obvious Mensur scar. This would be the envy of many, he said. He told me that the women will love it, not that I need any assistance in that department," he boasted.

"God, you are an arrogant piece of shit. No wonder you were challenged," I said. "I can see it, you probably got right into his face leaving the man no choice but to retaliate."

George's reluctant self-enforced short period of abstention from alcohol came to an abrupt end.

"Forget it now, let's have a drink." He called the waiter over and ordered Jägermeisters and large steins of beer for our table. I took the fiery, clear spirit and threw it back into my throat. It burnt its way down my gullet where it finally nestled warmly in my stomach. Those round the table then toasted him and congratulated him on his success. A few of them agreed that my brother had managed to draw the duel, a remarkable achievement against Hubner.

We stayed at the inn until midnight by which time we were both drunk as were most of the other students. We left the inn with the other students, some of whom had now become my friends, and we all strolled down the street in a line, singing German drinking songs. Still, I was lucid enough to realise that joining a Bund and getting involved in this blood sport was not for me. If a member of a Bund, it was certain that at some stage or other during the course of a year, you would be called to fight. Although in terms of the rules you are allowed to refuse, this had never occurred in the history of the Mensur. Clearly, none wished to be the first. I had no intention of sporting duelling scars so as to impress others, in particular the women.

CHAPTER FIVE

It took a few days and a number of visits to the university to work out a daily work program, but once I enforced this, life settled down to a daily routine. I actually started on a few of my subjects and made good progress.

The house was empty, everybody had left. Yes, Gustav was a manservant, but now that we had the house to ourselves, the overall formality of the relationship changed; though in the background, the owner-servant relationship still persisted. Admittedly, he was a lot older, more experienced, and certainly had a more mature outlook on life compared to my own. I eventually persuaded him to call me Matthias. He did this reluctantly. I called him Gustav as I always had. He saw to the cooking, the procurement of food and other household items, and being the chauffeur. He also devoted time to the upkeep of the garden, which was not too extensive. A young woman whom he had appointed a while back assisted him with the cleaning, the linen, and the dusting.

It had been a month since my brother had left for Mittweide when one evening Gustav approached the dinner table as I was about to rise and handed me a rather large officious-looking manila envelope, prominently emblazoned with the new German swastika on the left-hand corner. He said that it had arrived in the mail that day. I realised that it was from the Ministry of Defence and guessed that this could only be my call-up papers. Of course I had expected this, but certainly not quite so soon. I carefully studied the documents and saw that I had fourteen days in which to present myself with the completed documents at the local recruiting office. A sheet of paper listing the locale of the recruiting offices was included. Of course, it did not mean that I would immediately have to report for duty.

If I were to ensure that I was not to be assigned to an infantry or armoured regiment, it was obvious that I needed to pull a few strings. I had been told that once they had done this, that is placed me in the Wehrmacht, it would be difficult to get re-assigned. Flying was what I wanted to do. This is where Onkel Willi was to play a role, or so I hoped.

Later that evening I phoned Uncle Willi and when I informed him of the papers I had received he merely laughed.

"Of course, I've been expecting you to receive these. In fact, I've already made enquiries and have talked to a few friends, if you know what I mean," he said, sounding as if we were involved in a conspiracy.

"That's wonderful," I said, beginning to feel a lot more confident.

"In fact, I've arranged that your call-up will be postponed as it were, but you must join a flying school, or a flying club as they prefer to call it, and at your own expense in order to learn to fly. This must happen soon and should ensure your assignment to officer school with the right backing."

"Uncle Willi, that's expensive," I replied.

"Not for an Aschenborn. Besides, this is also subsidised by the government, or certainly to a degree. I've already written to your father. Meanwhile I'll see to the fees. Don't worry, your father will repay me. It is only for a month or two anyway. By then he will arranged for payment from his own sources."

"What must I now do?" I asked.

"I'll be sending you a letter from a Major Lutzow of the Luftwaffe, which has been given to me and which you need to hand to the senior recruiting officer in Kiel. I also have a letter from the Major addressed to the senior instructor who is also the manager of the airfield and the flying school at Husum. If you haven't heard of the place, it is a short distance from Kiel. Actually, it is a disguised Luftwaffe flight school, but the students are without uniforms for obvious reasons. It is commanded by Hauptmann Osterkamp who, as I said, acts as the manager. You may call him by his rank. This stems from the First Word War and should not cause embarrassment. Please, Matthias, don't be concerned, all has been arranged. Rest assured, with a pilot's licence in hand your entrance into the Luftwaffe is virtually a foregone conclusion."

I was surprised, never expecting Uncle Willi to go to these lengths. I thanked him profusely. He brushed my remarks of appreciation aside, reminding me that I was German and he knew that I would not shirk my duties to the Fatherland.

The Fatherland, I thought. I realised what had prompted his personal intervention. It was not his interest in me per se, but rather his intention to present the regime with another willing recruit. No doubt it would also enhance his standing in the Party if he had near family in the armed forces, particularly an officer in the Luftwaffe. Buying a commission in Germany was no longer possible but nepotism still existed and I had no idea what part my good uncle played in this new Germany. I realised he had to be more than just an ordinary Party member. The man appeared to have considerable clout.

I had to wait a few days for Onkel Willi's letter to arrive. This also contained the letter addressed to Hauptmann Osterkamp of Husum, the envelope also displaying a Nazi swastika stamped on it. It all seemed quite impressive.

The next day I had Gustav drive me to Husum. My arrival in a chauffeur-driven sedan did not go unnoticed and when I enquired as to whether Herr Osterkamp was there I was soon ushered into his office by a middle-aged man whose bearing indicated a military background, surely that of a non-commissioned officer from the Great War. I guessed he had to be or had been Hauptmann's adjutant.

That Herr Osterkamp was an officer of the old school was immediately evident. He rose from behind his desk, his back ramrod straight. He took my outstretched hand with a faint but perceptible bow. I, of course, in deference to his rank, shook his hand with a single downward jerk, clicked my heels, and bowed to forty-five degrees, announcing myself in the proper manner.

I estimated him to be in his mid-forties. His face was thin, his blond hair combed straight back and flat against the sides of his head as was currently fashionable. He had a scar on his left cheek. His ears were flat against his head and his nose thin and pointed. I noticed that he must have been wounded at some stage or had been in an accident as his left hand was badly scarred.

"Herr Aschenborn, you seem well-connected," he said waving the letter from the Major with a slight smile indicating that I should take a seat in the chair in front of his desk. "You wish to learn to fly and then, no doubt, join the Luftwaffe. Well, Herr Aschenborn, I cannot agree with you more. It's better than walking. I hear from Lutzow that you have expressed a dislike for walking." He laughed at his own comment. Lutzow probably had heard the remark from my uncle. He extracted a cigarette from a silver case and proceeded to light it, blowing smoke at the ceiling. He asked me about myself. I told him of my background, occasionally having to raise my voice as aircraft outside the wooden building were started up, or their engines taken to full power as they commenced their take-off runs. I told him of my initial schooling in South West Africa, the studies I had just commenced, and my desire to fly no matter what sacrifice was necessary.

When asked whether I had ever flown before I had to admit that I had not.

"Herr Aschenborn, I require two hundred marks upfront, plus you will need to pay for the manuals I shall give you. These you can collect tomorrow morning from my daughter. Unfortunately, she is not here now. I understand that the rest of your tuition fees will be paid from Mittweide. I am agreeable to that." He scribbled something on a sheet of paper which displayed the flying club's letterhead and slid this across the desk to me.

"You will need to go for a medical. Get this done as soon as possible. The doctor's name and address is on this. Go soon," he said. "I cannot permit you to fly solo unless have been certified medically fit. Incidentally, the same medical examination will suffice for the Luftwaffe. You will not need to go for any other examinations. In fact, the doctor in question is an appointed Luftwaffe surgeon. That will be all. Oh, by the way, your first lesson is tomorrow morning at eight. Buy yourself a warm padded one-piece overall. We'll provide you with a flying cap and goggles, but again, you'll have to pay for these."

He rose and shook my hand, "I'll see you tomorrow again. Ah yes, you should also know that I'll be your instructor. I only teach a selected few," he said. Did I detect a cruel smile? The man then pulled a document from a basket and proceeded to study it. I realised that I'd been dismissed.

Gustav promptly took me to the address of the doctor I'd been given who was to medically examine me. His receptionist gave me a two-hour appointment for three days hence. Of course, this was all being done in the guise of civilians whereas this was really a Luftwaffe operation. That it may have included a few civilians I did not doubt, besides this would probably lend this undercover operation more authenticity.

This sort of subterfuge was going on all over Germany. In reality, the conditions of the Treaty of Versailles were no more than a collection of words on pieces of paper. Germany was building ships of war, aircraft, and armoured vehicles. He had begun to train his armed forces, slowly adding thousands of men, the numbers continuously increasing. The strength of the German army was already well beyond the restriction of a 100,000 men as imposed by the Treaty of Versailles.

When I told Gustav that the appointment covered a two-hour period, he was flabbergasted. "Two hours! My God, what do they want to do with you? Give you an enema?" I shrugged my shoulders. I would soon find out. The overall was a problem and it took a while to find out who stocked these. I selected one my size and then saw fleece-lined black boots on display. I could not resist the temptation and bought a pair as well.

I hardly slept that night, my mind enraptured with the thought that I would be flying and controlling the aircraft myself. I imagined the wind in my face, the ground passing below and even the occasional cloud below me.

I was up early. In fact, for the first time, I rose before Gustav who was clearly surprised. I decided that I would not need a chauffeur. Even if I sat in the front, the car would still be seen to be chauffeur-driven, and to arrive for my flying lessons in this fashion would create the impression that I thought myself above others in the order of social standing. I'd have rather arrived in something less ostentatious but then we only had the BMW sedan. I told Gustav I'd drive myself. I was sure that I'd soon get used to driving on the wrong side of the road.

It was well that I made an early start. I drove slowly and still arrived well before time. I swung the car into a parking lot surrounded by hedges and parked amongst a motley assortment of DKWs, Opels, and Adlers. There were a few of the new Volkswagens and, surprisingly, a single Horch four-door sedan. I did not doubt that the Horch belonged to Osterkamp. I wondered how he had acquired it. It certainly was an expensive car.

The airfield was a grass field with a large concrete apron surrounded by a few squat hangars, a slightly raised control tower and then the office block constructed of wood, which housed Hauptmann Osterkamp's office. This all had been erected in one corner of the airfield. There were a few smaller wooden huts but I did not know what purpose these served.

It was a typical Baltic coast winter's day. The sun would only now and then break through the scudding low cloud, but this for never more than a minute or so. The wind was fresh and cold. The chill factor must have had the temperature close to the freezing mark. I would've been surprised if we did not receive rain or snow later in the day. I was glad I'd bought the fleece-lined boots.

I saw that the offices were still locked. I stood on the apron with my overall draped over my arm, my other hand clutching the boots and watched as the hangar doors were slid open and the men starting to push the trainer biplanes out onto the concrete apron and line them up.

I heard footsteps behind me and swung round and saw Osterkamp approaching, he already in his flying suit and wearing boots similar to mine. A red scarf was wrapped around his neck.

"Good morning, Herr Aschenborn," he said, and in typical German fashion we shook hands. "You are early which is a good sign but you should have been helping the students and mechanics get the aircraft out. Off you go and be quick about it and give them a hand."

Of course, I felt that first twinge of embarrassment and that distinct feeling you get when you've just been put in your place. Without a word, I trotted off towards the hangars, put my overall and boots against the hangar's wall, and rushed over to a biplane that two men were trying to push out of the hangar onto the apron. The one man at the aircraft's wing moved aside to make room for me. I watched where he placed his hands on the wing. I did the same and then put my weight against the aircraft. It moved and slowly rolled out. We manœuvred it until it too had joined the row of lined-up training aircraft, all biplanes seeming to be of every description.

When we returned to the hangar, there were only two aircraft left and both had their cowlings off.

The man whom I had assisted and followed back to the hangar, turned to me. He stuck out his hand. "Schmidt, Klaus Schmidt," he said, smiling. We shook hands both clicking heels. "I'm an aircraft mechanic. I help keep these overworked birds in the air," he said.

"Matthias Aschenborn. I'm a new student. In fact I was told that Osterkamp will be my instructor," I said.

"Really," he said. "What qualified you for that honour?"

I immediately realised that the use of the word 'honour' had some other sinister meaning.

"I would suggest that you wait for Osterkamp next to your aircraft." The mechanic indicated a two-seater biplane, a Focke-Wulf Fw 44

Steglitz trainer. I thanked him and added that I was happy to have met him. Little did I know that this was to be the beginning of a long, symbiotic relationship.

I quickly retrieved my pair of overalls and my boots and soon found out where the change-room was. I stripped down to my shirt and trousers and stepped into my overall, buttoning it up to mid-chest. The flying boots followed. I had a pair of gloves I usually used for driving and these I put in my pocket.

I strolled over to the Steglitz. It was painted silver with a few red stripes on the fuselage. Its registration number was stencilled on the body and rudder fin in black letters. I saw that the wheels had been chocked, the nose pointing slightly skywards, the tail resting on the tail wheel. It was powered by a 160hp six-cylinder inverted Hirth engine. The pilot and instructor sat in tandem in an open cockpit. A feeling of exhilaration overcame me as what was about to happen finally became a reality: I was about to take to the sky and learn to fly. Nothing else was of importance at that moment.

"Are you familiar with aircraft?" I heard a voice behind me. It was Osterkamp.

I was about to say I was, but thought better of it. "Only from what I read from the manuals," I replied.

"Well, let's start with a pre-flight inspection and at the same time I'll familiarise you with the flying surfaces and their purpose, similarly the controls and so on. I need you to take careful note, because at the completion of this exercise I will ask you various questions and only once you have answered these all correctly, will we take to the sky."

Slowly, but with exhaustive thoroughness, we made our way clockwise around the aircraft. We spent time underneath the aircraft, examining the undercarriage and above, inspecting the fuel tank in the upper wing and then the interior of the open cockpit. As he detailed every aspect to me and fielded my many questions, he expressed surprise at my knowledge and my grasp of things mechanical.

"I should have realised that you'd be rather knowledgeable about these things, you wanting to become an engineer," he said. For a moment, I thought the man actually was beginning to mellow.

He stepped away from the aircraft, removed his silver cigarette case from his pocket, and proceeded to light a cigarette.

"You'll be seated in the rear cockpit and I in front of you. We can speak through the speaker tube. You'll have no idea when I'm flying the aircraft. You are to assume that only you have control. If you freeze on me requiring that I forcefully take control, I will terminate the lesson. And take care, I might consider you inappropriate as possible pilot material. Please understand, I don't want to have to wrench control from you with you fighting me. Flying is a matter of feeling and being one with the aircraft. Just imagine you are caressing a woman and trying to gently coax her into doing what you want," he said.

"I understand," I replied.

"Good, in that case, run off to the office and buy your flying cap and goggles. Don't forget the manuals."

I never hesitated and quickly trotted over towards the wooden office building, climbing the three stairs with loud thumps from my heavy flying boots.

"Guten morgen," said a soft female voice. I tuned to see a young blonde woman standing on tip-toe. She had on a pair of grey women's laced shoes, the heels slightly elevated. She was dressed for winter, with woollen stockings and a thick, knitted jersey that reached to below her waist. But still, there was no concealing the curvature of her body, her slim legs, waist, and the thrust of her bosom. She stood on a low stool, sticking papers to a green, felt-covered notice board with drawing pins.

For a few seconds I forgot the plane and Osterkamp. This was the most beautiful woman I had ever seen. She was tall and willowy. She had to be about my age with beautiful blonde hair done in large curls. Her eyes were light grey. She wore no make-up other than a slight smudge of lipstick.

She turned to look at me, I immediately looking into her light grey eyes. I began to feel embarrassed and was forced to turn away. It was as if she could see right through me. I stuttered a greeting and for a moment was at loss for words. She smiled waiting for me to speak. It was with difficulty that I spoke, my mouth failing to react to my brain.

"Can I not do that for you?" I asked stumbling over my words.

"Not to worry. I'm nearly done. What is it you want?" she asked peeking over her shoulder while still affixing the last pamphlet.

"I'm Aschenborn, Matthias Aschenborn." I quickly added, "Herr Osterkamp said I should obtain a few items from his daughter."

"I'm his daughter, I'm Wiebke Osterkamp. What is it you want?" she asked.

I rattled off the list of items I sought, which included the flying manuals.

She stepped down from the stool and without a word disappeared into another room, immediately reappearing with my items.

"I understand that you'll be flying so I'll hold the manuals until you're back," she said and handed me the cap and goggles. I'm sure I discerned a slight smile play around her lips as she took in my obvious embarrassment. I couldn't understand why I should feel abashed. I was like a young teenage boy. Where was the nonchalance and confidence Tippi had bestowed upon me? I clutched the damn cap and goggles in front of my chest in a show of thraldom, like a little boy in wonderment. It was damn ridiculous.!

I left the office running towards the aircraft, Osterkamp still standing there waiting patiently.

"Herr Aschenborn, is everything okay?" he asked.

Did I detect a hint of sardonicism?

"Yes, yes, Herr Osterkamp," I said getting myself under control again.

"Good, get in."

Klaus Schmidt appeared. He looked into the cockpit and checked that I had strapped myself correctly into the wooden seat and that my feet were under the leather straps that locked my feet to the rudder pedals. We went through the ritual of starting the engine. Fortunately, this was fitted with an electric starter and soon the propeller was a spinning silver disc, the engine rumbling and spluttering, being still cold. The temperature in the cockpit seemed to drop another few degrees from the wind of the prop wash and I zipped up my overall to my throat. Schmidt came up to my cockpit again and thrust a scarf at me.

"You'll need this!" he mouthed at me over the din and smiled. Gratefully, I wrapped it around my neck.

My speaking tube was plugged in.

"Indicate to the board mechanic that he should remove the chocks," I heard Osterkamp say. I looked at Schmidt and gave him thumbs up. He acknowledged. I then waved my hand sideways. He grasped the rope attached to the chocks and swept these away.

"Slightly advance the throttle till she starts to roll, but as soon as she starts rolling, retard it slightly."

I gingerly inched the throttle forward; the revs increased and then with reluctance the aircraft rolled; I immediately reduced power. Slowly, we trundled forward.

"Using the rudder pedals, gently swing left towards the southern end of the field, don't exceed a walking pace. You need to occasionally weave so that you can see sideways past the nose where you're going," Osterkamp said. This would be necessary so as to see over the aircraft's nose, which now pointed slightly upwards towards the sky.

The aircraft obeyed my commands and soon we were at the end of the field. We went through the magneto and engine checklist and were finally ready.

"Push the stick slightly forward, and using the rudder pedals keep the nose pointed into the wind and ease the throttle all the way forward to the stop."

I did this. The noise of the engine rose to a crescendo, the propeller clawing at the air. The aircraft picked up speed, bouncing over the slightly uneven turf. Rapidly its speed increased, the tail coming up.

The torque from the spinning propeller took over, the aircraft wanting to turn left.

"More right rudder – not too much! Keep the damn ball in the middle as I told you!"

I briefly looked at the turn and bank indicator. The ball was not in the middle!

Suddenly, things started getting seriously busy. The airspeed indicator's needle was rapidly climbing. The aircraft swung left, then right, and then left again as my feet danced on the rudder pedals, the damn ball in the turn and bank indicator going everywhere but not staying in the middle. I suddenly felt his hands and feet on the controls. This was so unobtrusive. Immediately, all settled down as he for a few moments assumed control, the aircraft streaking straight down the field, just beginning to start to bounce as the wings began to acquire lift.

"Ease back slightly but be ready the moment she becomes unstuck and the nose rises, push slightly forward and keep the airspeed at one-ten."

I eased back and immediately the rumble stopped and the ground began to fall away, the seat of my pants telling me we were flying. I wanted to yell in exhilaration. I controlled the speed as he told me to, pushing or pulling the stick, keeping the needle on one-ten.

"The damn ball!" he again shouted.

'Christ,' I thought. The damn ball was out of whack over to the left again. I worked the pedals until I had in the centre, my manipulations making the nose yaw from side to side.

"Verdammt! Are you trying to make me ill?"

I made a mental note: I would watch this from now on. I was resolute this was not about to happen again. I recalled his euphemism about treating the plane like a woman.

We spent an hour in the air doing shallow and steep turns, stalls, gliding on reduced power; just getting a general feel for the aircraft and how it responded to the controls. Osterkamp seemed an excellent teacher. He was never really riled, was patient, and ran a continuous commentary on how best to carry out the numerous manœuvres.

It was soon over. We approached the airfield with the nose down, the throttle back and I trying to keep the needle on one-ten. We swept over the hedge, which demarcated the boundary, the field coming up to meet us.

"Wait," he said.

I thought the ground already too close.

"Now slowly, start rolling out."

I eased slowly back. The nose came up, and up, and up. God, we were looking at the sky. Damn! I'd overdone it. The aircraft had ballooned.

"Quick, stick forward!"

Instantly, I pushed forward, the nose suddenly dropping with the ground rushing up. I had to pull back again. Then everything went wrong and I felt him take the stick. He rapidly got us back to some resemblance of control, but again he suddenly just left me to figure it out for myself, removing his adept hand from the stick, leaving only mine controlling the aircraft.

The wheels struck the ground with a wham, the shock resonating through the airframe. The aircraft bounced back into the air and I rammed the stick forward trying to flatten out the flare. Keep the bounce low, I thought to myself. It was not to be. Again, we bounced, flew, touched, bounced, and flew again. Finally, the wheels stayed down and the aircraft rolled out.

"That was spectacular! Not even Richthofen could have given a better performance." Nobody needed to tell me that the remark dripped with sarcasm. His ironic reference to Germany's famous WWI fighter ace humbled me.

We taxied to the apron and shut the engine down. I allowed Osterkamp to clamber from his cockpit first and then followed. Schmidt the mechanic appeared ready to assist and placed the chocks in front of the wheels.

Osterkamp, who now stood on the concrete apron, went through a sequence of back exercises. Then he stood wide-legged with his hands in the crook of his back and bent over backwards. He looked at Schmidt saying, "God, my fuckin' back. I think it's broken. I want you to check this aircraft carefully. I believe we may have bent it. Also, rather give it to one of the other instructors to fly before you give it back to me. Rest assured, they're bound to complain if it's not flying right." He turned to me. "Aschenborn, you follow me."

God, this was the first time I'd ever flown an aircraft and I'd loved every second. I didn't think my performance that bad. Sure, the landing was lousy but, Christ in Heaven, this was a first flight. Osterkamp shouldn't really belittle me. That wasn't fair.

As I passed Schmidt he whispered, "I've seen worse."

'Was that supposed to be a consolation?' I thought.

We quickly walked through the reception area where I got a glimpse of Osterkamp's daughter staring at me before we disappeared into his office. We had both removed our goggles and flying caps.

"Sit down," he said. He moved towards a wooden cabinet against the sidewall, lowered a lid until it resembled a writing table, and plucked a shot glass from a small collection. From a glass decanter he poured himself a generous glass of what I assumed to be cognac which he quickly drank without offering any to me.

"For my back," he said. He left me with the impression that his back injury was entirely my fault, probably an excuse as to why I should not be offered to share a cognac.

"An abominable exhibition, I must say. Fortunately, we both survived. However, while I'm not prone to making comments concerning a student's abilities after the first lesson, let it be said that you seem to have a rapport with the aircraft. This is an essential ingredient if a man wants to be a good pilot. You may just be one of the few who have it. I'll continue to instruct you. You may go," he said.

'You may have it.' What was that? Some essential secret ingredient?

CHAPTER SIX

Time passed quickly – fast, so fast I had time for little else. My near daily appointment for flying lessons were made to fit in with the schedule of classes I attended at the university. Often I would be dashing back to the university straight from the flying school at Husum to attend lecturers or I would be rushing in the opposite direction. This had certain benefits. It forced me to fly different times of the day, which brought different weather conditions with it.

Invariably, and at my initial request, Gustav would join me every evening for supper. We would eat around eight, which still left me two hours to devote to my studies.

While I occasionally used the BMW for my daily trips to Husum and the university, I preferred Gustav's NSU motorcycle, which he insisted I use. He had become aware of my reluctance to use the sedan.

Using the BMW as a run-around would leave all with the impression that I thought myself in the Junker class, the old German aristocracy, amongst all the vons and zus. This is not what I wished and would have been embarrassed if any had thought that of me, especially those with whom I'd become acquainted at the airfield and in flying circles. At the flying school the men enjoyed a spirit of comradeship, irrespective of rank or class. I wanted to reimburse Gustav for the use of the NSU but he would not hear of it. I soon wrote to my father and told him of the embarrassing situation I found myself in and my reluctance to make use of the ostentatious BMW.

*

After seventeen hours of dual time with Osterkamp using the Focke-Wulf trainer during which I had been praised, cajoled, denounced, cursed, and sworn at, I was finally able to start the aircraft, fly it off the ground, and return it to Mother Earth in one piece without the assistance of any. In fact, I believed I did this with the required skill which probably matched that of most other pilots. Unfortunately, Herr Osterkamp did not share these sentiments. I still received repeated tongue-lashings. Imagine my surprise when, one morning, so early that small puffs of mist still wafted across the field and hoarfrost still covered the grass, he walked up to stand next to the fuselage watching me as I strapped myself in.

Of course, I need to mention that I'd passed the Luftwaffe medical examination with flying colours. The surgeon had put me through the mill and Gustav's comment regarding the imminent enema at the time of the appointment was close to the truth. Never have I been prodded, poked, squeezed, and embarrassed to such an extent before, and this with a young female nursing orderly looking on and assisting. I produced samples of blood, saliva, urine, and fæces. I had to hand these little rubber-corked bottles to her hoping she would not ask me what each contained. Fortunately, she was qualified enough not to have to do that. Had I been forced to do that I probably would have been even more mortified. What they wanted these all for I did not know and never ventured to ask. The nonchalance with which the female orderly handled these administrations surely qualified her well for the medical profession. She looked the no-nonsense type and had a physique to match. A blonde Aryan was an adept description, certainly not my type.

I was still considered a civilian student pilot but was told that the Luftwaffe was taking a close interest in my progress. I don't know what all the bluff was about but everybody seemed to be aware that this was a Luftwaffe-sponsored training school.

Once he saw that I was properly strapped in, Osterkamp stepped closer, his eyes nearly level with mine.

"Aschenborn, you're now on your own. Break you neck. Please, I require one circuit only, then land."

He spun round and walked away. He had long since dispensed with the more formal 'Herr' when addressing me, probably because it was then easier to disrespect and swear at me. During the last few weeks, I had come to dislike him intensely. I dreaded the moments after the final landing for the day. He would invite me to join him in his office where I had to watch him slurp his cognac. Alone, I might add. I knew that I was in for a lecture and at times would leave the office believing that I was barely capable of riding a bicycle, let alone flying an aircraft. More than once, I left his office white-faced, grinding my teeth, and biting my tongue, silently mouthing 'and fuck you!'

Once I had endured a particularly harsh tirade and had just stepped from the office, closing the door behind me, when I heard Wiebke Osterkamp's voice.

"I'm so sorry. I wish I could make it easier for you. He can be impossible, but remember, if he did not think you had talent, he wouldn't bother."

'Impossible?' I wanted to say that was putting it mildly. The man was a tyrant. What did this woman know about flying?

Just looking at her was enough to help calm me, my anger evaporating.

I greeted her and then asked, "Is that supposed to mollify me?"

At least I no longer suffered embarrassment and enthrallment when speaking to her. She clearly had no designs on me and I doubted whether she would ever be mine to have. Don't believe I was off women. I often recalled the time on the liner with Tippi, nearly overcome with desire, but simply not having the time. If I were to find somebody, it would be by accident.

Her eyes flitted around the reception area making sure that none could overhear her. "It may not appear so, but he likes you. For your training since you started and till now he has given you virtually full marks and advised the Luftwaffe. God, I shouldn't have told you that," she blurted, her hand moving to cover her mouth.

I could not believe what I had just heard but knew it had to be true. She was not the type to fabricate a remark like that.

"Don't worry, I'll never say a word," I replied.

Just then, Osterkamp's office door opened. "What's going on here?" he asked looking at his daughter a frown on his brow.

Before she could reply I blurted, "I just wanted to buy another pair of flying goggles."

He harrumphed, spun round, and retreated to his office, closing the door behind him. She smiled at me.

I bought another pair of goggles. My current pair did require replacing.

"Where is your BMW? " she asked.

"Oh, that's not mine. It belongs to my father in South West Africa. I'm using a motorcycle now," I said.

"Yes, so I've seen. So, you're from South West Africa. It must be wonderful there. I've often thought of Africa, with no snow, plenty of sun and wide-open spaces. What does your father do there?" she enquired.

She was looking up at me, her face radiating a picture of innocence. Her beauty was astounding and she wasn't even dressed to show herself off.

"Well, he's both a businessman and a farmer," I replied.

"Have you got wild animals on your farm? You know, lions and elephants?"

"On one of the farms we have many wild animals including those you've just mentioned. On the others, there is nothing like that, just buck, jackals, and a few cheetahs."

"You father has more than one farm?" she asked with a look that bordered on incredulousness.

"Yes, in fact he has quite a few," I replied.

She stared at me in wonder, her eyes round. She obviously found it difficult to believe what I had just told her. Clearly, she was trying to imagine a value that could be attached to such extensive ownership of land. She must have thought it a fortune.

I smiled. "It's nothing like you imagine. It's wild like the day God made it. Only some of the farms are fenced. Some don't even have a dwelling house. Most have no barns or anything as you would find here. It's just wild, hardly touched by Man, and the per hectare price is nothing like you'd pay for land in Germany."

"It sounds wonderful," she said.

"It is."

For a few seconds we said nothing. We just looked at each other.

"I'd like you to stay and talk but I think you really should go. My father would be upset if he came out and saw us still talking. We can speak again sometime," she said reluctantly, and for a moment I thought she was genuinely sad to see me go. This made me feel good.

*

Now that Osterkamp had walked off leaving me on my own, Klaus Schmidt came to stand next to the aircraft, a Bücker Bü 33, powered by an Argosy engine, also a two-seater biplane.

"Herr Aschenborn," he smiled, "your solo flight. This is indeed an achievement. Just take it easy. Just imagine him sitting upfront shouting the odds. It'll feel quite natural then."

He laughed and thumped me on the shoulder and then checked my straps. He stepped away from the plane and whirled his finger in the air. At the signal, I pulled the starter knob and the engine spluttered to life with an initial cloud of blue smoke which momentarily enveloped me as it blew back in the prop wash.

Steering the aircraft with the rudder pedals, it slowly trundled across the field towards the take-off point. Keeping a wary eye out for aircraft on their final approach to land as well as on the tower, I swung the plane round until it pointed into the wind. I had the field to myself. I raised my arm. A green flag was waved from the tower balcony. I eased the throttle forward, doing everything by the book. Soon I was airborne, the wheels free of the ground. Suddenly I was flying, flying on my own! I balled my fist and shook it triumphantly in the air above my head.

One circuit only, Osterkamp had said. He had been quite emphatic. He had walked away before my start-up. I wondered whether he was watching. I concentrated on what I was doing. Soon I had completed the circuit and turned the aircraft on final to land, the throttle barely open and the engine ticking over. I approached the end of the field in a shallow dive, the airspeed needle hovering on 110kph. The wind whistled through the wires and struts. As the ground loomed close, I pulled back at the right moment, the aircraft rounding out. The wheels kissed the ground without a bounce. Seconds later, as the speed died, the tail slowly descended until I felt it make contact with the ground, its harsh rumble audible, a quiver passing through the aircraft.

I taxied to where Schmidt was still standing, and pulled the mixture lever back and switched off the magnetos off. The propeller swung to a stop with a tick, tick. The mechanic chocked the aircraft's wheels, helped me out of the seat, and then from seemingly nowhere, produced two bottles of beer. We opened these and drank, toasting my success. Surely, it was my first meaningful, thrilling, and happy laugh since I'd arrived in Germany. I was ecstatic.

"Call me Matthias," I said to Schmidt, which now meant that we were close friends, he no longer having to address me with the customary 'Sie' but rather as 'Du'. Of course, the same applied to me when I addressed him. This type of familiarity was only found amongst close friends.

We finished the beers, Schmidt taking my empty bottle.

"Okay, Osterkamp asked that as soon as you landed he would like to see you in his office," Schmidt said.

As I walked through the reception area, Wiebke and another woman clapped hands. All seemed to be aware of my solo flight. I gave Wiebke a wink and a broad smile and strode into Osterkamp's office.

I was surprised. He actually grinned at me. In fact, it seemed a friendly grin! Then I saw the two schnapps glasses filled to the brim. Two! Well, that was a new one on me. He slid the one glass over the desk towards me.

"Congratulations, Herr Aschenborn." The fact that he had reverted to the proper form of address, the use of the 'Herr' prefix now evident, did surprise me.

"Not that I ever doubted your ability. I think you may just hold the record for going solo in the shortest number of hours. Seventeen, is it? You are a fast learner and it would seem a born flyer. Here's to you!" he said and threw the contents of the glass into his throat and replaced the glass on the table with a loud bang. "Well done, my man!" He then came round and shook my hand.

I could hardly speak, the schnapps taking my voice away, but I certainly did grin and happily accepted his commendations.

The lessons continued. My brief respite from his tirades and sarcasm were forgotten. Things reverted to normal again. We flew another two lessons together. Then he again sent me aloft alone. This became more frequent. We then tackled navigation, first a triangular flight with him followed by another alone.

We then started the most exhilarating aspect of my flying lessons and my quest for a pilot's licence, aerobatics. I loved aerobatics and even Osterkamp grudgingly admitted that this seemed to be my forte. I learnt to wring every conceivable manœuvre out of the aircraft: inside loops, climbing into the sky, the stick back, looking up at the top wing waiting for the horizon to appear as the plane zoomed to the apex of its loop. As soon as it did, I yanked the power back, the plane's speed increasing as it slid down the back end of the loop. I learnt to do spins, inverted spins, snap rolls, rolls, and four-point rolls, stall turns, Immelmann turns, and every other known manœuvre in the sky and then some more.

Osterkamp continued to devise new lessons. The next was to learn to fly really close to the ground, so close that at first I thought him insane.

We flew we nearly level with the cows in the meadows and lower than the masts of the small sailing boats on the Baltic Sea, the passage of the aircraft over the water, rippling the surface. On the ground he strung hydrogen-filled balloons floating no more than two metres above the clipped grass surface. I had to snag these with my wing, always with only one particular spot on my wing. I soon became quite adept at this game. Little did I realise that he was training me to be a Luftwaffe fighter pilot.

After that, I graduated to a Messerschmitt Bf 108 Taifun. This is a beautiful four-seater aircraft with a retractable undercarriage and a decent turn of speed. Thereafter, my night-flying lessons commenced flying the Messerschmitt, Osterkamp and I now sitting side-by-side as opposed to in-tandem, which was the case in the biplanes. After this, still flying the same aircraft I graduated to instrument flying. I spent hours under a hood flying the aircraft from the first roll of the wheels on take-off until the aircraft was about to touch down, this all done on instruments alone.

Osterkamp's favourite lesson seemed to be the recovery from awkward attitudes, those situations which can very suddenly occur in stormy weather when enclosed in a cloud with zero visibility. This was not the place to be flying by the seat of your pants. He would jam the hood down over my face and blind me and then seconds later lift the hood sufficiently so that I could see only the instruments.

A glance was sufficient to tell me we were in serious trouble. First, we had no airspeed. The needle hovered on zero. This is an unnatural attitude for an aircraft with wings especially at an altitude of 1,000 metres. Secondly, the aircraft also was banked at an angle of ninety degrees. And finally, that damned ball, Osterkamp's favourite instrument, was rammed up against the end of the tube. He shouted 'Recover!' in my ear, flashing some bright light, from where it came I knew not, simulating lightning strikes. To crown it all, the inclement weather bounced the aircraft around. The situation was precarious and if I tried to recover and did so incorrectly, the aircraft, which hovered on the edge of an incipient spin, would immediately enter a spin. That would not do.

This all had taken place in the span of a second or two. I had to imagine, as he would put it to me, that I had three passengers aboard. How would they feel about being involuntary participants of such an exercise? We would practise these recoveries repeatedly and eventually I could recover the aircraft from any attitude in any weather.

During the course of my training, I wrote a few examinations drawn up by the Air Ministry, all compulsory and incumbent upon trainee pilots. My final test flight was done with a government official, no doubt a member of the Luftwaffe in civilian clothes. I did the test flight in the Taifun. The man hardly spoke to me other than to issue instructions and busied himself with a clipboard as I proceeded to do the manœuvres he required.

Eventually we stepped from the aircraft. He turned to me.

"Congratulations," he said. "You are now a licensed pilot. It's something to be proud of." He saluted me and strode off to Osterkamp's office. Another Luftwaffe pilot in disguise, I thought.

CHAPTER SEVEN

Christmas and the New Year had come and gone. We were still in the full grip of winter. The snow in and around Kiel was more than a foot deep and every few days the coast would be battered by another cold front which would roar in from over the North Sea, sending temperatures plummeting and leaving a blanket of white in its wake.

The snow and ice on the roads made the use of the motorcycle hazardous. However, my father had come to the rescue and I was now the proud owner of an Opel Kadett. He had understood my reluctance to make use of the BMW. I do believe that Onkel Willi might have written to my father and explained my predicament regarding the BMW. Other than leaving the house to attend lectures or to take to the sky for an hour or two if the weather permitted, I confined myself to the house on Niemanns Street with Gustav my only companion. Since arriving in Germany, I had not once dated any woman and I had recently decided that it was time that I made some effort to find myself an accommodating female companion.

If I originally had had any designs on Wiebke, they had long evaporated. Of course, I still thought her one of the most beautiful woman I had ever seen, but Osterkamp was her father and my instructor and to suddenly become her beau may not have been beneficial to my flying career. That was assuming that his daughter would respond to my advances, which she had never done. Admittedly, I never came on strong so we would never know.

The occupants of the houses on our street had always appeared well-to-do and some even ostentatiously wealthy. A house, which was two houses down from us on the same side of the street, belonged to a Jewish family, the Eichbaums. The family, I had been told, that had for the past fifty to sixty years owned one of the larger department stores in the city. Whilst we were not house friends as it were, we would doff our hats to one another if we passed them in the street and would make small-talk and enquire about the weather and as to their well-being. The family consisted of the husband, the wife, and two daughters, the oldest of which was probably about fifteen years of age. Once when we past them on the street, Gustav had remarked on the daughter's beauty and said that given a few more years she would turn out to be an extraordinarily beautiful woman. I had to agree. It seemed that the Eichbaums were fortunate for we had yet to hear of any visits they may have had from the Gestapo and their goons.

The Jews were continuously harassed by the authorities who knocked on their doors in the middle of the night, demanding to see papers and just generally making their lives a misery. It was to the Gestapo and the SS that the task had been assigned of rounding up the Jews.

The Jews were leaving the country in droves. They had been left with little choice. Their property and assets were systematically being confiscated. They were barred from almost all business activities. They had to walk around with a yellow badge bearing the Star of David, proclaiming to all that they were Jewish. The government designated them as 'Untermenschen', a new word in the everyday German topics of conversation, and they were to be treated accordingly, a people without the normal privileges bestowed on the rest of the population. They were targeted by all to receive the worst of social treatment. Those who had not been so fortunate as to have been able to leave were systematically rounded up and taken to concentration camps.

We had seen and heard that on a few isolated occasions an academic or so-called wayward student at the university had questioned this abominable behaviour by the rank and file of the Nazi party, and some had even dared say that this constituted a crime against humanity. Within days, the glaringly obvious black cars of the Gestapo, a real giveaway, would arrive on the university campus where three or four men in long brown leather jackets would confront these individuals, scaring the living hell out of them and then whisking them away in their cars. Any who were foolish enough to voice objection or criticise were also dealt with in similar manner and driven off to God knows where. Without exception, all knew that it best to avoid Himmler's leather coat-clad henchmen. No longer did any German openly consort with the Jews lest they be seen to be sympathisers.

Hitler's closest deputies and henchmen suddenly had been elevated to the highest positions in Germany, which placed them on his right hand when he was appointed the Reichspräsident after the death of Paul von Hindenburg. They were never chosen for their academic prowess or their social standing. They were those drawn from the original riff-raff of the population that were unemployed and often uneducated by German standards. They were the followers and hangers-on who had supported Hitler during the political turmoil of the post-war years following WWI and the chaos after the Treaty of Versailles.

*

Dressed in my black overcoat and with my homburg pulled down over my eyes, I descended the steps from the front door to the street below, the snow crunching beneath my feet. I turned and noticed two black sedans parked in front of the Eichbaums house. I realised that it had to be the Gestapo but what I could do? We had all hoped the Gestapo would have left him and his family alone considering their standing in the community, but it seemed that this was not to be.

Just as I passed the gate from which a short garden path led to the front door, I saw the family being herded out of their front door, one of the Gestapo thugs even giving Herr Eichbaum a shove which nearly sent in stumbling down the few steps to the pathway. Herr Eichbaum looked up at me, his face pale, his expression that of confusion, fear and shock. Frau Eichbaum was in tears as were both their daughters. Each carried a suitcase. They were all bundled up in what seemed excessive layers of clothing. Clearly, they were being forced to leave, and for some time, I thought. My step faltered. I was on the verge of enquiring as to what was going on.

"Laufen sie weiter, mein Herr!" *Keep running, mister!* the tall Gestapo man who was in the lead shouted at me, he eyes hard, this obviously an order. I hesitated. This was not lost on the man.

"Bitte ziehen sie furnünftig," *Please keep moving properly*, he then added. I got the messagethat to interfere would have serious repercussions. I continued to walk without a backward glance, the hair in the nape of my neck erect with fear.

I would remember this incident for a long time.

*

Gustav had taken the weekend off to visit his family in an outlying village. He did this every few months. I was on my way to find a restaurant as I had decided that cooking was not for me and it would be simpler, and probably more pleasant, to sit down somewhere and order a meal. At the same time, I would see what the city centre had to offer. The fact that I had chosen to travel by tram was because I had little else to do and this would be a diversion. Also, I thought I just might take in some of the nightlife on offer.

The snow came down in flurries, some of it finding its way down the back of my neck. I turned up the collar of my overcoat and pulled my hat down farther. Just then, the tram screeched to a halt in front of the stop and I, together with a few others, ambled forward through the falling snow to board. I slid onto the first available seat.

I barely had relaxed when I heard a woman's voice behind me.

"Herr Aschenborn, what are you doing on the tram? What a surprise!"

I turned round to see Wiebke Osterkamp looking at me from the seat behind me.

"Fraulein Osterkamp, you too are a surprise, I never knew you lived in this area," I replied.

"Please Herr Aschenborn, you must call me Wiebke, I insist," she said. Of course, this would mean that I would use the 'du' form of address, which would imply a degree of familiarity in our relationship to any other who may be looking on.

"In that case, you will have to call me Matthias," I said. "What are you, at this time of the night, doing on a tram?" I asked.

She smiled at me, flashing her beautiful teeth. "I am rather bored at home. My father decided to go to Dresden and visit family. We mutually agreed that it would be a good idea if I remained behind and kept an eye on the administrative side of the office. You know, it's quite busy now. He said I was old enough to see to it myself."

I laughed. "I agree with him. You're definitely old enough to look after yourself, although what were you planning to do with yourself this evening, if I may ask?"

Again, she gave me a smile and then lowered her head coquettishly. "Well, he's not here and I thought that this time I may just do something that I would not normally do, go window-shopping or go to the cinema or even get something to eat. Maybe even look into one of those clubs? Although it probably would not be the right thing to do for an unescorted woman."

With all the turning around I was doing to look at her in the seat behind me, I was rapidly developing a crick in the neck. When the elderly man in the aisle seat opposite her stood to get off the tram, I immediately took the vacant place. At least it was now easier to look at her.

I looked at her side profile. God, I thought, she truly was exceptionally beautiful and she seemed to have matured over the last few months or was that because she had applied more make-up than usual? Why not take her out to dinner, I thought. It certainly was worth a try, I had nothing else to do, and I was feeling decidedly lonely.

"Please don't think it presumptuous of me, but why don't you join me for dinner. It should be quite pleasant. We could even go to the cinema," I said.

She looked at me from under lowered eyelids. "My father would probably not approve, but then it is I who am alone. Thank you, that is very kind of you," she said quietly.

Her acceptance came as a complete surprise. The tram wound its way through the suburbs while we discussed this and that, most of which was related to the flying school. She also mentioned that she had been trying to study but found this difficult what with her duties and having to keep house, her father being a widower after her mother having died a few years back.

"I suppose quite a few young men from the airfield and school have asked you out?" I asked

"Not really, I suppose they are afraid of my father. Most are student pilots just as you were," she giggled. "They're terrified of my father. I don't know why, he's actually a dear man," she added.

I believe that most of us did not share her sentiments. We had all fallen afoul of his sharp and sarcastic tongue.

Soon the tram entered the inner city. The shops' windows were lit up and small crowds were to be seen on the streets. Every now and then, I would see a shop front in darkness between all the other lit-up windows. These dark windows were crisscrossed with the white tape usually used to indicate that the owners were Jewish, the owners having been forced to close their business down. Every time I saw this, I experienced a fleeting spasm of guilt. Still, like many others, I did nothing. The whole of Germany did nothing.

We alighted from the tram in the city centre. This was nearly as bright as on a clear winter's day as a result of the reflection of the street and shop window lights off the white snow, light seemed to be radiating from everywhere. On the one corner of the city square I saw a cinema with a restaurant on each side of it, and through the windows I saw the guests sitting at their tables, clearly visible with their faces lit up by candles and small table lamps.

"Come, let's see what's showing and maybe we can find a restaurant that suits our fancy," I said gesturing towards the small complex on the other side of the square.

The huge back-lit porte-cochère of the cinema, which displayed the film's name and those of the main actors, revealed that it was an American gangster movie and indicated that it was with German subtitles. This suited me fine. She agreed. We crossed the square and entered the foyer, brushing the snow from our clothing.

I got us two decent tickets, not too far back from the screen. We handed in our overcoats with the hat-check attendant and made our way into the theatre itself. The film was about to start and the theatre was nearly full.

Now that she had removed her overcoat, I was able to get a better look at her. She was dressed in a light grey two-piece suit, the skirt ending just below her knees. She wore silk stockings, her shoes black and high-heeled, but sensible. Below the suit jacket, she wore a white blouse which was adorned with lace and buttoned to her throat. This all had been hidden by a black scarf which she had also handed in. Of course her face was now made up and this enhanced her appearance, the first time I had seen it so. There was no doubt that she was more mature than I originally thought and clearly a grown woman. Before, I'd thought her in her late teens. I guessed her to be in her early twenties. She also appeared to be more confident than I recalled. For over a year or more, she'd been working with groups of what had to be oversexed young men. To be sure, she must have been approached on a few occasions for a date. I had to believe that she was well schooled in ignoring or repelling the many advances a woman of her beauty would encounter. Well, I thought, at least I'd not been rejected. Or at least I hoped so.

We took our seats, she with what had to be the girlfriend or wife of a young sailor next to her and I with a uniformed soldier next to me. A good many uniformed military personnel were in the cinema.

The film started within minutes. This was a newsreel, the first feature covering the upcoming 1936 Olympics in Berlin scheduled for the summer and the preparations which were being made. The next, was a propaganda piece showing Hitler with his more important party members at a rally, a huge gathering of pomp and flags and thousands of followers. As Hitler appeared on the screen, the patrons in the cinema broke out in spontaneous applause. I noticed that Wiebke did not clap. There followed another feature, which showed Reichsführer-SS Himmler and the Deputy Führer Martin Bormann. They addressed a crowd in Berlin and expounded on the importance of maintaining the purity of the German race, giving reasons for the prohibition of mixed marriages between Christian and Jew. Jews were no longer considered citizens, but rather wards of the State. The degree of eagerness and ovation with which the crowds accepted these pronouncements defied reason. Germany was now a dictatorship and those in power now seemed to be irreversibly entrenching their power.

Wiebke leaned over to whisper in my ear, "Do you think this is good for Germany?"

I really did not want to reply. I merely shook my head but this did not deter her.

"My father says this is absolute madness. He says the whole world will end up hating us," she continued.

I had to say something. "That could well be true," I whispered in her ear, taking in her scent as I bent close to her ear. Our shoulders had touched and remained so, neither of us made an attempt to withdraw.

I hadn't been with a woman for ages and the nearness of her had a profound effect on me. I desperately wanted to touch or take her hand into mine. Our seats were separated by an armrest and I slid my hand under it and closed it softly over hers. She did not resist but lowered her head sideways until it rest on my shoulder. No word was spoken.

Of course, the Germans had followed the American example and introduced an interval before the main feature, referred to as a 'pause'.

Many left their seats, as did I. I bought a box of Swiss liqueur chocolates and returned, handing the box to her. She opened it and we each helped ourselves to a few silver paper-wrapped bonbons. No sooner had the lights dimmed when our hands again found each other's. The movie was good and we both became engrossed.

It was just after nine-thirty when we exited the cinema. We did not bother to don our coats but snuck into the adjoining restaurant to the cinema where we handed these to the woman attending the restaurant's hat counter. Soon the maître d'hotel approached dressed in starched shirt, black trousers, and tails. I requested a table for two, slipping him a five-mark note and asking that he try to give me a table which was secluded. He immediately understood my intentions, the banknote disappearing. He led us to a round table for four stuck away in a corner and with a half-round, red upholstered bench affixed to the corner wall provided seating on one side. Opposite to this, there were three chairs. We ignored these. The only source of light was the candles on the table, the wall lights had been dimmed. We slid onto the bench until we were sitting next to each other, both of us making sure we remained close, again taking each other's hand.

"Your father's in Dresden and you have the house to yourself for the next few days. You don't have to rush home so don't look at your watch. Just enjoy yourself," I said.

She smiled. "You're treating me like a teenager on a first date. I'm twenty-two years of age and will be twenty-three in the next few months. I don't have to account to my father for my actions," she said.

I was surprised. I never imagined her true age. She withdrew her hand from mine and placed both on top for all to see, that's if anybody bothered to look. I felt her leg touching mine.

"I'm rather surprised to find that you are without a partner," I said.

"I was involved for a few years. It didn't work out. I found out that he had another on the side. Somebody, let's say, who was more accommodating than I," she said.

The waiter arrived with our menus and the wine list. We ordered a bottle of Riesling and this being Kiel we both opted for fish.

The waiter bent conspiringly forward and in a subdued voice said that he had something special, a little pricey but excellent. Where we interested? I nodded.

"I have a fresh Norwegian salmon. It is served poached, to be shared by two, this in a delicious white wine sauce, with creamed spinach, boiled potatoes and ratatouille."

Wiebke winked at me and smiled. I said we'd go for it. Soon the wine arrived.

"What were you planning to do in town after you had eaten? Go to the cinema?" she asked.

74

"No, I wouldn't go alone. I would be uncomfortable. I would've just walked around and looked at the shops," I said.

"Liar. Young men like you can't resist a visit to one of these clubs," she retorted.

"Well, maybe then we would've accidentally met at one of the clubs," I ventured mischievously.

She drew in her breath and rounded her eyes in mock shock. "How dare you," she whispered, "I would never frequent a place like that! But to be honest, and for the sake of curiosity, I wouldn't mind knowing what goes on there. My friends have told me, but I found what they said difficult to believe. I would've liked to have seen for myself."

"Brave words. Well, seeing that there are no prying family eyes in Kiel at the moment, maybe we can arrange that." I grinned.

She glanced sideways at me. "Do you think I'll be shocked?' she asked.

I laughed. "Are you easily shocked?" I asked, my voice a little hoarse. This woman was pushing my buttons.

"It depends, by what and by whom. But then, I may just shock you."

That got me thinking.

The meal was excellent and we finished it off with coffee and liqueurs.

"Just remember, the last tram leaves at eleven-thirty," she said, taking my arm as we left the restaurant.

During the past few years, the Germans had again learnt how to enjoy themselves after the trying times and unemployment which had followed the Great War. We walked to that sector of the city centre known for its nightclubs and late-night revelry. The sidewalks were crowded with people moving in and out of the bars, the latest American Jazz tunes filtering out of some of the doorways.

I saw a place that I thought was what I was looking for. A large garish neon sign above the doorway winked on and off intermittently. This displayed a rather voluptuous woman holding one of those ridiculously long cigarette holders, the front of her dress cut to reveal her bosom while the rear plunged to her ample derrière. The was the Black Cat, *Die Schwarze Katze*, a rather well-known watering-hole, dancehall with cabaret, and scantily-clad women or so the sign advertised.

"This should suit your fancy," I said playfully.

"It's not bad, is it?" she asked, a concerned look on her face.

I laughed, unable to contain my amusement.

"No, nothing is bad. It may be just a little graphic for you. In a number of the shows the women strip off their clothes."

"Good God! Really?"

Before she could hesitate, I pulled her into the entrance where the door attendant eagerly ushered us inside, making sure we wouldn't change our minds. The entrance fee was exorbitant but I did not mind. I had a feeling that my lovely Wiebke was also playing her own game. God, I thought, what would Hauptmann Osterkamp think if he knew his daughter was consorting with Aschenborn in a Kiel nightclub?

It was rowdy. The bar was lined with men and women, while others danced, and a woman in a shimmering silver dress on a small stage sang to the music of a five-piece band. The lighting was subdued except for the small table lamps, the shades of which were dark, only illuminating the surface of each table. The tables were small, designed for two, just. However, there were larger tables for groups. The waiter led us to our table. We sat down. He was about to flash a menu at me. I shook my head.

"Two coffees and four Dom Benedictine liqueurs," I said. I looked at her. She nodded her approval. I knew I was going to baulk at the price as this was how these places made their money. If it weren't wine or beer, you paid the earth.

"I see that you've already got your C2 licence as well as a KII aerobatics licence. That must have cost a bit. You should soon get your papers to report to the Officer Cadet School at Berlin-Gatov. This is now the new Luftwaffe Fighter Weapon School, or so my father says."

This came as a surprise. She was well-informed. She must have had sight of documentation between Hauptmann Osterkamp and the Department of Defence or the Luftwaffe directly. Of course, I thought. She probably typed his letters. Surely, she realised that mentioning this to me constituted a breach of security. Good God! Fighter training and officer cadet school, for what more could I wish?

I took her hand, brought it to my lips, and kissed it. "I can't tell you how glad I am that you've told me. You've given me the best news." I then leant across and fleetingly brushed my lips across hers. "I'll never tell a soul that you've told me, so don't worry. You've given me the best news. I knew I was going to be conscripted, but I certainly won't be walking. A Luftwaffe officer? Jesus Christ. A German glory boy. A dream come true."

We danced, moving well together, our bodies touching and our thighs occasionally brushing. During the evening, she lost that slight degree of reserve she had initially displayed. Here was a woman who would not pretend about anything, I thought. If something were not to her liking, you'd know. I seemed to have figured a little higher in the attraction stakes than others and I was sure that if I were to ask her out again, she would not refuse. Actually, I hadn't asked her out. Our getting together had been an accident.

By the time we were ready to go home, the trams had long stopped running for the night. It took a while but eventually I found a taxi. It was convenient to drop Wiebke off first. She instructed the driver and we set off, we both sitting close together on the rear seat holding hands. Too soon we arrived outside her home, a two-storey apartment similar to others in the street, built one adjoining the other.

"I'll walk you to the door," I said.

"Will we do this again?" she asked.

"Of course," I replied and took her in my arms and kissed her, this for no more than a moment or two.

She opened the door and with a wave disappeared.

*

The taxi dropped me off at the house. It had not been a cheap evening considering that I was still a student. Still, over the last months I had spent little and getting to know Wiebke had been worthwhile. Also, what pleased me was that she appeared not to be taken up with the fanaticism that seemed to be sweeping Germany. I had the feeling that this could be her father's doing and being a member of the old school he may not be an ardent supporter of Herr Hitler.

Wiebke had been right. Gustav had returned and, a few days later, an officious large envelope arrived in the mail. This contained papers from the Ministry of Defence advising that my conscription had now become effective and that, upon completion of my current semester, I was to report to the flight school at Berlin-Gatov but not later than the 31st of March. Well, that gave me sufficient time to finalise my studies at Kiel. There were various other documents attached. They included the basic requirements in terms of clothing and other items, a brief description of the regulations that applied in terms of conduct and dress, and the name and address of the local tailors who specialised in military uniforms. The military did issue ready-made uniforms to its officer cadets but it was commonly believed that an officer should have at least one tailor-made uniform, which was referred to as an *Ausgangsuniform*, his dress uniform, as it were.

I had seven weeks to prepare myself before my departure for Berlin. Little did I know that this would change my life.

*

I sat for the semester exams and was pleased to have passed my engineering subjects. I was in the top ten of the faculty. That I was able to achieve this and still learn to fly and obtain my pilot's licence I thought commendable. My father thought so as well. Hauptmann Osterkamp returned from Dresden and was aware of my imminent induction into the Luftwaffe. Surely, he would have had something to do with this. I wondered, would they have also asked for my reports?

Of late, I had noticed a change in the man's attitude towards me. He was more friendly and occasionally even given to long discussions with me on matters not related to flying at all. He spoke of the Great War and its tragedies. The millions of young men who had died, and the millions of lives lost even affecting the country's manufacturing abilities. There were simply no workers. He spoke of the aerial battles in aircraft made of wood, string, and wire as he put it, flying without parachute and the ever-present danger of fire, every pilot's greatest fear. He told me of the loss of his wife a few years back to cancer and his daughter who kept house for him.

I found out that he had been a man with a mission, pushing me in order to see that I accumulated the necessary hours and that I moved from the A1 certification on my licence to the current C2 with the aerobatics KII. I was sure that this had something to do with my Onkel Willi. What I did find out was that he had been awarded a Pour le Merit, he had downed 21 aircraft. He was an ace and a German war hero.

"Don't look so surprised," he had said one morning in his office when we were unable to fly due to the inclement weather. I had mentioned that I thought he had relentlessly driven me to obtain the qualifications I now held. "The Luftwaffe covered most of your expenses once they established that you did have some talent. Certainly, somebody had to tell them that you had talent. Well, I did. Now, it will be up to you not to let me down in Berlin."

"I won't," I said.

"You know, I've enjoyed your company." Then he added with a smile, it as if this was merely an afterthought, "and so has my daughter."

He smiled at the look of amazement that crossed my face.

"Don't concern yourself. I'm pleased."

A feeling of relief passed through me. I'd no idea how he would react knowing that Wiebke and I had been out while he had been away.

I walked out of the office and closed the door behind me. Wiebke looked up from behind her desk. There was a stack of papers in front of her. I walked over.

Quietly, making sure I could not be overheard I said. "It's Friday. How about going out with me tonight?" I asked.

With her eyes, she indicated her father's office. I brushed this nonchalantly aside.

"Don't worry about him," I said and laughed. "He knows and seems quite happy with it."

She showed surprise.

"I thought so," she replied. "Well, in that case, it's yes. Where are we going?"

"To a restaurant and dancing," I said and then bent down and lowered my voice to a whisper, "I'm going away to Berlin very soon. The restaurant and dance is actually being held at my house. I'll collect you a seven-thirty. Are you happy with that?" I asked.

At first, she appeared dubious and undecided but then smiled and nodded. Un-chaperoned to single men's house was not condoned. Were people to know, this could result in embarrassing scandal.

God, I could have taken her there and then into my arms and kiss her passionately and let one thing just lead to another. I was thrilled and infused with a feeling of expectation. She'd actually agreed! Did she understand that I was planning an evening of sexual incitement? She had to., it had to be that obvious.

When I arrived home from the airfield, I immediately sought out Gustav and asked him whether he did not wish to go home for the weekend. I could hardly contain my excitement.

"I wasn't planning to do so," he said, looking at me unsure of what I was up to, but then I saw it dawn on him that I wanted him out of the house.

He smiled. "It's a woman, isn't it?" he asked.

I squirmed and looked away, reluctant to say anything, neither did I want to lie. Fortunately, he read my mind.

"Don't worry, I actually do have to go and was planning to do so next week, but now would be as good as any. Are you planning to have supper?"

Christ! Yes, I thought. I told him so. "Supper for two", I said.

"Don't worry, the train leaves at six. I have time. Let's see what I can do. You don't have to worry about anything. It's all here."

"Thank you, Gustav. I do appreciate it."

At about five, he called me into the kitchen.

"It's all done. Anyway, this was supposed to be our supper," he said and pursed his lips. "It's actually sauerbraten with dumplings. You know, beef marinated for a few days and then roasted in the oven. Everything is already cooked. You just have to warm up the meat in the oven and stick the dumplings in boiling water. When they rise to the top they're ready. The sauce is in the pot on the stove. Just heat it and, voilà, you'll have a perfect meal. There's Apfeltorte and cream for dessert."

The good woman was in for a surprise, I thought. Gustav shook my hand, took his case and left.

At six, I poured myself a stiff whiskey from my father's stock, added plenty of ice, and took this up to my bedroom. I stripped and got into the bath, luxuriating in its warmth, sipping my whiskey and thought about Wiebke. There was no doubt that she was special but it was a pity that with the relationship just about to move up a notch, I had to go to Berlin. I would not be able to see her that often. Berlin was far and really too far to travel to every weekend from Kiel. I would have to come up with something.

I shaved, brushed my teeth, and put on black trousers, my best, a snow-white shirt, and a black sports jacket copied from America. I appraised my reflection in the full-length mirror. I thought I looked rather snazzy.

Dressed in my overcoat, gloves, and a hat, I backed the BMW out of the garage and drove off in the direction of the Osterkamp residence.

Osterkamp opened the door, this time with a pipe in his hand and clad in a blue smoking jacket. I noticed that his ever-present military demeanour had vanished.

"Herr Aschenborn, punctual as usual. Impressive," he greeted me jovially. "Did you know that punctuality is a reflection of a man's character?" he said, leading me to the drawing room. I wondered whether this was not his manner in indicating to me that he approved of me.

"Please take a seat. Wiebke will be a while. She's a woman, what can you do?" he said, also sitting down in which was clearly his seat, the side table containing his tobacco pouch, matches and a pipe scrapper, and the book he must have been reading.

I let my eyes casually take in the room. While it was quite pleasant, I thought it did not reflect the Osterkamp image. It was not what I expected. He seemed to perceive my thoughts.

"This is really not our home. It's temporary, provided by the military for my use. Our home is actually in Dresden," he said sounding apologetic. Again, another snippet of privacy I was privileged to hear, or so it seemed.

For a temporary residence and obviously provided inclusive of the furniture, the place wasn't bad at all. The furnishings were tasteful, as were the carpets and paintings. But somehow they seemed out of character, impersonal, similar to those in an upmarket hotel.

"Let me offer you something to drink.How about a brandy and soda? I know her, she'll be a while."

"That'll be fine," I replied.

He busied himself with the drinks at a small buffet and without turning around said, "I'll not be here long, may be just another few months, but keep that to yourself. I, too, might go to Berlin or Dresden. I believe I'm to be promoted to major. One hears these things if you have friends in the right places."

"Congratulations."

"No, it's not time for that yet. I'll believe it when I see the shoulder boards on my uniform. Incidentally, that bit of information is also confidential."

It was good brandy. We chatted for another ten minutes. I heard a door close upstairs and turned towards the staircase. Wiebke appeared at the top and smiled at me. She was gorgeous. She'd done her hair, this style a little different from what she usually wore. It shone in the light of the chandelier. She wore a red cocktail dress, the hem no higher than her knees, revealing her beautiful legs. The swell of her breasts were just discernible above the neckline of the dress.

I needed to greet her but I was not going to walk up and kiss her in front of her father. I shook her hand murmuring a greeting and smiled, which she returned.

"Your look magnificent," I said.

Her father also murmured a compliment. I thought he said, 'very nice'. I helped her into her coat which she had brought downstairs draped over her arm.

"Are we ready to go?" she asked as if it were not herself that had held up the proceedings.

I stuck out my elbow for her to take my arm. "Shall we?" I asked.

Osterkamp had risen from his chair. "Enjoy yourselves. You're not working tomorrow, so get back whenever you wish," Osterkamp said walking up to his daughter and pecking her on the cheek. He then said goodnight. I led her out of the front door to the car.

"My god, he seemed to be saying you could even get back after dawn," I said.

She giggled. "I told you, he's not as bad as you think. Besides, he knows I'm a grown woman. I do as I wish, although he occasionally does object."

I didn't need reminding that she was older than I. I realised that this woman was not to be taken advantage of. She had a mind of her own.

After helping her into the car, I came round to my side and slid into the driver's seat. On impulse, I then leant across and softly kissed her on the lips, lingering there for a few seconds, our tongues touching. She was not surprised and never hesitated, she immediately responded.

"I missed you," she whispered. "But you'd better go. He'll wonder why you haven't driven off."

I started the car and we moved off, but once I turned the corner, I again pulled over to the kerb. Without invitation, she fell into my arms and we kissed passionately. Her nearness consumed me, my lips running over her face, eyes and ears. I then kissed her again. This carried on for two or three minutes. Finally, we drew apart.

"Mein lieber Gott!" she whispered. "This certainly wasn't planned." I realised that she had her hand in my lap. She quickly drew her hand away.

I just laughed and drew her to me again. For the last few weeks whenever I had an erotic thought, she would invariably play the leading role. Now this was no dream, this was reality. My need for this woman was so intense I found it difficult to speak, my words seeming to be stuck in my throat.

"Let's not sit here. You said you're taking me to dinner. I hope it still at your house and that we're not going anywhere else," she said.

Clearly, she had shed any inhibitions she may have had and we both knew where this was leading.

"It's still the house," I replied.

We drove the short distance to my home with her leaning against me, her hand on my upper thigh and her head on my shoulder, I so aware of her. This woman had me aroused and I had to make an effort to concentrate on my driving.

We had hardly walked through the front door when she asked, "Are we alone?"

I nodded. She fell into my arms and kissed passionately. Instinctively, I ran my hands over her body and drew her hard against me. I then helped her out of coat and removed my own. These we just draped over the armrest of the nearest armchair. A coal fire burnt in the hearth, shedding its warm glow over the room. She moved back into my arms and then, still caught up in our passion, we slowly moved on to the large rug in the living room, shedding items of clothing as we haltingly moved nearer to the fire. We both were oblivious of our surroundings.

Once in front of the fire, we sunk to our knees but still on the thick rug. By then all I still wore were my trousers and shoes. My belt buckle was undone and hung from the trouser loops. Wiebke wore but a bra, her panties, and a suspender belt. I reached up to unclasp her bra but she pushed my hands away and looking into my eyes, reached behind, and unclasped it letting it drop to the floor. Her breasts were beautiful. They stood proud of her body. I took them in my hands and lowered my head, my lips closing over a nipple. She groaned letting her head fall back. My mouth slid down her stomach, kissing her. Slowly I lowered her upper body to the floor until she lay with her back on the carpet. I removed her stockings and suspender belt and then pulled her panties over her feet and tossed them on top of the other clothing.

She had unbuttoned my trousers. I stood and removed my shoes and trousers and slid off my underpants. She reached out a hand and touched me. I kissed the flat of her stomach just above her pubis and then her inner thighs. She arched her back and drew in her breath through clenched teeth with a hiss. She emitted a long slow moan, took my hand, and forcefully placed it on her pubis. She was wet and ready to my touch.

"Um Gottes willen, Liebling. Warte doch nicht so lange!" *For goodness sake, don't take too long!* she whispered hoarsely in my ear.

I buried my face in her neck and felt her hands fiercely grip my shoulders. The hiss of her sharp intake of breath was loud in my ear. A minute later, she again arched her back and let out a howl, so loud that for a moment I thought somebody might hear it. Then I shuddered as my own orgasm overtook me.

Spent, we lay there in front of the fire, our eyes closed, waiting for our breath to slow, the sheen of perspiration on our bodies reflecting the light of the fire. She lay next to me on her side, her face nuzzled into my neck.

"I love you," she quietly said.

"I know, and I love you," I replied.

A smile crossed her face. "I think I started to love you from the first day I saw you when you came in to buy your goggles and flying cap. You were so shy. You looked so young and inexperienced and I remember how resolved you seemed to become a pilot. It seemed so important to you," she said.

"God, I remember. You were so beautiful I could hardly talk."

She chuckled. "I then watched you for weeks as your confidence grew and how you learnt how to handle my father, steeling yourself for his inevitable verbal onslaught without losing your temper. You know, nowadays he seldom, if ever, instructs. Somehow and for what reason I wouldn't know, he singled you out. On the day you saw him for the first time and left the office he said, 'That man I will instruct myself'. I felt so sorry for you, knowing what you were in for, but you handled it. One evening we were talking about you and he said, 'Aschenborn will one day teach me how to fly, he has that much talent'. Then you became aloof, instead of me getting closer to you, you just moved out of reach. It was as if you never saw me. It nearly broke my heart."

Again, I laughed: "And I thought you had no interest in budding young pilots who were not yet men."

"I'm hungry. Let's eat. What do we have for supper? After that, we can do this again, but slower this time." She said rising from the floor. She picked up my shirt, which lay on the floor at the entrance to the foyer, and slipped it on, buttoning it part-way until it reached nearly to her knees.

I slipped on my trousers and my vest. We both padded barefoot into the kitchen.

Everything was on the table, the oven still hot. She removed the cloth that covered the prepared food.

"Sauerbraten! My favourite!" she exclaimed with mock delight. "Just stand back. You wouldn't know what to do." She busied herself around the stove, sliding the baking pan with the roast into the oven. She put on the dumplings to boil. The gravy pot was also placed on top of the stove to warm up as well as a pot that contained shredded red cabbage. I sat there in a kitchen chair and watched this extraordinary, uninhibited, beautiful woman who'd somehow taken over my heart. Already, I was thinking what I would do when in Berlin and she either here or in Dresden. How was I going to get us together?

"I need you to come to Berlin to be with me," I said.

"I can't leave my father. He needs me," she replied, giving me a quick glance over her shoulder. I realised that this was a resolve from which she was not to be persuaded.

The food was ready and we dished up. The smell of the marinated roasted piece of meat was mouth-watering. With the laden plates in my hands, I moved towards the dining room.

"Uh-huh! Back to the fire. Give me your plate. You just find the wine and the glasses. We'll eat on the carpet and afterwards we can carry on where you left off, but this time I'll control the tempo. No more zim-zam stuff."

What could I do?

I opened the bottle of wine, a red from the Rhine Valley, the colour warm in the light of the fire. The roast was sumptuous as were the dumplings. The gravy made from the juices of the meat and the marinade, which had oozed from it while roasting, just crowned it all. We followed this with coffee and liqueurs.

I could not keep my eyes off her as she moved around the kitchen naked beneath my shirt. Inadvertently or may be even surreptitiously, she permitted me glances of breasts and her dark triangle.

She noticed my arousal. "Not now," she said, "but keep it, you'll need it later."

When we had eaten and had drunk our coffee and liqueurs, she pushed the dishes aside, then approached, stalking me like a lioness on hands and knees, a mischievous smile on her lips to where I sat cross-legged on the carpet. She shoved me back with the flat of her hand until I lay flat on the floor.

"Now let me show you how it's done," she whispered and slowly started to kiss me.

CHAPTER EIGHT

I awoke with a start. The first signs of daylight showed through the chinks in the bedroom curtain. It had to be past seven.

"For fuck's sake," I gasped, aware of her asleep next to me. I jumped from the bed. "It's bloody morning already. Your father's going to shoot me."

She opened her eyes and looked at me. I realised I was stark naked with everything on display. She started giggling and the bed shook.

"God, you should see yourself," she managed to get out between laughing.

"Come on, get up," I shouted.

Christ, I realised that our clothing must still be strewn all over the place. I returned minutes later with my arms full of her and my clothing. The damn woman was asleep again.

"For God's sake, Wiebke, get up," I shouted again.

"Come back to bed. We'll get up later," she mumbled, her face buried in the pillow.

"Your father, what's he going to think?"

"Well, whatever it is, rest assured he's already thinking it. Now be quiet, I want to sleep." She turned her back on me and stuck a pillow over her head.

Just then I heard a bang and clutter. "Oh my fuck," I said. "It's the bloody maid." I had completely forgotten her. Here was a scandal of immense proportions brewing. The maid was going to love this. "Please, sweetheart. Just get up," I pleaded.

Wiebke threw the covers off and slid from the bed. "Oh, all right, but what good is it going to do. You'd have to be a total idiot not to realise what went on here, so live with it. Pretend nothing happened."

I dispensed with a bath, I just wanted to get dressed. This was not the time to be undressed and with a woman in your bedroom. I shaved, brushed my teeth, combed my hair and got dressed all in record time.

Wiebke had to wear what she had worn the previous night. Nonetheless, the overcoat hid most of it. As we descended the stairs, the maid appeared and greeted us. She never blinked an eye at the picture of us before her. I dreaded to contemplate what she had to be thinking. She merely enquired whether we would be having breakfast.

"Coffee will do for the both of us," I said. "Just bring it into the drawing room."

*

I drove Wiebke back home. Obviously, I was apprehensive. She may be twenty-two years of age, but I was expecting Osterkamp to make issue that I had kept her out for the night without informing him and leaving him concerned for her safety. I wasn't sure how I would handle it if he confronted me. Wiebke did not appear perturbed. At near twenty-three, she probably thought it none of my business and convinced that I would not say a word.

"Have you been through this before?" I asked.

"Don't be ridiculous. I only stayed because I love you and I'll tell him so if need be. That'll shut him up." She smiled, "Anyway, whatever he may say, we both know it was worth it." She leant over and kissed me on the cheek. If this young woman had previously had any inhibitions, they had vanished.

With her own key, she opened the front door to the house and we both entered the drawing room. It was just after nine in the morning and Osterkamp sat in a lounge chair already dressed with a cup of coffee on a side-table and the morning *Allgemeine Zeitung* newspaper on his lap.

"Good morning, you're back I see."

If that was a reprimand it did not sound so, I thought. Osterkamp continued, "Well, rather late than never I might add. I take it you had a pleasant evening?" he said with a smile. Wiebke went over to him and bent down to kiss him. "Morgen, Vati," she said.

I mumbled a 'good morning', still stunned by the nonchalance and pleasant greeting from the man. I had expected some dissatisfaction with our late return.

"I'm going to bath and change," she said and left disappearing up the stairs.

"Tell me, Herr Aschenborn, " he waved the newspaper at me, "do you believe this man Adolf Hitler is Germany's salvation?"

I hesitated. It was not a good idea to speak out against the Nazi Party. All Germans knew this except for a reckless few. However, I had already gathered that Wiebke was anti-Nazi and it was a good bet that her feelings were a portrayal of his own, she being his daughter.

"Herr Osterkamp, to be honest I would've preferred a Germany that was a true democracy. Yes, I'll admit that dictators have brought wealth and glory in the past, look at Napoleon, but unfortunately history tells us this is always short-lived. I believe all should have a say in government. The system in the United States appeals to me. You know the bit about 'all men are created equal' and if you don't like the way those in power are running the country, you can always vote against them in the next election. And no president seeks to serve more than two terms."

"A good answer," he said cynically, "and probably the right answer given the times."

"Come, please sit down. Seldom do I have male company in my own home, besides it would seem that you and my Wiebke are now an item. Is that correct?" he asked.

"I love him, father," she shouted from the landing.

"Well, she sounds quite sure doesn't she? And you?"

I felt ridiculous, never expecting to pronounce my feelings for his daughter in quite this fashion. I felt embarrassed.

"Yes, I feel the same."

I'd be damned before I said that I loved her to her father!

"Excellent! I am pleased." He beamed. "Now, back to the paper. We know that Hitler is gearing up to make Germany a world power again, particularly in Europe. I'm not saying he is planning war but should that ever happen, he wants Germany to be ready. Now, as a military man, I can't fault that, but there lurks the danger. I see this as power without morality. You need just look at this nonsense about the Jews, and worst of all the Germans seem to believe the propaganda that Goebbels's mob is spreading. During the war, Jews died like Germans in the trenches, dead Christian and Jew lying next to each other. For Christ's sake, I had one Flugzeugwart during the whole war and he was a Jew. God knows how many times he patched up my aircraft, loaded my guns, and probably saved my life, he was so methodical. Now I'm expected to treat him like a piece of shit because he is Jewish. I can't do that. Unfortunately, he died a few years back, natural causes, but I could've never sold him down the road. Germany has no loyalties to its own or its friends anymore, we believe this no longer necessary."

If he was looking for a reaction from me strongly supporting what he was saying, I was not ready to give it. I had decided that it would be better if I didn't get too involved. This was the typical attitude adopted by most.

"I would rather adopt a wait-and-see attitude. Give the Nazis a chance, so far they haven't done a bad job," I said.

He just stared at me for a moment over the rim of his cup. I looked back without averting my eyes.

Finally, in a lowered voice he said, "Maybe yours is the right attitude for a budding Luftwaffe officer, but I hope that there is a lot more decency in you which you are not revealing. Be careful, the Luftwaffe has its fair share of political socialist fanatics."

He then moved away from politics saying that in view of the fact that I'd soon be going to Berlin, both Wiebke and I should make the most of the opportunity and see each other a lot more often. I did not believe that this statement contained any sexual connotation, but I'm sure it must have crossed his mind. I did not miss the slight smile that crossed his face.

Finally, Wiebke descended the stairs and helped herself to coffee. It was amazing that she showed me such affection in front of her father, coming across to me and leaning against me with her arms around my waist and her head on my shoulder. He took this show of uninhibited affection in his stride. "I'm very glad you two are happy. She is my only child and if she's happy, so am I," he said, smiling broadly.

Well, that certainly put a stamp of approval on things, I thought.

*

We returned to our Niemannsweg house before noon and, for the next few weeks, she would commute between her home, my home, and the airfield, but most nights she spent with me. Gustav took this new development in his stride, never raising an eyebrow. Besides, Wiebke treated Gustav as if he were a grand-uncle. He loved every moment.

I soon realised how deeply in love I was with this woman, but she was not to be dissuaded. She would return to Dresden with her father. Berlin was not an option she was prepared to consider.

CHAPTER NINE

I drove to Berlin in my Opel Kadett. I was in no rush and planned a two-day trip. Although it was now spring and the first green leaves had begun to show, most of the snow had melted but the sun remained hidden for most days, the occasional shower still encountered.

I was amazed at the number of military vehicles I saw and how many men appeared to be in uniform. A few times, I was stopped in police roadblocks. These were manned by police and occasionally the Gestapo, their men in leather coats. I presented my papers and once they realised to where I was going, immediately let me pass.

The Luftwaffe complex at Berlin-Gatov was huge. It spread over a vast flat area, all dominated by the airfield itself. The complex was oval in shape and permitted take-offs from all directions. It was a requirement in the old days when it was essential to take off into the wind because biplanes of string and wood were difficult to handle in the slightest crosswinds.

I stopped at the main gate. Two Luftwaffe infantrymen with rifles barred my entry and demanded to see my papers. A non-commissioned officer appeared and took my papers, carefully inspecting these.

"You are a day early. Your detachment needs only to arrive by tomorrow at three," he said.

I said I knew, but came earlier to ensure that if anything went wrong, such as with the car, I could make it in time.

He harrumphed, clearly surprised at my answer. He gave me directions to where I had to go and then let me through. I drove slowly, the roads were clearly-marked with signs forbidding speeds above ten kph. Squads of men dressed in fatigues could be seen marching to the commands of their Unteroffiziere whose dissatisfaction with their performance I could clearly hear, audible through the car's open window. I began to realise what I was in for.

I drew up in front of the office block, which was the office of the commanding officer of my detachment. Another armed soldier walked up to me and enquired whether I was a new intake. I said I was. He then asked whether this was my car. I said it was.

"Sorry, you can't park here." He gave me directions to the car park for candidate officers.

"That's quite a way. I've a lot of stuff," I said.

"Sorry, you'll just have to carry it," he said.

I didn't argue and drove off. I found the car park. At least it had covered parking, a few rows of wooden sheds open to one side which had been erected for this purpose. There were only a few cars. I barely could carry the luggage I had and slowly hauled it to the office block having to stop numerous times to rest.

I had stopped when another fellow dressed in a suit and with only one large suitcase stopped next to me, he having caught up with me. He was just short of six feet, with blond hair combed right back and held in place by a generous application of hair oil which made it shine in the light. His eyes were strikingly blue and he sported a faint blond moustache.

"Helmut Kleber from Hamburg," he said sticking out his hand. "I'm also new. I'm assigned to Detachment 4."

We shook hands.

"Matthias Aschenborn, also Detachment 4."

"Come, let me give you a hand with this stuff. I just brought absolute necessities. The buggers have to give us everything else. Why bring it?"

I let him relieve me of a few pieces and we walked towards the office block. Once outside the building, we neatly packed our luggage in a pile, straightened our clothing and entered the offices where we were promptly stopped by another non-com.

"New recruits," I said.

"You mean Luftwaffe cadets," the man said, clearly looking at us with contempt. "Stand here! Don't move until I get back. Your papers, please."

The man walked off.

"Fuckin' asshole!" my companion whispered.

I liked him already. When the Luftwaffe tells you to wait, you wait. This was to be my first experience. Many others were to follow. About half-an-hour later, we were still standing in the front office. If they intended pissing us off on our first day, they achieved that. Finally, we were led into the office of an Oberleutnant, both of us displaying an air of impatience.

"Aschenborn and Kleber. What're you looking so shirty about?" he asked with an affectation that implied that we were nothing more than an irritant that he was forced to deal with. Any display of impatience we may have had immediately evaporated.

We nodded.

"The reply is 'Jawohl, Herr Oberleutnant'!" he shouted. "You best remember that!"

We both shouted the proper term of address and came to attention clicking our heels. Not dressed in uniform there was no need to salute.

He scrutinised the papers and expressed his satisfaction.

"Aschenborn, I see that you are well-qualified already. C2 and KII? I daresay, that's impressive. Kleber, you've managed it to C1, not bad. Now let's see if you can fly a Heinkel."

He called for a sergeant who arrived with a salute and a click of heels. It was a normal salute, not a Nazi salute.

"Feldwebel, let them drop off their personal effects and then present both of them to Hauptmann Bähr. Best take them to Ordinance and get them into some sort of uniform first." He turned to us, "Be warned, Detachment 4's commanding officer is the good Hauptmann Bähr and today he is acting like a bear, which is not unusual," the Oberleutnant said with a wicked smile.

I wondered what that implied.

We followed the Feldwebel to our barracks. Fortunately, cadet officers were not packed into one large barracks like sardines. We clearly were being afforded some deference, even if initially not much. Two cadets to a room was the norm for candidate officers. Spartan would adequately describe our new residence. There were two beds and two lockers, these quite large with hanging space and a threadbare carpet on the floor. A few faded photographs of WW1 planes hung on the walls. A single light bulb hung from the ceiling with a small Bakelite shade. We were to share a common bathroom and the latrines with the cadet officers in the other rooms.

We were given a minute to drop off our stuff and then marched off to the Ordinance Section where again a burly Feldwebel and his clerk confronted us. First they passed a critical eye over us, murmuring amongst themselves, and then proceeded to pass equipment and clothing across the counter, ticking the items off on a list. There were two uniforms, two pairs of boots, one pair of which were fleece-lined, caps and flying caps, gloves, underwear, canteens, steel helmets, padded flying suits, and other insignia.

"What about the leather flying jacket?" Helmut asked.

The sergeant's face turned a bright red, clearly enraged. He leaned across the counter and I was expecting him to grab my new friend by the lapels. When inches from his face, he barked, "You're not an officer yet, just a whippersnapper. You might not even stand up to the rigours of the course. You're still nothing. Understand?"

Helmut turned away, his face screwed into a grimace and then stepped back to stand next to me. The sergeant continued to stare at him as his clerk shoved our kit across the counter at us.

"Halitosis," Helmut whispered nonplussed, "bad enough to kill a fuckin' Hamburg tramp."

I saw the sergeant's head jerk. "What did he say?" he demanded.

"Just that he'll get his leather jacket when he graduates," I intervened.

"Take your fuckin' stuff and get out," the sergeant screamed, sliding the documents across the counter for us to sign. I scrawled my signature. Helmut did the same.

We took our bundled-up kit, which we hardly were able to carry, and stumbled out of the building.

Our sergeant spoke for the first time. "Now, that was a good start. No doubt, you'll be hearing more from him. I'll look after you. I hate the bastard. Be careful, he'll have singled you both out."

That was a consoling thought. At least somebody would look after us, I thought.

"What if this doesn't fit?" I asked.

The sergeant waved me off. "You can sort it out with your companions. You just swap." I knew it pointless to argue, that this would only aggravate the situation.

"Officious fuckin' idiots," Helmut whispered as we returned to the barracks.

"Where did you grow up, Hamburg docks?" I asked.

The man's language was atrocious.

"What do you mean?"

"Forget it," I said. Christ, my remark was lost on him. His choice of words and expletives was yet to land us in a load of trouble.

In the barracks, the sergeant waited while we dressed. Of course, the uniforms were not pressed and did not fit. I did swap a few items with my roommate and finally we were ready to present ourselves to Hauptmann Bähr. The uniforms were still creased, nothing had been cleaned and the boots had not even seen polish. Still, we were marched off to his office, a pathetic looking pair of rumpled-looking wannabes.

"Remember, to come to attention and salute," the sergeant said.

We waited in the fore-office while the sergeant disappeared for a minute. We heard him come to attention, the click of his heels loud enough to penetrate the closed door. A minute later, he re-appeared and beckoned that we enter. We marched into the office and came to attention. Of course, our timing was out, the heel clicking sounding like a tap-dance and the salute out of sync.

The Hauptmann lifted his right hand to his temple in return. It was a movement, not a salute.

"My God, what is the Luftwaffe going to take on next? You both look like something that was scrapped off the pavements of the Hamburg Reeperbahn. This is not the Wehrmacht. This is the Luftwaffe," he stated, a grim look on his face.

He took two files off the top of a pile on his desk and studied these for a minute.

The man was impeccable in his light-grey blue uniform with the three spread-winged gulls, one below the other on each lapel against the yellow background. There were various insignia attached to his tunic. The most striking aspect of him was the eyes. I'd never seen anything like them before, silver grey and although I did not think him yet thirty, his hair had already greyed but he still carried a full head, combed straight back and slicked down. His features were chiselled, the jaw square, a straight nose and a strong mouth. Although I didn't know it at the time, this man was already a legend amongst the women of Berlin who were trying to find themselves a Luftwaffe officer to marry.

He placed the files back on his desk and looked up.

"The only thing that can be said in your favour is that you've come here partially qualified with pilot's licences, saving us a lot of trouble trying to teach you basics. No doubt, you still can barely fly an aircraft and it will be left to us to teach you. Do you think that flying Bückers and Stieglitzes is anything like flying a Heinkel 51 or Messerschmitt?

God, you're in for a surprise." Again, he ran his eyes over us, "Sergeant, get them out of here. When they line up for first inspection day after tomorrow, I want to see Air Force candidate officers, not some Hamburger dock riffraff. You're dismissed."

We returned to the barracks and spent the rest of the day and most of the next preparing ourselves for the first official day. We scrubbed the room until the floorboards looked like the planking on a naval ship, cleaned the windows, polished our boots until they shone, and ironed everything. We were adamant that nobody would find fault with us on our first day of induction.

We watched the other candidate officers arrive. They were going through the same ritual as ourselves, all being crapped on from officers and non-coms, and being issued with equipment and uniforms that did not fit. The barracks took on the semblance of an Arabian bazaar as clothing and boots were tossed around from room to room as the now twenty or more men tried to find their right fit. Of course, those of us who already had been through the initial introduction forewarned all with the result that until late that evening the barracks was a hive of activity as all prepared themselves for their first day.

We soon found out that all in Section 4, which comprised twenty-five candidate officers, had flying experience and at least a C1 rating, which was a multi-engine rating with time as Pilot-in-Command. These men were experienced flyers by civilian standards. Not all were in the early twenties, some were already in their thirties.

At seven the next morning, we mustered on the parade ground in front of our barracks. Hauptmann Bähr arrived with his Feldwebel in tow. They slowly proceeded along the line of assembled men without the expected cajoling, but rather speaking civilly to some, asking about their origins and where they learnt to fly.

Finally, he stopped in front of me.

"Aschenborn, where did you learn to fly?"

"Husum, Herr Hauptmann," I replied.

"Ah yes, Hauptmann Osterkamp's base," he said.

"He personally instructed me, Herr Hauptmann," I volunteered, hoping to extract some positive comment from the man.

"Well, in that case you might just know something, but we'll find out, won't we?" he said and walked on.

Well, I thought, at least he knows who Osterkamp is. Hopefully, this could mean something in the long run.

Again he took up position in front of the assembled men.

"For the next six weeks you'll undergo basic training: how to march, how to salute and how to behave like officers. Normally, for those without the type of flying qualification you all have, this would be three months. You are fortunate. Thereafter we will commence flight training, slowly moving onto fighter or multi-engine aircraft. You'll also be subjected to some theory on aerodynamics and aeronautical engineering. And best of all, which I'm sure you will enjoy immensely, you'll undergo intense physical training. We'll have to get rid of those threatening beer-bellies I see. Of course, you'll be subjected to a battery of examinations, which you must pass. Welcome to Flight Training School, Berlin-Gatov."

We gave him a ragged salute which he returned and then strode off.

For three weeks, we were not permitted to leave the base. We marched and we ran an obstacle course repeatedly until I could recognize every blade of grass, stone or bush. Initially, the run would so exhaust me, left me gagging and vomiting as my chest heaved for breath. We did callisthenics and then we ran some more. We were treated no better than raw recruits off the street were. The sergeants never gave us any respite.

Every night we fell, exhausted, into our beds. Inevitably, inspections were a surprise and took place at any time of the night or day. We had to be prepared at all times, everything had to be spick and span. Again, we had to submit to further medical examinations. Our eyesight was again tested. The base had an altitude chamber. In this weird contraption with its thick-glassed portholes, we were subjected to ever-decreasing air pressure, the oxygen starvation effecting our coordination and thought response. Those that could not do specific tasks at certain induced altitude variations would not be allowed to continue flight training.

During the initial period before actual flight training was to commence the contingent was down to eighteen men as those who could not make the grade were weeded out. Selection was merciless. There were no exceptions. Even the son of one of the highest-ranking Nazi Party officials was forced to pack his bags. After six weeks, all that kept me going was sheer guts and determination. In the beginning I had often thought of giving up, but if that's what they wanted, I was not about to give them the satisfaction. Helmut was a pillar of support. The word 'surrender' was not part of his vocabulary.

Finally, those of us who had survived the gruelling rigours of basic training and the round of endless tests were advised that we had to attend a swearing-in ceremony where we would formally become members of the Luftwaffe. It was then that we knew we had made it, provided we did not cock-up during the aircraft training phase. Please, we were trained pilots. Why should we?

After that, we were given a pass to go home for a few days. On our return, flight training was to commence in earnest. We took the oaths swearing allegiance to the Führer, Adolf Hitler, and to the German Empire. At that stage, we were so glad to have seen the end of our basic training I think we would've sworn allegiance to the Devil if need be.

Helmut Kleber and I had developed a close friendship and during the trying and exhausting past few weeks had often come to one another's assistance or found ourselves encouraging each other to survive the rigours of the training program. When utterly exhausted and lying in the mud, the rain coming down in buckets, and you are frozen and convinced that another step was not possible, the encouragement from another was usually sufficient to instil that final additional sliver of determination. It was just enough to get you up on your feet to continue and finish.

*

We both decided to go home, he to Hamburg and I to Kiel. We would both be sharing the same train, at least for a while. I found out the departure time and sent a telegram to Wiebke.

We had exchanged a few letters but often I was just too exhausted to write and I hoped she would understand. The train pulled into the station. I looked out of the top of the half-open window and saw her standing on the platform anxiously looking at all the faces as they passed. Then she saw me and her face lit up with delight. She waved frantically while she followed the coach until the train came to a halt. I jumped down onto the platform, dropped my valise, and took her in my arms and kissed her. The feel and smell of her heightened my awareness, reminding me of how much I had missed her.

"God, it's good to have you back, even if only for a few days," she said while I held her close.

"I missed you," I said.

"Come, let's go. My father won't be home until after five. We'll go to my house, there's nobody there," she said.

In the taxi, we sat very close and kept kissing each other. I was dressed in my Luftwaffe Ausgangsuniform. It was a perfect fit but still with little in the way of insignia, it clearly indicating that I was still in the Offizierkadettenschule. The taxi driver found our display of affection amusing.

"You're on furlough, aren't you?" he said.

"Yes, I'm just out of basic training," I replied.

He laughed. "It looks like it. You seem not to have seen the Fraulein for a while."

The car drew to a halt outside the Osterkamp residence. Wiebke paid the driver and gave him a handsome tip, he wishing us a pleasant and happy weekend. We stumbled into the house still hanging on to each.

"Come, come! Just leave your bag. I've a surprise for you," she said, dragging me towards the stairway. We were in such a hurry to climb the stairs we stumbled halfway, both collapsing on the carpeted staircase. First, we laughed, and then I rolled on top of her, kissing her passionately. I undid the buttons of her blouse and pulled her brassière cup down until her breast popped over the top and kissed and licked the erect nipple. It felt as if my entire existence was concentrated on my groin. Already she had undone my fly and held me, I as hard as a policeman's baton. I had my hand under her skirt and pulled her panties off, spread her legs, and let her guide me into her. I seemed like only moments when she suddenly shuddered under me just as I went into spasm.

After a few minutes during which I recollected myself, I asked, "What about that surprise you were talking about?"

Wiebke burst out laughing. "You're a naughty boy. You took it before I was ready to give it to you."

"But, I'm ready for my real present," I countered, a look of mock disappointment on my face.

"Silly man, I know you are, but first lct's eat. I'm sure you're hungry after all that Luftwaffe food."

She had set aside an assortment of cold meats, pickled herring, and cheeses on the kitchen table covered by a cloth. There were crisp German bread rolls, Brötchen, these still fresh with a bowl of real farm butter. I got stuck in, I was starved. She ate with me. For a while we did not talk, we just stared at one another both chewing slowly, both elated to be together again even if it was only going to be for a few days. After the meal, we retired to her bedroom where we spent the next few hours and then finally emerged to catch the tram to Niemannsweg.

Gustav opened the house's front door and beamed upon seeing me. He shook my hand vigorously and then hugged Wiebke

"My God!" he said, "You're a picture of health."

I was. I'd not been in such good shape ever before. God! I felt as strong as a stevedore.

"Gustav, if you knew what I've been through you'd never believe it. I barely survived, but at least that's now over. From now on it's all flying and lot less of the physical stuff," I said.

We talked some more and then I asked what was the latest news, having heard nothing from the rest of the family.

"Well, your brother George is engaged to a woman from Mittweide in Saxony. She is Fräulein Ruth Borchard. She comes from a farm in the district of Brandenburg. I gather he's deeply in love, which is strange. He was always the playboy type.. But, as you know, when it comes to the matters of the heart we're all continuously surprising each other. However, just look at you two," Gustav said in a jovial manner, throwing his arms outwards, glad to see us.

Gustav was quite taken with Wiebke. She was a beautiful and vibrant woman and seemed relaxed in Gustav's company, even accompanying him to the kitchen to assist with getting coffee, greeting the maid, and making herself at home. There was no attempt to play the girlfriend of the owner's son. I went upstairs to get out of my uniform and into something more comfortable.

'I'm actually concerned about your brother George," Gustav said when I returned.

"Why's that?" I asked.

He took his cup from the coffee table and sipped before he answered. "Well, something occurred in Mittweide. It had to do with Ruth's parents. It really was about her mother. She got into an argument with some SD stormtroopers who were keeping watch on an old established Jewish business. Apparently, Ruth's mother insisted on making her purchases there no matter what, and would not allow any to dissuade her.

The Nazis didn't like it and now have the Borchard family under investigation," he said, his brow crossed with a frown.

"How's George involved in this?" I asked.

"You should know your brother by now. He wanted to take a swing at one of them – called them thugs, I understand. It started off when Mrs Borchard said that her family had been buying from this shop for the past 150 years and had always received the best service. She then said she would be damned before she'd let a little guttersnipe in a ridiculous uniform tell her what to do and when to do it. That's the words I'm told she used," Gustav sighed. "You can imagine the can of worms that has opened up. I heard that the Gestapo called on the farm. Old man Borchard is a war hero; he was badly wounded at Ypres. He apologised on his wife's behalf. It would've worked, him being a war hero, but she wasn't having any of it. She chased them off the farm with a bloody shotgun."

"Jesus Christ! The bloody woman is insane."

"I know. I hear she's a tough lady," Gustav said.

We were all silent for a while, thinking about the ramifications that were sure to follow and whether these we have any influence on our lives. I was particularly concerned that this could somehow have an influence on my acceptance to the Luftwaffe.

"What's George going to do?" I asked.

"He wants to get Ruth out of Germany. It doesn't seem as if they yet know who he is – they never got his name although they half-heartedly enquired. He wants to send her to Oubaas in Windhoek. He wants you to see him in Mittweide. I've an address for you. He asked that you do so as soon as possible." He leant across from his chair and whispered, "Matthias, don't mess with the SD, they're dangerous. Talk some sense into your brother. You know what he's like once he gets himself worked up. This is a shitty business."

Things were going very badly for the Jews in Germany, that was evident, and I did not need my brother trying to champion a cause that favoured the Jews. I knew that to be an exercise in futility. Somehow, I also knew that this could impact on me. I mentioned this to Wiebke.

"Well, you can't blame him, he's right. We can't treat the Jews like that," she said with a touch of vehemence.

"Now listen, sweetheart. This is none of my business and I don't want to be involved. Why doesn't he just leave it alone?" I said, annoyed that my brother always seemed to want to make other people's business his own. Why did he always want to champion the underdog's cause?

Wiebke came to stand next to me and took me by the sleeve.

"Matthias, be reasonable. The man's in love with the woman. He has to be seen to support her if she decided to side with her mother on this. What I think you should do is ask for two days' special leave, go and see your brother. May be you can talk to him or help him, convince him that it's important that he take a neutral stance. Go and see what you can do," she said.

Gustav had gone out and we were in my bedroom, both lying on my bed.

The conversation got round to my brother again. He was a concern.

"Come here," I said. She rolled towards me and I took her in my arms. "I'll try and help George. That's all I can do. After that, he's on his own."

I then told her the story about the Mensur duel my brother had with Oberscharführer Hubner, both of them requiring surgeons to stitch them up. This too had been the result of an argument and an exchange of insults.

*

I had to leave early Monday morning for Berlin. Both Gustav and Wiebke's father realised that we wanted time to ourselves. We spent most of the time at Niemannsweg, other than going out to dinner on Saturday and seeing another American movie.

Osterkamp invited us both out to Husum. He knew that I hadn't flown for weeks and knew the exhilaration that I'd feel at flying again. He made arrangements for Sunday morning. We drove out to find that Schmidt, the aircraft mechanic, was also there and had already given a brand-new Bücker Jungmeister a thorough pre-flight check. He had two flying caps, gloves, and overalls. It took a while before I realised that one set was intended for Wiebke. So, I thought, she was going to fly with me. That would be fun, although I was sure she must have flown many times with her father.

*

102

It was a beautiful spring day. The sun was up with only a slight scattering of cloud. A light wind blew in from the North Sea. Soon we streaked across the short grass of the airfield, the aircraft showing the first signs of lift. The wheels bounced and then we were airborne. We climbed slowly, flying over the old town, the famous old Realschule that came into existence in the sixteenth century, and the picturesque small harbour. I could see that the tide was out, the fishing boasts lying on the mud.

"I'm sure you've flown before. You take her," I said into the mouthpiece and let go of the stick.

I felt Wiebke's hands take hold of the stick. The plane didn't even twitch. She kept it in the exact same attitude as I had handed it to her. It was clear that she had flown before. Slowly we continued to climb until about 4,500 feet above the coastline, Husum now behind us and the border with Denmark in front of us.

Gradually the aircraft started to nose-down, the airspeed increasing, and the needle hovering just below the 200 kph mark. What was the woman doing? I readied myself to take control. Suddenly, I was pushed down into my seat, my cheeks sagged from the g-forces as Wiebke hauled back on the stick, the nose passing the horizon as it rose. I heard full power being applied to the engine. Dammit, I realised the woman could fly. She was taking me into a loop or so I thought. At the top of the loop with us inverted, the countryside and sea spread out below, she wiped the stick to the side. The Jungmeister rolled perfectly and the next moment we were flying perfectly level in the opposite direction we had been flying seconds ago. She had just executed a perfect Immelmann manœuvre.

"You little devil, you," I shouted. "Why didn't you tell me you could fly?"

I heard her laugh. "You never asked. I've a B2 licence with a KII aerobatic certificate."

That flabbergasted me. This woman could fly.

"All right, give me a performance," I said, sitting back in the little cockpit plywood seat with my arms folded over my chest. There was no denying her expertise. She put the small aircraft through every manœuvre as if she were flying in an aerobatic competition, and she worked the controls and the throttle at the right moments, never over-revving the engine, quite a feat in itself. We did loops, stall turns, chandelles, figures-of-eight and finished off with an inverted spin, which she let flatten, a dangerous manœuvre, and then expertly worked the throttle to pull the nose down before attempting recovery. An expert could not have done it any better. I was dumbfounded.

"Take us home," I said.

She greased the aircraft on the ground in a perfect three-point landing. We taxied to where Schmidt and Osterkamp were standing in front of the hangar, they both clearly amused. I was sure they had put her up to it.

She shut down the engine and we clambered out of the cockpits, the two men walking up to us.

"That was quite a display, my dear," Osterkamp said laughing.

"Jesus Christ, I didn't know she could fly," I blurted.

"You never asked," she retorted.

For a moment, my thoughts fleetingly returned to South West Africa and I imagined arriving in the country with this woman on my arm, a pilot. The Flying Couple! That would really be something.

"Shit, that really was something, not to mention the surprise. I just wanted you to feel what the controls felt like, give you your first experience at flying a plane."

All thought this hilarious.

*

Sunday night was to be our last night together for quite some time and we both knew this. Gustav left the house early leaving us on our own. We'd had a large lunch to which Gustav had invited Herr Osterkamp. The Hauptmann had mellowed considerably. He treated me like a son, confiding in me his concerns for Germany and the dangers of Hitler and his henchman. He even suggested that I call him by his Christian name, Hans-Jürgen. Doing this would have publicly implied a very special relationship, akin to father and son, which some would view with suspicion. I flatly refused to do so, saying that I thought others would believe me forward and impolite.

Osterkamp and Gustav had left together as if they had conspired to do so, and left Wiebke and I with the house to ourselves knowing that we wished to be alone.

We settled for a light supper of rye bread and an assortment of sausage, pickles, and cheese. Just before eight, Wiebke retired to take a bath while I waited to listen to the news on the radio, nursing a cognac.

I listened to the rhetoric of the German propaganda ministry which exalted the Nazi Party on its achievements, reminding the population of the danger the Jews represented and that this matter had to be dealt with. They spoke of the civil war which was being waged in Spain between Franco's Nationalists, who were renowned Fascists, supported by Hitler and President Manuel Azana's Republicans, who had the backing of the Russians. This was also an important news topic. Germany was providing Franco with men, armaments, and aircraft and already Luftwaffe pilots were taking to the air in Spain to bomb and strafe Republican positions. Even amongst the student pilots of Detachment 4, some had expressed the hope that some could be sent to Spain to acquire aerial combat experience under real battle conditions. Germany appeared to be coming out in open support of the Fascists.

"Are you going to listen to that propaganda shit all evening? I've already run your bath and its getting cold," Wiebke called from the landing above.

I swallowed the remainder of my cognac and turned the radio off, doused the downstairs lights, and slowly climbed the stairs, wondering whether the Luftwaffe would send us to Spain to fight as part of the Legion Condor, the name given to the aerial assistance that German men and machine gave the Spanish Fascists.

I strode into the bedroom. Wiebke stood in front of my chest of drawers above which hung a large ornate mirror. She was doing something to her face and watching my reflection. She wore a full-length terrycloth gown which reached to the floor. I realised it was mine.

"Get into the bath," she commanded.

I stripped off my clothes and hung these over a chair and then completely naked walked into the adjoining bathroom to the large bath, which stood on four clawed cast-iron feet, steam rising from the hot water. She watched my every movement in the mirror.

"Isn't that circumcised penis of yours going to get you into trouble? They'll think you're Jewish," she asked.

"That's already happened. But I'm blond, I was baptised and confirmed in the Lutheran church and the only reason I'm circumcised as are a few other Christian Germans is because my mother has this fetish about cleanliness and had both my brother and me snipped immediately after birth. Sure, it's frowned on and some do stare in the showers, but what can I do?" I replied as I gingerly lowered myself into the steaming water.

"Just don't lie there all night. I've got something to show you when you're out," she called through the open door.

I soaked a good twenty minutes in the tub and eventually washed, emerged, and dried myself off. My robe was gone, so I walked naked into the bedroom. Wiebke lay on the bed reading a magazine still dressed in my robe, and looked at me.

"That snipped putz of yours actually looks quite appealing," she said. Her reference to that part of my anatomy in Yiddish surprised me.

"Where did you learn that word?" I asked.

"I went to school you know. There were quite a few Jewish girls. We shared everything except our religious classes. Like boys, women discuss things of a sexual nature. How else can we learn?" she asked, her lips slightly pouted.

She rose from the bed and then untied the terrycloth belt and let the robe drop to the floor. All she had on was a black garter belt and white stockings, these clipped to black silk ribbons that hung from the belt. It was so sexy I was immediately aware of my arousal. She raised her eyebrows questioningly as she saw my sudden surprise at her recently shaved pubis. I clearly saw the cleft of her sex.

"You like, no?" she whispered, mimicking a French accent, and then pirouetted. Her breasts jutted out from her and jiggled with every movement.

"Sis is vot the French girls do to ze leetle Jeweesh boys in Paris," she said, still playing what I presumed was a French whore. She sunk to her knees in front of me and took me into her mouth. The feeling was exquisite. I pulled her to her feet, swung her into my arms, and carried her to the bed. I kissed her, our tongues probing. Then I ran my lips over her body and as I kissed her inner thighs, she raised her pelvis in anticipation, giving a low moan. When my lips touched her, she emitted a low guttural sound, primitive.

Her hands groped for me, she then held me firmly. I could no longer contain myself, my need for her was overpowering.

We made love a few times that night. If Gustav came back, we never heard him.

I had to rise early. My train was to leave at seven. I persuaded Wiebke to remain in bed as I quickly bathed and dressed. By six-thirty, I was on my way to the station, my brother's address and telephone number in my pocket, and my heart heavy at having to leave her.

CHAPTER TEN

Our return to Berlin-Gatov from our first furlough signalled a change in our training. There was now little emphasis on any physical training, except the mandatory morning calisthenics. We were split into groups of five men and were subjected to intense instruction in aircraft mechanics, navigation and other theory related to aviation. Helmut Kleber and I had bad luck. Our immediate superior and lecturer was the Feldwebel Hannemann, the non-com that Helmut, during the issue of our kit on our first day of arrival, had with derogative intent referred to part of the sergeant's anatomy, the comment obviously overheard.

The Feldwebel was middle-aged, already with a pronounced paunch, certainly too large to allow him into the confines of a trainer or fighter's cockpit. He wore his slightly grey hair cut short, no more than a centimetre from his scalp. He also wore glasses for reading purposes. His turnout was immaculate. His uniform was pressed and his boots gleamed.

We were all in the small lecture room standing and ready to commence.

"Please sit down, not Aschenborn and Kleber. I want you two to immediately change into your fatigues and steel helmets and then to report outside the armoury. You have exactly five minutes."

Christ, what was the bastard up to? We both stormed out of the room and managed to present ourselves at the armoury where we were confronted by another Feldwebel, this being Feldwebel Fiebig, the known friend and companion of Hannemann.

We were both issued full infantry kit as well as two 8mm Mauser rifles and a twenty-litre can filled with water, which we were instructed to insert into our rucksacks.

Once we were properly laden with all our equipment and the rifles at port-arms, Fiebig said, "Right, you two. I want you to run once around the circumference of the airfield confining yourselves to the perimeter paths. You are not permitted to rest and if you as much as try and walk, I'll add another circuit. Every time you pass a sentry, you will shout the following: 'This is what one arsehole can do to two other arseholes.' Do you have that? Shout it out loud, I want to hear it," Fiebig said.

Helmut and I shouted.

"That's not loud enough. Again."

We shouted again. I am sure that everyone on the airfield could hear us.

"Better. All right, off you go. Make sure you maintain a fair tempo, otherwise another circuit."

I'd done a quick calculation and thought that one circuit was about five miles. We had not run a third, by which time we were panting, the shoulder straps biting into our shoulders, and the perspiration trickling from under our helmets. My clothing clung to my body and my inner thighs were rubbed raw from the rough cloth of the fatigue pants. The chaffing burned because of the sweat.

"Let's not make a fuckin' cock-up," Helmut said amongst gasps for breath. "Another circuit is going to kill us. Oh, he's such a cunt. I'm going to get him. Just watch me."

I didn't want to talk, but only wanted to concentrate on putting one foot in front of the other. This was not the time to be thinking of how we were going to take revenge on Fiebig and Hannemann.

"Don't get smart. They'll throw us out of the academy. Fuck, let's just get this over with," I shouted back at him.

We had not gone halfway when we heard a vehicle approaching with a large tank affixed to the rear. As it passed, two men on the back with hoses sprayed a steady stream of water on us until we were soaked and then continued to do so for the next minute or two. I shouted at Helmut, "Just keep running, don't stop." I realised what the bastards were trying to do. They were trying to force us to stop.

It was only with the greatest of efforts that we completed the circuit and as we passed the armoury, we both stumbled and fell to the ground, utterly exhausted and fighting for breath.

The sergeant stood wide-legged with his hands on his hips and looked down at us sprawled in the dirt, still exhausted and gasping for air. "Next time you won't be so lucky. We'll get you yet. Just wait," Feldwebel said with utter contempt.

Before Helmut could say anything, I shouted, "Don't." I didn't want him setting them off again with some snide remark or crude expletive. He knew what I meant.

It was important that we both concentrated on our studies as every week or so Hannemann would call for a test. Of course, these test results found their way to Hauptmann Bähr's desk. The theoretical courses required a fair amount of study, but the two sergeants would constantly single us out for some minor misdemeanour which would invariably influence our study time. They had us either washing the communal bathroom and toilets or running a few circuits of the barracks. This kept us from lectures at times or absented us from studies, necessitating the borrowing of study notes from our fellow cadets and forcing us at times to apply our minds to our books well after midnight. Then, to crown it all, we found our papers subjected to unfair marking.

Somehow, we persevered and got through the tests, barely. During an inspection parade, Hauptmann Bähr stopped in front of me and said that I was a disappointment in that he had expected me to do well in the written exams. How I wanted to tell him it was because of the doings of his sergeants.

Training on aircraft had commenced in earnest and the transition from the 150–180hp-powered aircraft to a Heinkel 51 with its V12, 750hp BMW engine was similar to the change from a pedal-powered bicycle to a large two-cylinder motorcycle. The first thing you learnt was that everything happened quickly. This aircraft roared into the sky with a rush of speed requiring lots of torque correction on take-off, it being capable of nearly 400 kph at full speed. It had none of the forgiving traits I had encountered in the numerous civilian aircraft I'd flown. Do something wrong and it could bite. Fortunately, I soon mastered the aircraft and my instructor was quick to get me started on air combat training.

In the classroom, we would study the various attack and escape manœuvres, learn about coming at the enemy from out of the sun, and how to shake him from our tail if he somehow had managed to latch on. We would then take to the sky with some of the aircraft piloted by the sergeants, officers, and instructors; practise how to take evasive action when attacked, and to apply the attack tactics we had learnt in proper air combat conditions.

For identification purposes, the officers and non-coms would fly a coloured streamer from a tail or wing. One afternoon I was attacked by another He51, with a streamer trailing from its tail. We dived, rolled. and looped across the sky. I managed to break away from my opponent and get into an attacking position only to be thwarted again as he carried out an unexpected gravity-defying manœuvres that extracted him from what I thought was a sure-kill situation. This happened on a few occasions. The g-forces we pulled were so severe that at times, I thought the wings would come off, and I was nearly blacking out.

After the simulated dogfight, he came up alongside, waved to me holding up his hand making an 'O' with thumb and forefinger, and gave me thumbs up before breaking off to land. I wondered who the pilot was.

When I had landed and taxied to the front of the hangar the Flugzeugwart came up to me and said that I should report immediately to Hauptmann Bähr. It was with a good deal of apprehension that I walked to the office complex and came to attention in front of the Oberleutnant's desk in the front office.

"It's you again, Aschenborn. What shit have you got yourself into this time? Go through, the bear awaits you," the lieutenant said.

This didn't sound good at all. I racked my brains trying to think of what I may have done wrong during the last few days.

I clicked my heels and gave the lieutenant a salute, and walked passed him through the door to the bear's office, coming to a rigid attention in front of his desk, clicking my heels again and saluting smartly.

"Aschenborn reporting, Herr Hauptmann. I was told you wanted to see me."

The man leant back in his chair and let those silver-grey eyes roam over me, a slight smile on his lips. He dispensed with returning my salute.

"Osterkamp was right, you can fly. For a moment up there, I thought I was up against an ace. How do you account for that?" he asked me, nonchalantly extracting a cigarette from a cigarette case. "At ease, Aschenborn, relax and sit down." He leant forward and offered me a cigarette. I declined, sitting ramrod straight in my chair, my cap on my lap.

"Aschenborn, both Kleber, von Kletzen, and you in particular, have shown a particular aptitude for flying. When you pass your final theory in the next few weeks or so I will consider issuing the three of you your Luftwaffe flying licences and present you with your Fliegerausbildungszeichen. However, from Feldwebel Hannemann I hear that you and your companion Kleber have a total disrespect for authority. How is that?" he asked and then drew on his cigarette.

For a moment, I was at loss for words. I knew I had to be careful how I replied.

"Herr Hauptmann, it would seem that for reasons unbeknown to me the sergeant misinterpreted or misheard a comment that Kleber made, believing this to be a slight on his character. It was nothing of the sort. However, the sergeant continues to believe otherwise," I replied.

"And you believe this accounts for his bad reports on your performance?"

"Herr Hauptmann, I believe that this is a factor."

"Hmmm." He stared reflectively at the ceiling for a moment. "I would then suggest that Kleber and you, who appear to be the good sergeant's whipping boys, do something rapidly to change his attitude towards you, if you know what I mean. I should add that we are looking for young pilots to send to the Legion Condor in Spain. Do something soon if you wish to be considered. Okay, you're dismissed."

I stood outside in the sun and could not believe what I had just heard. Do something? What were we to do?

That evening when together with Kleber I told him what had happened.

"He mentioned you and von Kletzen. He wants to send us to Spain. Well, that's what I understood, but apparently, Hannemann and probably Fiebig are the problems. The bastards are screwing us," I said dejectedly.

"Don't worry. I found something out today," Kleber said, slapping me on the back. "Rumour has it that they're Hundertfünfundziebiger."

"Hundertfünfundziebiger? What the fuck's that?" I asked.

A smile broke out across his face. "Hannemann and Fiebig are queer. You know, poufs." He said making a wavy motion with his hand. "They give it to each other from behind." He was clearly happy with what he had just found out. Christ! He certainly had a propensity for crudeness. The bastard seemed devoid of any common decency.

Although shocked to hear this, I could not imagine how this could possibly help us.

"So what? That's not going to help us," I said.

"But it is. We are going to catch them at it on camera. Take a photograph. Just one will do," Helmut replied.

"You're crazy. They'll lock us up for that. God, I heard somewhere that queers get sent to concentration camps," I said.

Helmut cackled loudly, "The Nazis put poufs in concentration camps? You're sure? That's just the place for them," Helmut replied, making a lock-clicking sound implying that they would be locked up.

We had a further discussion and decided that after lights out, we'd watch them like hawks. Kleber said he'd find a camera with a flash. He said he'd also find keys to fit their quarters. Their rooms were next to each other and they shared the same ablutions.

I continued to remain dubious. Imagine Hauptmann hearing that we had photographed two queers at it? God, what a sordid scandal that would be, and we the initiators. They'd crucify us.

"How're going to do that?" I asked.

"Christ, I'm from fuckin' Hamburg. Don't you know what we can do?" he retorted.

Helmut was a genius. For two nights, he remained out until the early morning hours. He had asked for my car keys with which I had reluctantly parted. Two days later, he handed them back and I must confess that I snuck down to the car park to inspect my Kadett. Fortunately, it didn't have a scratch on it. That evening after dinner when we were back in our rooms, he produced a Leica camera complete with flash attachment and a few flashbulbs. Then, with some enacted fanfare and imitated trumpet-blaring, he opened his hand to reveal three keys. One each for the rooms and the small adjoining bathroom. He also had a stethoscope around his neck.

"What the hell is that for?"

He removed it from around his neck, stuck the two ends in his ears, and then walked over to the panelled wall that separated us from those next door.

"Come, just listen," he said beckoning me over.

I saw that there were little chinks and tiny gaps in the planking. He had placed the scope against a small hole. I stuck the ends in my ear. I could hear the talking next door clearly.

"That's your job. You listen and when we think the groaning and grunting reaches a peak, I'll slowly open the lock, swing the door open, and take the photograph. Of course, we'll then have to run like hell," he laughed as if this were a big joke.

I did dare think of the consequences we'd face if we were caught. They would have us up for something serious, probably attempted break-in and theft. We'd have no evidence to support any claim we made. We'd be arrested.

We needed to keep a vigil on their barracks building. These were all constructed of overlapping planked pine, the buildings standing on short stilts about a foot or so above the ground. As Helmut had said, every night I dressed in my grey pyjamas and with a loose blanket over my shoulders, the nights were damn cold, would crawl under the barracks facing the two men's rooms. For three nights, I watched well-past light outs waiting for one of them to make a move. At just after midnight, with nothing having happened, I would make my way back to our barracks to try again the next evening.

On the fourth night, the sky was clear with a half moon. It was exceptionally cold and I wore a pullover over my pyjamas. I saw Fiebig walk a few times back and forth between his room and that of Hannemann. Every time he opened the door to Hannemann's room light music would filter out. It seemed that they were also drinking, I once even heard the word 'Prosit'.

It was late when Fiebig disappeared into his room only to reappear in his pyjamas and walked the short distance and then disappeared into Hannemann's room. Being no more than a few metres away, I distinctly heard the spring-loaded latch click shut. The light in the room was still on. Using my elbows, I crawled until I was directly below the room. I could see slits of light above me where the floor planking showed minute gaps. I took the stethoscope and placed it against an opening.

I could not hear everything. Only every now and then did I catch an phrase or word, but it was sufficient to enable me to get a gist of what was being discussed. There was no doubt the matters of a carnal nature were seriously being contemplated above me. Fuck, what the hell was I doing, eavesdropping on a pair of homos? I got back to our room as soon as I could. Of course, I had to wake Helmut who had fallen asleep. He was up in an instant. He grabbed the camera and the keys and we returned quietly to the sergeants' quarters. I sneaked up to the wall and placed the scope against it where I had previously noticed a larger than usual chink in the woodwork.

There was no mistaking the sounds. I handed the scope and let Helmut listen. He beckoned me away.

"Christ! Somebody in there is snorting like a pig. What the hell is he doing to the guy?" he whispered, his face an expression of intrigue.

I had to smile.

Helmut stifled a laugh. "You wait here," he whispered. "Get ready to run."

I couldn't help the feeling that overcame me. This was a damn mistake, but it was too late. Helmut already stood on the landing and inserted the key in Hannemann's door lock. The next moment there was a loud bang as the door was flung open immediately followed by a camera flash. There followed a loud yell of surprise, or fury.

I didn't wait. I ran straight to our room, dodging around the other barrack buildings with Helmut's loud steps close on my heels. I put my pullover under my pillow and crawled into the blankets, pretending to be asleep. I tried to control the pounding of my heart. I heard Helmut do the same.

We had planned this escapade in the utmost secrecy. None knew about it and my absence from my bed had previously gone unobserved. The two sergeants could not have known who was responsible. Anyway, the flash would have momentarily blinded them. They were not able to see who the culprits were, or so we hoped.

We could clearly hear a commotion outside and there were a few shouts. After a while footsteps approached and our door was opened, the light switched on and then off again, but not before Helmut had uttered a few classic expletives about arseholes who inconsiderately woke others up.

The next morning while at muster and at breakfast, it was obvious that the two sergeants had something on their mind. They appeared concerned.

A day or two after my return from Kiel I had asked for special leave, which Sergeant Hannemann had refused. I needed to see my brother but dare not give the sergeant a proper explanation. I merely said that my brother would soon be returning to Africa and that it was imperative that I get away to see him.

Again, Helmut disappeared for the whole night only returning just before muster call the next morning. It was obvious that he had not slept and he was forced to feign the onset of flu to ensure that he was not ordered to fly.

During the morning, while we were alone, he pulled out a photograph from his tunic pocket and handed it to me with a leer on his face.

"Look at that, the bastards," he said.

I looked. Oh my God, I thought. They had been caught in the act, both naked in bed, bare to their midriffs, the rest hidden by a sheet. Both men stared at the camera with startled expressions. It had to be the most undignified snapshot I'd ever seen. There was no mistaking them.

I was bewildered. We couldn't hand these to anyone as our careers would be scuppered. I said so. I also told him it was pornography. We would be arrested.

"That's not what I'm going to do. I'm not handing it to any authorities. I'm going to hand it to Hannemann himself and tell him I found it on the parade ground. Of course he'll know, but believe me, he won't say a word. Remember, the negatives. He'll shit himself and so will Fiebig."

Initially, I opposed the idea but then thought it the best way. Helmut insisted that I be standing nearby clearly visible when this was put to the sergeants.

*

It was after breakfast and before flying was to commence. The two sergeants were smoking a cigarette, standing together talking softly but earnestly with each other when we approached. Helmut came to attention and clicked heels giving them a smart salute.

"Herr Feldwebel, I just want to report that I found this on the parade ground," he said. He pulled the photograph from his pocket and handed it to Hannemann. For a moment the sergeant blanched, actually rocking back on his heels. His face was a picture of total shock. Fiebig stared over his shoulder, his mouth forming an 'O'. Before he could speak, Helmut saluted again, did an about turn and walked away. I joined him. We walked. I was waiting to hear an order for us to stop and return. None came. After a few yards, I ventured a look. The two men just stared at us.

All day I was expecting an order to report to Feldwebel Hannemann and was surprised that this did not happen. However, the following day, as we were exiting the lecture room, Feldwebel Hannemann summoned me, and to my dismay recalled the request I had made a few days before for two days leave. He granted me a twenty-four-hour pass and not a two-day pass, solely because it was close to final exams and at this point any absence would raise questions. He felt he could explain a one-day absence.

For the first time his attitude was devoid of any maliciousness, in fact, it was quite strange to find him helpful. Helmut and I had won the first round. We had to be holding the trump card, but I was certain that the incident with the camera and photograph would not be forgotten. They had to know that it was us.

*

I had phoned the number I'd been given for my brother, George. A woman answered the phone who identified herself as the owner of the Gasthaus. My brother was out but she promised to leave him a message that I'd be arriving about nine that evening at the Gasthaus.

At around six that evening, I dressed in my best and left the base and drove to Mittweide, about a two-hour journey. The town was home to about a thousand or more students. The university, the Hochschule Mittweide, was one of the renowned science and engineering universities in Germany. Twice I had to ask directions, but eventually stopped in front of the Gasthaus.

This was a students' residence. There was some activity and a few men and women were sitting in the common room. I soon found George sitting at a table with a woman and another couple.

We hadn't seen each other for a while and we heartedly greeted each other. He introduced me to the others with whom I shook hands. He indicated the woman next to him. "Matthias, this is my fiancée, Ruth Borchard," he said, looking at me for a reaction.

She was a strikingly beautiful woman of average height with auburn hair cut short in a bob. She had an oval face with large brown eyes, high cheekbones, and a sensuous mouth. She was dressed in a dirndl, which was typical for a country girl with its wide skirt and tight waist. When she spoke, it was with a Saxony accent.

After some small talk, George made excuses and explained to the other couple that we wished to discuss a matter of a private nature which was urgent and would they please excuse us. We vacated the table to find another where we could speak privately. Ruth joined us.

"I heard you are having trouble with the authorities," I said sitting down.

"It's not me, it's actually Ruth's mother. She took it upon herself to disregard instructions from the SD regarding a Jewish shop in town. The incident has now erupted into a proper mess and it seems the Gestapo has gotten involved. They're involved in everything these days. It's incredible how things have degenerated so rapidly in the country. They're thugs, beating the people with truncheons, making old and young clean the streets, swearing and cursing. It's out of hand. Frau Borchard took the opportunity to tell the SD what she thought was wrong with the Nazis. The SD got nasty, and you know me and my temper. I wanted to thrash the squad leader but fortunately another student restrained me. The SD squad leader demanded my name and you can guess what I told him. I've been lying low ever since and I've Ruth with me. I can't let her return to the farm. We don't know what could happen there. I'm planning to send her home."

I looked at George. He wasn't the usual man I knew. Clearly, the latest developments were taking their toll. He appeared stressed and was not his usual jovial self.

"Home? You mean Windhoek?"

"Yes."

George lent across and took Ruth's hand.

"Have you written and told Oubaas?" I asked.

"No, I'm not going to. I'm going to get her across the border into Belgium and then from there to Southampton and onto a boat for South Africa," he said.

"Christ man, what about money?" I asked, looking anxiously at him.

"I've got it, compliments of our grandmother," he replied.

"I mean, are the authorities out to arrest the Borchards?" I asked, giving Ruth a sympathetic look. The poor woman, she looked drawn and nervous.

"God, who knows? All I can tell you is that Frau Borchard has been instructed not to leave the farm. They served some document on her from the local Gauleiter, which says that she is considered a threat to peace and the community or some nonsense to that effect. The bastards!"He spat."That's serious," I said.

"I know, that's why I've got to get her out of the country and soon," he replied falling back against the armchair's backrest with his hands behind his head, staring up at the ceiling.

"I take it that she has papers?" I asked.

"You won't believe it. Of all the people, Uncle Willi arranged these. Very reluctantly, I might add. The man's now a full-blown Nazi official, but I'm grateful he helped. God knows what would happen to us if we weren't family. He believes Hitler is the best thing that ever happened to Germany."

I looked at Ruth and realised that she was terrified.

"And you, Ruth. How do you feel about this?" I asked looking around. There was nobody nearby.

"I have to leave. It's dangerous here. I'm a Borchard. We're marked. You've heard of the Sippenhaftung practice. If one does wrong, they can arrest all members of the close family. God, all my mother wanted to do was buy from the same shop she's always bought. The way the SD carried on you would have thought we had stolen something or tried to murder someone. It's all going crazy here," she said, close to tears.

"Okay, George. Tell me what I can do.""I want to use your car. I'm going to drive her to Belgium. First to Kiel, of course," he said.

That was simple. I agreed to that. I told him that I had to be back at the base before six the next evening. He said he'd drive me there. He told me that he had Ruth staying in a boarding house in the town. He did not want to send her back to the farm, he was afraid the authorities could restrict her movements and not allow her to leave the property.

"Where did you two meet?" I asked out of curiosity.

Ruth smiled weakly for the first time. "It was at a dance with some friends where we were introduced. We danced, went out together a few times, and that's it," she said with a shrug of her shoulders, as if to say their meeting was ordained.

We walked Ruth home and I waited outside the boarding house for a few minutes while they both went inside. After that, we decided to go to beer hall and have a drink.

"Just be careful what you say. The Nazis believe the students are possible dissidents and have infiltrated the Bunds and classes with sympathisers. Every week we hear of some poor fellow being hauled up before the authorities and cross-questioned about the most ridiculous transgressions. If the Jewish question arises, say nothing. Okay?" he said.

"Of course."

A lot of beer had been consumed and the place was rowdy. The barmaids were scurrying around clasping three or four mugs in each hand, delivering these to the tables. Here and there, I could see a few uniforms and thought them probably men off-duty.

The next day, the three of us went shopping. Poor Ruth had little in personal items, these being still on the farm to which she dared not return. Her brother Heinz attended the local Realschule and they had asked him to bring a few of her personal belongings from the farm, which he had done over the weekend. George bought clothing and other items but only those considered essential. He said he'd rely on our parents to sort the rest out once she got home to South West Africa. It was difficult for Ruth; she was unable to accept that she was fleeing her own country. In fact, she personally seemed to have no stance on the situation regarding the Jews and had been a mere bystander to her mother's outspoken criticism of the system. Clearly, the old lady was not going to relent and none knew where this would eventually end.

"You're sure you've got enough cash?" I asked George.

"Don't worry, I've enough. I told you about what grandmother gave me, and Dad owes Onkel Willi a bloody fortune, but I couldn't help it, I had to take from him. I'm sure we'll finally sort this mess out," he said smiling but I could see he was concerned.

That afternoon they drove me back to Berlin-Gatov. We stopped outside the gate and shook hands.

"George, be careful," I said.

"Don't worry about me. I'm worried about you. The way our Führer is carrying on, God knows what's eventually going to happen. Some are already speaking of war," he said.

"Don't believe it," I replied.

*

Near fourteen years passed before I would see my brother again.

Ruth made it safely to South West Africa. Yet, when she had arrived in Windhoek, my parents were not even aware that George had sent her out from Germany. Inexplicably, my brother's endeavours to communicate with his parents broke down. They never received his letters and

120

telegrams. Fortunately our family is well known in the country and the taxi driver whom she found at the station dropped her off at the house in the Bismarckstraße.

I was told that when the doorbell rang, my mother opened the door to be confronted by this strange young woman who, when asked the reason for her being here, just blurted out that she was George's wife. Apparently, my mother required a few minutes to recover from the shock. They had got married before she left Germany. I believe this was not well accepted, especially by my mother, George being her first-born. Of course, once the reasons were given for the subterfuge, all were pleased she was safe and was accepted in the family as one of their own. George remained in Germany for another six months waiting to graduate after which he left and returned to South West Africa.

CHAPTER ELEVEN

The situation at the Luftwaffe Fighter Weapon School had changed drastically. With both the sergeants now being very accommodating, my marks suddenly showed a dramatic improvement, sufficient to persuade Hauptmann Bähr to make a comment regarding my rapid and unexplained advancement. This time he even spoke to Helmut about his remarkable turnaround.

Fighter training progressed in earnest and we were flying at every available opportunity with emphasis on both the air-combat and ground-attack roles. Finally, the day of graduation arrived. We were ceremoniously handed our Flugausbildingszeichen and pilot certification, and received our commissions as second lieutenants in the Luftwaffe. We were referred to as Leutnant as opposed to a full lieutenant who is referred to as an Oberleutnant.

CHAPTER TWELVE

The participation of the two fascist countries, Germany and Italy, in the Spanish Civil War was seen as an opportunity to test weapons and aircraft in battle conditions. The Spanish General Francisco Franco, who headed up the Nationalist movement, had requested Hitler to provide assistance. It was on advice from Herman Goering that the German Minister of the Economy conferred with Field Marshal von Blomberg, the commander-in-chief of the German armed forces. The Führer decided that Germany would come to Franco's aid against the Spanish Republicans who were being backed similarly by the Soviet Union.

Germany's burgeoning arms industry required essential raw materials and these were available in Spain, where large iron ore deposits and deposits of tungsten and other metals could be found. It was believed that if General Franco could eventually control the whole country, this would ensure a steady supply of these ores to Germany and their source would be safe in fascist hands. Also, were a fascist government to retain power in Spain, Germany's long-standing enemy France would find herself surrounded by fascist powers on her borders and the Nazis believed that this could promote the fascist cause in France.

The German Luftwaffe sought volunteer pilots for Spain. However, being aspirant fighter pilots, all volunteered. None wished to be tagged as having refused service. In addition, all pilots knew that having been attached to the Spanish Legion Condor had acquired a special standing in the Luftwaffe and with the German public. Additionally, Spain presented a perfect training ground and an opportunity to find distinction as a seasoned combat pilot as well as the chance to fly the most modern German fighters in real war situations.

Helmut, von Kletzen, and I had hardly received our wings and officer commissions when we were asked whether we wished to volunteer. This was put to us by Hauptmann Bähr. We sat in front of his desk now dressed in our new Luftwaffe uniforms resplendent with all the regalia of an officer. I was imbued with a feeling of accomplishment. I had actually made it. I was now Leutnant Matthias Aschenborn. Even the sergeants were forced to congratulate us. Of course, they now also had to salute us.

"Well, gentlemen," Bähr said, "here's an opportunity to prove yourselves and get proper combat training. I'm told the Russian fighters are no match for our Heinkel 51s. Those pilots we've lost never died in combat but in accidents. What say you?" he asked.

None hesitated. We all said that we wanted to go.

The Luftwaffe wasted no time. The three of us were assigned to Jagdgruppe J/88 but were given a week's leave after which we were to report to Berlin-Gatov with orders that when we reported back, this should be in civilian clothes.

The unexpected announcement of a few days' leave came as a godsend. I immediately left for Kiel, arriving in the early evening. From the station, I took a taxi to the Osterkamp residence where my unannounced arrival was greeted with much joy. Wiebke ran into my arms and we hugged and kissed as an amused Osterkamp looked on and when finally the opportunity presented itself, he stepped forward and shook my hand, adding that it was good to see me again.

When asked the reasons for the unexpected furlough, I explained that we had been assigned elsewhere and this was an opportunity to see our families and loved ones before we departed. Of course, Osterkamp knew to where I had been ordered, and said so. I neither confirmed nor denied it as we were told not to discuss this with others. However, it was sufficient to bring a look of sorrow and disappointment to Wiebke's face. She asked for how long this would be. I merely shrugged my shoulders. In any event, none of us had any idea how long the assignment would last.

At the house on Niemannsweg, I found my car where it had been left by George. Gustav told me that he had arrived with Ruth and that they had left for Belgium. There was no message, so I assumed his plans were on track and that they had not encountered any problems.

Wiebke took a few days off work, which her father happily granted. We spent this short time going to the cinema, to dinners and making love at every possible opportunity.

I had to leave again and a tearful Wiebke saw me off at the station. We didn't know when we would see each other again.

*

From Berlin, we pilots left by train for Hamburg where we were to board a ship for Genoa in Italy. Helmut and I did not believe the destination when we heard it. Surely, this destination had been chosen to confuse anyone who was curious.

There were quite a number of military men from the Army, Air Force, and a few from the Kriegsmarine on the train. They were all in civilian clothes but still I thought it a rather ineffective disguise. The whole operation was quite a military arrangement but then the idea was probably that whoever saw the proceedings could think what they wished but couldn't prove it. However, for the sake of appearances, we were said to be part of some travel group although this too appeared to be rather ridiculous, we all being men of similar age.

Anyway, if this were intended to mislead the world it would have little effect as all already knew that Germany was assisting Franco in Spain and Morocco, and on a grand scale as well. Germany had already airlifted Franco's Africa army including his Moorish auxiliaries from Spanish Morocco to Spain in Ju52 German tri-motor transport planes, all flown by German aircrews. These aircraft were, for appearance's sake, part of an air transport company's fleet in civilian markings but, of course, this was merely done to distract attention from Germany's military intervention.None believed it.

If it was thought that the embarkation and general conduct of the men would be orderly and organised as one would expect from military personnel, it was not so. Discipline seemed to have fallen apart. All the soldiers, air mechanics and pilots were in civilian clothes and funnily enough, once out of uniform and they no longer appeared to be part of some military establishment. Rigid conformance to order had disappeared into thin air, the civilian clothes not distinguishing officer from non-com or ordinary troopers. The troops degenerated into an unruly mob and it was clear that nothing could be done about this until they were back in uniform. This was still a while away. The officers and non-coms had little choice but to live with the situation provided it did not get out of hand.

In Hamburg, we boarded a tramp steamer. When I first saw the ship, I could not believe that Germany would have even considered using a Panamanian-registered tramp. oO reflection, if the intention was to mislead the newsmongers, it probably was a good idea. The ship had a displacement of about four or five thousand tonnes with a tall, thin single funnel which belched black coal smoke. It was a rust-bucket and certainly not the type ship Germany should be using as a troop-carrier. I thought it some relic from the beginning of the century. Apparently, it had previously been used on the same route to transport all sorts of war materials, trucks, armoured vehicles, tanks and knockdown aircraft to Franco. I saw that the holds had been converted to living quarters with bunks and ablution facilities erected, but still this was as primitive as it could get. The bulkheads and ship's steel sides sweated moisture, rust was everywhere, the air circulation was poor, and we were to be crammed into these facilities like sardines. Nonetheless, all were excited and in good spirits. We were told that the voyage would take no more than a week or so.

I would not say the voyage was uneventful. At least more than half of the men will never forget the voyage. Some actually expressed a death wish. The tramp wasn't fast. I didn't think she could make more than ten knots at best. Once off the coast of western France, we encountered the first warnings of what was to come as we entered the Bay of Biscay. The ship was a bitch. She tossed and rolled constantly. Once we entered the Biscay, we were greeted with the inevitable storm. Most of the men were always seasick. The walkways between the bunks were slick with puke and the stench was overpowering. Those who could not make the rail in time spewed their guts out. The storm was relentless and, as I said, most would have welcomed Death right there and then and not have waited for Spain. Below decks it was a mess. All semblance of order had deserted the men. As officers, we had a duty to ensure order. It was pointless. The men could not even function. They just lay there, their faces pale, some with part of their stomach contents splattered on their clothing, some giving an occasional dry retch, oblivious of the world around them. They would have ignored orders from even Hitler himself.

When the ship finally docked in the port of El Ferrol in the northwest of Spain, very few of the men who disembarked looked anything like the cream of Germany's armed forces. They all had but one wish and that was to put their feet on firm ground.

The Basques in northern Spain were fighting to force their own autonomy, wanting to break from Spain and create their own country. They sided with the Republicans and controlled part of the coastline along the Bay of Biscay and the borders with France. The Republicans also controlled what used to be the Spanish Navy, as well as the more important ports on the eastern coastline of the country which included the harbour of Bilbao and the city of Barcelona. Part of the front between the opposing forces split the country down the middle, the Communists also controlling Madrid.

From El Ferrol we travelled by train, a stop-start journey that seemed to go on forever before we arrived in Vitoria. It was situated in Nationalist-controlled territory, south of the Basque-controlled enclave along the French border, where the Fighter Group's headquarters were stationed. From there we were driven to Avila, an old fortified city surrounded with walls that went back hundreds of centuries. It was picturesque and romantic and when we entered the town, it was as if we had stepped back a good few centuries in time. We were billeted in an old monastery. The monks were still active but did not appear to be put out by our presence and just continued to go about their business and religious duties as if we did not exist. Our commanding officer was an Oberleutnant Ernst Tallant, who had arrived a few weeks before. We were known as the 'Mickey Maus squadron'. All our He51 aircraft sported this American comic emblem on their fuselages. We had no radios but communicated via hand signals and shared the ground support role with the Italian Aviazone Ligionaria, the Italian equivalent of the German Condor Legion, who also flew biplanes, their Fiat CR32 similar to the He51.

We were given two days to acclimatise during which we were issued with our new Spanish uniforms and rank. We were all upped by one rank. Captains became majors and second lieutenants, as both Helmut and I were. We suddenly found ourselves Teniente, this being the rank of a full lieutenant in the Nationalist forces as they did not have a rank for a second lieutenant. Of course, an Oberleutnant became a Hauptmann or Capitán.

The Heinkel 51s suffered losses against the Fuerza Aérea de la República Espanola, the Second Republic Air Force, which was supported by the Soviet Union who had supplied them with a variety of aircraft, mostly biplanes. The Soviets also supplied pilots, the intention being that they, too, acquire first-hand combat experience in Spain. Surprisingly, the Republicans also had well-trained pilots of their own. Not all military personnel supported Franco and these came from the Spanish Air Force before the civil war. The legendary 'Rata', a

Polikarpov I-16, a Soviet monoplane had also arrived on the front and these played havoc amongst the Heinkel 51s, outperforming the biplanes in all aspects. Other squadrons in our fighter group had received the new Messerschmitt 109E, better known amongst crews as 'Emil', a monoplane fighter. In order to minimise He51 losses, they would, when it was considered necessary, form a protective umbrella over us when we went into the attack.

As good and as wonderful the He51 biplane was, it had a number of faults. That it could not out-perform a Rata was simply because the other was a more modern fighter, and a monoplane too boot. It had better speed and rate of climb and had considerably less drag, only one wing without struts or an undercarriage sticking out.

A major problem with the He51 was the heat generated by the V12 BMW engine up front. In summer, this blasted through the firewall and it became unbearably hot in the tight confines of the open cockpit, some pilots even flying in shorts and bare-chested, often returning from a sortie on the brink of heat exhaustion. They joked at the possible embarrassment of being shot down and captured clad only in bathing costumes or shorts. Surely, the Republicans knew that anyone clad only in shorts and walking around the countryside had to be a downed He51 pilot.

Attacks on ground targets were to become the bane of our lives. These necessitated coming in at a low-level and the forces on the ground, which appeared to have to have no shortage of flak batteries and machine guns, threw everything at us. Often we would return having lost an aircraft or two to ground fire, others with their fabric-covered wing, tail and fuselages punched full of holes and the pilot glad that he had survived the curtain of fire. The He51 was fitted with two machine guns and could carry half a dozen 100lb bombs fitted to under wing racks. We tried bombing from higher altitudes but this tactic was ineffective unless we passed over the target in close formation, all dropping our bomb loads simultaneously thus creating an improvised carpet-bombing technique.

The Republicans anti-aircraft fire was intense and was the cause of most of the losses the Legion's bomber groups suffered. The Me109 would escort the bombers over the targets and took on the Republican's fighters which rose to intercept them, but it was left to us to take out the numerous anti-aircraft batteries and machine gun emplacements that surrounded the targets. These would throw a hail of lead, steel and fire at us and every attack left me overcome with fear, sure that this would be my end. An attack by a Republican Curtiss or Rata evoked the same feeling. This aircraft was far superior to the biplanes and once on your tail difficult to shake off, so we were forced to take our aircraft deep into the valleys and gorges in an attempt to out-manœuvre the enemy. Trying to get behind one of them was rather pointless as they were able to increase speed until out of machine gun range.

Other than those moments of abject fear that we experienced in the air, and the heat of summer and the cold in the winter, our stay in Spain was as good as a holiday. The countryside and towns were as they had been for hundreds of years and the population looked upon us as heroes and treated us accordingly. Spanish women may not be blonde but certainly were the most beautiful with those dark, sultry looks and with a mysterious aura around them. This was aggravated by our near inability to communicate, our knowledge of Spanish rudimentary to say the least. The food and wine was excellent and with the truly beautiful women added to it, the place was a near paradise for the officers who were held in awe. Developing any relationships with the women was difficult. We were being moved around the country so often, forever having to look for new billets, until it was finally decided to billet us on a train. This simplified matters and when advised of a transfer to a new location, it merely required that the coaches and wagons be loaded with all our equipment, other than the aircraft, the whole train then hooked behind a locomotive, and off we went.

*

It was early in the morning, the valleys still with traces of mist hanging low over the streams below and still cold, when we took off to attack a Republican strongpoint which overlooked a strategic bridge. The aircraft were armed with the usual bomb clusters but because the enemy was entrenched on the slope of the valleys overlooking the bridge, we would be required to come in low along the valley floor. This was not something to look forward to. They were bound to throw up a curtain of anti-aircraft fire which we would have to penetrate to get to the bridge.

We were four aircraft, piloted by Helmut, von Kletzen, another recent arrival from Germany, and me. Although still cold, I was dressed only in a shirt and short trousers. The damn engine up front would soon heat things up in the cockpit. I also had a few bars of chocolate, which would invariably be soft within a short while. I also had a sidearm, just in case I was shot down and was forced to walk home dodging Republican patrols. Our target was near Guernica, a town the bomber group had recently raided, killing a large number of civilians, many of them women and children. This gave rise to an indignant outcry throughout the world, branding Germany a cruel and callous murderer. Photographs of the bombed town had been circulated by the newspapers. New instructions were strict: avoid civilian targets.

We approached the target in a diamond formation but, as we got close and descended into the valley, we changed to a line, one behind the other with me in the lead. Already we were under attack and took some fire from the slopes of the valley. Had the enemy known what our true intentions were, they probably would not have fired so as not to reveal their positions. They obviously believed the bridge our target and opened up with seemingly everything, which was what we wanted. Their tracer bullets revealed the source of their flak and machine gun emplacements which were our targets. I realised that someone in our high command considered our lives a price worth paying to ensure our bombers a safe passage to the bridge.

I banked towards a spot from where I thought the most AA fire emanated and dived on it firing my machine guns. As I zoomed low over the concentration of guns, I released my cluster of bombs. I then dragged the stick back, desperately clawing for altitude to clear the top of the mountains, the g-forces shoving me down into the seat. I felt return fire impact on the aircraft but the engine never missed a beat. It hauled the biplane effortlessly over the top of the mountain, the ground fire abruptly breaking off. I banked to see into the valley and watched Helmut drop his bombs on another anti-aircraft nest on the slopes. I then looked to see what the others were doing, but by then Helmut was already zooming up the side of the mountain.

Christ! I immediately saw that our recent addition to the squadron was too damn close. He was right on von Keltzen's tail, both flying low in the bottom of the valley. It struck me that they were too close, presenting a concentrated target to the gunners who seemed to have opened up from all sides. Correctly, von Kletzen started to jink the aircraft, sliding from side to side, but this manoeuvre slowed him down slightly. The pilot behind did not consider this, or so it appeared, his biplane rapidly catching up with von Kletzen. As if in slow motion, I watched, realising what was about to happen next. As if it were so ordained, I was unable to stop the inevitable end. Whether he was powerless to stop or whether he was distracted by the intensity of the anti-aircraft fire, frozen with fear in the cockpit and incapable of taking evasive action, I'll never know. I couldn't do a thing but watch as the drama unfolded, the newcomer's biplane drawing nearer and nearer until he flew into von Kletzen, the aircraft's propeller chewing up von Kletzen's tail assembly. Pieces of wood, aluminium, and fabric visibly spewed out by the spinning propeller blades. Horrified, I watched as von Kletzen's aircraft started to slide off one wing like a mortally wounded bird, its nose dipping as it started to spiral towards the ground, which it struck at speed followed by an enormous fireball. The whole incident had taken place at so low an altitude that it would have been impossible for von Kletzen to bail out.Tthe other aircraft still flew, the propeller still spinning, but the hope that his biplane was unscathed was short-lived.

Because of the collision, he had broken off the attack and now had insufficient speed to enable the aircraft to zoom over the mountains that paralleled the river on both sides. The mountains would protect the aircraft from anti-aircraft fire. He continued straight on drawing fire from all quarters. I saw that the enemy machine gunners had homed-in. Pieces flew off the aircraft as their machine gun fire impacted. Suddenly the aircraft, still with the bombs attached to the racks, reared up as if it were about to start a loop, but then fell off a wing and spiralled down until it, too, crashed into the mountainside. An enormous explosion followed.

I was stunned. Helmut came up alongside and I signalled that we should return to base. Von Kletzen was a sad loss. We knew him from flight school, he was a friend and his loss was devastating.

CHAPTER THIRTEEN

We landed on our makeshift airfield and it was evident to those expecting us that we had suffered losses. I was approached by von Kletzen's Fleugzeugwart. He was wearing his overalls and ready to start preparing the aircraft for its next sortie. The man looked at me. I slowly shook my head. I sadly watched as the man's face changed to a picture of anguish and distress. He lowered his head and stared at the ground and then turned away.

For me at was a solemn moment when I stepped aboard the passenger coach.

This had been shunted onto a small siding that adjoined the station of the small town. The coach contained Oberleutnant Tallant's headquarters and offices. Three compartments had been converted into an office for him. It was long and narrow and as it was already hot outside all windows had been opened, the slight breeze requiring the stacks of papers on his desk to be held down with a variety of paperweights. I gave Capitán Tallant, my commanding officer, a perfunctory salute which he returned with a wave of a hand. I was stilled dressed only in a vest and shorts, short socks, and boots. Other than that were my helmet and flying goggles. I was splattered with a mixture of oil, soot from spent cordite from the guns, and dirt from the ground thrown up by the propeller. The same applied to my upper torso.

Tallant offered me a cigarette. "Matthias, tell me what happened," he said, flicking a petrol-lighter and lighting it.

I drew the first breath of smoke deep in my lungs, holding it for a moment, and then expelling it in a steady stream.

"Truly, a total fuck-up and I'm not sure whether I should take the blame. I should have realised that the new man, Hoffmann, wasn't ready. Christ, he just flew into the back of Hans-Joachim. Sure, they were under fire, but still. There wasn't a damn thing I could do. Hans Joachim, I mean von Kletzen, jinked, trying to avoid enemy fire. Fuck, the bastards were throwing everything at us. He didn't even know what was happening until his tail disappeared."

This was not the first pilot we had lost, but Von Kletzen had been a close friend of ours. The three of us had carried on as though this could only happen to others, but never to us. I knew that this was war, but still his death hit me hard.

"Well, you boys aren't going to be flying for a day or two. You know Hans-Joachim's girlfriend, that Spanish girl he met a month ago, they were besotted with one another. I need you to go and break the bad news to her," Tallant said.

I nodded. God, that had to be the shittiest of jobs.

"Somebody's got to do it. I know it's early, but let's have a cognac. Tell Helmut to join us."

Helmut was standing outside. I called him into the office. He was similarly dressed, both of us looking ridiculous in comparison to the correctly dressed Capitán Tallant in his Condor uniform.

Tallant handed Helmut a cognac glass which contained an unusually large tot. "Helmut, I'm sorry," he said.

I could see Helmut's rigid jaw line as he clenched his teeth trying to show no emotion.

Tallant held his glass up high, both Helmut and I following suit.

"To Hans Joachim von Kletzen. A comrade and friend, may we never forget him," Tallant declared.

All three of us downed the cognacs in one shot.

There wasn't much else we could do other than the paperwork, which Tallant and the Gruppenführer would attend to. Von Kletzen's orderly would clean out his room and see to it that the man's personal belongings were packed for dispatch to Germany.

A month earlier, Von Kletzen had met this astoundingly beautiful Spanish girl. She was already a young woman whose age I guessed to be about twenty. She had those dark, smouldering Spanish eyes and a sensuous appearance about her that drew your immediate attention. When I first saw her, she was dressed in a thin cotton dress that revealed her long and slender legs, the colour of light nutmeg, as was her face. When she walked in the near skin-tight light dress she had worn, it revealed her buttocks, which quivered with every step. Her face was serene with long eyelashes, dark eyebrows, and high cheekbones, her lips red and wet. When she smiled, her perfect teeth were in sharp contrast to her near-olive complexion and red mouth.

Helmut found out that she lived in the nearby town with her elder sister. Both their parents had been killed months ago in the lead-up to the Civil War. Her sister ran a small local laundry which she had started in order to generate some income. She now worked for her sister. Helmut had met her one evening at the local restaurant where she had arrived to collect dirty table linen. Her name was Isabelle Garcia and her father had been a local olive merchant. The family business had been ransacked and destroyed when the Nationalists had routed the Republicans from the area. The moment Helmut had laid eyes on her, he was bowled over and had then doggedly pursued her until her sister had relented and permitted Helmut to take them both to dinner, she with them as a chaperon. The chemistry between them had been near-instantaneous and, a few weeks thereafter, he started talking about marriage. Initially we had laughed this off and thought it premature but soon realised that the man was serious.

I reluctantly strode up the short driveway that led to the Garcia residence. The property and buildings showed all the signs of war with most of the windows broken and boarded up, the wall pockmarked with bullet impacts, and one corner partially collapsed, either by a bomb or artillery fire. It was evident that in its heyday the family was an important entity in the community, the opulence of the building, notwithstanding the war damage, indicated this.

I stood outside the front door and pulled on a rope which hung from the small portico roof and heard a bell ring from within. The door was soon answered and I was confronted by a tall, attractive woman in her mid-twenties.

She looked me up and down in my Condor uniform with my black boots which shone in the sun these recently polished.

"Good day, Senorita," I said in my broken Spanish. "I'm Teniente Aschenborn of the Condor Legion. I am a friend of Teniente Hans-Joachim von Kletzen."

She smiled. "Good day, Teniente. You can speak German, I understand a little. I know you, I've seen you before."

She must have realise that something was amiss. I saw the friendly expression slowly disappear from her face.

"Oh no! Something is wrong!" Her hand flew to her mouth. "What's happened to Hans-Joachim?" she asked in a whisper. It was clear she was expecting the worst.

I told her. Immediately she was distraught, fighting to keep her emotions in check.

"Madre Diaz," she exclaimed in Spanish and then switched to German. "This will surely destroy my sister. What am I going to do?" She bowed her head and pinched the bridge of her nose, her eyes screwed tightly shut.

"Celeste, who is that?" I heard being called from inside the house.

"Not to worry, I'm dealing with it," she shouted back, stepping forward so that she could pull the door closed behind her.

"Please, you must go now before she sees you. I will contact you. Your name is Aschenborn, am I right? Please go," she said. "I'll tell her."

I got the message. I left immediately. I had not yet reached the driveway entrance when I heard a loud wail from the house. Celeste had told Isabelle. I could have cried with her. The woman's agony stabbed through me and, for a moment, I too was overcome by a feeling of despair.

*

It was four days later and I had just landed after another sortie against Republican ground forces. I had clambered out of the cockpit when my Fluzeugwart said that a young woman was waiting to see me. He said she had refused to enter the base but was waiting at the main gate. I whipped off my helmet and goggles, put on a shirt, and strode off to the main entrance, which was guarded by a sentry.

As I approached, I saw that it was Celeste. She was sitting on a large rock under a tree, her long black hair falling over her shoulders, nearly reaching to her breasts. It was hot and clammy and she was dressed only in a thin, floral cotton dress with a small smudged white apron tied to the front. She obviously had come straight from work. Her legs were bare and her feet were stuck in a pair of leather thong sandals. She rose as I approached.

We greeted each other perfunctorily. She looked at me and afforded me a weak, tired smile.

"You smile? It does not seem that you want to smile," I said.

"You are right. There is nothing to smile about. But you, you look so strange. You look funny," she said, her face breaking into a broad smile as she ran her eyes over my attire.

I realised that I must look comical. I had owl rings around my eyes where my goggles had been. My oil-and-soot-smeared face, my ridiculous shorts, my arms blackened but my hands white where they had been protected by my gloves.

"I'm sorry. I came immediately after I landed," I said taking a seat on another round boulder close to her.

"Do all aeroplanes make you this dirty?" she queried.

"No," I said, "only the ones that I fly." Then we laughed, both of us trying for some humour at this still-tragic moment.

"It is very bad at home. Isabelle is overwrought and hasn't stopped crying for days. I don't know what to do. She just lies in her room and cries," she said, the initial expression of amusement gone, her face now a picture of concern.

"I'm sorry, but what can I do?" I said patting my pocket for cigarettes. There were none.

"I'm asking that you come and speak to her. I'm sure it will help. You know, you being his friend and having been there when it happened."

I did not want to be mixed up in this. Yes, it was tragic but there was little I could do. This was war and it spared nobody. Still, it would cost nothing to try to help.

"Okay, I'll come this evening. At about seven. Is that all right?" I said.

"Thank you," she said, and then seemingly as an afterthought added, "Come for supper."

Just then, one of the base's trucks approached the gate, probably on its way to town. I waved the driver down and asked him to give Celeste a lift.

"Go with him. It's too hot to be walking," I said helping her into the cab.

*

A few of the pilots, Helmut and I included, had between us bought two motorcars. I managed to commandeer one for the evening without any difficulty, especially when some heard my reasons. I arrived at the sisters' front door dead on time. Celeste opened, ushered me in, and guided to me to an expansive lounge with upholstered settees and chairs, gold-rimmed mirrors on the walls, and the décor typically Spanish. It was beautiful.

136

"As you know, this was my parents' house. It's now ours. A lot was stolen by looters," she said.

"Are you managing?" I asked.

"Yes, we are. The laundry makes just enough to enable us to live, which is the main thing. We have some money, not much, but we don't keep it in the country." She gave no indication where this was kept.

She was dressed in a striking red dress, its décolletage quite revealing. I was able to see the prominent swell of her breasts. It was a warm evening and her arms were bare as were her legs. She wore high-heeled, sandal-type pumps.

"Sit. Let me get you a glass of wine," she said and, with that, disappeared.

It was still light but I realised that this would be a candlelight affair. There was no electricity, the power generators that fed the local area also having fallen victim to the war.

She returned with two glasses of wine.

"How is Isabelle?" I asked.

"She's a little better but still cries at the slightest provocation, like when she hears your planes pass overhead," she replied.

"Where's she now?"

"She'll be coming down."

It was a quarter of an hour later before Isabelle appeared. She had done her best to look presentable. She was smartly dressed, but I could still see the puffy eyes. She managed a weak smile when she saw me. She approached and I hugged her. She sobbed once and then issued another ragged half-sob, half-sigh and her shoulders shuddered for a moment.

I told her how sorry I was, but did not want to dwell on the subject lest she became overwrought again. I could see that she fought back the tears.

"Come, sit down next to me," I said patting the settee seat. She did so but squeezed herself against the armrest leaving a considerable gap between us. Celeste brought her a glass of wine which she refused with a wave of her hand.

"Come, drink a glass with me," I said.

Reluctantly she then took it and sipped tentatively.

"I've done my best with supper, but you know with the war, meat is difficult to find but I've managed a mutton stew," Celeste said.

"That's terrific, I'm sick of the Air Force's food," I replied, trying to be conversational.

Celeste stood up from her chair and bent over to retrieve the glasses from the low coffee table. I caught a glimpse of her breasts. I must've stared because she brought her hand up to cover the view down the front of her dress. I felt myself colour with embarrassment and hoped that they had not noticed. I had not been with a woman since Germany and that was months ago. For a while, my libido had begun to remind me of its needs and they were gradually becoming more strident. At this moment, sitting here in the presence of what I thought to be the most beautiful women in Spain, the sight I had just beheld was enough to awaken a stirring in me.

We sat down at the table. Celeste had only set one end of the long table which was covered with a white tablecloth, polished cutlery, and white plates with a gold emblem embossed on the centre. The glasses were crystal. I was suitably impressed and said so, mentioning that it made one forget the war for a moment. She told me that she had managed to save this from the looting. This was the first opportunity she'd had to use it.

"In that case, I'm truly honoured," I said, smiling, and raising my glass to the two women.

She had insisted that I sit at the head of the table. She and Isabelle then brought the out the tureens containing the stew, vegetables, and sauce. A large, freshly-baked loaf of bread rested on a board. The two women took a seat on each side of me. I saw that Isabelle's demeanour had slightly improved.

Celeste briefly placed her hand on mine and said somewhat solemnly, "You are the man of the house now. You can say grace."

I was quite taken back, never expecting this. I'm not the religious type. I'm one of those who only calls on the Almighty when in serious trouble, like when confronted with life-threatening stuff. I did not withdraw my hand, but lowered my head and mumbled a Lutheran prayer, which I recalled from my distant past, giving thanks for what we were about to receive.

As an entrée we had broken bread dipped in olive oil with what I thought was flavoured balsamic vinegar. There was also a salad with olives. Simple, but just right as a starter. I saw Celeste watching her sister quite intently although trying to be unobtrusive in the process.

When Isabelle started to eat, her sister's face lit up and she bumped my leg with her own under the table, slightly arching her eyebrows she clearly telling me how pleased she was that her sister had started to eat again.

Was the pressure of her leg on mine merely to draw my attention to her sister or was I to read anything else significant in it? Again, I felt her leg touch. I looked at her, but she just smiled and did not remove her leg. Was she aware of what she was doing or not?

It was evident that Isabelle was ravenous. Now that she'd started eating, she must have realised how hungry she was. We started the main course. The mutton stew was excellent and when the empty tureens were revealed we all laughed. We had eaten everything.

"Even if I did cook it myself, this was the best meal I've had in a long time. It must have something to do with the company," she said pressing her leg hard against mine again and leaving it there. This woman's intentions could now not be misread. She certainly had my attention. From my response, she had to know that I would not require much to ensnare me.

Isabelle's attitude appeared to be improving by the minute, her eyes now less puffy, and she even smiled from time to time, clearly having forgotten Hans-Joachim for a moment. It was important to keep her busy and talking. She rose and started gathering the used plates and stacking these.

"Come, let me help you take these to the kitchen," I said. I rose from the table, reluctantly moving my leg from Celeste's, but giving her a knowing look.

Celeste jokingly admonished me telling me that I was not to go to the kitchen and should sit down. I thought Celeste would then help her. Celeste realised what I was thinking. She shook her head.

"I'm staying," she said. "I made the supper and did the rest, cleaning up is now her job. You stay," she commanded and led me by the hand to the sofa, indicating that I was to sit down next to her. "Isabelle will bring the coffee now."

Keeping Isabelle busy was obviously the right medicine. She was nearly her old self again. I truly believed she was over the worst of her grief. Life must go on. The thing was to keep her mind off the past. She soon returned with a tray and proceeded to pour coffee which was accompanied by Orujo, a powerful Spanish liqueur made from grapes.

Isabelle came to join us.

"Listen, if there's anything I can do for you, you must let me know. Helmut was my friend and I will do what we can. We know how difficult life must be for you at the moment," I ventured.

"Thank you, we understand," Celeste replied.

Finally, I thought it time to go. I thanked the two women and said that I hoped to reciprocate soon but not wanting to make a definite time as I not sure how Isabelle would take it. Celeste said that she'd walk me to the car. Isabelle said goodbye and came over to me and pecked me on the cheek with a whispered thanks. She did not attempt to accompany us outside, saying that she still had things to do in the kitchen.

The two of us stood outside, standing in the dark next to the Citroën. There were hardly any lights and those that we could see were from candles and oil lamps. We could barely see each other.

Celeste took my hand and held it. "It was kind of you to come. Isabelle seems to have improved. I was worried." She seemed to hesitate: "I would like you to come again," she said.

I ached to take this woman in my arms and press her body to mine and passionately kiss her. My need for her was overpowering. She took a step closer, turned her head up and kissed me. I drew her close and pulled her body to mine.

Slowly, I pushed us apart. "I must go," I said, "but I'll be in touch." I just had to get away. I couldn't let anything happen. Wiebke was the love of my life although, it seemed that the rest of my body didn't think so.

CHAPTER FOURTEEN

It wasn't a good day for flying. The weather had taken a turn for the worse with a rapid cumulus cloud build up, which was sure to bring scattered thunderstorms with it. I wondered whether our squadron leader hadn't thought of cancelling the mission. Again, I looked at his He51 diagonally ahead of me as it bobbed slightly up and down in the air currents created by the clouds. I doubted whether the bombers would even find their target, weather conditions were deteriorating rapidly. This time we were dressed appropriately. In these conditions, it suddenly could get very cold with rain and even hail, not pleasant in open cockpits.

Again, our leader rocked his wings, pointing his arm right indicating that we were to swing around another cumulus cloud build-up that barred our passage.

I kept swinging my head around, looking about me, up and down. This was the perfect weather for an ambush. The Russian I-151 biplanes could pop out of nowhere. If these included the new Russian Ratas then, in my opinion, it would be best to high-tail it for home.

The terrain below looked familiar and I knew that our Capitán was still on the right course. For a moment, my mind began to wander. It was a few days since I'd had dinner with Celeste. My thoughts kept returning to her and what was so bizarre was the carnal and erotic nature of these. Of course I had Wiebke, but I could not help thinking that Celeste was ready for the taking. Letters are fine and well and Wiebke and I continuously expressed our undying love and devotion in these, and we had exchanged many. But I longed to touch and explore a woman and Celeste was now the woman within reach.

Of late, I had been aware that I was experiencing a period of heightened libido, not an unusual situation considering that I had been without a woman for a considerable time. I yearned for Wiebke, but it seemed she was months and miles away. And as ridiculous as it may seem, my thoughts were constantly being assaulted with the thought that I could die not having been with a woman of late, but certainly not as bad as to die and never having had a woman.

I saw the first of the bombers with which we were to rendezvous. These were Dornier Do17Es, a twin-engine aircraft. We called them Flying Pencils as their fuselages were so thin. We began to surround the bomber flight in groups of four. However, our main purpose was not the interception of enemy fighters, this we would leave to the Me109s, which were faster and were in formation thousands of feet above us.

We had crossed the front line. This was heralded by the arrival of a swarm of Soviet-built I-151 biplanesand a scattering of Russian Ratas. Our new Me109s broke formation to intercept them while we held our position to take on any of the enemy that managed to break through to the bombers. Our ultimate target was the anti-aircraft flak and machine gun batteries that surrounded the target, the same assignments we'd done time and time before.

The first puff of black smoke mushroomed just ahead of me. The flak batteries had opened up. This was followed by more airborne shell-bursts, the shockwaves bouncing and rattling my aircraft, and I continuously corrected to hold my position.

Our leader again waggled his wings and pointed down. He peeled off over one wing and dived down at a particularly active flak battery, his machine guns chattering, sending out a steady stream of tracers. I rolled the He51 until nearly inverted and pulled the stick back, the nose coming round to point at the ground, the airspeed rapidly increasing, the wind screaming in the wires. I took a bead on another gun emplacement, watching my leader out of the corner of my eye. The aircraft rocked slightly as I released the bombs. I drew back on the stick, the biplane zooming skywards.

Suddenly, something struck the engine cowling in front of me, ripping off a piece of it. A huge hole appeared in my right upper wing. I realised that I'd been hit by an explosive shell. The instrument panel in front of me had also shattered. The aircraft began to vibrate. Something crucial had been hit. The vibration was violent so I cut the power. The plane lost airspeed, the nose dipping down and the controls getting mushy. I had also banked, heading back towards our lines, this an automatic reflex. I certainly had no intention of bailing out with a parachute.

A quick inspection of the terrain below revealed it to be rugged in places interspersed with the occasional chestnut grove. These trees were large and the areas below their canopies quite dark. These orchards nestled amongst the hills and mountains with the occasional cultivated square patch that was green with row upon row of what looked like grapevines. I also saw a number of sloped meadows with cattle grazing on them.

There was a loud bang from the engine and smoke began to pour from it, this now streaming past the side of my cockpit. The propeller did not even windmill in the slipstream but came to a complete stop. Clearly, the engine had seized. The sudden near silence was eerie. All I could hear was the whistle of the wind through the wires and the now-stationary propeller.

The aircraft lost altitude and approached the ground at an alarming rate. I looked round for a place to put the biplane down. There was no area nearby that was flat and large enough to accommodate a landing. I had a general idea from which direction the wind blew. I worked the stick and rudder pedals and brought the plane round so that it flew into the wind. I saw an open patch and chose it, realising that I now was committed. It was far too short and I no longer had sufficient altitude to look for an alternate spot. The plane skimmed the top of the chestnut grove. I worked the controls to put the aircraft into a sideslip to kill some of its speed and lose the last of its height. At the last moment, I pulled on the stick to lift the nose and round out. Christ, then only did I see the rocks and stumps. This was part of a cleared chestnut grove.

The wheels touched, one strut colliding with a chestnut stump, the aircraft's momentum shearing it off. The left wing dropped and skidded along the ground, this, too, colliding with a stump slewing the aircraft to the left and causing the right strut to break off. The aircraft was now on its belly, sliding sideways. The rough ground was tearing the fuselage open under my feet. Seconds later, I'd run out of open ground. The plane slammed into the first trees of the next grove. I was flung forward and blacked out.

I opened my eyes. I was hanging upside down in my harness, my head a few feet from the ground. The fuselage was partially suspended in between two of the chestnut trees, upside down with its nose in the air and the rudder resting on floor of the grove.

Fire! That was my immediate thought, but I heard no hissing or spitting although I saw that petrol trickled from a wing tank. I must have banged my head. My left forehead ached like hell and I was sure the skin was cut. I also was rapidly developing a stabbing headache.

I released the harness and, with some difficulty, let myself slide out of the cockpit until I could swing my feet down and was at least upright. It was easy to drop the few feet to the ground. Fire was no longer a concern. The engine and exhaust must have cooled down after the engine came to a stop. I heard the sound of an aircraft engine and looked up. A He51 approached at low-level and rocked its wings as it flashed overhead. It was Helmut's plane. I waved. He pulled the plane up and rocked the wings again, and then disappeared over a hill. There was nothing he could do.

I realised I must look a ridiculous sight in my flying jacket with a vest beneath, dressed in shorts and wearing flying boots. I removed my cap and goggles and felt my forehead. It was already swollen and I brought my fingers away with blood on them.

I had to get out of the area. I was in Republican territory and no more than a few miles from the fortified position that had started throwing the anti-aircraft fire at us. They were sure to send a patrol to investigate. I had a general idea in what direction the front line lay. Front line was actually a misnomer. It did exist but was not a continuous line of foe-facing-foe. Rather, it was a series of dug-in pockets of infantry and machine guns with gaps of miles in-between where you could pass through, provided you knew where these were.

I set off towards our own lines trying to put as much distance between the wrecked aircraft and myself. I debated whether I shouldn't set it alight, and then abandoned the idea because I had nothing with which to ignite the fuel. Besides, I knew that a fire would just give the enemy a good idea of my exact location.

I must have walked a good twenty minutes when I stepped out of the chestnut grove and found a flat expanse of grassland in front of me, dotted with a few trees and small rock outcrops. I saw a few head of cattle. It was surrounded by hills and mountains. About a half-mile from where I was, I saw a large farmhouse surrounded by corrals, barns, and tall trees. I didn't want to be seen and decided to skirt quite wide around it. It was just past midday but fortunately the sky was overcast and rain threatened. At least this kept the day cool. I knew I would have to find shelter soon as it was bound to rain later during the day, probably towards evening. In the distance, I saw a truck approaching, trailing a rooster-tail of dust. I backed into the grove of trees and dropped down behind some scrub.

The truck neared from my right in a half-circle, travelling slowly on a road that skirted the edge of the grove. When a few hundred yards from me, it squealed to a halt. Seconds later, from its rear, about a dozen men armed with rifles dropped to the ground, fanned out, and entered the grove in a line abreast. I realised that they had to be looking for me and were heading towards where the aircraft had crashed.

They all passed to the side of me while I made myself as small as I could. They were about forty yards from my position. This was Basque country and any downed Condor Legionnaire could expect no mercy if caught. The Condor Legion had bombed Guernica, the centre of the Basque culture, killing over a 1000, many women and children. The planes had also strafed the streets with machine guns. The bombardment had gone on for hours. They weren't about to forget that. Retribution was what they wanted and any downed Nationalist pilot was unlikely to survive if he fell in their hands.

Better I stick to the mountains, I thought, and when certain that it was safe, I moved towards the edge of the hills and mountains. I found a small stream of clear water that bubbled and trickled down from the high ground. If it rained this would become a torrent. I drank some water and then ate one of the chocolate slabs which were now just a brown congealed mass from the heat in the plane. I had hardly moved off from the stream when I walked into a herd of sheep intermingled with a few goats. I dropped to the ground certain that there had to be somebody shepherding the animals.

I heard a stone rattle and when I turned round, I found an elderly man standing a few feet behind me with a double-barrelled shotgun pointed at my back. He just stared at me, neither of us moving. He was dressed in grey woollen pants and wore a misshapen jacket. The beret on head hid most of his hair but what I could see was silver-grey. I thought he had to be at least sixty years old. His face was criss-crossed with age lines. His eyes were a dull grey and his grey moustache was stained by nicotine.

He said something to me in Basque Spanish, called Euskera. It was actually a language of its own, the dialect so pronounced I never understood a word. He was being careful but did not look like the type

145

who would just shoot me out of hand. The gun never wavered. He had it pointing at me all the time.

For a few seconds I did not quite know what to do.

"Allemane," I said in Spanish, saying that I was German. With that, I slowly extracted my helmet goggles from my jacket, and held these up for him to see. The automatic in my jacket worried me.

He stared at me. I added, "Falangist."

He whistled loudly through his teeth and seconds later a large hound came bounding towards us. I had never seen an animal like that before. It was large like a Great Dane but that was where all similarity ended. It had a ragged shaggy coat which was grey with black, I thought it some kind of wolfhound. He said something unintelligible to the dog which just gave me a snarl and fell in alongside the shepherd who, with a jerk of the shotgun barrel, indicated that I should walk in a particular direction. They both took up station behind me. I had no idea where he was taking me but I did notice that he had chosen a route that did not take us into the open where we could easily be detected.

We had walked no more than a half mile when he shouted something in Spanish. indicating with his hands that I should get down. I understood and flung myself down lying flat on the ground. He indicated some dense bush nearby and, imitating a crawling motion, said, "Go." I got the message and crawled to the dense bush and forced myself into it, ignoring the thorns and oblivious of the pain they inflicted during my frantic attempt to hide.

Soon I heard voices and tried to peer through the dense foliage. The dog had kept station with its master. Four men appeared. They were a rag-tag lot dressed in different clothing, not looking like soldiers at all, some with berets. They greeted one another after which a conversation ensued that I could not understand. During all this, the large dog would occasionally growl, the soldiers keeping a wary eye on the animal. I then saw the old man point in a direction close from where we had come. This seemed to satisfy them. They then greeted one another and the foursome left. When he had indicated that I should hide, I had hoped he was trying to help me and, after seeing what had transpired with the four Republicans, I realised that this was so. But this was Basque country and it was out of character coming from someone who definitely was a Basque.

He waited a good while before he called that I should come out of hiding, but still keeping his shotgun on me. We resumed walking, he behind me with his dog.

We came over a slight rise and I saw a shepherd's hut with a smudge of smoke rising from a chimney. It was just a square abode with weathered ochre tiles on its roof. There were two corrals alongside and I saw a well with a water-trough. The whole scene was dominated by an exceptionally large oak tree, half of which hung over the cottage. The scene had to be hundreds of years old.

He herded me through the door where we were met by an elderly woman. Her hair was also grey and she was dressed in grey blouse and a long skirt that reached to the ground. He indicated that I should sit at a large table in the room with an enormous hearth on one side. The two spoke to one another, I now and then catching a phrase or two. He was telling her that I was a downed Falangist pilot from Germany.

The woman approached me and slowly spoke to me in Spanish, her dialect not as pronounced as that of the man I presumed to be her husband. It was a tiresome exercise, she having to repeat words and phrases, but eventually I got the gist of what she was saying. They were Basques but had lost their son who was only sixteen years old when the Republicans had press-ganged him into their army. She said that if I was captured, the Republicans would shoot me. Since the bombing of Guernica, they were shooting any enemy pilots. She told me that I was to hide for a few days until the troops stopped looking for me. She indicated a small loft upstairs in the roof. She gave me a plate of food, which appeared to be a stew of mutton or goat with olives and beans. It was delicious and I was ravenous. I was also given wine. The old man left again, leaving me alone with the woman.

After the meal, she brought me a change of clothing once meant for her son. The fit was tight but acceptable.

I asked in slow Spanish how far it was to Vitoria. I knew the area to be in Nationalist hands. She said about forty kilometres, which meant that I could not be far from the front line.

The woman left me sitting in the kitchen and went about her business. I tried to make conversation but she answered in monosyllables, and I quickly got the message that she didn't want to talk.

At sunset, I heard the clinking of bells and realised that the sheep and goats were returning. This would be the old man. The animals were herded into the corrals and then the old man stood outside the door beating the dust off his clothing before entering. He nodded in greeting and walked over to a rough wooden buffet where he poured himself a generous glass of red wine. With the red wine jug, he motioned if I wanted to drink. I shook my head. He then came and sat down at the table with me. I offered him a cigarette from a packet I had in my jacket, which he gratefully accepted. I took one as well but indicated that I had no matches. He produced these and we lit up.

He started speaking to me very slowly trying to use Spanish. He often had to repeat himself. I gathered that in a few nights from now he would take me to the enemy lines but that I must remain in the house until then and sleep in the loft. I was not to leave the house as it may be watched.

*

I spent three nights in the house and never ventured outside. The food was plain but good. The woman had cleaned up my head wound and, by the second day, my headache had disappeared. Most of the time I spent in the loft sleeping as much as possible. There little else to do.

On the second night just after dark, a vehicle drew up followed by a loud knock on the door. In a flash, I climbed to the loft. It was a detachment of Republican soldiers still out looking for me and wanting to know whether the man had seen anything suspicious. He conversed with them for a while. They occasionally laughed as they drank the cups of wine he gave them. After that, they drove off again. It took a while before my heartbeat returned to normal.

On the fourth night, I said farewell to the old woman who wished me luck. I could see she was glad to see the last of me as I represented a danger to them. It was a dark night with a clear sky and just a small sliver of moon. I could barely see where we were going in the starlight but the old man seemed to know. I kept behind him with his back in front of me. He carried his shotgun and I had the automatic. Having found out I was armed, he had not asked for or removed the weapon from me.

We must have walked for at least two hours. All the while, in the stillness of the night, I heard the sound of an occasional artillery exchange. This could be but a few kilometres way. I could also see a few campfires which were placed so that the light was hidden from the enemy either by a high mound, a crumbled wall, or they had been made within the walls of a shattered building, only the orange glow visible. We had passed a few, sometimes no more than a hundred yards distant. This was when old man would proceed with a great deal more caution. He would stop me with a show of his hand, then alone move from black shadow to black shadow. He finally waved me forward, I imitating his movements from shadow to shadow.

He stopped.

"I can go no further. This is the line. You have to go on alone," he said. I didn't catch it all, but sort of pieced the sometime foreign words together and so would get a gist of what he was saying. Pointing with his hands he indicated: "This is a gap. Just follow the stream but you must be quiet." He had brought his finger to his lips to emphasise this point. I nodded. He held out his hand to say goodbye. I took it and we shook.

"Adios, Señor," he said, and then added, "Buena suerte." *Good luck.*

"Gracias, Señor," I replied. "Cuánto le dobo?" *How much do I owe you?*

"Cien US Dollars," he said and laughed.

I didn't have a cent on me and he knew it. It had been a joke. Hell, I didn't even know his name.

I walked in the direction he had indicated and kept looking back until he disappeared in the darkness.

I proceeded with the utmost caution. I could see a campfire about a mile away, this being the nearest to me. There was another but more distant. My eyes had adjusted well to the dark and I kept to the path we had followed. I tried to be as quiet as possible but every now and then I would tread on a stone or twig, the sound so loud that I would freeze and listen.

I kept on moving tentatively, frequently stopping for a mile or more, sticking to the path that followed the stream, but fortunately encountered no danger. The fires I had seen were now behind me and I could see no light at all, although occasionally there would be a flash on the horizon. I knew I was in no man's land and was trying to be extremely quiet, moving slowly and cautiously. My heart was in my mouth and any second I expected a shot to ring out and a bullet to hit me. This was a very frightening experience. I had no idea where I was. I could not help imagining that I was surrounded by the enemy and I wondered whether I was not stumbling into the enemy's positions where they were dug in. I was jumpy, imaging all sorts of disasters, and believed that I could die at any moment from a bullet, bayonet, or knife.

"Quién va?" rang out in the night. *Who goes there?*

This was a challenge and I froze. I was terrified. I wasn't quite sure where this came from but it was from up-front. It could have been Nationalist or Republican, I didn't know. Either way I knew I was a sitting duck out here in the open. They obviously had seen me. I didn't hesitate; I had to take the chance.

"Yo soy un piloto republicano," I shouted

"No se mueva o que se disparan," was the shout back. *Don't move or I'll shoot.*

I did as told.

I heard the crunch of boots on gravel and three shadows emerged from the dark with rifles levelled, the bayonets glinting in the weak moonlight. I had pulled my helmet and goggles from my pocket, held these out in my hands, and hoped that this would help persuade them that I was what I maintained I was.

Nothing more was said. Two of them moved to stand behind and he who seemed to be in charge led the way, saying that I should follow.

We followed the path for a short distance, veered left, and, after a short while, dropped into a deep hollow. A small fire was burning and this was surrounded by quite a number of men, most of them asleep in blankets. A bunker had been dug into the side of the hollow with an entrance protected with a tarpaulin. This was pulled aside as I was led in. Two oil lamps illuminated the bunker. There was a table with a large chart spread out on it with a few officers around it, some standing and others sitting. The very first thing I noticed were the uniforms. They were Nationalist.

"Gracias a Dios," I exclaimed. "I'm from the Condor Legion. Jagdgeschwader 2 88 near Vitoria. I'm Teniente Matthias Aschenborn."

A man stepped forward out of the shadows. He too was in a Condor uniform.

He spoke German. "I'm Hauptmann Graf. I'm an adviser with the infantry."

I saluted him.

"What happened to you?" he asked.

I then told him where and when I'd been shot down, the help I had got from the old man and his wife, how he had brought me during night to the front line, and then had shown me a path through the Republican positions.

"You're a very lucky man. He quite easily could have shot you. That's what usually happens," he said.

I said I realised this and did consider myself very fortunate.

"I'll have these people make contact with your unit. We'll take you to the nearest village behind the lines where you can wait for them to pick you up. Meanwhile our first-aid man can look at your forehead."

"I think it looks worse than it actually is," I said.

"No matter, Leutnant, let him look at it."

*

That morning, I was taken by truck to the village where I hung around until one of the squadron's trucks arrived to pick me up. I was glad to be amongst familiar faces again. Of course, once we arrived at the base, I was congratulated by all, my return considered a near-miracle. They believed that I had fallen into enemy hands. That night we broke out the Spanish cognac and beers and had ourselves a serious party.

During the evening, Helmut hauled me one side.

"That piece of Spanish fluff was at the gate looking for you. She was told that you had been shot down and gone missing. Apparently, she was beside herself." He paused. "Matthias, what the hell did you do to her? What about Wiebke, man?" He asked, but not without a grin on his face. Playing the women was one of his favourite pastimes.

"Helmut, just leave it alone. It's none of your damn business," I replied.

"Oh, oh! What do we have here? Another budding romance?" he said, then emptied half the contents of his beer bottle into his mouth, gulping the liquid down.

There was no romance but I could not deny that I seriously desired this woman. The way I felt I'd have taken on any attractive woman. It was a damn sex thing, something I just could not ignore.

If a pilot managed to make it back after being shot down, it was usual to be granted some leave. Of course, this was insufficient to get back to Germany for a few days. Besides, Capitán Tallant had said that I could have two days only. This was significant, I had stepped ashore in Spain exactly a year ago today. Perhaps this did call for a celebration.

CHAPTER FIFTEEN

I opened my eyes. I was lying on my bunk in the private compartment of one of the four passenger coaches of the train that had been shunted onto a siding and served as accommodation for the squadron. The sun streamed in through the slats of the wooden window shutter I had pulled up the night before. This was my first day of my two-day leave that Tallant had granted me.

Dressed only in shorts and with a towel over my shoulder, I made my way down the narrow corridor to the shower. This was a first-class carriage and had all amenities. The only other person I saw was the Capitán's batman, who greeted me as we passed in the passageway.

The first thing I decided I would do was call on the two sisters. I dressed in my uniform and, after twisting the officers' mess cook's arm, was served a late breakfast of poached eggs and bratwurst with fresh rolls. All serviceable aircraft had taken off on another raid so there were few if any pilots on the base. I took the Citroën and drove to the sisters' house. I was about to ring the bell when the door opened.

An incredulous Celeste stared at me. Her eyes and mouth were round with surprise.

"Madre Diaz," she said, "It's you!"

I smiled. "Yes, I made it back. My plane got shot down. I crashed in an orchard and I had to walk back through the lines with the help of an old Spanish gentleman."

It took a moment for her to get over the shock of having seen me.

"I thought you were dead, wounded, or captured," she said and then reached out and took my hand.

She turned round and shouted through the open door, "Isabelle, come, look who's here."

The younger sister appeared in the doorway with an expression of unconcealed surprise. I was glad to see that the puffiness around her eyes had disappeared. Her life had begun to return to a degree of normality, notwithstanding the war and its hardships and sorrow. Celeste gave me a hug and quick kiss as did Isabelle.

"Come in, come in," Celeste said, pulling me into the entrance. "Sit down. Let me get you a cup of coffee. We want to hear what happened."

I told them my story in a few sentences adding that I'd been lucky. They brought coffee on a tray and some biscuits.

"Come for supper tonight," Celeste said.

I knew that civilians seldom were able to find good food and I did not wish them to make sacrifices on my behalf. Even the coffee they'd served me was a luxury for them.

"I'll only come if you let me bring the meal. You can cook it. I'll come early," I said.

"No, we'll do it all. We'll find the food and cook it," she said.

"In that case, I won't come," I replied, but she wasn't quite certain whether I meant this or not. "I tell you what, I'll find some ducks. How's that?"

She pondered this. Isabelle dug her in the ribs and nodded her head at her.

"All right. We'll cook ducks, I know how to make a fabulous meal out of them," she said.

I thought my uniform would help, yet finding ducks to purchase in Vitoria proved difficult. I had to part with a considerable amount of money, buying these on the black market, but at least they gave me three. I scouted around for some good wine. In so doing, I walked past a market stall that sold all sorts of what I thought to be exquisite pieces of women's clothing. I bought two beautiful scarves and drove back to their house with my purchases.

At the house, I handed all to Celeste.

The scarves were gratefully accepted and I was rewarded with a kiss followed, surprisingly, by another. She lingered before withdrawing her lips.

"The first was from Isabelle, the second from me. My sister's busy with a delivery and will soon be back. You know, there's so much here," she said looking at the items I had brought. "Why don't you invite your friend to join us? What's his name? Helmut?" Initially I baulked at the idea. I couldn't have him playing havoc with an already broken heart. His feelings didn't concern me, it was Isabelle I was thinking of. Then I thought, surely he can't be that damn callous?

"I'll think about it. I don't want Isabelle hurt again," I said.

"Well, it's up to you but I think it's just what she needs. She's still young and needs to put the loss of von Kletzen behind her," Celeste said.

She said she still had work to do and I left.

*

"How would you like duck for dinner?" I asked Helmut.

"I take it that would be with the two sisters at the Garcia's place? Will one of the sisters be on the menu?"

"Don't be damn ridiculous," I snorted, already regretting the invitation.

"No, I'm serious. Does the invitation come with a bit of Spanish puta for dessert?" he asked, laughing.

"Fuck off, Helmut. Have a heart. Isabelle was Hans-Joachim's girlfriend. Christ man, don't be such a callous bastard. She's still trying to get over his death. You know that.""Sorry, no offence intended, it was just a joke. Sure, I'll tag along," he said.

*

It was Helmut's turn to use the Citroën so we were lucky and got to use the car

That evening, we swept into the Garcia's driveway in style, both resplendent in our Condor uniforms. Celeste met us at the door.

For most of the evening, Isabelle was withdrawn and, I have to admit, Helmut was the proper gentleman. Celeste and I were a different duo. The groping and footwork under the table were taking on a new intensity, my desire for this woman reaching greater heights.

There was a moment when the women had gone to the kitchen during the meal. Helmut and I were alone and he laughed at me.

"God, what the hell are you two doing to each other under the table? It's damn obvious, you know," he said. "Actually I'm embarrassed," he added humorously.

I shrugged my shoulders. I was so turned on I didn't care what he thought.

We ended the dinner with coffee and Orujo liqueur.

Helmut invited Isabelle to take a drive into town with him, inventing some pretext as to why he had to go, but then the man could be quite ingenious. I don't think Isabelle really wanted to go but realised Helmut wanted to give Celeste and me an hour or two to ourselves. I thought that rather generous of him.

155

With the sound of the departing car still in our ears, Celeste fell into my arms, kissing passionately, her body pressed hard against mine. She stepped back and sank to the sofa with me hovering over her, sliding my lips over her face and neck. I took her breast in my hand and gently kneaded it, still covered by the bodice of her dress. She slid her hand down my body and over my belt until she felt me and half rubbed, half stroked me. I wanted to open her dress but did not have the foggiest notion how the damn thing was held together.

"Silly, it has hooks at the back," she whispered.

I unhooked her, the front of her dress falling open to reveal her magnificent breasts, the nipples pointing slightly upwards, the darker areola prominent against the silky smooth lighter skin. I kissed a hard nipple and then took it into my mouth. She moaned softly.

"Come, let's go to my bedroom," she whispered hoarsely.

In the bedroom, I helped her out of her dress and underclothes until she stood naked before me. She was beautiful, with long sleek legs, a thin waist and those splendid breasts. She stepped nearer and undressed me, finally slipping off my shorts, then taking me in her hand. We fell onto the bed. I slid my hand between her thighs, my fingers sliding over her pubes and into her cleft. She was wet and ready.

From deep within her, she groaned and lifted her midriff as if to solicit me into to taking what she offered. I cannot describe that feeling of intense desire that overcame me prompted by her surrender to my caresses and kisses. Finally, I entered her, our lovemaking violent as if we wanted to lose ourselves in each other, she climaxing with a loud half-squeal and half-gasp and I following seconds later.

We lay spent on her large bed trying to catch our breath. I was damp with perspiration. Yes, I did have a nagging feeling of guilt, even if this was only slight. I wasn't in love with this woman. I just wanted her, something to soothe my own desire. However, I knew that I could not have both. I would have to give up one. I also knew that I could return to Germany at any time. She would just become a vague memory once I saw Wiebke again. Hideously cruel, I thought, but everything seemed cruel in this stupid war.

"I love you," she whispered in my ear and laid her head on my chest, wrapping an arm over me.

Illicit love affairs always seem to get complicated. It's difficult to share delirious, unbridled eroticism with women and not step over some invisible line and get emotionally involved. Yes, this woman had grown on me and I was involved but I remained silent.

By the time Helmut and Isabelle returned we were back in the drawing room. When they entered the house, I saw that they'd both lost some of the stiffness they had displayed when introduced. They joined us, sitting on another sofa, but continued with the conversation they were having. I hoped that this could develop into something more permanent, but this would mean Helmut would have to give up his other women of leisure. That remained to be seen.

CHAPTER SIXTEEN

The Basque-controlled territory stretched from the northwest corner of the Iberian Peninsula just east of the Nationalist naval port of El Ferrol, along the coastline of the Bay of Biscay, to beyond San Sebastian, and a very short distance into the land border with France, which is separated by the Pyrenees. This enclave resembled a horizontal oval quarter circle that penetrated south into the hinterland a hundred or so kilometres. The Nationalists had slowly driven the Republicans back, the Nationalists trying to take Bilbao, a strategic port on the Bay. The Nationalists, with the help of our Condor Legion, resorted to carpet-bombing, breaking through a front line known as the 'Iron Belt' which surrounded Bilbao at a radius of about forty kilometres. The terrain was rugged and this area saw vicious and heavy fighting.

The carpet-bombings wreaked havoc. Following these raids, the Republican troops were unable to regroup fast enough, allowing the Nationalists to take Bilbao in June, 1937. This heralded start of the campaign's final collapse in the north of the country.

It was with disappointment that Helmut and I learnt that we would again move to a new airbase a hundred kilometres or so to the south where vicious fighting was in progress as the Nationalists tried to wrench control of the city of Teruel from the enemy.

An intimate relationship between Helmut and Isabelle had blossomed. For the first time, he a one-woman man, if that's how it could be put, which I thought totally out of character but nonetheless immensely pleasing. Isabelle was again a young vibrant woman in love with this dashing airman.

Eventually the base moved to a spot about forty kilometres from Teruel, the process taking days. Our mobile accommodation was shunted all over the countryside, sometimes being held up while the rail line was repaired. We had flown ahead to where we were accommodated in atrocious conditions near our new airbase while we awaited the arrival of our coaches.

We left two sad and dejected women behind, but promised to return at the first available opportunity. This new development was so untypical of Helmut, having promised Isabella his true love and devotion. This surprised me, his seeming resolved to do so.

After we had said goodbye to the women and returned to the airfield to fly the aircraft out of Vitoria for the last time I said to him: "Tell me friend, was that promise you made from your heart, head, or dick?"

He just smiled. "From all three. I truly love the girl."

"Well, I'm glad to hear it because if you hurt her in any way I promise I'll beat you within an inch of your life." He laughed. "You mean you'll try."

"Fuck you, I mean it."

Again he laughed. The bastard, I thought. I meant it at the time.

We did see the two women as we had promised, thought not as often as we'd like. Capitán Tallant was not impressed with our periodic requests for the use of an aircraft or aircrafts to spend a day in Vitoria. As he so bluntly put it, good military airmen did not allow themselves to be distracted by what he said were sexual needs. Actually, his wording was a lot more descriptive. I bitterly disputed this but he did not relent. Nonetheless, we did occasionally get the use of an aircraft. We would arrive over the sisters' house and buzz it announcing to all and sundry that we were back. Invariably, we ensured that we brought foodstuffs and drink, which we would leave with the sisters and, of course, share with them while we were there.

Soon after the agreement between Hitler and Chamberlain at Munich in 1938, when France and Britain agreed to the concession of Czechoslovakia, when Chamberlain infamously proclaimed 'Peace in our time'. Helmut, a few others, and I were recalled to Germany, supposedly to permit another group of pilots to accumulate some flying experience in battle conditions.

The unfortunate aspect of this was that we were given very little time in which to take farewell of Spain and, in particular, those two lovely women. I have to admit that I wasn't emotionally prepared to part from Celeste and doing so had a profound, heartfelt effect on me. Yes, we did promise that we would see each other again but deep down in my heart I knew that this was a final farewell. I believe that she knew the same. Surprisingly, Helmut had a hard time and got deeply involved in making arrangements and buying tickets to have Isabelle join him in Germany. He would have married her in Spain but there was insufficient time and the local Roman Catholic diocese would not hear of it. Shotgun marriages were definitely not in their religious program, there a number of prerequisites. I'm not saying she was pregnant, but many believed this. During all this, Helmut's behaviour was quite strange and not like him at all.

Celeste never requested to come to Germany and I never made any such offer. To put it bluntly I slept with Celeste but still yearned for Wiebke. Is that possible?

CHAPTER SEVENTEEN
JULY 1944

When Helmut and I returned to Germany from Spain, we were again stationed at Berlin-Gatow where we converted to the latest Messerschmitt 109s. Thereafter we spent a year training and learning to fly various types of the latest aircraft in the Luftwaffe's arsenal. In the winter of 1938, we were posted to a new squadron, this situated on Germany's border with Poland. To many of us, it soon became evident that the country was preparing for war. The build-up of artillery, armour, and troops was discernible from the sky. Shortly thereafter the invasion of Poland began. This was followed by the Blitzkrieg against France and the Low Countries.

*

When we left Spain, we had been accredited with a number of kills. I had shot down three aircraft, these being Russian I-151s. Helmut had bagged two. We were both awarded the Spanish Cross, which was not an award to be sneezed at. This was accompanied by a set of cufflinks and a campaign medal from Spain. So, as you can well imagine, we returned with a somewhat elevated status of our abilities as opposed to those pilots who had missed out. We were battle veterans as it were.

The Polish campaign was rapid and within a short time the country was overrun. Later, the squadron was moved to western Germany.

The advance through Belgium and Holland was rapid, the squadron flying numerous sorties and engaging the enemy in the air and on the ground, destroying the aircraft and airfields. We then took on the English. The air battles over the English Channel were different. The English and their allies, the air forces of which had fled to English soil, were fighting for their very survival. Losses on both sides were heavy as we pitted man and machine against each other. Finally, the losses the German bomber forces suffered made these attacks on England too costly and the planned invasion of Britain by Germany, Hitler's Operation Sea Lion, became no more than a pipe dream.

Helmut was shot down over the Channel but bailed out. Fortunately, he was picked up by a German E-boat before he succumbed to hypothermia.

I was hit by shrapnel that lodged in my shoulder. I just managed to make it back to friendly territory, landing the aircraft when on the verge of losing consciousness. But I botched the approach, ploughing into the airfield on the aircraft's belly. I recuperated for three months before I could take to the air again.

For us, the pattern of warfare changed again. Now we started flying sorties against the huge American B-17 bomber raids, which meant flying at altitudes in excess of 20,000 feet, with oxygen masks clamped to our faces and an outside temperature of -30°C. The bombers often left contrails, so many of them that they seemed to fill the sky. As you initiated an attack on the densely packed bomber fleet, the gunners on these aircraft opened up, spraying a curtain of machine gun fire, with tracers criss-crossing the sky looking for their targets. We devised various tactics, all intended to allow us to get into a firing position and present their gunners with the smallest targets and this for a shortest period possible. The Americans suffered huge losses, but finally, the North American P-51 Mustang appeared. This was a formidable fighter, rated amongst the very best in the world with well-trained pilots. These now flew escort to the bombers and were ready to take on all adversaries.

Those of us who were chosen to protect the skies over Germany were decimated one-by-one as we fell to the enemy's fighters. Many of those who died were accomplished and decorated pilots but were replaced by new pilots who had not yet learned the necessary air combat skills. The flight training schools were releasing them for active duty too soon, without the abilities a fighter pilot required to stay alive. The shortage of fighter pilots was too acute, leaving the German High Command little choice. Most soon succumbed to enemy fighters. The enemy had a continuous source of pilots and aircraft, or so it seemed and the odds against surviving were now staggering. For many, death was merely a question of when.

'Die Alten', the Old Ones, had by now flown over a thousand sorties and we truly considered ourselves lucky to be still alive. We were all going to get shot down, or have an accident either taking off or landing, and realised that it was just a matter of time. Maybe a very lucky few would make it through the war. As I said, the question was only when. Tempers were short, the stress incredible, and fear a constant companion.

Helmut and I were inextricably bonded, always watching out for each other. He had brought Isabelle to Germany where they married, to everyone's surprise. They had found an apartment in Hamburg, situated more on the outskirts of the enormous city, into which Helmut had also ensconced his mother. A first child was born in 1941. He would run off home at every available opportunity. On her arrival in Germany, Isabelle had devoted herself to learning to speak the language. She was now employed in the local offices of the German Abwehr, they having sought her out for her fluency in Spanish. Helmut's mother looked after the child.

Herr Osterkamp, now an Oberstleutnant, was assigned to Austria where he commanded a group of flight training schools. Since her father's transfer from Kiel, Wiebke had moved back to Dresden. I had repeatedly asked that she remain in Kiel but she had desisted.

Helmut and I were again transferred, this time to Jagdgeschwader 27. We were now flying Bf 109Gs from airfields in Russia, trying to stem the relentless march of the Russian armies to Germany. The Russian advance was a juggernaut. It was unstoppable, an army of seemingly uncountable numbers – millions of men, thousands of tanks, and Russian and American aircraft. It slowly dawned on us what the inevitable end would be. We were fighting insurmountable odds. The Allies demanded an unconditional surrender. Germany was lost. It was just a matter of time, not that any dared say it.

While involved in the European theatre of war, we knew little of what was really going on behind the scenes. Yes, we knew that the Jews were in concentration camps but the atrocities that were carried were not known to us and we viewed these camps as no more than holding facilities for those who were dissidents and undesirables: the Jews, communists and Bolsheviks, criminals, and others who were out of step with the Nazi ideology.

Once stationed in Russia, we were to hear differently and were soon confronted with the truth. The stories that were whispered about the rounding up of the Jews by the SS Einsatzkommandos and the mass execution of them could not be contained. None dared speak out or question these actions. We heard of whole trains of cattle trucks transporting these people back to Poland. Men, women, and children were summarily executed in Russia, shot and buried in mass graves. We all knew. There were simply too many stories and rumours, but still we considered it best to remain silent.

Of course, the Luftwaffe was never involved, but this did not exonerate them. They adopted an attitude as if this had nothing to do with them. Nonetheless, in retrospect, by their very silence they also condoned this. On occasion, we would come across these detachments, which were invariably busy rounding up a ragged bunch of shocked and terrified human beings and carting them off to no one knew where. Sometimes, when coming into land or flying at low altitude, I would see long throngs of people guarded by these men as they were marched or sometimes trucked to their final destinations. It was difficult to believe that there was a God in times like these, the sheer horror of it all just impossible to grasp.

In the summer of 1944, an attempt on Hitler's life by the elite of the German officers' corps brought massive reprisals, with scores of officers and their families arrested, some executed after show trials, others simply thrown into concentration camps. We all soon learned that it was dangerous to speak out against Hitler and the Nazi Party. No one questioned the activities of the SS and their Sonderkommandos.

Klaus Schmidt, the Flugzeugwart, the mechanic who had originally attended my aircraft when I was learning to fly in Kiel, had been seconded to our squadron and was again my Flugzeugwart, but he was now also a non-commissioned officer. This had been engineered by Osterkamp. He thought it best to keep those he cared for somehow together.

We flew hundreds of sorties. Both Helmut and I had, over the years, added to our number of kills. Now that we were up against the Russians, these increased substantially. They had so many aircraft, many still inferior to our own, and the pilots not so well-trained. I now had fifty-six kills to my name, that is, enemy aircraft destroyed. We both were decorated with a Blechkrawatte, a 'tin-collar', the term pilots preferred over Iron Cross. We had both been promoted to major.

The rigour of the first winter spent on the steppes of Russia was an experience I will never forget. Let it be said that I know exactly what Napoleon's armies went through when they retreated from Moscow in 1812. The cold was incredible, the aircraft engines having to be started every hour for a bit so as to stop the oil from solidifying. from the cold.

If not, petrol had to be added to dilute the oil in the engine. The thinner viscosity enabled the engine to be turned over and then started. Once the engine started to warm up the petrol would boil off, but none were happy to do this. This was done by the sleep-deprived ground crews and not the pilots. All we did was look for a place that provided warmth, food, and sleep.

I had been shot down. A Russian Yak fighter blew a hole in my aircraft's radiator. Within minutes, the glycol spewed out and the engine overheated and seized with an enormous shock, nearly ripping the engine from its mountings. Thick smoke poured from it and I expected at any second it would burst into flame. I had no choice. I had to get out unless I wanted to be consumed by fire. I jettisoned the canopy, rolled the aircraft on its back, and let gravity drag me from the cockpit. The parachute's canopy opened with an enormous crack and I swung back and forth in the frigid Russian air as I descended to the ground. Fortunately, I was back over friendly territory and was soon picked up. As the men neared, backed up by a half-track, I saw the double lightning flashes on their helmets and realised that they were SS.

I was without injury and so pleased when I was bundled into the warmth of the half-track, away from the searing cold wind that blew over the steppes.

They drove east following a used track in the snow. Soon we approached a wooded area, the half-track following the track into the trees and then into a large clearing. There were a few large log huts. Nearby, a huge fire raged, surrounded by a number of SS troops. None could approach nearer than ten or fifteen yards, the heat so intense. There was a god-awful smell reminding me of something I'd smelt before.

The soldiers led me into a hut where it took a few moments for my eyes to adjust to the gloom. I soon saw that I was standing in front of a major, an SS Sturmbannführer, the death-head on his cap and the twin flashes on his tunic collar.

I saluted the man, who gave me a Heil Hitler salute in return.

"Welcome Major," he said, "I'm glad, as you should be, that we found you before the Russian partisans got hold of you."

"Major, I'm grateful. Please tell your men."

The major took in the Iron Cross with its ribbon that hung from my collar in place of a tie.

"They'll be glad to know that they rescued a war hero," he said.

With my noise wrinkled, I asked, "My God, Herr Sturmbannführer, what's that awful smell?" But I'd seen enough, the fire said it all.

"Those are the bodies of those we've rounded up. Jews, partisans, and other riff-raff who were executed. We're cremating them."

I was aghast. I had seen the pyre, the huge, broiling flames and smoke. The stacked logs with the bodies intermingled was enormous and must have contained hundreds of bodies. The sight burned in my mind was the most horrible sight imaginable. The SS Sturmbannführer smiled," "Come Major, don't be so put out. You people are so squeamish. They're were all enemies of Germany. What else to do with them? Our camps are already overflowing. Incidentally, I'm Fassbinder and I'm unfortunate enough to have been given this awful job. I would've much preferred to be in command of a Waffen-SS battalion on the Western front fighting the Amis. Those American troops are no match for the Waffen-SS and our King Tiger tanks." He stretched out his hand and I shook it but only after a second's hesitation.

"Aschenborn," I replied.

Just then, a Sharführer in camouflage uniform entered the hut, a Heckler & Koch MP-40 Schmeisser machine pistol dangling from a strap around his neck. He was pushing a young boy of no more than fifteen ahead of him.

The man saluted. "Herr Sturmbannführer, We missed him. He was hiding under the tarpaulin covering your Kübelwagen just outside . He's a Jew."

The boy's hair was long. He was dirty as were his clothes. His face was smudged, the dirt on his cheeks streaked by his tears. He cowered, petrified with fear. God knows what atrocities he had witnessed.

"For God's sake, man, don't bring him in here. Just get rid of him and make sure the body is destroyed," The Sturmbannführer responded with annoyance.

"Jawohl, Herr Sturmbannführer," the soldier responded and then dragged the boy from the hut.

"Damn Jews. They're forever trying to escape," The SS officer muttered.

I felt as if I were in a surreal world. The cold-blooded, insensate display shocked me to the core and left me numb. But I knew that to show any emotion could have repercussions. Expressing revulsion was one thing, but to show support for the victims or to question the morality of these executions could lead to being arrested and incarcerated in a concentration camp or assigned to a punishment battalion. None were known to provide a long life.

Minutes later I heard gunfire. Whether this had anything to do with the boy who was dragged away I did not know.

As a senior officer, it would have been discourteous to attempt to leave the hut and it required all my willpower to remain and drink his coffee while making small talk with this callous and inhumane man. I was overcome with a feeling of despair and ineffectuality. There was nothing I could've done to assist the boy and this made me as guilty as they were. I felt nauseated and wanted to scream to dispel the feeling of dread and shame, but I knew had to maintain an appearance of indifference and exude a touch of boredom while I waited to be collected by my comrades.

It took nearly two hours before the squadron's half-track arrived. I was surprised to see Schmidt sitting next to the driver. I profusely thanked the Sturmbannführer for his hospitality and climbed aboard, glad to be getting away from this place of horror.

We sat two rows behind the driver, the roar of the half-track's engine loud.

"You just cannot imagine the horror that I was forced to witness in that damn SS camp," I said

"I saw enough," was all Schmidt said.

"Just face it. All is lost." I covered my face in despair. "Matthias, think of something else. You've got to put this out of your mind, lest you go insane."

Addressing me by my Christian name, which he very seldom did, was his way of trying to share my torment and distress.

"But Klaus, for Heaven's sake, that's precisely the problem."

"So, what are you going to do about it?"

I didn't answer.

There was nothing I or he could do.

*

I was not the only one who had been lucky. Helmut also had his narrow escapes, belly-landing on the airfield, the aircraft bursting into flame. But he too was lucky and the aircrews and fire fighters extracted him quickly enough, with him suffering only some singed hair and a few superficial burns.

CHAPTER EIGHTEEN

I felt vulnerable as I sat in the cockpit of the Messerschmitt Me-262. Some called the twin-engined jet fighter 'das letzte Hoffnung', the last hope. It was sleek and fast, considerably faster than anything the Allies had, and it truly was, as one of the German aces had said, as if the angels pushed.

There was no longer hope. We all knew the war was lost, yet we said nothing and stoically applied ourselves to the job at hand. Many of us convinced that death was near, having seen so many of our fellow pilots succumb to the Allies. For every one aircraft we had, they must have had twenty.

We had again been transferred, this time to an airfield near Munich. It was surrounded by forests, which enabled the ground crews to hide the aircraft amongst the huge trees, away from the seemingly ever-present American Thunderbolts and the clusters of rockets slung under their wings.

*

I taxied to the take-off holding point, knowing that until I'd gotten the aircraft off the ground and gained some altitude and airspeed, I was a sitting duck. There is no substitute for altitude and speed in aerial combat. When taking off and landing you're at your most vulnerable. Sure, an umbrella of German fighters was aloft. These aircraft were part of the Platzschutzstaffel, composed of Focke-Wulf 190 fighter aircraft. Their sole function was to stop any sudden attack by the American Mustangs and Thunderbolts as our jets were taking off or landing.

The Me-262 was an incredible aircraft, faster and better than anything the Allies had. They were the very first true jet fighters in the world. Yes, it was plagued by faults. The two jet engines under its wings were temperamental.

I looked to the side. Helmut kept pace with me on my left. Two weeks before he'd experienced an engine flame-out on take-off and was forced to pancake the aircraft in an adjoining field. He'd had insufficient altitude to bail out but still managed to walk away from the wreck. It was then that he had likened the jet engines to two French prostitutes from the Place Pigalle in Paris who, on a whim, could unexpectedly terminate their services, leaving you otherwise at the most crucial of moments.

I swung the nose of the aircraft round so that it pointed down the runway and advanced the throttles, the engines slowly spooling up. This was a drawback of the jet engine. It took a while to spool up properly, a good few seconds, more like a quarter minute. I felt the strain of the thrust of the engines at full power and released the brakes. At first, the aircraft started to trundle awkwardly and slowly forward but then it began to gather speed but still required a considerable length of runway to attain flying speed. Slowly I felt the controls begin to bite and then, as the plane gained sufficient airspeed, I felt it acquire lift. I pulled the stick back, the nose rotated upwards, and suddenly the wheels came unstuck. I was flying. Behind me on my left, Helmut followed.

Six of us formed up in formation at 27,000 feet. We were then given coordinates to enable us to intercept a formation of American B-17 bombers. It was reported that these were en route to Munich, or so it was thought. We were told that they were being escorted by Mustangs and that other German fighters had already engaged them.

Flying at near 750 kph, we approached the formation with an altitude advantage. The Mustangs swung to engage us, most already having dropped their auxiliary fuel tanks. Those that had not yet released these also did so.

We broke formation. Keeping an eye on the approaching Mustangs, I chose a bomber and started to close with it from the front. I got the cockpit area of the massive aircraft into the gun sight and then slightly lowered the nose and squeezed the button on the joystick. The cannon's tracers burst from the nose in multiple flashes, the jet fighter streaking towards the bomber, which flew straight into the deadly stream of fire, a classic deflection-shooting manœuvre.

I saw the shells impact and saw bits and pieces of the aircraft break off. I pulled up, zooming over the top of the bomber, barely missing its enormous tail-plane. The bomber nosed down and broke formation. A wing started to droop, the aircraft beginning to roll. The bomber appeared out of control and lazily entered a death spiral towards the ground. Black dots spilled from the doomed plane and then parachutes blossomed.

From the side, two Mustangs had latched onto me and although I had lost some speed by zooming skywards. I still had a slight speed advantage, which made it impossible for them to manœuvre into a firing position. I rolled the jet and then pulled it towards the bombers, the Mustangs still behind me. Relying on my speed advantage, I managed to keep them away from me. Now I was approaching the bombers from the rear. As I got into gun-range, it seemed as if every machine gun turret on the bombers opened up, streaks of tracers approaching from each and every direction flashing passed my cockpit. I manœuvred the aircraft until my jet's gun sight hovered on a bomber's inboard port engine, and I squeezed the firing button. Again, the cannon blasted away and smoke poured from the huge radial engine which then burst into flame.

Machine gun bullets stitched a row of holes across my wing, the work of a P-51 Mustang. I pushed the stick to the left and forward, diving to increase speed. This kept the Mustang out of gun-range. I knew my plane was wounded. Fuel leaked from the wing tank, leaving a trail of white vapour. I swung the aircraft towards home with the hope that I would make it. Under normal flight conditions the Me-262 used fuel at a prodigious rate. Damaged, this would be worse. I hoped it would last and get me to the airfield.

I soon realised that the fuel loss was serious. I thought I could see the fuel gauge falling. Soon, I approached the airfield. The Platzschutzstaffel fighter umbrella over the field was involved in a wild dogfight with the enemy, the American and German fighters trying to out-manœuvre each other. I had no choice but to fly right in to land and ignore the dogfight. The jet was flying on the last fumes. I wasn't even sure I could make it. I concentrated on my approach, hoping to get the jet down before the engines cut, praying that the German fighters would keep the American Thunderbolts and Mustangs off my back.

I lowered the undercarriage and dumped the flaps. About two or three miles ahead of me lay the runway. I flew straight towards it, the jet still about 1,500 feet above the ground.

The aircraft shuddered and I realised I was taking hits. I felt the impact of the gunfire against the rear armour plating of my pilot's seat. Something smashed into my left foot, which was torn from the rudder pedal by the force of the blow. The canopy was holed and a shot or two had smashed my instrument panel. I knew the plane wasn't going to

171

make it to the runway as I took another salvo from an enemy I couldn't even see behind me. It was only when a Thunderbolt overshot me and then zoomed skywards that I saw him, a Focke-Wulf 'Dora' behind him, with his guns blazing as the German pilot desperately tried to protect me.

I jettisoned the canopy, the slipstream ripping at me. Something was wrong with my foot, it wouldn't work properly. I pulled the stick back to lift the nose and maintain some altitude for a few seconds. With my hands and on one foot, I lifted myself out of the cockpit and then let myself fall over the side onto the wing, the slipstream immediately whipping me off into the empty sky. As I fell out of the cockpit, I had my hand on the ripcord and the moment I cleared the cockpit, I pulled. The parachute blossomed, followed by a sudden jerk, and I then floated serenely towards the ground with an air battle raging above me and my jet disappearing in a massive fireball as it hit the ground.

For the first time I had an opportunity to see my foot. It looked a mess. Something had penetrated my flying boot and I saw blood oozing from it.

The ground was rushing up. I was over a meadow. My feet struck the ground. I felt an excruciating pain and then lost consciousness.

CHAPTER NINETEEN

The doctors told me I had been fortunate. I had taken a .50 calibre machine gun bullet through my foot. It had missed my ankle but shattered the bone just above it.

At first I was admitted to a Luftwaffe Lazarett near Berlin. But because of the continuous bombardment from the air and the approaching Russian Army, those of us who were expected to be there for a while were moved to a smaller Lazarett just east of Dresden. This was probably because this city had never once been bombed during the entire war. From talk and rumours, I heard that refugees were pouring in from the east ahead of the advancing Soviets, these cities bulging at the seams with the mass of humanity they were absorbing.

The doctors had operated twice and I was again mobile, albeit it still on crutches. I was assured that once properly healed, my foot would be as good as new and I'd have no limp, maybe just an ache or two if the weather were cold.

Wiebke came to visit me as often as she could. She worked for the Food Ration Control Centre in Dresden. I would have preferred to move further east towards the advancing Americans. My stint in Russia had taught me that we Germans could expect little mercy from the Russians and it would be far better to be captives of the British or Americans, for surely we soon were all going to be captives.

Wiebke had visited me the day before but could only stay a short while. Transport had become a major problem and there was forever the fear of being strafed. I told her that if I could get a discharge from hospital, which the Luftwaffe doctor still refused, we should go to Kiel. It was by a miracle that the house on Niemannsweg had withstood the bombing of the city and, except for a few broken windows, was as it was before. Wiebke refused. She felt she still had a duty to her job. Many people relied on her. I told her it was over, but she would not relent.

On the night of the 13th February, 1945, the Royal Air Force bombers carried out a saturation raid on Dresden using incendiaries which caused the city to be engulfed in a firestorm that lit up the sky. We in the Lazarett forty miles away could see the glow from the fires from our window. This raged through the night, its position revealed in the morning by the smoke that still hung over the city.

I was beside myself with concern for Wiebke. She had an apartment near the centre of the city and although I was sure she would have taken shelter from the raid in one of the enormous bunkers that had been built for that purpose, this did little to console me. An atmosphere of fear and gloom descended on the hospital. Many of the staff had family in the city and as the first stories filtered back it was obvious that the death and destruction wreaked by the bombers and the ensuing firestorm had been far worse than originally imagined. Already it was said that the deaths were in the tens of thousands. Rumour had it that many had died of asphyxiation and not explosion, the firestorm depriving the surrounding air of oxygen and those in the bunkers suffocating to death.

I was appalled. I begged the doctor, an Oberstleutnant, to release me. He refused and told me that if I did not heed his order, he'd court-martial me on the grounds of desertion.

"There's nothing you can do in Dresden, Herr Major. The city is destroyed. In your condition, you'd merely be a hindrance. Stay here, we'll hear soon enough. I, too, have family in the city," he said in a voice that was close to choking. I realised he was dead serious.

For two weeks, my mind floated in a mist of despair, hope and anguish waiting on word from Wiebke. I didn't know whether she was dead or alive. I had appealed to all to get me news. It seemed an impossible task, there simply were too many deaths and the situation was aggravated by the thousands of unknown refugees in the city, many of whom had succumbed in the firestorm. It was soul-destroying, the anguish unbearable.

It was ten in the morning and I was seated with others in a glass-enclosed porch. My foot was still in plaster, which was due to be removed in the next week or so. I had dozed off.

I opened my eyes and found Oberstleutnant Osterkamp sitting in a cane chair facing me with the saddest of expressions on his face. He looked older than his age. I immediately assumed the worst.

"Dear God," I whispered. "She's dead. Are you sure?"

He just nodded and then stretched forward and laid a hand on my arm.

"I'm absolutely sure. She was found and identified. I'm so terribly sorry," he said.

For days, I had prepared myself for news of the worst, but this was an enormous shock. I was paralyzed with grief. Now, it was as if my life had become meaningless. I had lost her, the only thing in this world of war and carnage that meant anything to me. What had I done that she should die and me to lose her?

"I'll leave you alone for a while. I'll be back, we need to talk," he said rising from his chair and walking away.

Osterkamp did not return until the next day. I had recovered from the tragic news faster than I thought, probably because I had partially conditioned myself for news of the worst while I waited for word on her.

I was on the porch when Osterkamp arrived. He greeted me, pulled up a cane chair, and sat down.

"I thought I'd let you sleep on it. You clearly had a bad shock. Well, for me there is nobody anymore. They're all gone. This fuckin' war and that fuckin man. With all that we've done to people, Germany is not going to be a nice place for a long time," he said with resignation.

"Maybe the Stabarzt will discharge me now," I said.

Osterkamp smiled weakly for the first time.

"I must confess that it was at my request that you remained here. Dresden was no place for a man on crutches with the use of only one leg. The place is in total ruins. The destruction is incredible. Everything I had is gone, as it is for most others. The conditions the survivors have to contend with are horrific. Please, don't make a performance. The Stabarzt is a personal friend of mine."

In the light of his remarks, he probably did have a valid point. Nothing I could do would bring her back.

"Matthias, Germany is finished. The war is over. The Russians are fighting in the outskirts of Berlin. We have to think of ourselves. Your plaster cast is ready to come off. My friend thought it a good idea to leave it on for a few days longer. They'll take it off today and you'll be discharged. I've a car and driver. We'll drive east to the American lines. They've halted their advance, probably to allow the Russians to penetrate Germany. The stupid Americans want Ivan to enjoy his share of the victor's glory. Watch how they will regret this one day. It would be better if they were to keep them out," Osterkamp said.

True to his word, a nurse soon wheeled me into a surgical ward where a doctor and nurse removed my plaster cast. I was given my uniform in which to dress, my Fluzeugwart, Klaus Schmidt having delivered it to me weeks before when he had visited me. He had told me that many of my comrades had fallen but Helmut was okay. He laughed that my friend had more lives than a cat. He had shot another four aircraft down and had achieved 101 acknowledged kills. He was an ace, up amongst the very best. I didn't envy him.

The Stabarzt issued me with a discharge document which also indicated a fair amount of furlough for recuperation. This was necessary if I were to be stopped by the Feldgendarmerie, who, in the closing stages of the war, were continuously on the lookout for deserters, especially those of the Offizierskorps. All seemed to be fleeing. Fighting to the very end was pointless.

Still using crutches but letting my injured foot take some of my weight, Osterkamp and I exited the Lazarett and made our way to the black Mercedes staff car, the door of which was being held open by a man in a Luftwaffe infantry uniform. The man smiled and saluted smartly.

"Christ, it is you, Klaus," I shouted, forgetting to return the salute but shaking the man by the hand.

It was Klaus Schmidt, my Flugzeugwart. I couldn't believe it.

"How the hell did you pull this off?" I asked Osterkamp, still dumbfounded.

"He is now our driver. It's amazing what you can do if you have friends. My good friend, Oberst Tallant, intervened and had him posted to me."

I was overjoyed to see the man. He was pleased himself. He wanted to get to Kiel and this was an excellent opportunity. The good Colonel Tallant had seen to it the Klaus Schmidt had been issued with the appropriate papers.

We set off with the car travelling east, keeping a constant lookout for American aircraft which would strafe anything that resembled a military vehicle. Quite a few times we were forced to pull into the trees that lined the road as American Mustangs or Thunderbolts roared overhead. We saw no German aircraft. We did pass a few mechanised German columns travelling east, obviously sent to stem the advances of the Russians. Parts of the road were lined with destroyed German army vehicles, some still smouldering. Crowds of refugees moved west trying to get away from the advancing Red Army. Fortunately, the American Air Force was not into attacking civilians.

Klaus Schmidt swung round. "Herr Obersleutnant, there's a roadblock ahead."

Osterkamp leaned forward to get a better look.

"Christ, it's an SS detachment and they've military police with them. This could be a problem," he said.

The roadblock had been placed under a group of large oak trees which provided a degree of cover from over-flying American aircraft. There were about ten to fifteen uniformed SS troops, all armed with machine pistols, and then a few Feldpolizei, Military Police. A portable boom had been placed across the road. Affixed to it was a large white signboard, which read 'HALT!' in black letters, and below that the twin lightning flashes of the SS.

The Mercedes came to a stop with a faint squeal of brakes. An Obersturmführer approached the car's open back window. He was flanked on both sides by two camouflage-uniformed troopers in their brandishing their automatic weapons. The Obersturmführer bent down to look at the occupants. At the sight of the two high-ranking officers, he immediately came to attention and shot his right arm out in a Hitler salute.

"Heil Hitler!" he said.

Osterkamp casually returned the salute and then immediately produced papers, which included those given to me by the Stabarzt from the hospital.

"I've just collected my companion, Herr Major Aschenborn, from hospital near Dresden and we are on our way to Ainring, an airfield in the Berchtesgarden, Upper Bavaria to meet up with Jagdgeschwader 44."

"Herr Oberstleutnant, I regret that I cannot let you proceed. I have my orders," the SS lieutenant said.

"Herr Obersturmführer, what do you mean you cannot let us proceed?

"Colonel, I'm sorry. Our orders come directly from the OKH. No military personnel are permitted to leave their current station."

I looked at the officer with his fair hair and chiselled features. The SS had chosen well, this individual would not let us pass. He was an elite soldier to the core. His face and bearing said it all. No way were we going to persuade him otherwise.

"Herr Obersturmführer, are there no exceptions?" Osterkamp asked.

"None, sir."

"Then what do you suggest I do?"

The officer indicated a side road, which led off at a ninety degree angle, lined on both sides with enormous oak trees which formed a near continuous canopy over the road.

"Herr Oberstleutnant, I would suggest you follow this road to our headquarters, which are bivouacked in a small village, and talk to my commanding officer, Sturmbannführer Stechel."

"Thank you, Obersturmführer," Osterkamp replied and then indicated to Schmidt that he should follow the side road.

I saw that the Waffen-SS had dug themselves in all along the high ground, all of it extremely well-camouflaged. We could still see the occasional anti-tank gun emplacement and soldiers armed with the Panzerfaust, an anti-tank weapon which can be operated from the shoulder. The drawback with this weapon was that you had to allow the tank to get perilously close before you could effectively fire it to penetrate a tank's armour.

Klaus Schmidt drove with care. The road was criss-crossed with tank tracks and I wondered whether these were not visible from the air. It was evident that a large force was dug in among the various large copses of trees. We approached a village after about four miles. It was nestled in a valley and, at first glance, seemed a picture of rural tranquillity, revealing no war damage and with cows still grazing in the adjoining pastures. On closer inspection, the preparations for war could be seen: tanks were covered with camouflage netting and branches. There were a number of half-tracks and squads of Waffen-SS in camouflage gear lounging under the trees, most with automatic weapons. A truck from which antennae sprouted gave away the position of the commando post. The SS had taken over the local inn but had made sure that nothing could be detected from the air, there being no vehicles or men in the quiet streets.

As we approached, a soldier appeared and waved, indicating that we should park under a large tree. We climbed out of the car and were directed to the inn. This was a one-storey building, clearly quite old, which bordered on the main street. As tranquil as it appeared from the outside, the interior bustled with activity, with maps spread out on a large table, these being studied by a few officers. On another table there was a powerful radio set manned by two men. I saw that an adjoining room had been converted into an office, the desk and chairs visible through the open door. They led us straight into the office where a Sturmbannführer sat, whom I presumed to be Stechel himself. The man came to his feet and gave us a Nazi salute which we returned.

Osterkamp repeated our reasons for being on the road.

"You are brave men. A staff car in daylight in these times? The Ami Thunderbolts and Mustangs would have shot you up had they seen you," the Sturmbannführer said lighting the cigarette which Osterkamp had offered him.

"Major, it is vital that we get to Ainring to join up with Jagdgeschwader 44. You're at liberty to contact Oberst Tallant if you wish," Osterkamp said and then gave our names to the Sturmbannführer.

"I'm sorry, gentlemen. My orders come from our Oberstgruppenführer himself. Clearly you will understand that I cannot ignore these. You must remain here. However, I will in the meantime try to get permission so that I may allow you to proceed. I don't think my high command expected any high-ranking Luftwaffe officers to make an appearance. Also, I'm sure your squadron needs you. Meantime, relax, you're my guests." He motioned to his aide and asked that we be brought something to eat and drink."

Both Osterkamp and I realised that to argue was pointless. I hoped that the Major would soon make contact with our squadron and his commander.

Three hours passed and still there was no reply from Ainring. Suddenly a soldier burst in from outside.

"Take cover," he shouted. "Raketenangriff!" *Thunderbolts!*

Everybody stormed out of the building, running to a few slit trenches that had been dug under the trees about a hundred yards away from the buildings, these not visible from the air. The air was loud with the howl of the aircrafts' engines as these in pairs dived down on the village. I looked up just in time to see the first rockets leave their launch pods on an aircraft. I dived into the slit trench and buried my head into the ground. At the same time, the aircraft opened up with their six half-inch machine guns. I heard the chatter and thump as the bullets churned up the ground, sending clumps of clay and mud flying into the air. This was followed by a series of explosions around us as the rockets struck the terrain, the concussion of the explosions hammering our eardrums. A second or two later the ground shook from a few massive explosions. The pressure bursts pounded our ears and pummelled our bodies. It rained earth and stone. I realised that the aircraft had dropped bombs as well.

We heard the drone of the aircraft recede in the distance, which signalled the end of the attack. We climbed from the trenches, brushing the layer of dirt from our clothes. The inn was no more. It had received a direct hit and crumbled. Two of its outer walls had collapsed and so had the roof. The shouts and calls for stretcher-bearers could be heard. There were dead and wounded.

The Sturmbannführer took control, ordering that the inn be searched and whatever had survived the attack be taken to another building situated further down the road. An Opel Blitz ambulance truck materialised out of the trees and the wounded were quickly loaded. I wondered where they would take these men. The few dead were laid down on the ground in a neat row, covered with whatever was handy, a greatcoat or blanket.

Fortunately, the three of us had emerged from the rocket attack unscathed. As evening approached, we found ourselves a deserted building and, after scrounging around for some blankets, prepared a place to spend the night. Klaus Schmidt found a narrow mattress which he surrendered to Osterkamp who only accepted this after we repeatedly insisted that he take it. Klaus and I made ourselves makeshift pallets from some old sacking I found in the cellar. From the soldiers we received some ration packs which would serve as supper.

That night I realised that these were the final days of the war. The sound of artillery could be heard in the west and in the east. The enemy was closing in on us from both sides, the Allies from the west and the Russians from the east. Fighting had become pointless but, for some, especially in the SS, fanaticism prevailed. It seemed we would resist to the last, irrespective of the lives that it would cost, their sacrifice futile and unnecessary. Sheer madness, I thought.

The next morning, as the first light began to streak the sky, we found that we were now in artillery range, the first shells falling on the town. The shelling came in from the east. This had to be a Russian artillery barrage.

We remained in the cellar for two hours while the town was bombed, the shells whistling in, the ground below us shuddering with every impact. Finally, the cellar of the building in which we had taken shelter, took a direct hit. Debris and dust fell upon us as we hunkered down on our makeshift beds with our hands over our heads.

I was terrified, never knowing whether the next few seconds would be my last. The constant concussion waves of the explosions became unbearable. My head pounded and I felt disorientated. I forgot those around me as I was taken up with my own abject fear.

Just when I thought I couldn't take another explosion, the shelling stopped. The smashed interior of the building filled with an eerie silence. A few minutes later, we heard the sound of machine gun and small arms fire interspersed with the lesser explosions of hand grenades and mortars.

We knew what was happening. Ivan was coming. The town was being defended by the Waffen-SS who could expect no quarter from the Russians. The atrocities committed by the SS against Russian civilians and Russian prisoners of war were legend. This would be a fight to the death.

"Quickly, dust yourselves off. Make sure your Luftwaffe insignia is clearly visible. It is our only hope. These bastards are going to shoot every SS soldier out of hand," Osterkamp shouted at us.

Frantically, we cleaned ourselves as best we could. We beat the dust from our caps and stood with our backs against the wall and waited. My greatest fear was that a soldier would toss a grenade or two down into the cellar before he ventured down the stairs. I said so. They just stared at me. To venture outside would be madness as some trigger-happy Ivan was bound to open fire at sight of us. I didn't think white flags would be of any use either.

Already the fighting was in the streets, from door to door, the sound of machine-pistol and rifle fire clearly audible and closing relentlessly.

Suddenly we heard movement above.

"he стрелять. Мы - чиновники Воздушных сил!" Osterkamp shouted in Russian three times. *Don't shoot, we are German Air Force officers!* I prayed to God that this would be sufficient to dissuade the Russian soldiers from shooting us at first sight. I was numb with fear, powerless to move my limbs.

From above we heard shouts. I didn't know what they were saying, but I knew the Osterkamp understood.

"Lie down flat on the floor, on your stomachs. Do it now," Osterkamp said hoarsely, his fear as apparent as my own. I prostrated myself on the ground with my arms stretched out in front of me and looked sideways out at the corner round which anyone coming down the stairs would have to approach.

There were noises on the wooden staircase and then the muzzle of a Russian machine-pistol slowly began to protrude, followed by an arm clad in a green khaki uniform. A face appeared, showing only one eye and taking in the whole cellar. Then only did the soldier step forward and reveal himself. He did this with caution. I saw the blond hair that peeped from under the Russian helmet and the insignia on his shoulders, the red epaulette with the double gold stripe and CA, he was a sergeant, a European Russian.

"Hände hoch!" he shouted in heavily accented German.

Maintaining a 'hands up' position while lying stretched out on the ground on your stomach is difficult but we did our best, raising our arms slightly off the floor while expecting him to open fire at any moment.

The sergeant was followed by four soldiers. They all entered the cellar pointing weapons at us. With a wave of his machine-pistol the sergeant indicated we should rise, but again shouted, "Hände hoch!" We got to our knees and then slowly stood, our arms pointing straight up. The sergeant spoke to one of his soldiers who then left the cellar. For minutes, we just stood there looking at each other. We could still hear gunfire, bursts of automatic fire and distant shouts.

It was five or more minutes later that the soldier returned with an officer in tow.

The officer looked at us and then spoke.

"You are Luftwaffe?" he asked in German.

"Yes, lieutenant. All three of us," Osterkamp quickly replied as we still stood with our arms in the air.

They led us up the stairs through the rubble of the building, most of which had collapsed, and then out into the open. I saw Sturmbannführer Stechel and two of his junior officers standing to one side. There were four Russian soldiers standing a few yards away with their weapons trained on them. I heard another burst of automatic fire and turned to look. I was horrified to see four men who had stood next to a wall crumple to the ground as some Russian soldiers summarily executed them.

"They're SS," the Russian lieutenant said matter-of-factly, as if the execution of these was justified.

I looked at the SS officers and saw in their faces that they already knew their fate. I wondered if this was to be ours as well. A feeling of total despair and defeat overcame me. There was no escape from this. Death seemed certain.

A soldier indicated to the three SS officers to start walking. The three men marched to the wall, having to walk around their fallen comrades. At the wall, they turned to face those who made up the firing squad, a few Russian soldiers who had formed a ragged line armed with machine-pistols. The SS officers formed a straight line and turned to face the soldiers, making no sound. The air was rent by machine gun fire again, the three men collapsing against the already bloodstained wall. My body jerked as the bullets stitched across the men, raising dust from their tunics. The horror of it was nearly unendurable. Even if these men were members of the feared SS, they died brave men. They died silently, making no objection or sound. It was tragic. The war was long lost and Germany was finished, but still they had to die. It was such a waste of life.

It was our turn now. The Russian officer spoke to the men who then prodded us with their weapons, forcing us to walk towards where the dead SS officers and non-commissioned officers lay. The other SS soldiers, the ordinary infantry, had been rounded up and were encircled by men with weapons. The dead lay everywhere, both German and Russian.

The same Russian lieutenant who had originally confronted us in the cellar after the initial Russian attack broke away from the small group of Russian officers and approached Osterkamp. We assumed that he was probably the only one who spoke German. He spoke to Osterkamp.

"You are now the ranking officer amongst the prisoners. Take a few of your SS men and your fellow officer," he indicated me, "and collect all the identification tags of your dead. Use a few of the soldiers to help you, the rest are to start digging a large grave," he said, indicating a meadow nearby. "Use a shell crater to start, just enlarge it. Then place all the

German dead in it and cover it up. Between the two of you, you supervise the detail."

The lieutenant then called a Russian detail over and spoke to them. They were to guard the SS soldiers and us to ensure that none made a break for it.

The Russian attack on the town had been on a narrow front, which was no more than about two miles wide.

We started at one end, removing the discs and moving the dead to a spot near to where the mass grave was being dug. Between the Russian and German medics, they supplied us with a few stretchers and the laborious task of collecting the dead began. Osterkamp and I were accompanied by two guards as we systematically inspected the dead and removed their dog tags. The soldier who removed these handed them one by one to me, some covered in blood. Soon my hands were red. It was a grisly task.

We were busy the whole day and it was only at dusk when a T-34 Russian tank arrived, this with a scraper-scoop attached to the front. It was used to shove the heaps of dug-up soil into the mass grave, covering the dead until it was filled and the ground level with the surrounds. The tank then drove back and forth over the ground in order to compact the earth.

We had been at it all day and during that time were given nothing to eat. Some of the German SS still had a few ration packs which they surreptitiously dished out amongst us.

The Russians herded the surviving SS soldiers and ourselves into the local Lutheran Church which still stood. It was only marginally damaged by the Russian artillery bombardment. Most windows were blown out and some masonry shattered, but at least it would provide adequate shelter against the elements for the night. The Russian officers organised a strong presence of guards who kept a round-the-clock vigil while we tried to make ourselves as comfortable as possible. Osterkamp and I were now the only German officers in the group.

I awoke the next morning to the shouts of the guards. It was barely light and freezing cold. I had wrapped myself in my greatcoat and curled up on one of the church benches, as had Schmidt and Osterkamp. I groaned as I tried to work my stiff, cold joints. I needed to relieve myself. There were no latrines other than a single toilet attached to the church, which did not function. The Russians had made no provision for field latrines and when we stepped out of the church, we saw the adjoining meadow dotted with squatting soldiers, both Mongol and German, who were relieving themselves while the guards looked on.

"Christus! This is just a foretaste of what we'll have to contend with. These soldiers are from the southern steppes and deserts in Russia where very little has changed in the last few hundred years. You're naïve if you're expecting them to come up with anything remotely sophisticated. I don't think the word 'dignity' is in their vocabulary," Osterkamp said as he wrinkled his noise in disgust.

I realised that I had better follow the example of the SS soldiers, as another opportunity may not present itself before the evening.

I sighed. "Well, I don't have an alternative. Look the other way, I've got to go!" I said and strode off towards the meadow.

We marched for three days, finding shelter every evening in some disused and damaged buildings or churches. The fed us once a day, a small loaf of bread and a large bowl of kabushka to share. This was supposedly a cabbage soup, though what the exact ingredients were we did not know. All were so hungry they ate it anyway.

From the few signs that we could still find on the roads we realised that we were being taken east towards the German border.

On the morning of the fourth day, there was no order to resume marching. We remained confined to the building in which we had spent the night. The guards let a dozen or so of us out at a time to attend to our personal ablutions. During the three-day march, we had been joined by other long columns of German prisoners. There were a few walking wounded, none serious. A few men did collapse, not many. The other soldiers would just pull them to the side of the road and lay them down on the verge. A Russian guard would be assigned to remain behind with the man. We noticed that after an hour or so the guard would catch up with us again, but without the prisoner. We had no idea what had happened to him and any questions were met with a silence. Whether true or false, though never substantiated, it was soon believed that to collapse was tantamount to a death sentence as once the column was out of sight and earshot the prisoner was executed. Those who dropped out were never seen again.

At noon that day, a convoy of canvas-covered trucks arrived. The guards forced us aboard, the vehicles then taking off with two guards assigned to each vehicle. We were unable to look out of the sides but could see out of the rear of the vehicle. Still, we saw enough to see that the towns and villages we drove through all bore the scars of war and destruction. Women and children were seen searching through the rubble, and some even called in German for food as we passed. The situation in the occupied east part of Germany was a catastrophe and many more were sure to die.

Notwithstanding the ordeal I had to contend with, I was fortunate in that my leg improved each day, the pain slowly diminishing. The three of us stuck together, sharing everything we had. At first the Russian officers were not happy that Klaus Schmidt was constantly in our presence, but eventually they accepted that he was Osterkamp's aide as it were and he was permitted to remain with the officers.

*

After days of stop-and-start travelling, this during the day and some of it during the night, the trucks drew up in front of a large building that adjoined a railway line swarming with hundreds of workers repairing the track. A contiguous building was adorned with a few large Soviet flags. The sides and entrance were encircled with sandbags and machine gun emplacements on the two street corners. Word spread like wildfire, we were in Poznan in Poland and the building housed the Soviet military courts for the forward lines.

"Military courts. This definitely has an ominous ring to it. We are German prisoners of war. I don't trust these bastards," Osterkamp whispered.

The building we were herded into contained hundreds of bunks, three to a tier. We were each issued with a blanket. These were dirty and used. But we all were dirty and stank, many having not washed for days.

We stayed a week, hearing different rumours every day, never knowing whether these were true or false. Each of us was interrogated by whom we thought was the Russian NKVD, the military secret police. We answered their questions supplying whatever details they requested. The questions were not those I expected and did not relate to armaments and troop movements, but our names, rank and units, and where we had seen service during the war. We also found out that some officers were to face

186

a court-martial in order to establish whether they should be tried as war criminals.

We were soon to learn that the Soviet definition of war crimes was all-encompassing, and that most German high-ranking officers often received a sentence for committing crimes against the Rodina, the Russian motherland and its people. These sentences were anything between ten and twenty-five years, but amongst the SS these were invariably death sentences. However, these were rumours and difficult to verify.

We were housed in a section of the detention camp reserved for officers and Klaus Schmidt was finally separated from us. We were still able to speak to him from time to time from across the wire that separated us.

We were in Poznan for four weeks during which we heard that Hitler was dead. None knew how he had died but it was rumoured that he had committed suicide in his bunker in Berlin. Hostilities had ceased except for a few sporadic outbursts in the Caucus Mountains and Yugoslavia. The Russians had taken Berlin.

Osterkamp and I were hauled before a military court, the proceedings no more than a sham. We were without representation and charged with crimes against the Russian motherland. We both sentenced to ten years imprisonment with hard labour. We knew this would mean transportation to a gulag somewhere in Siberia. It was a farce: we were never even asked to plead, no evidence was led, our officer status condemning us. They had our names and where we had served and to which squadrons we had been attached. That was sufficient. The three-man tribunal conferred for a minute or two and the sentence was then read out. No questions were permitted. The sentence was final.

We were escorted back to our bunks and allowed to collect the few belongings we had. From there we were transferred to another detention camp, the officers were separated from the men. All the inmates already received sentences. This camp was also in Poznan, not far from the railway line.

The camps were enormous rectangular barbed wire enclosures containing hastily erected long wooden huts built in rows which stood off the ground on stilts. The huts filled by the day as more and more prisoners arrived. Of course, the German prisoners were wholly reliant on their captors for everything. There was no German army left and the German command structure was no more. Most soldiers just wanted to go home to their families and loved ones, not knowing whether they were still alive. German soldiers were being picked up by Russian patrols all over the country and sent to these holding centres for processing.

The railway line from the east, which had been damaged in multiple rocket and bombing raids, was finally repaired and the first train arrived. It crept along the hastily repaired line, by a steam locomotive with a long line of cattle trucks attached to it. This was loaded with various goods: bundles of barbed wire, timber, crates, and other items which the Russians had the prisoners offload.

The next day all of us, the officers and men who were in our enclosure, were herded into the cattle trucks, each with our blanket and canteen. The Russian guards packed each cattle truck with about thirty men. They provided each truck with a drum which was to serve as a portable toilet. This was to be emptied at every stop. It was a disgusting and foul arrangement. The rapidly repaired rail line was uneven and the wagons would sway alarmingly, the nauseous contents of the drum sloshing over the sides. Thirty men to a wagon was a tight fit and when we all lay down and you needed to visit the drum, this required stepping over your indignant comrades who protested. All did their utmost to find a place to lie down as far from the drum as possible and this further reduced the room available.

We were now mixed with other officers, most from the Wehrmacht but a few from the Kriegsmarine and the Luftwaffe. All occupants of our wagon had been sentenced to hard labour. The unhygienic conditions during the past days and the cramped quarters we experienced in the holding pen eventually took its toll and we had to contend with an outbreak of lice, which spread like wildfire. The Russians provided a disinfectant in powder form. From the labels on the tins, we realised that this was of American manufacture. This did help contain the spread but was not a cure in itself. Those who had fallen ill while in the detention camp had been removed from the enclosure, but none knew where they had been taken. They, too, we never saw again. There was a Luftwaffe surgeon in our enclosure, who also boarded our wagon, but he was without any medical supplies whatsoever and almost powerless to treat those that had fallen ill. He was only able to offer comfort.

For a month, the train was our home as we slowly moved eastwards and then north. Often the train would stand for a day or night without moving, or we would spend hours being shunted around in some large marshalling yard. Periodically, we were permitted off the train to stretch our legs, to eat, and on two occasions were afforded the luxury of a shower. It was then those who had succumbed to hunger and malnutrition, from old wounds that became infected and never healed, those who seemed to have given up on life were removed from the wagon. Nobody did a count, but during the period of transport scores died. The Russians didn't give a damn but we thanked God that the Russians had not turned their tommy-guns on us as they had done to so many other Germans simply because the German prisoners were considered a nuisance.

*

The weather was now colder, particularly the mornings and late evenings. Fortunately, it was not yet winter which was still a few months away. If it had been, then I'm sure many more thousands would have died in these cattle-wagons.

We had travelled deep into Russia, bypassing Moscow, or so it was rumoured, and then travelling northeast. We entered the taiga, a boreal forest which stretches around the world in all countries between the desolate tundra wastelands and the temperate zones. In Russia, this is a forest of conifers. Fir, pine, larch, and spruce grows in the semi-permafrost and the harsh taiga winters.

We seemed to have travelled thousands of miles. Our daily fare consisted of tea, bread and kabuska, that cabbage gruel, in which we would occasionally find some protein like salted fish or unknown meat. Sometimes it even contained potatoes and turnips. It was said that as officers we fared better than the ordinary soldier did.

One morning we awoke to find the train again stationary. We peered through the planking of the cattle trucks and saw that we had halted on a siding. The wagons had been pulled onto a spur line which led into the forest. On one side of the track, there were a few buildings to be seen, all with smoke spiralling from their chimneys. Evidently this was a small settlement which had been built in the taiga. The buildings were devoid of any paint, the rough wooden planking already bleached a light grey. All the buildings stood on stilts, about foot or so off the ground, each with a few small windows. Osterkamp explained that the windows were always small because in winter the glass provided insufficient insulation and allowed the heat within to escape. He added that they also closed the shutters in winter to retain the heat. The other side of the track was taken up by huge stacks of logs and bundles of sawn timber, which were piled parallel to the rail line. The logs were already de-branched, de-barked, and cut into long lengths to be loaded on the train.

The cattle-truck doors were slid open and all prisoners were ordered out to form into columns of four with a hundred men to a squad. We saw that we had new guards. They were in different uniforms, still the same green khaki but they wore boots of felt, and some had dogs on leashes. All carried automatic weapons. Most had Mongolian features, thus seeming from another world, and unlike the European Russians at all. It was difficult to establish a basic rapport with them. Their Russian was rudimentary and they spoke no German at all.

Trying to sort the men out went on for an hour, with Germans mingling amongst themselves and moving from one squad to another, some looking for a friend with whom to team up. The guards became frustrated and angry. Eventually it was announced, in both German and Russian, through a loudhailer that we had two minutes in which to take up our positions. Any who moved thereafter would be considered an escaper and shot. This had the desired effect. All came to order and within minutes the count commenced.

It took an hour before the Russian officers were satisfied. Then the officers decided that we should be sorted. All Luftwaffe personnel were to form their own squads, as had the Wehrmacht and Kriegsmarine. It was decided that in view of the very few naval prisoners, they should be thrown in with the Luftwaffe. Again we were counted and by the time the order was given to move out it was past midday.

It was with relief that we started moving. The gnats and mosquitoes swarmed around us as we swore and slapped at insects. The new guards flanked us on both sides, as did the guards with the dogs who were placed at regular intervals along the column's sides.

It was well past seven in the evening when the gulag itself came into sight. At this latitude, we were close to the Arctic Circle and the twilight would last until ten in the evening. Vast areas around the gulag had been cleared of trees. This was huge, ringed with barbed wire, and even with high wooden fences in places. Watchtowers surrounded the camp. They were always in sight of one another and there was no area of the camp's perimeter that could not be seen by any two watchtowers. Each tower was manned by two guards. Machine guns could be seen these covering all accesses to the fence.

We marched through the huge gate where each squad was met by a three-guard contingent, one of which was a non-commissioned officer, and then led to their barracks. These contained rows of two-tier bunks. A large central area was dominated by a huge potbelly stove. From the stove, recessed pipes led to the walls, leading to radiators at regular intervals along the walls around the barracks. It seemed an efficient heating system, certainly a necessity in the harsh Siberian winters. There were rough wooden tables and chairs around the enormous stove and a long row of wooden lockers against the centre portion of the opposite wall. The steam pipes also led to an ablution block with showers and basins. The amenities were not as primitive as we expected.

We spoke little Russian and the guards spoke even less German. Communication was going to be a problem.

Osterkamp and I chose a bunk tier, which we would share. I insisted that I'd take the top. Folded on each bunk were two blankets, a small towel, a spoon, and a mug. There was also a set of basic summer clothing and a pair of felt boots similar to those worn by the guards but of a different colour. These were grey.

Again there was much shouting from the guards in Russian and we soon realised that they wanted us to fall in alongside our bunks. Again they did a count and only when satisfied did they leave.

For a few days, we did little but acclimatise. The food we got was similar to what we had received before. We soon learnt that a considerable trade was being done in the camp. Various private items could be sold and exchanged for just about anything. The fact that our barrack was composed of officers certainly ensured that a degree of honour was maintained which seldom was transgressed. To break that honour amounted to immediate ostracism. All knew it. Therefore, never was anything stolen. This was a godsend considering that in other barracks theft plagued all.

About a week later, we were included in a work detail which marched daily from the camp to the forests a few miles away. Here we would cut down trees, trim them, and then load these on trucks. The logs were transported to a timber yard situated near to the rail line. They were then de-barked, the machinery operated by the prisoners.

It was hard work. All the tasks had to be carried out manually without the assistance of power-driven tools. We were not worked to exhaustion and we were never beaten. We were fortunate in that we had a good few summer months to acclimatise before the winter set in.

*

As it approached winter, it got colder. Then one morning we woke to a howling wind. It was freezing cold, thus heralding the first of winter. By this time, we had prepared ourselves, heeding the warnings we received, and ensured that we had complemented our issued clothing with other winter garments bought and bartered from others. Still, the first days of winter were a total shock. The temperature plummeted to well below freezing, often down to -20°C. In the forest, you heard the occasional loud wooden crack as a tree froze and succumbed to the cold.

Winter brought with it other dangers. Everybody was more careful. To be injured in winter, however minor, was to be avoided at all costs, as it brought a host of other problems with it. While we did receive medical attention, it was primitive. In this freezing weather, all wounds healed slowly and were more prone to infection. Added to that you ran the risk of being sent back to work before you'd properly healed. Klaus Schmidt was separated from us. We would see him regularly on work detail or in the main camp compound when we would daily have to muster for a count before leaving in the morning and returning in the evenings.

The food was never good or adequate but we heard that it was a great deal better than what the Russian civilian prisoners were given in the neighbouring camps. It was rumoured that hundred died from malnutrition. Their conditions were said to be abominable.

There were few escape attempts and these were not encouraged by the inmates. Firstly, the German border was thousands of miles distant and, secondly, after each escape, there inevitably was some form of reprisal from the Russian commandant, which affected all inmates. This could be a cut in rations for a while, the withholding of food parcels for months, or something else that would bring extreme hardship. In addition, we never knew for how long these extreme measures would be inflicted. Twice a week, we were compelled to listen to lessons on Communism.

The Russians hoped that in time we would see the evils of capitalism, as they continuously put it to us. Added to this, the NKVD would make regular calls on the camp in their search for war criminals. If there were the faintest suspicion, the victim would be transferred to another special camp to await processing and interrogation. We all knew that conditions in these holding camps were atrocious. The inmates guarded by the NKVD were shown no mercy whatsoever.

Osterkamp was born in the early 1890s and had served in the First World War, flying biplanes manufactured from wood and wire. He was a war hero, a German fighter ace, and a recipient of the Pour le Merit, Germany's most prestigious medal at the time. He was the most senior officer in our bungalow, although rank was now meaningless. Still, most looked up to him and acknowledged his leadership.

He was many years older than I , but we seemed to share an affinity and would always be found together, probably because we both had lost Wiebke whom we had loved very much. He assumed a quasi-father figure and I was comfortable with this. Irrespective of rank, we were now all considered criminals by the Russians, no longer prisoners of war, and therefore not subject to the rules and conditions of the Geneva Convention. Also, it was not wise to wave the German flag as it were. The Russians harboured a deep hatred towards us and this could only serve to further antagonise them. Things were bad enough. We were never allowed to forget that we were a defeated nation who had inflicted the most heinous of crimes on the Russian soldiers and population. Unfortunately, we all knew this to be true.

*

After the first year, the first mail arrived, that is if a letter once every six to nine months could be seen as an exchange of mail. I was writing to Inge, my sister in Kiel, who had married before the war and now had four daughters. She in turn, kept the rest of the family abreast of developments as these related to me as well as giving me the latest news. At that time, all Germany suffered and my sister was fortunate in that the family in South West Africa sent food parcels as often as was permitted. I learnt that George was in South West Africa, married to Ruth, and with a child.

Also, the first of the Red Cross parcels began to arrive in the camp. We probably only received one out of three. The others, no doubt, were intercepted by the Russians and kept for themselves. The everyday contents of these were considered luxuries by not only ourselves but by the Russians as well. Many of the items contained therein were not yet available to those who lived deep in the taiga which, to a degree, made them prisoners as well. In a sense, all inhabitants of the taiga were prisoners, Russian and German alike. There was nowhere to go.

*

It was in 1948 that Osterkamp became ill, but this was after a long bout of melancholy and depression. By then the medical attention in the camp had improved and for the first time antibiotics in the form of penicillin had become available. The Russians also introduced a system whereby doctors from the cities of Russia would spend a year or more at a camp after having received their degrees.

Osterkamp was hospitalised. We were never told what was actually wrong with him but were eventually informed that he had wasted away from some incurable disease, his condition rapidly deteriorating until he finally passed away. I never believed that his death was a result of ineffective health care as many others did. I knew he had just given up and wanted to die.

I was devastated. I hadn't realised it but he had become my life buoy and now was gone. I moped for months, shunning the companionship of others, and became slowly and surely withdrawn, not wanting to mix. I developed into a true loner.

Of course, every conceivable string was being pulled in Germany to persuade the Russians to release those prisoners of war they still held captive.

Even we prisoners in the camps were aware of the emergence of the Cold War and saw this as just another hindrance to our timely release. It seemed that we would never return home. The despair that many felt robbed some of the will to live and once this was lost, their demise was inevitable, some even taking their own lives.

The Russians had long learnt that to staff the kitchens with prisoners to do the cooking was an invitation to wholesale theft. The ingenuity of the prisoners knew no bounds. Therefore the decision was taken to staff all kitchens with women. As far as we knew, these women were not prisoners but rather were locals who were actually seconded to the gulags as staff, part of the gulag's personnel as it were. It was believed

194

that some had been banished to live in Siberia after being caught for a small misdemeanour.

Contrary to general belief, the Russians had more than their fair share of beautiful women and some had found their way to camps and villages in Siberia. Even the camp hospital had two or three female doctors and a few nurses who rated high on the one-to-ten looks scale, and although most of us would have given anything for a carnal moment with them, they considered us untouchable and to have a liaison with a prisoner was unthinkable. After all, they still saw us as the enemy.

However, the women in the kitchens were another matter entirely and actually ran a lucrative sex trade. Every six months or so, all hell would break loose as the camp commandant and his officers tried to stamp this out. It would soon resume, these women accommodating both soldiers and prisoners, there being an unwritten law that no soldier would report a prisoner and vice versa. All were happy with what was considered a rather amicable arrangement.

I thought that the more successful of these women must have accumulated a fortune in watches, lighters, rings, and other items they bartered for their favours. Unlike the doctors and nurses, these women were not well-educated. They were rough in their general demeanour and appeared to see humping as an activity like eating and drinking, only with added benefits. The sex-starved inmates' ingenuity as how to get to these women knew no bounds and the goings-on in the kitchens remained a favourite topic of conversation amongst the men who found it the basis for many a good laugh.

I still maintained a very close bond with Klaus Schmidt, and though he was not in my bungalow we would see and talk to each other almost every day.

Klaus and I were sitting in my bungalow at a table near the stove drinking tea. He had scrounged a handful of sugar cubes from one of the women in the kitchen and we were drinking our tea in Russian fashion with a cube clenched between our teeth, drawing the tea through it as we sipped.

"Christ Klaus, you've become a fuckin' sex-maniac. You've nothing of value anymore, no watch, no lighter, even your ring is gone. You've bartered the whole fuckin' lot," I said loudly, unable to disguise my disbelief and amazement.

He continued to sip his tea, this still through his teeth, and finally put the mug down and smiled.

"Matthias, what can I say? I'm a man, I can't help it," he said quietly.

I shook my head in disbelief. "Which one of those Babushkas is it?"

"It's Tanya," he replied.

A vision of Tanya came to mind. She was a Nordic blonde with clear blue eyes, generally well-padded, and a magnificent bosom which initiated many a lewd comment from most of the men when they saw her from a distance.

"God, the way you're going at it, you're fucking your way to oblivion," I said.

"I'm not. She no longer demands payment. She's in love with me and I'm in love with her," he said dejectedly. "I wish I could marry her. She doesn't consort with other men anymore."

I looked up at the ceiling in despair.

"Jesus Christ, you're mad. Doesn't consort? For God's sake, she's already had them all."

I did not want to even imagine what the commandant would say if he were to hear about this.

Klaus just shrugged his shoulders. "Whatever," he said, not giving a damn about my tirade.

"Klaus don't be ridiculous. We'll go home one day. You have to believe this," I said.

"Go home to what? I've no family. Those that I had died in the bombing of Bremen. Now I have no wife and no children. No. I'd rather stay here with Babushka," he insisted.

"My God, man, that's insane. This country is the arse-end of the world," I said.

"Is it? Look, it's all I've got and she's everything I want."

I threw my arms up in despair. I realised that this was no time to remonstrate with him. He was infatuated with the woman. There was nothing I could do.

*

Six months later, their ardour for one another had not cooled and by then all were aware of the relationship, both the Russians and the prisoners. Strangely, nobody objected. That was surprising. Liaisons between prisoners were frowned on. The men were all German prisoners of war. The Russians never allowed German prisoners to consort with the convicted political or criminal elements in the camp. The Germans were never brought into contact with them. The only exception was the occasional Russian women employees in the camp's hospitals and kitchens.

Babushka fell pregnant and Klaus, without any prompting, assumed the role of father-to-be. He petitioned the camp authorities saying that he wished to marry her and wanted to remain in Russia. There was disbelief when we heard that they actually were given permission to do so. Thereafter, they were released and allowed to travel to Minsk, Babushka's hometown.

Later, it was rumoured that Klaus was assigned to the Soviet Air Force, his experience with jet aircraft considered invaluable. At least he had finally attained a degree of happiness, something that still eluded me. I never saw him as a traitor.

CHAPTER TWENTY

It was the middle of winter in late 1948 and it was the work force's first morning out again after a particularly violent blizzard. The ground was covered in two feet of snow which now had a hard crust on the top, making movement difficult.

During the last year, a small degree of mechanisation had been introduced to assist with our work in the forests. Also there were now trucks to transport us to and from the furthest of our workstations in the forests. We also now had a skidder, an all-wheel drive vehicle, specifically designed to pull large logs from where they had been felled to a depot amongst the trees, where they could be loaded onto trucks to be taken to the mill. The skidder often broke down but today it was working.

We were trying to move a stack of particularly large logs to a depot and were using the skidder and a few teams of horses to do so. We dragged the logs through the snow and over the frozen ground. The going was difficult. I had the reins of a three-horse team in my hands and was walking just behind them to one side. They were pulling a large log when the skidder came alongside with three logs attached with chains behind it, ploughing through the snow. The skidder passed me quite closely. Suddenly, one of the logs snagged on something below the snow, the skidder coming to an abrupt halt. The chain snapped with a loud crack and, although seemingly impossible, the chain snaked through the air. The one end smashed into my lower thigh, whipping my leg from under me, and I crashed to the ground.

Feeling quite dizzy, I lay there in the snow, my leg numb. The driver of the skidder jumped from the vehicle, ran towards me, and tried to help me up. I screamed. The pain was excruciating. I had broken something as my lower leg was at an unnatural angle. They left me lying there while they fetched a stretcher. Three men manhandled me onto it, carried me to the back of a truck, and drove me back to the camp's hospital. A month or so before, we had received a new rotation of medical staff. The chief medical officer was a Lieutenant Doctor Novikov. We soon learnt that she was from Leningrad and a survivor of the nine-hundred-day siege of the city by the Germans. This had not enamoured her to the Germans at all. In fact, she harboured such an intense dislike for Germans that she was always screaming at the patients and those prisoners assigned to assist the hospital staff in their duties. Amongst the prisoners, she soon acquired a nickname: 'Zahnziege', Goat's Teeth. Her breasts, which no uniform could hide, were magnificent. In fact, the manner in which the Russians wore their tunics, outside their trousers and cinched at the waist with a wide belt, emphasised her assets. Unfortunately, that was the only pleasant thing any had to say about her. To aggravate matters, she was a lieutenant to boot and all did their best to avoid her. She dished out punishment duty at the slightest provocation.

A hospital nurse had given me an injection and while I waited to be attended to, I faded in and out of consciousness.

The stretcher I was on had been placed on a gurney which two prisoners wheeled into a pre-theatre as it were, where smaller injuries and examinations were carried out. In its centre it had an operating table with a huge lamp above it. They manœuvred the gurney next to the table and then, with the assistance of a nurse, they slid me across onto the table.

Shortly afterwards Doctor Novikov entered. It was the first time I had ever seen her close-up. I thought her a startlingly beautiful woman, the drab Russian uniform unable to blend her in with the many. To me, she stood out from the rest. Her close-cropped black hair shimmered in the strong light of the operating lamp. Her waist was narrow and, of course, that bosom …. She bordered on being voluptuous. There was no doubt that she had Slavic blood, with her high cheekbones, the dark distinct eyebrows, slightly perky nose, and full red lips.

Over the last few years I had learnt to speak plausible Russian. This was near-fluent with a trace of an accent.

"Strip him," she ordered in an abrupt manner.

The nurse had been joined by another. They removed my boots and were trying to remove my clothes, a difficult process with me lying prone on the table.

"Don't mess around, cut off his clothes," the doctor snapped. "I'll be back in a moment."

The nurses' faces showed no hint of resentment at the tone in which they'd been addressed. It was evident that they tried to keep their expressions neutral lest they awaken the doctor's ire. She was well-known for her sharp tongue.

The clothes that I was dressed in were my working clothes. They were filthy and smelt of sour sweat and the unwashed. None of those who did manual work in the forests had the luxury of clean clothes. They actually lived in their clothes, sometimes not taking these off for days. In places, they were worn through and torn. The same applied to our footwear. Soon I lay on the table clad only in my worn underwear. Everything had been cut off me with scissors. The doctor had returned and was now dressed in a white gown with a white waterproof apron tied to the front.

"He stinks. Get that filthy underwear off him and wash him," she commanded.

Within seconds, this was removed. I was humiliated, lying on the table on my back with my genitals exposed for all to see.

She wrinkled her nose in disgust. "Wash him," she repeated and again disappeared.

I was embarrassed. They brought bowls of hot water, pieces of towelling, and soap. I watched them with a wary eye as they proceeded to wash me from head to toe. The nurse who washed my genitals raised her eyebrows, smiled, and smirked, then said, "Now, doesn't that feel better?"

Thank God I was too far sedated and embarrassed to react at all. My leg throbbed, the painkilling injection not able to take the pain away entirely.

"Do you understand Russian?" the doctor asked, bending over my leg.
I nodded.

"The x-ray machine is not working, but I'm going to try and set your leg as best I can. It should be all right. Who are you?" she asked.

"Matthias Paul Aschenborn, Prisoner 914763/7," I replied. I never mentioned my rank. I wasn't a prisoner of war, none of us were. We were considered war criminals. She covered my groin with a towel which she laid crosswise over my waist. She looked up at one of the nurses.

"See if we've got a file. Bring it here."
I repeated the number. The nurse wrote it down on a clipboard.

She moved my thigh trying to set it correctly. I thought I could actually hear the bones grate together. I winced and then yelped.

"I think the bones are now nearly properly aligned," she said and then moved my thigh again trying to improve the alignment. Again I cried out.

Meanwhile my file had arrived and she briefly studied it.

"Huh, I see you were in the air force. You were a major. Did you shoot down a lot of our planes?" she asked.

"A few," I replied.

I watched what she was doing and was fascinated by her fingers. These were long and so clean. I hadn't seen fingers that clean in years. Her hands were soft and the nails showed a small amount of white clean cuticle where these had been trimmed. It was clear that she cared for them. When had I last seen such clean fingernails? I realised that I probably stank and thought it had to be abhorrent for her to work on us. Comparatively speaking, we were filthy.

She came round to the other side of the table and bent over to inspect my thigh. In so doing, her blouse opened a small gap between the buttons and I caught a glimpse of the soft, pale swell of her breast where it was cupped by a khaki brassière. That first brief glimpse was titillating and erotic, its affect akin to a mild electric shock.

She lifted her eyes for a second and looked at me. I knew she had to have seen what I had been staring at.

I looked away and muttered in German: "I'm sorry." It was a reflex and I was not expecting her to comment. Besides, it was in German.

The briefest of a smile passed her lips.

"We are going to give you another injection so that we can put a cast on. This could be painful," she said. Already the nurse was handing her the injection. She approached my good side and with the help of a nurse, half rolled me onto my side and injected me in my buttock. A minute or two later I was out.

*

For three weeks I lay in the makeshift hospital with its wooden walls and dark ceiling. My leg was suspended from pulleys attached to a framework above the bed. She told me this was to ensure that my broken leg did not become shorter than the other did. It was uncomfortable, especially at night while trying to sleep.

Every bed in the hospital was occupied and there was tremendous pressure on the hospital staff to vacate the beds of those still recuperating so that others requiring medical attention could take their place. The suspension of my leg created a unique situation and I had been given a bed in the corner of the large ward where the ceiling rafters were still quite low.

I had heard that Dr Novikov's first name was Klara. Every day she would stop by, take my pulse, wrap the blood-pressure instrument around my arm, and diligently record the results on a clipboard. The situation was ridiculous. I found myself looking forward to her daily visits, dreading the day when I would be discharged. I thought that this was because I had not been with a woman for a long time.

More than two weeks had passed when I was let out of bed for the first time. Using my own crutches, I was allowed to go to the latrine at the end of the building. She told me that I'd be on crutches for at least another six weeks. Then, surprisingly, she said that I could stay in the ward and help with light duties. The was camp no place for somebody on crutches with the daily roll-calls, the queuing for food, and sleeping in narrow bunks. She added that they'd find me a space where I could bed down at night in one of the storerooms. As I said, I had learnt to speak Russian and I could now read it as well. After a few weeks, in order to give me something more constructive to do, the doctor had given me the job of sorting and renumbering cabinets of archived files in an office adjoining her own. I had to ensure that these were correctly labelled and sorted in proper alphabetical order. There were twelve cabinets and whoever had been responsible had left a mess.

One morning, she flew into her office at about nine in the morning. I was busy with the damn never-ending files, trying to fix years of accumulated mess and confusion. The door between the doctor's office and the records room was open. She stepped into her office and slammed the door behind her, throwing a bunch of keys on the desk along with her shoulder satchel. She removed her ushanka, a special item, made from karakul fur and having some military medical insignia depicting a Soviet star attached to the front of it. This she threw on the chair. She was pale and her eyes flashed with anger.

"Cunt. The commandant is an idiot. Somebody should shoot him," she said loudly to herself in frustration. She sat down in front of her desk with her elbows on the top and dropped her head into her hands. It was not the first time I had heard someone call our dearly beloved commandant a swine. I wasn't sure whether I heard her sob or not, but if I did I was sure it signified fury or despair and not sorrow.

She sat like that for a few minutes without moving. I continued to sort files and then dropped a few folders, which I had sorted in proper sequence, into a cabinet drawer, which I slammed shut.

She looked up and stared at me, she then only aware that she was not alone.

"You've been here all the time?" she said, her expression showing slight concern.

"Yes, I've been here since before you arrived," I said and paused, and then quietly added, "Don't concern yourself. I heard nothing."

She stared at me for a moment as if she doubted me and then smiled wryly. "Even if you had, I'd still say what I said. He's a peasant. They gave him this post because they didn't know what to do with him. But enough,– it's no concern of yours." I saw that tears had rolled from her eyes down her cheeks. She wiped these with the back of her hand. "He's a cunt."

That was a new word for me. "What's that, Doctor?""Somebody who tries to touch women who'd not invited him to do so. At first, I wasn't sure but now he does it openly, and then he even leers evilly as if I should enjoy it. He frightens me," she said, "but I shouldn't tell you this. Forget about it."

"If you say so."

"A man like that could ruin my career, you know, if I try and be difficult. What am I supposed to do? Just let him do it? You men are all the same.""We are not all like that," I said not looking up from the open cabinet drawer. This conversation was going where it could only mean trouble. Speaking against the commandant or any other Russian officer was treated seriously.

She seemed to get hold of herself, her usual mien returned, and she again hid behind her professional façade.

After her unintentional display of emotions on that morning, her attitude or at least that towards me seemed to undergo a subtle change. If we were alone in her offices, she would now award me a morning greeting.

Then one day, she asked me where I came from and what I had done before the war. When I told her that I was actually a South African and how it had come about that I landed up in the Luftwaffe, she was surprised. She was or at least feigned interest in my life in South West Africa, wanting to know about it.

About a week after the incident she had with the commandant, she rushed into the office and looked for the medical file on one of the guards who, while drunk, had fallen from a watchtower and had multiple injuries, having struck the ladder on the way down. The damn file was not to be found and we were both rummaging in the few cabinets, which I had yet to sort out.

She came to stand next to me to help find the file. I was acutely aware of her nearness and her smell. Although I tried my best to appear nonchalant and unaffected, this was impossible. My demeanour was beginning to display that awkwardness and slight turmoil of one whose senses are affected by the closeness of an attractive woman.

I had difficulty on concentrating on what I was doing. She could not ignore what her nearness was doing to me, the slight change in my demeanour and actions surely were that apparent. She turned and looked at me, she holding my own stare. She turned away and continued searching through the files. At that moment, my eye fell on the file we were looking for and I extracted it from the drawer.

"Here, Doctor," I said holding the file out to her. I was embarrassed to notice that it shook in my hand, which she noticed. Again, she looked at me strangely and then took it with a quiet 'thank you'.

The moment she was out of the door I sat down and waited for my emotions to return to normal, realizing that the tingle of exhilaration I had experienced could become addictive.

She returned to her office that afternoon and looked at me. I realised that something had changed. I wasn't sure what it was, but things were now different.

"That cast of yours, I'm going to remove it tomorrow," she said.

I realised that six weeks had past. This would mean a return to the prisoners' quarters. My feelings were mixed. I could not wait to have the cast removed, but the return to the barracks was another matter. I dreaded the thought.

She personally oversaw the removal of the cast. The exquisite feeling of relief when the last of it came off was indescribable.

"I still want you to use your crutches for a few days until your leg gets used to you moving around on it again. I don't need you falling or doing anything else that might injure you. You are to continue working here until I say otherwise." I had finished the files but to keep appearing to be busy, I had begun to re-label them, taking my time about the job, trying to prolong my sojourn in the hospital. I still slept in my temporary quarters.

Escape was not an idea that was seriously entertained by any. The distances were too vast. The camp was situated near Ust Tsilma near the Pechora River just south of the Arctic Circle, the islands of Novaya Zemyla no more than 600 miles north in the Barents Sea. In winter, the conditions were incredibly harsh. The temperatures for weeks were below freezing, even reaching -30°C to -40°C with regularity, and without shelter none could survive the long night. Yes, there were rumours of the occasional attempt in the summer. These had never been successful and, as a result, vigilance was lax. The watchtowers, the guards, and machine guns were probably placed there more as a deterrent than anything else.

These gulags were dotted all over this area separated by fifty miles or so. As the forests were cleared, so some of the watchtowers were moved to create new boundaries. The authorities offered rewards to guards who shot escaping prisoners, which led to the guards devising many an ingenious scheme to shoot a prisoner for attempting to escape. A popular ruse was to send a prisoner to somewhere on the outskirts of the cleared forest to collect something a work party had supposedly left behind and then to shoot the prisoner for attempting to escape, the guards then sharing the reward.

One morning she arrived at the office carrying a cardboard box, which she handed to me.

"This is for you," she said.

I opened it and saw that it contained a near-new used prisoner uniform with underwear. On top of the folded clothes there rested a new toothbrush and toothpaste plus a bar soap. All prisoners considered these luxury items, and were keenly sought after. New clothes, even if only near-new, were impossible to acquire.

I thanked her profusely but must have appeared perplexed by this sudden generosity.

"Those who work around me must be clean and neat. After all, I'm a doctor," she said, her voiced tinged with authority. "Under the clothes is a new pair of boots," she added with a smile.

*

My leg healed completely and in time even my limp disappeared. I continued working for her, she now giving me other duties, more those of a secretary, and I eventually looked after most of her paperwork. I continued to sleep in the hospital, making use of its baths and showers.

One morning I was busy in the filing room, as we referred to it, when the camp commandant, a Colonel Popovich, flung the door open and strode into the doctor's office with a lieutenant in tow. The commandant was tall with a heavy build and an already-developing pronounced paunch. I estimated him to be in his forties, his hair starting to grey.

I came to attention, standing ramrod straight, my arms against the seams of my trousers. I saw that they were both drunk.

"Where is Doctor Novokov?" he shouted, a fleck of spittle flying through the air.

I was terrified. I pointed towards the wards.

"Fetch her," he screamed.

I scuttled off, making sure I limped, hearing them both laugh as I rushed out of the office. This was no time to be in their vicinity.

Normally, I would not approach the doctor while she was in the wards but would wait until I caught her eye, and only in circumstances demanding her urgent attention. This time I flew into the ward. I rushed right up to her where she stood around a bed with two nurses in attendance, and blurted out that the commandant awaited her in her office immediately. She paled. She whispered to the nurses that they should continue and then scampered from the ward. I followed, but she waved me back.

A corridor led from the wards to her offices. I slowly approached and when I heard loud voices I ducked into a side room that contained a few wheelchairs, bedpans, jugs, and other hospital paraphernalia.

I heard the commandant talking to her. He was demanding that she now accompany them to Vorkuta, which was about one hundred miles away. They were to leave immediately. This was a town that originally had been a gulag but had grown so large that it was now classified a town. It was no longer a prison, primitive, but nonetheless a town with a few shops.

"I will not," she shouted. "You are both drunk. One woman and two drunken men is not a good idea."

"That is an order," the commandant shouted.

"I will not," she shouted.

"You bitch, I'll have you court-martialled for refusing an order." This was followed by the sound of a hard slap and then the sound of falling furniture. "Yes. Cry, you stupid bitch. It won't help you. Let's go." Footsteps followed and then a slamming door.

I waited a few seconds and when I heard nothing further, I crept out of the storeroom and down the corridor to her office. I peered round the doorframe. She lay on the floor, a chair which had also fallen over was lying next to her. I could see a faint trickle of blood flow from her nostril. Her one cheek was bright pink, definitely beginning to bruise.

"Christus," I said and ran into the office, bending over her to see whether she had any other injuries. "Are you all right?" The concern in my voice was unmistakable.

She groaned.

I didn't know what to do. To touch her was not allowed and could have serious consequences. Consequences be damned I thought, somebody had to help her. From behind her, I put my arms under her armpits, lifted her up, and then dragged her over to one of the chairs. She groaned again and opened her eyes slightly. Leaving her, I went to an enamel basin and jug on a commode. I wetted a small towel, wiped the blood away, then placed the towel against the back of her neck.

"The bastard," I said with contempt.

She laid a hand on my arm. "Don't say anything. You'll get into trouble and I wouldn't want that to happen. I don't want them to know that you had seen or heard what happened," she whispered. "Men do strange things when they're drunk."

I then heard the roar of a Russian GAZ-67 4x4 all-terrain vehicle, similar to a Jeep, as it roared out of the camp. The officers had left for Vorkuta, thank God, without her.

"They're gone," I said.

"Well, we won't see them for two days. Come, help me to my quarters," she said.

None of the officers' quarters were forbidden to the prisoners provided they were accompanied by an officer or guard. She hung onto my shoulder and we slowly walked out of the hospital towards her quarters. She leaned against me and I was again aware of her nearness. A sentry standing guard outside in the quadrangle surrounded by the huts came running forward.

"It's all right, comrade. I'm not well. He's helping me to my room. I accidentally fell in my office," she said, no doubt feeling that she needed to give the man an explanation.

The man gave her a perfunctory salute, looked strangely at me, but made nothing of the fact that she was leaning on me and then returned to his post. He had seen her bruised cheek. It would not have seemed too strange to him. I was what was referred to as a 'monitor', a trusted prisoner, one of the few who were allowed to move freely around the camp. We had both left the hospital without our gloves or hat and it was freezing cold. I had not yet reached her quarters and already my ears and hands were like ice.

I had never been to the officers' quarters before and she directed me. We got to a double door.

"In here," she said. We passed through the anteroom and again through double doors which were designed to keep out the cold when the doors are closed. A long corridor led off to various rooms for the single officers, not that there were many. The camp probably had no more the four or five officers, the rest being non-commissioned officers and privates.

We stopped in front of a door. She extracted keys from a pocket and handed these to me. I opened the door and we entered a large room containing a bed, essential furniture, and a desk and chair. There were radiators against the wall for heating and, to add a female touch, the window had curtains with a floral design. The room was dark. The shutters were shut.

I guided her towards the bed and let her sit down. I then stepped a good few paces back.

"Is there anything I can do?" I asked.

"Yes, just stay a while," she said, her voice barely audible, and she looked at me with eyes that still seemed frightened.

"I don't think I should do that," I said furtively looking at the door.

Please."

I moved to sit down on a wooden chair.

"No." She patted the bed next to her. "Sit here next to me. I just need somebody near me for a while."

I felt that tingling feeling of expectancy that usually accompanies the onset of sexual arousal. The atmosphere was charged, she had alluded to what her inner feelings were, there was no doubt. Considering the circumstances, this was a dangerous game. Already the commandant was not pleased. For him to find out that his advances, even though rather crude, had been rejected in favour of a German prisoner of war could only produce a vicious response. Subtlety was not one of his known characteristics and I could imagine the type of retaliation that would be aimed at me.

"Doctor," I said, "I think not. I would give anything to sit next to you, but it is too dangerous."

"You are shunning me," she said. All inhibitions had disappeared, we now revealed our true inner feelings.

"Never, I'm crazy about you but would not want to see your career come to harm or the commandant start an action against you. You know he could court-martial you for fraternising with a prisoner.

She gave me a dismissal wave without looking up at me, "Go then."

All I wanted to do was what I'd set my heart on and that was to survive one day at a time in the hope that eventually I would be released and could return home. If I were to achieve this, it would be vital that I keep my nose clean, not draw any attention to myself, and definitely not become a target against which a person of authority could vent their personal hate or frustration. What was now happening went against the grain of everything I had resolved in order to survive. If I lived or died didn't matter. In the Russians' eyes, I was just a statistic.

I left her quarters and slowly walked back to the hospital, passing the guard who had previously confronted me.

"Is the doctor all right?" he asked, his expression concerned and confused, probably still wondering why the doctor had used me, a prisoner, to assist her.

"Yes, she just wishes to rest," I replied.

I returned to the office where I made sure that I busied myself in the records room.

Other than to grab a cup of tea and eat some bread and soup, I never ventured out of the records room and proposed to stay there until it was time to sleep. The day had been far too unsettling and it was best to stay out of everybody's way.

It was about seven in the evening and it had been dark for the past three hours. A cold wind had arisen and it moaned and whistled through the hut's eaves. I heard the door to the office open and knew that it had to be she who had returned. She would know that I was here, the lights were on. I heard her remove her coat. I turned as she entered the records room and stopped in the doorway, leaning against the doorjamb staring at me. Her expression immediately told me all. She was here because of us, not work.

A feeling of apprehension coursed through me. I had turned from the row of wooden cabinets to face her. She strode towards me and came to stop inches from my face, our bodies nearly touching, her face upturned, she looking into my eyes.

"What kind of man are you, that I feel this way?" she whispered and then placed her lips on mine.

For a few seconds I was speechless with shock, but then her tongue probed mine and I put my arms round her as I drew her close. I mentally threw off those resolutions I had so vehemently stuck to that were supposed to help me to survive this seemingly endless period of incarceration and hardship. I lost myself in the taste of her, her smell and warmth. At that moment, just holding her and aware of her feelings for me seemed the most important thing in my life and with the best will in the world, and despite the enormous risk this entailed, my mind was no longer master of my heart.

I grabbed her by the buttocks and crushed her pelvis to mine, she surely aware of my arousal. She emitted a soft moan. Again we kissed, this not tender but fierce and demanding.

I pulled away. "Dear God," I whispered, "I'll be shot."

"Never would I allow them to do anything to you.""Please, Klara, for my sake, you must go. We can speak tomorrow," I said, this the first time I had dared address her by her name.

"All right, but remember you and I have unfinished business." She kissed me again and then left.

*

By the next day, she seemed to have recovered from her ordeal with the commandant. Yes, we did occasionally touch and there were a few surreptitious kisses to the lips but no more than that. The commandant returned after two days, going about his business as if nothing had occurred, or so I gathered from Klara. He usually inspected the hospital once a week and I ensured that I was absent whenever this happened. Invariably, warnings of the commandant's movements preceded him.

During the next two weeks, my need for this woman was overpowering. Every time we were together or passed, we both felt this incredible feeling of physical attraction. The stolen hugs, kisses, and fondles in the record room away from prying eyes merely intensified our arousal. I kept on trying to come up with a plan which would allow us to be together without putting ourselves at risk. Little did I know that the gods were to intervene.

The commandant had been called to the district's headquarters and his protégé, Lieutenant Spirodonova, had assumed temporary command of the camp. Unfortunately, his drinking bouts made him a dangerous man. Klara had left him in no doubt that he was not welcome near her but the lieutenant eventually found a female companion in a senior nurse who was also the camp's optometrist.

A massive gale moved in over the Barents Sea and across the North Cape bringing with it a blizzard of howling winds, plunging temperatures, and deep snowdrifts. The outside temperature nudged -35°C. The prison workforce was called in to dig through the huge snowdrifts that isolated the hospital from the administration, officers' quarters, and other essential areas of the camp. The storm had struck in the early morning hours, the snow falling continuously.

That evening we found that we were completely isolated from the outside world with a temperature at -40°C. With the blizzard still blowing, it was decided that those in the hospital would not venture through the storm to their quarters.

Both Klara and I were in her offices when the building was plunged into darkness. I realised that the power lines were down or that there was a problem with the camp's generating plant. This was not unusual, and fortunately we did not rely on electricity to keep warm as the camp's heating requirements were met by fired boilers. There were a few emergency oil lamps in the hospital but barely sufficient to supply emergency lighting.

When the lights went out, the offices were plunged into absolute darkness, there being neither moonlight nor any other source of light.

Klara had just come into the office and I was sitting at an additional desk which she had found for my use. I knew that we had an emergency lamp. The problem was to find it. I starting groping around in the dark trying to find my way to where I thought the lamp had to be. I had no matches.

"Shit. The lines must be down," I said.

"Can you get the lamp?" Klara asked.

"I think so but I need matches," I said.

"I've matches in the bottom drawer of my desk."

I turned in what I thought was that direction and bumped into Klara. She giggled and then grabbed me round the neck and kissed me hard on the lips. I placed my hand on breast.

"No wait. Let me find out what's happening about the electricity," she whispered.

I felt her move away from me and after a while, I heard the whirr of the hand-operated telephone on her desk as she cranked the handle.

"Is that Sergeant Terekhov? Good, this is Doctor Novikov. What's happened? Is the hospital is in darkness?"

The telephone conversation continued for another minute and I heard her raise her voice. She was obviously angry. Then she put the phone down.

"The idiot. He's also drunk. I could hear it. He said their lines were down, maybe the snow or trees, he said. He told me that he refuses to go out in this weather. He'll only go tomorrow." He heard her giggle naughtily again. "Aren't you happy?"

She stumbled into something as she made her way back to me and when she touched me, she moved in close against me and kissed me again.

"I'm going to lock the office. Nobody will come looking for me in the dark. They'll think I've gone to my quarters," she said, her voice now slightly hoarse.

She found the door in the darkness and locked it. We kissed, she grinding her lips into mine. She grabbed my one hand and placed it on

212

her derrière, she forcing herself against me. I cupped a breast in my hand. She writhed against me and then slid her hand down the front of my body and under my clothing reaching for me. We both sank to the floor, facing each other on our knees. I slid my hand under her heavy woollen winter skirt and up her thigh to where her thick stockings ended. My fingers touched the soft, warm flesh of her inner thigh. I felt her shudder. She now had a hand inside my trousers and her fingers closed around me. As my body went into momentary spasm, I simultaneously jerked. A low groan emitted from deep within me. I unbuttoned her tunic and unclasped her brassière and felt for her breast with my lips which then closed over her nipple that stood hard and proud as I rolled it between my lips and tongue.

My trousers dropped to the floor, I drew down her winter bloomers and gently lay her backwards. My fingers touched her and I felt her wetness. As I thrust into her, she softly moaned and her nails dug into my back. "Too soon," she shrieked loudly in the quiet office. I placed a hand over her mouth. Seconds later, I exploded in her.

We both lay on the planked floor gasping for breath. Reality soon returned and my first thought was that we could be caught.

"Come, Klara, we've got to get up. Somebody could come," I said. I was terrified.

"Don't worry, my love," she whispered, "we're safe here. Nobody will be looking for us."

This did not console me. I was in a near panic. I broke away from her and sorted out my clothing.

"Come on, Klara," I insisted. "Please get up and get dressed.""You're being silly," she said, but I could hear her getting dressed. We soon found the lamp and she got the matches from the drawer. The office was now bathed in light and we were able to look at each other.

"Heaven, you look like you've seen a ghost," she laughed.

I was so wound up I didn't think it was amusing. I imagined myself being dragged outside by Russian soldiers, put up against a wall or tree and summarily shot for raping a Soviet officer. I was terrified. No explanation could save me. It would be ignored. I moved away from her and sat down at my desk lest somebody would arrive and notice what we had done.

"I'm going to my storeroom," I said and left without waiting for a reply. I knew that she would bed down in a special room set aside with cots for the nurses doing long duty.

The corridor was dark and I could hardly make out where I was going. In the storeroom, I removed my outer clothing and crawled into my makeshift bed. Only then did the turmoil and fear within me dissipate. I could still smell her. I still felt the warmth of being inside her and I still hungered for her. This was insane. We would all die for this, I thought. Eventually I slept.

I was awakened by the blankets being lifted. There were no corridor lights so the lines still had to be done. I felt Klara slide into the cot, her body next to mine, the cot really too narrow.

"Klara, you're mad. We'll get into trouble," I whispered.

"Maybe I am, but when will we ever get a chance again?" She softly slid her hand onto my groin. My response was quick. I groaned a mixture of concern and pleasure. The cot could hardly accommodate two but we were not aware of this as we took in each other and made love. We then both slept and when I awoke, it was still dark and she had gone.

*

We all realised that something was definitely afoot. Conditions in the camp improved, the food was better, which gave rise to the bizarre comment that they were fattening us up before slaughter. Better medicines were made available and the German Luftwaffe surgeon, who previously was seldom allowed in the facilities of the hospital, now assumed an important role in the care of the more seriously ill prisoners. He was supplied with medicines, operating facilities, trained personnel, and unrestricted access to the hospital.

The many rumours and the change in our treatment told me that I was going home. I prayed to God that this were true.

Klara and I continued our clandestine love affair. We slept together whenever opportunity presented itself or when she could manipulate the system so that we could be alone without too big a risk of discovery. This was not very often but I cherished these moments and vowed never to forget them.

It was a sad affair. We both knew how it would end. She would often cry.

CHAPTER TWENTY-ONE

In the spring of 1950, we heard that some might be going home.

It was still no more than a rumour but this had originated from the Russian officers, which gave the story a lot more credence than from where these rumours usually came. It was said that the GUPVI, the Central Administration for the Affairs relating to Prisoners of War and Internees, was involved and handling the matter. Both these units were subordinate to the NKVD. But with the NKVD involved, the likelihood remained that we would never be released.

We heard that Germany had been divided and that Dr Adenauer, the first chancellor of the new Federated Republic, had ceaselessly petitioned Stalin and his communist counterparts for the release of the thousands of prisoners of war still held by the Soviets. From the odd letter received in the camp, we heard of other prisoners of war who had made it home. However, none had ever been released from our camp. The release of my crew chief, Klaus Schmidt, and his marriage to Babushka, were unique as was his absorption into Russian society and his appointment to the Soviet Air Force.

During the summer of that year, it was officially announced that we were to be released. It came as a surprise to all. Sets of better clothing were dished out and we were ordered to make ourselves more presentable. Most of the camp was to be released, but there were a few who were to remain behind as they were still under investigation by the NKVD. Little did we know how lucky we had been. Tens of thousands would never make it home, having died in captivity.

An arduous journey by train and truck followed as we travelled through Russia and Poland to Soviet-held Eastern Germany. The Red Cross assisted with the processing of our release, advising families, many of whom were waiting expectantly at the border crossing where these releases would take place.

On morning we were herded onto trucks and driven to a border post between West and East Germany, the countries separated by high barbed wire fences and watchtowers at regular intervals, these manned by Russian and East German soldiers.

After a wait of a few hours, during which further processing took place, we were then led one by one to a small gate where we crossed into West Germany.

The elation I felt was indescribable and I could not hold back the tears of joy as I stood for a moment just a few yards within the boundary of West Germany, now a free man. A Red Cross official quickly took me by the elbow and led me with purpose to a border post building, which was converted into a debriefing hall. German officials sat us down and debriefed us, looking for our names on lists of Germans who were thought still to be held in Russia. The Russians had never fully cooperated with the Red Cross and the true figures relating to prisoners of war had continuously changed and were never properly confirmed. There were questions on treatment, on what atrocities we had witnessed, names of those that we knew had been removed from the camp by the NKVD, and names of those we knew that had died.

For all the joy I now experienced, the last separation from Klara had been heart-rending. I loved her as she had loved me but we both knew that to have allowed this to become publicly known would probably have kept me in the camp and certainly would have ostracised her from the rest of the Russian officer corps. It would have led to a court-martial and she could become a prisoner in the gulag system herself. Still, we both agreed that her position would not be put in jeopardy nor would we compromise my release in any way.

Finally, the process of release was complete. I was issued with temporary papers, given some money which would keep me in funds for a while, and then led through to a huge hall where we were to meet those who had come to welcome us back to Germany.

It was a beautiful day without a cloud in the sky. It was hot and the windows of the hall had been opened. I walked through the large entrance that led into the hall, dressed in the clothes which had been issued to the prisoners who were to be released. There was nothing smart about them. They were barely adequate and did not disguise the haggard, emaciated look of the long-term criminal just released from jail. The faces and hands of the men bore the scars of overwork and malnutrition. The prime of their youth was gone forever. Their sunken eyes with dark rings below. The hair badly cut. The yellow teeth that had not been seen to by a dentist for years.

"Mein lieber Gott! Das ist Matthias," I heard a female voice call and turned to see from where this had emanated. It was my sister Inge. The first thing that struck me was that she was older. She rushed forward and hugged me. The slim attractive woman that I had known had lost her hour-glass figure. She was heavier and her cheeks were puffy. She wore no make-up and her appearance was that of a severe, middle-aged woman. She was dressed in a plain black dress, her arms covered by long sleeves. Her shoes were sturdy with only a slightly raised heel. She had a black leather bag slung over one shoulder. Two other men stood behind her. One was my brother-in-law, whom I had met with on numerous occasions during the war, and the other, to my utter surprise, was my brother George.

George walked up to me, took my hand, and then rather awkwardly hugged me.

"God Matthias, you look fuckin' awful," he whispered, "but it's wonderful to see you again." We then thumped each other on the back.

"You look like you could do with a schnapps," he added as we drew apart.

I hadn't seen my brother for near on twelve years or more. He was now middle-aged, deep into his thirties, and this reflected in his appearance. The previous lean, hard look I recalled was now replaced by some padding, and he was also developing the beginning of a slight paunch. The hair was thinner but the eyes had not lost their twinkle. He was dressed in a light summer suit, obviously brought from home in South West Africa as the tailoring was different. The shoes were light tan brogues. He looked a little like a tropical dandy, although the African suntan was unmistakable.

George took my arm. "Let's get you out of here, away from anything that can even remotely remind you of the past years. We've booked a table at a local restaurant here in Herleshausen. This is the border town where most of the German prisoners of war are released into Germany. We drove here from Kiel in Joachim's car."

He led me outside into the sunshine to a parking lot that was filled with cars. He opened the door of a black Mercedes 180 sedan. We all climbed in and drove off. Of course with my grey pallor and dressed in my drab clothing, I felt totally out of place in this sudden opulence which I'd forgotten, the clothing, the cars, and driving to a restaurant. I must stick out like a sore thumb, I thought.

The restaurant was situated on a side street just off the main road that passed through the town. We came to a stop outside a building with huge bay windows. This was built on a large piece of land, the rear of the building overlooking a large meadow which was dotted with trees.

George led us inside and spoke to the maître d' who guided us to a large table set for four next to one of the bay windows overlooking the park. The man realised that I must be a prisoner just released.

"Sir, welcome home. Please eat and drink what you wish, there will be no charge for you. Mein Gott, those bastards," he said his eyes taking in my appearance, "we can immediately recognize one of you. I've seen quite a few in my time. If I may ask, what were you? Let me guess, Luftwaffe?"

I nodded my head.

He left the menus. George placed our order for drinks but insisted that the waiter bring the men each a Jägermeister schnapps to go with our tall glasses of beer.

I hadn't had anything to drink for hours and this was my first beer in years. It was divine, like honey. At George's insistence, we knocked back the Jägermeisters and chased these with beer. Ten minutes later, I was decidedly inebriated to the amusement of the others.

"Sorry about that, you'd better slow down. Obviously, the Russians never gave you alcohol," Joachim said, laughing.

"I wouldn't say that. We made our own version of home brew, which was strong enough to peel the skin off your gums, but it was too little and was seldom available. Even the Russians were wary about drinking the stuff. I think they thought it some sort of German sabotage." All laughed as did I. It only now dawned on me for the first time that I was actually free. The ordeal that seemed without end was over.

George brought me up to speed with regard to the family. My father was well, heavily involved in his cattle ranches and engineering business. George was running the foundry and engineering works. While still in the gulag, I had learnt of my mother's death from ovarian cancer. He said that it was only recently that our father had begun to recover from the shock of his loss. Joachim and Inge already had four children, all daughters born one after the other. Apparently, he was some bigwig in a

Kaufhaus in Kiel and was doing very well for himself. They were now living in the family's home on Niemannsweg in Kiel.

"I've booked us both on a flight to Johannesburg. The departure date is about a month from now. It was hellish difficult and damn expensive to get these tickets. Aircraft seats out of Europe are booked months ahead. We'll be flying KLM. You remember, the Royal Dutch Airlines?"

"So soon?" I exclaimed, unable to hide my surprise.

"Oubaas wants you back in South West Africa as soon as possible. Our father doesn't want us hanging around here. He says it'll take twenty years before Germany really recovers and he's convinced the Americans and Russians will be at each other soon enough," he replied.

The food was exquisite. I started with a Fleißsuppe and I chose this simply because for years I'd been starved of meat and this soup was all meat with herbs. Thereafter, I had an enormous New York-cut sirloin steak. It was thick. Of course, I had another beer but this time without the accompanying schnapps. I forced myself not to rush. Eating quickly was a habit developed in the camp, hoping to be one of the first to finish in case the cook had something left.

George paid the bill we both thanked the proprietor profusely for my free meal. He waved off my thanks with the words, "It's always a pleasure to welcome a hero home. I hear your received the Ritterkreuz during the war. You should be proud," he said.

Where had he heard that, I asked myself? I wanted to say that I did not do that to please Hitler, but then thought it inappropriate. No doubt Inge or her husband must have said something to the proprietor.

*

The Germans were still efficient. Within four weeks, all my papers were in order and George and I left for Amsterdam. I was kitted out with a wardrobe of new clothes but only enough to keep me within the meagre baggage allowance the airlines permitted. Being able to fly from Europe to South Africa was a novelty. It only a thirty-hour flight, and that with all the refuelling stops included. Before the war, all travelled to Africa by ship.

When we departed Holland, I was still trying to adjust to a new life. My brother, true to form and as I knew him from the past, tried to introduce me to the nightlife in Amsterdam but I waved the offer off. I wasn't ready for it. In Germany, it had been the same. There the number of women outstripped the men by far and finding a willing and able woman would have presented no problem at all. He tried to persuade me to find a woman for the purposes of a brief flirtation and sexual fulfilment. I still felt too detached from reality and I was still trying to get to grips with my new-found life and freedom. My brother seemed to think that the sooner I resumed a fulfilling sex life, the sooner I would recover from the horrors of the gulag.

Once on the aircraft, a Douglas DC-6, the exquisite beauty of the stewardesses was really something to behold. George told me that all young women aspired to become a stewardess and the airlines literally put them on show. They were chosen for their beauty and poise, and their ability to speak foreign languages.

Still, it was with relief that the aircraft landed at Palmietfontein International Airport in Johannesburg, late in the evening at eleven. We stayed over in a hotel for the night and the next morning flew from Rand Airport, Johannesburg to Windhoek in a Lockheed Lodestar. This was a full all-day trip, the aircraft flying over the Kalahari Desert. We looked for shade under the aircraft's wing during the brief stopover at Upington in the Kalahari Desert while it was refuelled from forty-four-gallon drums using a hand-operated pump. The place was like a blast furnace with a strong wind and a temperature of 40°C in the shade. The dry desert heat told me I was home. The airport was devoid of any buildings except the corrugated hut that housed the airport refuelling equipment. The further west we flew the more primitive it became.

My father was at Windhoek airport to meet us. He hugged me, his eyes glistening with tears and softly said, "Thank God you survived, thank God. Many a time I thought I'd lost you, but I continued to pray. Danke Gott."

Of course, my father had prepared a celebration. I arrived at the house on the Bismarkstrasse amidst the preparation for the party that my father had organised and to which he had invited his closest friends. We drove into the rear of the property grounds and entranced the house through the kitchen, the front door being only used for special occasions.

I strode into the kitchen where I was confronted by Moses, a Heroro whom I had known from childhood, his hair now grey as he approached old age. He was my father's right-hand man, doing the cooking, buying in for the kitchen, cleaning the house, and supervising the other two servants, one of whom was Josephina, also a Herero. She was a woman of immense proportions, clad in traditional dress which reached to the floor. At every occasion, she wore an enormous folded cloth headdress sculptured so that it had the appearance of an anvil crosswise on her head. They both spoke fluent German but, for once, they broke out into Herero, unable to contain their exuberance at seeing me. Josephina's shriek surely was heard the entire length of the street. Ruth, my brother's wife, was also in the kitchen. She approached and hugged me and then kissed me on both cheeks telling me how glad they were to see me again. Her daughter Catherine stood next to her looking at me with big round eyes, not sure who this man was upon whom so much attention was being heaped. I thought her to be about twelve years old.

I saw that the dining room contained two huge tables each seating sixteen. A long buffet was crowded with an assortment of liquor bottles – whiskey, brandy and schnapps. The kitchen veranda was lined with a row of galvanised zinc baths filled with ice and dozens of beer bottles from the two breweries in the country.

The servants had all returned to their duties in the kitchen, the stoves covered with pots in which various dishes bubbled. Both ovens contained pieces of beef and mutton, and pans of potatoes, all roasting. There were fresh German rolls, hams and salamis, and a variety of salads.

"Good God, Oubaas!" I said in consternation, "What's this for?"

"This is for you, my boy. I have plans for us, and all my friends want to welcome you back. Many believed that I would never see you alive again. I've also invited some of your old friends." His eyes twinkled for a moment. "Also, some of the little children you may remember from before have turned out to become beautiful young women," he added.

"I don't know whether I'm quite ready for that," I said hesitantly.

"Rede nicht Scheiße," *Don't talk shit,* my father said. "Every man needs a woman and so do you. At least you'll know you've returned to the real world. A good fuck is what you need. They'll help you find your rightful place in this world." Of course he laboured under the belief that I had not loved a woman for the past five or six years. He also firmly believed that copulation ensured a healthy, long life. This he classified on the same level as burping and farting. These, in his opinion, were essential in terms of health. He believed there were two worlds: one a man's, the other for women. Man never lived in a woman's, he only visited, and when there, a different set of rules applied, and under no circumstances was man to overstay his welcome. Believe or not, he lived by these principles.

For a moment, my mind dwelt on Klara, as it still did from time to time. It was then that I would feel a pang of loss. I wondered briefly what his reaction would be were he to know of my relationship with Klara.

I couldn't imagine what any young woman would see in me. I still looked gaunt and wasted. It would take at least four to five weeks and a good couple of fabulous meals to ensure that I added the vital additional pounds to my frame before I attained a shred of acceptability. To adequately fill out would still take months.

The sun was about to dip below the horizon when the first guests began to arrive. They were the Sterns. Alex Stern was my father's best friend. They had two children, a son and daughter, both in their early twenties. I recalled them as children. Henry, the son I recognised from his still unruly mop of red hair, from which his nickname Ginger originated. He'd inherited the hair from his father who now had little left and was nearly bald. Sharon, the daughter, had grown into a true beauty with raven black hair that glistened in the light. It fell to her shoulders, framing a face with high cheekbones, full red lips, and a smooth unblemished skin. She was tall with a narrow waist and long beautiful legs. The cocktail dress revealed some décolletage and the enticing swell of her bosom was unmistakable.

After them, there followed Hans and Rezi Wirtz. A Feldwebel in the Imperial Schutztruppe when the country was still a German colony, he had fought the indigenous Herero tribe. The Germans driving them back into the Kalahari Desert where they had perished in their thousands – men, women, and children. Hans's ability to consume litres of beer in one sitting was legendary. One particular occasion came to mind when the three men had left to on a hunting trip for a weekend. This was well before the war. They had not returned by the following Wednesday and their wives were now agitated and concerned. In desperation, the wives approached the police for assistance. A search party was dispatched and the men were finally found camped in a riverbed sitting on camp chairs. The young police officer, who was in charge of the few black constables that made up the search party, approached Hans and came to stand in front of him, assuming a somewhat overbearing manner. Apparently, my father said, Hans just sat there staring at the police, the worst for wear.

"Why did you not send for help, Meneer?" the Afrikaans police officer had asked without being able to hide his annoyance.

"Constable, you're not serious, are you? My God man, we still haven't finished the beers," was the indignant reply. The two others in their chairs nodded in agreement. "Besides, our vehicle has broken down. Sorry for being rude, would you like a beer?" Hans asked, bending down to extract a quart bottle from a wet jute sack filled with straw next to him and holding the bottle out to the police officer.

The indifference the three men displayed with regard to their plight, and the fact that a search party had to be sent out was in itself sufficient to start a rumour. However, their refusal to seek help with beers still to be drunk had propelled the tale to near mythical proportions, with the story doing the rounds in every pub in the country. For a while, the three basked in their new-found notoriety.

Within minutes, the three men, as did George, Ginger, and I had tall glasses of beer in our hands, the moisture beading on the glasses. The women had glasses of wine.

My return from Russian prisoner of war camp was no longer a novelty. My father's friends had known for weeks. The conversation drifted towards karakul farming and the current pelt price, which was at an all-time high, averaging forty-four shillings.

The conversation had gravitated towards farming as it invariably did when the men got together.

"That Afrikaans idiot, de Jager, whom I had as a ranch manager, hasn't got a damned clue. About a month ago, I got rid of him. He was also farming a few of his own sheep on the farm and another pelt buyer, you know Steinmetz, well, he told me that the man seemed to be having a good deal of trouble trying to distinguish what were his and what were mine. Apparently, he preferred to err in his favour. It just shows you, if you want to run a business it's better to place your own family in charge. You can't trust these other arseholess, they all steal," my father said in a disappointed voice.

"Who're you going to send to replace him?" Alex Stern asked, and then took a huge swallow of beer, draining his glass, its stem pointing at the ceiling.

"I don't know."

"Why don't you send Matthias?" Stern suggested, looking at me.

Before I could say anything, my father replied with some bluster.

"Jesus Christ, Alex. The poor man probably hasn't even had a fuck since he got back. Hell, I can't just send him to the bloody middle of nowhere. Besides, he still looks like a scarecrow. We've got to fatten him up first." None seemed to know whether my father said this in earnest or in jest. There were one or two embarrassed chuckles.

They all looked at me with sympathy and knowing expressions as if they shared my anguish. Alex then whispered something to my father.

"What's that?" George asked.

"If you must know, Alex says that if Matthias goes anywhere near Sharon before he's terminated his long bout of celibacy, he'll kick his bloody arse and relieve him of his balls," my father replied.

All roared with laughter.

Alex turned to look where his wife was to ensure that she was out of earshot, then turned to me and whispered. "I can fix you up with something."

"You don't have to. Believe it or not, I had this Russian officer in the camp."

My father stepped backwards his eyebrows raised. "Christ! Were you … you know what …" He waggled his hand to describe some sexual act. "You shouldn't have told us this," he said, his face a caricature of disgust and disappointment. Was this another joke intended to ease the atmosphere?

"For God sake, father, it was a Russian woman officer," I said. I was about to add that I was in love with her but then thought better of it.

"That's better. For a moment I thought you'd crossed the line," he replied.

I then realised that this was another attempt at humour. Everybody laughed again as men do when covertly discussing matters of a sexual nature.

Other couples arrived; many I knew from years back. They were now married with children.

It was warm and all the windows and doors were opened as is usual in the tropics to allow the evening breeze to blow through the rooms. The sun had disappeared and the short twilight was in its final stages.

Joseph and Josephina had changed from their kitchen garb and were now dressed in black slacks and white shirts with red sashes over their shoulders. Two other servants who had joined them were similarly dressed. They moved amongst the guests with trays of canapés, crackers with smoked venison, smoked fish, some with steak tartare, rare roast beef, and salami. The popping of champagne corks could be heard and the first flutes of the sparkling wine appeared. All had come to celebrate and express their joy that I was back, some asking to see my Ritterkreuz and asking me to tell them of my experiences in the gulag. I told them that I no longer had the Ritterkreuz, which was true. I had never bothered with a copy and the Russians had relieved me of my original. Besides, I did not believe it wise to flaunt the fact that I had been decorated. After all, we were a defeated people. As far as my experiences were concerned, I proposed to forget these as soon as possible.

It was two hours later when dinner was announced. A name card with each guest's name, this written with Gothic script, had been placed at each setting. I guessed that Ruth, my sister-in-law had to have been the calligrapher.

I found myself seated next to Sharon Stern and her father. A prominent doctor and his wife sat opposite me. Dr Eggers had attended to the sick in our family for years and had accompanied my father on a number of his infamous hunting trips.

Already the waiters were placing the first course in front of us, a thick creamed mussel soup and a minestrone soup for those not into crustacean foods.

"Those bastards, I can't believe they kept you a prisoner for so long. Whatever enticed you to stay in Germany when it was becoming evident that war was inevitable?" Alex Stern asked me.

"I don't think we all realised the seriousness and the possible consequences that it could lead to. I was so taken up with flying. At the time I still saw it as a bloody adventure," I responded.

"My god, look what they did to the Jews," he exclaimed. I saw Sharon turn to look at me with a troubled expression on her face.

I was again overcome by a feeling of guilt, which surely had to be felt by any self-respecting German aware of the atrocities carried out by the Nazis in the concentration camps and the crematoriums. You could not say, 'I didn't know'. We all knew. Yes, it was dangerous to object, it could cost you your life. It was easier to look the other way. Many fell back on the feeble excuse that they did not know the true dimensions of what was nothing but genocide.

I looked down at my plate. "Herr Stern, I have no excuses. All I wanted to do was stay alive. After three years of war it was evident that Germany's fortunes were about to change. The airmen died like flies. There was a continuous shortage of pilots. We were sent up against an enemy that grew by the week. Friends and fellow-pilots died around us. It never crossed your mind to raise objection to what you did not like," I said in a voice that bordered on denial.

"Please, Matthias, I'm certainly not suggesting any direct involvement on your part. I only brought this up out of curiosity. I mean, the bastards murdered some of my family! I know there are good Germans, your family is a case in point, but then you see some of the other ex-SS who have come here and swagger around as if they are heroes. The South African government should not have allowed them in and, added to that, they are now immigrants who've been given resident status, for God's sake," he said with a trace of exasperation.

"George told me that a lot of the Nationalist Afrikaners were interned for the course of the war because they were sympathetic to the Nazi cause. Actually, probably not so. They sided with the Germans simply because they were fighting the British and we all know how the Afrikaners hate the British. Now the Afrikaner rules in South Africa promoting its own type of socialism and that's why they've allowed these ex-SS men into the country. I wonder how many of them have done things they would rather now forget. Maybe Wiesenthal, the Nazi-hunter, would have a field day here," I said.

Our conversation was interrupted by the serving of the main course.

"I don't blame you at all. I just wondered why you didn't come home. When Marie ... ah, your mother, knew she was dying, she realised that she would not see you again. It broke her heart," he concluded.

Sharon put a comforting hand on my arm. "Matthias, it's over now. Forget it. Just be glad you're back, as we are," she said and smiled.

At two in the morning, the first of the guests started to leave and by three we had the house to ourselves again. The three of us retired to my father's study for a nightcap.

"Well, that was a roaring success," my father said, sitting down in a leather chair with a brandy snifter in hand.

"Oubaas," I said, "Stern tackled me on the persecution of the Jews."

He harrumphed. "I knew he would. He lost most of his family in the concentration camps. Matthias, please, you can't blame him. But we didn't do it, and he knows that. He's still my best friend. Don't believe he thinks you had anything to do with that," my father added.

Still, this was a feeling of guilt that I could not just wish away. I was not about to forget my stay with the Sturmbannführer Fassbinder and the face of the young boy as he was dragged from the hut to be shot.

"So, Matthias, what are you going to do?" my brother asked, more to change the subject than anything else.

"I've decided. He's going to Gelwater to take that idiot's place. You know, that farm manager, de Jager, the bastard who stole from us," my father said with finality.

"Christ Oubaas, Matthias just got back," George blurted.

"It doesn't matter. There's nobody else to send."

I wasn't going to argue. He seemed to have rapidly forgotten his recent concerns regarding my sexual needs and the need to recover from my incarceration. I was still taken up with the euphoria of being free and maybe a short while alone on a farm surrounded only by the indigenous workers would do me a world of good. I could adjust to society again in my own good time. This would permit me to meet the world at my own tempo as opposed to being steam-rolled.

"No," I said, "I think it's a great idea." I took a sip of my cognac.

My brother, also seated in a leather chair, leaned across and quietly said, "Well brother, it would seem you're not going to get that fuck after all. There's nothing available out there, unless of course ..." he said with an evil grin.

"Fuck you, man," I replied. God, the bastard hasn't changed, I thought.

He laughed.

CHAPTER TWENTY-TWO

Gelwater was one of three farms my father owned. The farm had derived its name from the muddied yellow waters of the rivers that most summers would flash flood for a short duration. The farm was situated 300 miles from Windhoek and about forty miles off the main road from Windhoek that joined with Cape Town in South Africa. All roads in the country were dirt roads, these regularly graded. It was only roads out of Windhoek to the capital that were tarred and that for not more than the first ten to fifteen miles.

The farm measured nearly 25,000 acres. It straddled the confluences of both of the major rivers in the south of the country, the Fish and the Lewer. The landscape was arid with rolling desert savannahs of sparse grass and small bush. In the afternoons of the dry winter months, the area was prone to dust storms. It was then that none could believe that thousands of sheep grazed this land.

The rivers had gallery forests, their roots fed by the underground water. The Fish River was expected to flow every year during the rainy season. Unfortunately, the Lewer River flowed less often, as its source was in a drier region, its course bordering the desert.

The banks of the rivers were given over to the cultivation of alfalfa in those areas where the water table was shallow and the water easily pumped from underground. The alfalfa was important because the total sheep population was near 5,000. This placed undue strain on the available grazing. In the event of a dry year, the animals' grazing had to be supplemented. The farm also grazed a few hundred head of cattle and a small herd of goats. The meat from the goats was used to feed the workers and occasionally the house as well. Normally, a goat would be slaughtered once a week, this considered sufficient to see us through. The farm was divided into camps although most had yet to be fenced. The only complete fence was the perimeter fence. Various boreholes had been sunk and this was where the outposts were established. There was little to these outposts, merely a primitive hut for the two shepherds, a windmill with a reservoir and a drinking trough, and corrals for the sheep. These were imperative in order to protect the sheep from marauding cheetahs, leopards, and lynxes. This was particularly so on the western portion of the farm which encroached into the Swartrand Highlands, an area of rugged kopjes and mountains with deep gorges. It was covered with a dark red-brown slate rock with surprisingly good grass and bush growing from every crack and cranny. Over eons these rivers had cut deep into the soft slate rock. The water was hardly able to seep away and became trapped in pools ensuring thicker bush and trees along the watercourses.

The total number of workers on the farm numbered no more than twenty, most of whom were contract labourers doing a one- or two-year stint before going home again. The usual salary was one pound and ten shillings a month plus rations of meat, maize meal, and tobacco. Once a year they were issued with a set of clothing, a shirt and a pair of short khaki trousers. They were predominantly from the Ovambo tribe who lived in the far north of the country near to the border with Angola and fell under the control of SWANLA, the South West African Native Labour Association. It was only through this concern that the black Ovambos could get work. If they deserted their place of work they were pursued by the police, being in breach of contract and trespassers in unauthorised areas, both criminal offences. They were not at liberty to either choose or resign from their place of work. Their 'employers' were chosen by SWANLA. In reality, this was no more than a government-subsidised form of slave labour.

Fortunately after the party, we did not leave immediately for the farm. I spent a week with my father in the city. He presented me with a brand new Ford ¾-ton pickup with cattle railings around the loading deck. New vehicles were still in short supply, all agents still with waiting lists. But my father had pulled a few strings. It was navy blue in colour, not ideal but then it was really a matter of beggars not being choosers. Most of the furniture on the farm was our own, but still we loaded a few additional pieces, plus rifles, groceries, personal workshop tools, and the most important item of all, one of the new-fangled kerosene-fired deep freezers. At least I now would have a consistent meat supply. My father informed me that until I resurrected the vegetable garden I would have to rely on tinned foods.

We left early in the morning before sunup, travelling south on the gravel road which wound its way through the Aus Mountains and eventually reached the Rehoboth Plains, then went south through Kalkrand, a true one-horse town with only a small bank, hotel, general dealer and a garage. There was also the stationmaster's house and that of his assistant. After, we passed Mariental and finally reached Asab, where we would branch off on to a badly maintained washboard track that led to the farm.

Asab was a collection of a few small buildings with corrugated iron roofs, which were haphazardly spread out over the flat plain. It was evident that it owed its existence to the main railway line, but was no more than a siding. It provided loading pens for cattle and sheep, the siding lined with corrals and ramps that led up to the cattle trucks of the train when alongside.

It was a hamlet with a hotel which had a liquor licence and therefore a liquor store. It was small but adequate for the local population, most of whom were black and lived in makeshift shacks and crumbling mud houses situated a few hundred yards from the village. Another building housed a general dealer store with a single petrol pump. There was a small community hall, a police post with a solitary police pickup parked outside, and the house in which the sole owner of the town lived. The hamlet belonged to a family who I recalled had owned it even before I was born. They were able to trace their family back to the first settlers in the then-German colony. My father had acquired the farm during the late 1800s for a pittance when the Imperial German government was desperate to settle families in this remote region of the country.

My father refreshed my memory with regard to the owner of the businesses as we pulled up at the petrol station, the north wind blowing our own dust back over the stationary vehicle. It was hot.

The Kraft family, that is Peter Kraft and his wife Uschi, and their two sons Bernd and Otto, shared all the work associated with the business. Mrs Kraft looked after the hotel and liquor store, assisted by Bernd, while Otto helped his father in the garage and general dealer shop. The two sons had never been keen on furthering their education and had left school after Standard 8. Their scholastic achievements inadequate, they were not able to gain access to a university, not that they aspired thereto. Both were in their mid-to-late twenties and it was accepted that in time they would take over the running of the businesses.

The community hall had been built at the insistence of the government who had contributed to its construction. This was built to create a meeting place for the district's locals as well as a venue for weddings, church services, and other informal social gatherings. My father told me that once a month the hall would host a dance for the local white population and that this had become quite an event amongst the ranchers. Of course, this was fully supported by the hotel as it saw this as a source of revenue in terms of liquor sales and food. The owners made every effort to make this an enjoyable occasion, which it invariably was. I laughed as I envisioned these dances, accompanied by sakie-sakie music, the instruments the ever-present concertina, accordion, guitar, and drums. The origin of the music was true Afrikaner pioneers, the Voortrekkers. It was similar to the early dances of the American mid-west, the couples moving across the floor in long steps, the men invariably pumping their partner's outstretched arm up and down to the tempo of the music, all seemingly disjointed and not likely to ignite any spark of amorous intent. Invariably the folk would dress in their near-Sunday best for the event.

"What's so damn funny?" my father asked.

I told him.

"Don't laugh," he said, "Christ, this is where you may find the love of your life. You'd be surprised to learn how many local marriages had their origins at a dance in the local hall," he said.

We both laughed heartily.

It was near noon when my father and I stood outside the bar entrance beating the dust from our clothes with our hats.

"Come on, let's have a beer," my father said, looking at me through eyes squeezed to slits against the harsh sunlight reflected off the ground and the whitewashed buildings.

Surprisingly, it was cool inside. There were only two other customers, both sitting on stools at the bar. My father shook hands with Otto Kraft, one of the owner's sons, and introduced me, telling the man that I'd be taking over the running of the ranch, that they were to supply me with everything I needed, and that they should bill the company in Windhoek.

"No problem, Herr Aschenborn. What will you have?" he asked.

Soon we had two quart bottles of Windhoek beer in front of us. My father knew the two other occupants at the bar and introduced me to them. One of them, Dirk Kotze, was a middle-aged Afrikaner. He owned

231

the farm Falgras which adjoined our own, it also bordering on the Fish River. The man's hunting activities were notorious. He was said to shoot indiscriminately, whether protected game or not. My father had reports that the man made regular forays onto our land as there was little game left on his. My father turned to him. "I'm told that you regularly drive on my land and shoot springbok and kudu." He stepped up close to the man, "I warn you, if we catch you on our land without permission, we will shoot," he said and there was no mistaking the menace in his voice. "I'm telling the police. They've been trying to catch you anyway."

Kotze glared at my father. "I'll shoot back," he said.

"You do that. Shooting at us on our own land will make it a lot easier to explain when we kill you on Aschenborn property," my father replied. He then took his beer and moved to the other end of the bar. I followed.

Once we were seated, he turned to me.

"You're going to have trouble with that man. I'll take you to the local police sergeant, better that you know him. Sergeant de Vries is his name. He hates Kotze and has already had run-ins with him. Cattle theft, drunken brawls and family abuse. He hits his wife. You know what I think of that. He's better dead." The savageness of my father's statement surprised me. His eyes burned with hatred.

"Of course, you really don't expect me to take a pot-shot at him, do you?" I asked.

He slapped the bar top hard enough to draw attention.

"Of course I do. He may even shoot first. He's capable of that. Was up for manslaughter once, killed one of his labourers. But was exonerated from blame. Not guilty the court said, but we all know it was fuckin' bullshit. Whites who shoot blacks just somehow never seem to be found guilty." I turned to get a good look at the man. He was thin and tall, at least six feet three inches. He sported a short blond beard with a moustache. He wore khaki shorts and a faded denim shirt. His feet were shod in high lace-up brown boots which were badly scuffed and probably had never seen polish. He had an evil-looking sheath knife with a one-foot blade on his belt. His prominent eyebrows were bleached white by the sun rested over his hooded, piercing blue eyes. The man's features were rugged. There was nothing soft about him. I saw that the hand that clutched his drink was large and calloused, the knuckles scarred.

After downing another beer, we stepped outside into the blinding sunlight, screwing up our eyes. My father led me to the local police outpost where he introduced me to Sergeant de Vries. I was surprised. The man was well into his forties, somewhat corpulent and nearly bald. He had a wide, flat nose and sported a walrus moustache. His face was sunburnt with white lines radiating from his eyes.

He beamed at seeing my father and came round from behind his desk and shook hands with us, clearly delighted to see my father. I realised they knew each other well.

My father introduced me. The man knew of my existence and expressed his elation at hearing of my release from Russia. My father told the police officer that I was taking over from de Jager.

"I take it you've told Matthias of the run-ins you've had with your neighbour Kotze?" the sergeant asked.

"I have."

The police officer turned to me. "Watch your livestock and your game. I desperately would like to catch him, but must have evidence. Telling me that you've heard a couple of shots means nothing. Make sure you always have a witness and be damn careful, the bastard will shoot if provoked," he said.

We said goodbye, my father promising to stop by on the way home to Windhoek.

We drove to the farm over a rather bleak landscape, most of it belonging to Kotze. It was overgrazed and barren. We saw no game or livestock. Eventually his farmhouse came into view on the right hand side of the track. It was without a garden and seemingly neglected, the veranda overlooking a flat piece of ground, gravel and dust. Both the walls and corrugated iron roof of the house were in need of paint. A carport constructed of the same material as the roof was empty. At the approach of our pickup a woman appeared in the kitchen doorway and watched without a wave or greeting.

"That's his wife," my father said. "His daughters all left the house as soon as they could, most marrying very young. I'm sure they did this to get away from him. He's a tyrant and, when drunk, would beat the hell out of them and his wife."

Eight miles further on and now on our own soil, the farmhouse came into view. It was a large house with an excessively steep roof painted a dark red. The walls were whitewashed and a porch surrounded the house on two sides. The house was fenced in the front, this containing a garden with flowers and bushes in bloom. It even boasted a small rectangular lawn. The garden also enjoyed a brick-built reservoir which served as a swimming pool. It was fed with water from a windmill which adjoined the house. At the rear of the house was a four-car garage and workshop and a good hundred yards away was the black foreman's flat-roofed house, which was no more than a large hut. On the other side, a smaller house had been built. It, too, had a veranda and garden but much smaller, usually reserved for the manager.

From the rear of the house and beyond the outer buildings, the ground then fell away towards the river, finally meeting with the first of the large majestic camel thorn and acacia trees that made up the river's gallery forest. The width of these gallery forests on both sides of the river varied from fifty to about a 150 yards in width, the grass and scrub between the trees, this lush and dense. A large flat area, actually the backyard, stretched out from the kitchen veranda. This resembled a courtyard, it being surrounded by the few buildings. Other than a steel latticework tower on which a water-tank perched, the yard was bare, comprising flat, hard-packed gravel. On a mast erected on the roof of the house, a wind charger whup-whupped in the wind, recharging the batteries used to light the house after dark. In one corner of the yard were two slightly sloped concrete tables with taps at one end. This is where the day-old karakul lambs were slaughtered and skinned, the sale of their pelts the main source of the farm's income, truly a hideous business. This was not to be watched by the uninitiated and those queasy-stomached.

The foreman, a black named Joseph, and two farmhands approached the pickup to off-load the vehicle. They greeted us with deference but none shook hands as this was not customary. In this country, the blacks were strictly segregated. Joseph produced an envelope containing the house keys which he handed to my father.

We entered through the kitchen. The refrigerator door stood open and was completely bare. Obviously, it had not been used for a long time. In the sitting room and dining rooms, all furniture was draped with large bed sheets to protect them from dust. It was stuffy and hot in the interior and we opened the blinds, curtains, and all windows to allow the air to circulate. In the bedrooms, all the beds had been stripped. Within an hour a fire roared in the woodstove in the kitchen, the sheets had been removed from the furniture, the kerosene fridge lit, and two maids, one of whom was Joseph's wife, were busy cleaning the house and making up the beds in the bedrooms.

The fridge and liquor cabinet were stocked as was the pantry. By six that afternoon, my father and I relaxed on the veranda, each with ice-cold quart bottles of beer, the afternoon sun behind the house.

"I'm leaving tomorrow night. You'll have to drive me to the station. I'll use the train. It gets to Windhoek the next morning," he said.

I protested, saying that he should stay longer and I'd drive him back. He was adamant and did not want to hear of it.

"I want you and Joseph to take an inventory of what's in the manager's house. There's a list hanging behind the kitchen door. I just want to make sure de Jager didn't clean us out. There's also a list in the gun cabinet, check that as well. You can expect him to have used some of the ammunition. If there's anything untoward, just phone me from Asab," he said.

"Joseph tells me that we've lost a few goats and sheep, and especially lambs to leopards," I said.

"I know, I heard, but you'll probably find that it is a single marauder that's discovered our animals to be an easy kill. When it's hungry enough, it gets into the corrals at night and takes out a few goats. You're going to have to deal with it but be bloody careful. Find yourself a few dogs, don't even think of taking any dogs from the blacks. Their dogs are vermin and should be shot on sight," he said, taking a swallow of beer.

"Where am I going to find dogs?" I said.

"Go next door to Kabias. The Herbsts breed fox terriers, they're good hunting dogs."

Kabias was a neighbouring farm, not far. I made a mental note to do so.

We retired early.

The next morning, an agitated Joseph took us down to the corrals. We'd been visited by the leopard again. It had killed four goat kids during the night. I hadn't heard a thing.

My father and Joseph inspected the goat carcasses. They all had their throats ripped open, the other animals in the corral keeping a distance from the carcasses. They carefully inspected the ground outside the corral

"It's definitely a leopard. Look, it actually killed five and dragged only one off. That's typical," my father said, taking out a pipe and carefully filling it with tobacco from a pouch.

Once he had the pipe going and was encompassed in a cloud of smoke in the still morning air, he said, "We'll go to Kabias today, this morning, in fact. It'll also give us a chance to charge the Jeep's battery by driving it there and back. Anyway, you need to be introduced."

The Jeep was parked in one of the garages, the battery dead. We pushed the all-wheel drive vehicle out of the garage and then using jumper cables connected it to the new Ford pickup and got the vehicle started. First it spluttered and snorted and then settled down to a steady fast idle, the ammeter showing that it was charging.

"You drive," my father said. We hopped aboard and set off for Kabias on the two-track farm road.

The vehicle was ideal. It was one of the few US Army surplus vehicles brought to South Africa and sold here. It came complete with spare jerry cans, spade, and in military colour but showing no insignia. It was still new.

The road followed the riverbank of the Fish River and I was pleased to see two large flocks of guinea fowl with at least a hundred or more birds to a flock, a few kudus in the trees, duiker, and a fair herd of springbok.

"There's still a lot of game around," I shouted to my father over the find.

"You're right, but with Kotze around and his shooting, they'll soon disappear for somewhere safer. The animals aren't that stupid. Look at this lot, it's already gun-shy," he replied, clearly unhappy.

No further word was spoken until we drew up to the yard of Klaus-Peter Herbst, the owner, who was standing on his kitchen veranda expecting us, having heard the vehicle's approach.

The two men greeted each other. My father introduced me. While he may now be a dirt-farmer and rancher, Klaus-Peter was known to be a cut above the regular farmers with regard to manners and etiquette, this to an extreme, never succumbing to the laid-back attitude so many of the other colonialists had assumed. Ingrid Herbst, his wife, came out to greet us with her newborn son in her arms. The baby was no more than a few months old. I saw that the baby's ears were pinned back by strips of plaster. I thought that strange and curiosity got the better of me.

"Why the plaster? Was something wrong?" I asked.

"No, no," she said, smiling, "that's just there to ensure the boy doesn't develop airbrakes."

Well, that was a new one on me. I thought that perhaps my mother should have done the same to me. My ears standing out ever so slightly but sufficiently that in an unusually strong wind they would begin to strum a little.

My father and Klaus-Peter stood to one side, deep in conversation, no doubt exchanging the latest news. Ingrid welcomed me home, telling me how distressing it had been for all, knowing that with the war already over years ago, I was still imprisoned.

We all walked over to the kennels, which were no more than a wire enclosure with a few wooden kennels. There had to be at least ten fox terriers in the enclosure, all rushing towards us barking with excitement. I saw their tails had been cut, just stumps and already healed. My father was insisting that I seek out four dogsthat were not fully grown. I resisted. I was not a four dog man. One animal would suffice. It would be easier to bond with one dog.

"Father, all I want is one dog. Not to attack wild animals, but to warn me of danger, to sleep on my bed and be my companion." He wasn't happy. "You should get yourself a woman for that." Ingrid thought the comment amusing.

I remained stubborn and my father relented. We left with only one dog, which I was allowed to select. I liked the dog from the start. When I picked him up, he growled. I interpreted this as indication that he was his own master and not ready to be pampered by everybody. This was to become one of his strongest traits, many would learn to their dismay. I decided that I'd call him Foxie.

My father drove back to the farm while I was in charge of the dog. The dog insisted on standing on my knees with his paws on the fold-down windscreen ledge, staring through, ever observant. The claws of his hind legs dug into the top of my thighs.

On the way home, we encountered a few ostriches standing next to the road. At the sight of them, the dog was galvanised into action. He began whimpering, yowling, and groping for traction on the ledge of the windscreen with his forelegs, wanting to give chase. I rather liked that. My father did not, saying that the dog would ruin the new pickup's dashboard within a week. He was right. This would become a rather amusing bone of contention which my father would comment upon each time he entered the pickup.

That night the dog slept at the foot of my bed. I'd coaxed him to jump up.

The next day, we spent most of the morning going through my father's list of things to be done. It was evident that we'd be busy for quite a while. There was a lot to do.

At lunch he insisted that he be taken to Asab in the early afternoon, as he wished to spend some time with both the senior Mr Kraft as well as Sergeant de Vries. Foxie accompanied us in the Ford. which sustained its first dashboard scratches. My father endured the dog's hind paws digging into the tops of his knees. The dog's perception was astounding. Cattle and sheep were ignored but it reacted to any game and the occasional black walking along the road. We both noticed this. At one stage, just after the dog had indicated his dislike for blacks for a second time, my father harrumphed and grudgingly admitted that the animal might just turn out to be an excellent watchdog after all.

I dropped him off at the Sergeant's office and took my leave when I saw the officer withdraw a near full bottle of Kommando brandy from a cabinet with three glasses. I knew they'd finish the bottle. I was sure my father would have no problem sleeping on the train.

CHAPTER TWENTY-THREE

I acclimatised to the life of solitude on the farm, maintaining a strict employer relationship with all the hands. There was a great deal to do and boredom never was a factor. I had subscribed to various magazines: the American *Flying* and also *Motor Trend* magazines, a couple of German magazines; and I would dutifully listen to the news on the shortwave radio every evening.

Joseph, the foreman, was a good man. Unfortunately, he had a penchant for a locally-brewed moonshine made from maize, sugar, and yeast, usually left to ferment in a five-gallon drum. It was a home-brewed beer with an alcohol content that bordered on that of distilled moonshine. Of course any home-brew was illegal. Two mugs of the stuff were enough to reduce most men to blithering idiots. Any who drank it would soon exude a distinct sour smell of fermentation and this mixed with the smell of perspiration which would begin to ooze from the person's skin, it becoming overpowering.

At such times, Joseph became incoherent and it was best to avoid him, but unfortunately it was then that he wanted to take his duties seriously, much to the amusement of the other hands. When drunk he would vehemently disagree with me, putting on a show. He would wave his arms and argue at every opportunity about nothing at all. Eventually, during one of his sober moments, I took the man aside and told him that I'd had enough. He was to get his drinking under control, failing which I would fire him, banning him and his family from the farm. For a while, this seemed to have the desired result, the man was sober from Monday to Saturday midday. Mondays were invariably bad days. The man's hangovers would reduce him to a state of uselessness, to the amusement of the other labourers.

Sporadically we would still suffer attacks from the marauding leopard, the corrals being an easy source of food. Finally, we had no option but to deal with it.

We would have to do this at night although I thought I'd attempt to find out where its lair was. The farmhouse complex fell within what it considered its territory which it demarcated by squirts of urine.

During my next weekly visit to Asab, I purchased a box of 12-bore, heavy buckshot shotgun cartridges, just the right combination for close quarter use. Every night, I stationed a young contract Ovambo on the roof of the workshops with a promise of a one-pound bonus if he warned us of the leopard.

Since I'd been given Foxie, I had been training him. Now he was more obedient and would heel at my command irrespective of what he was confronted with, only emitting low growls. But his whole body would quiver in anticipation of the command to give chase or attack. Once he was off, there was no calling him back. I simply had to wait while events took their course. He would return an hour or two later wagging his stump and panting, his tongue lolling out of the side of his mouth with a look that signalled satisfaction. He never displayed any remorse at not heeding my commands to come back.

*

It took two weeks before the leopard returned.

Invariably I slept with all the house doors open it was so hot. Foxie would warn me of any intruders.

I awoke to Foxie's loud growl.

"Baas, Baas," I heard someone call.

It was the guard on the roof. He now stood on the veranda at the back door.

"The leopard is here," he said, his eyes flashing white in the moonlight.

I returned to the bedroom, got into a pair of shorts as well as slipping my feet into a pair of sandals. I grabbed my improvised battery pack, slung it over my shoulder, and fitted the lamp with its elastic strap to my forehead. The light was powerful. I grabbed the Sauer & Sohn 12-bore shotgun, this already with two cartridges in the breech, took another few loose cartridges from the box and stuffed them in my pocket. I put a leash on the dog and was ready.

"Let's go. You get Joseph. I'll wait for you at the workshops," I said, hoping that he understood me.

The night was warm. There was a three-quarter moon which cast a pale light over the back yard.

I knew the leopard wouldn't stay. It would kill a few goats, probably kids, and then drag one off for its meal. This is what they usually did when attacking goats or sheep in a corral. Fortunately, the two men

240

returned quickly and the three of us descended the slight incline to the corrals with me leading, shotgun at the ready. The leopard was still there. The goats were skittish and all bunched up in a corner of the corral as if trying to avoid something at the opposite end. Foxie strained on the leash and I had to keep pulling him up. He would then stand for a moment, his whole body shivering and him whimpering.

There was little sound, just the slight drumming of the goats' hooves on the compacted goat dung and the occasional bleat from a kid. We were no farther than twenty yards from the corral when we heard a staccato low growl, a warning sound from the leopard. I placed its source in the corner farthest from the goats, the nearest corner to my left.

I cautiously approached, the lamp still off, trying to gauge the precise whereabouts of the animal. I couldn't see it. It was time to switch on the light. I pressed the button on the battery pack and a bright shaft of light stabbed out from the lamp. For a split second, I saw the leopard's two eyes before it turned and moved, emitting one loud cough. It was directly behind the wire mesh of the corral. I brought the shotgun to my shoulder, pulled the hammers back, and squeezed the forward trigger, firing the left barrel. With a loud report, the gun slammed into my shoulder and a cloud of dust rose around the animal and from the wire fence. I saw the leopard bound for the opposite side. I fired the second barrel. This, too, seemed to have no effect. It did not hesitate in its flight, the goats scrambling to get out of the way. In an instant, it had clambered over the wire and disappeared into the darkness.

Everything had happened in a matter of seconds. The adrenalin coursed through my veins and I was still hyped, my reflexes taut as a bowstring ready to be sprung, my breath quick and shallow. Foxie had held his ground, the leash slack in my hand but now that the leopard had made a break for it, he could no longer contain himself and took off with a series of wails, nearly jerking me off my feet.

I hung on and shouted, "Heel."

The shaking dog sat, still whimpering.

"Baas, you hit it first time," Joseph said excitedly, walking forward past me.

We walked around the corral to where the leopard had cleared the fence. I shone the lamp on the ground and we were rewarded by bright spots of blood. The cat was wounded. To chase it in the dark was out of the question. Wounded, it was doubly dangerous and sure to ambush us, or so I thought.

"We will wait until tomorrow. How many goats has it killed?" I asked.

Baas, I see three," Joseph replied.

"Okay, get them out of the kraal. We'll start tracking at first light," I said.

The remnants of the adrenalin surge kept me awake. I tossed, turned and finally slept fitfully. At the very first hint of dawn, I was awake. In the bathroom, I threw water on my face, dressed in shorts, a bush jacket, and sturdy hiking boots. The choice of weapon was another matter. At close range, the shotgun was an ideal weapon, especially if the leopard were to make a charge. A wounded leopard had to be the most dangerous of animals – devious and incredibly fast. It was sure to charge from a concealed position. The hunter would need lightning fast reflexes. I didn't think I wanted to chance that. I decided I would carry a Mauser 8 x 60 Express with open sights. Joseph could carry the shotgun just in case it were needed.

We set out from the house to pick up the trail from the corral. The same Ovambo who had awakened me took the lead following the blood spoor, I behind him and Joseph behind me holding the shotgun and the dog's leash.

It was difficult to judge how badly the animal was wounded but the blood trail was faint. Unless the animal was bleeding internally, I doubted that it was mortally wounded. The blood trail would lead us towards the dense gallery forest along the riverbank. This would provide the best concealment but also meant that we would be right on it before we were aware of it. My apprehension grew by the minute. This was getting dangerous.

As we entered the trees, I swapped guns with Joseph, realising that when I did see the leopard it would be damn close. I also took the dog from him. I was beginning to give serious thought to abandoning the pursuit.

Usually in the early mornings before the day begins to warm the forest is filled with the sound of birds calling to one another. There is a continuous warble, twitter, and screech. Now it was nearly silent, ominously so, as if an atmosphere of impending doom hung over the river.

We walked through the knee-high grass, the fine powdered silt underfoot raising a small cloud of dust with each step. Except for the slight rustle of grass, our passage was silent. Every minute or so, I would briefly stop while we all took a careful look around. I kept one eye on the dog.I believed the first warning would come from Foxie. The dog was attentive but not excited.

"It's nearby," Joseph whispered to me in Afrikaans, his voice husky. He had no knowledge of firearms and I had given him strict instructions that on no account were he to attempt to fire the rifle. If we spotted the leopard, he and the Ovambo were to slowly withdraw to safety. I wanted a clear radius of fire.

Joseph was right and Foxie's hunting instincts came to the fore. He whimpered and strained at the leash. He knew the leopard was close. I tapped the Ovambo on the shoulder and indicated that he take up a position behind me with Joseph. I looked at the dog again and hoped that the direction in which he pulled on the leash indicated where we could expect to find the leopard. He was pulling in the direction of a particularly dense copse of shoulder-high bush, the centre of which was dominated by a huge camel thorn tree with thick branches. I stopped. I knew it was here somewhere.

The Ovambo laid a hand lightly on my arm in warning and then pointed upwards into the huge tree. I looked along the line he indicated but could not see anything but leaves and branches and patches of sky. The leopard had to move before I would see it. The distance from where I was to the tree was far enough to put it at the limit of the shotgun's effective range. It would have to be a rifle shot, but I needed to see the animal first. Why didn't the damn thing move? At least, I would then see it. All it needed to do was flick an ear. The Ovambo kept pointing to where it was supposed to be. Still, it eluded me. The man tutted softly with impatience and disappointment.

The lower branches of the tree exploded with movement, the leopard jumping into focus as it scampered along a thick bough. I saw that it was a large male. A shotgun shot was a distinct possibility, it was that close, but the animal was too fast. By the time I had brought the shotgun to my shoulder, it had hopped down from the branch where it had lain and with the next bound disappeared in the ground foliage. All we were left with was the sound of the receding rustle of leaves and branches as it made its escape.

"Shit," I said, realising that to follow now would confront us with an especially alert animal who had every advantage in the dense bush. It was not about to leave the cover the gallery forest provided. The odds had now changed in favour of the leopard.

"It's too dangerous. I'm not going after it," I said to Joseph, looking at him to see his reaction and hoping that he did not think me a coward.

He nodded his head. "Baas, I agree. We must wait a few days and see what happens and then find the leopard and track it. Maybe its wound will heal and it will move on and find new territory." Did I perceive relief in his eyes?

We turned round and retraced our steps.

"Joseph, make sure that none of the children play in the river. They must keep away for a while, it's too dangerous. Let them stay near the house for a few days.""I will tell them," he replied.

Foxie did not want to return and kept on tugging at the leash. I was forced to drag him along.

"Stupid bloody dog. The damn leopard will kill you," I shouted, jerking the dog back on the leash.

The two black men laughed, relieved that we were postponing the hunt to another day.

*

For a few days, the leopard was nearly forgotten as we concentrated on resurrecting the vegetable gardens along the riverbank. These were about a mile from the house. Using the tractor and temporarily employing a number of the wives to assist with the cleanup, we ploughed the ground, removed the weed and brush that had taken over and prepared the soil for seeding. Joseph had worked the gardens before. He knew what would flourish here. We had abundant water and now that we had cleared the irrigational canals of all the dirt and muck which had collected since last used, we could plant just about anything that would grow in this hot climate. There was no doubt that in this arid country our produce would find a ready market in Windhoek. Most fresh produce was railed in from South Africa at considerable expense.

I decided that we should devote at least an acre of the garden to tomatoes. In this harsh sun, I thought it a good idea to put up some shade cloth, a full day's worth of sun was probably too much for the tomatoes. The cloth I ordered from Windhoek and I expected the arrival of the consignment in Asab within the next few days. We also planted pumpkins, cucumbers, and watermelons. The rest was given over to potatoes.

We started growing the tomatoes and cucumbers in compartmentalised seed boxes from which we then transplanted the seedlings. The rest of the seeds we simply put straight into the ground, ensuring that these were properly spaced and in proper rows. We dealt with the seed potatoes in a similar manner. The ground we used as a garden had long been in use for similar purposes years before when trees had been planted around its circumference. For quite a few years it was neglected, the bush beginning to take over, but the high water table ensured that the trees received water and thus flourished. They were now tall and stood in rows just within the garden's perimeter fence.

The birds and baboons were a problem and we needed to ensure that we could keep them at bay. We placed scarecrows at strategic places and tied anything that would flutter at intervals along the fence in the hope that this would also deter them. Long strips of plastic were ideal as it made the baboons nervous. For a small sum per week, I employed one of the wives to spend every day at the gardens, making her presence known, walking through the vegetable plots periodically. That would keep the baboons away, or so I thought.

In the early morning on specific days of each week, the shepherds at the various outposts would keep the karakul sheep corralled until I arrived with Joseph. This was usually before seven. The first thing we did was count the herd to ensure that no sheep had been lost. On these occasions, we would provide the shepherds with their ration of maize meal and meat, tobacco, and matches, and whatever food supplement we had. We would return with those lambs that were to be slaughtered for their pelts. If a lamb's pelt was to be saleable, the animal had to be slaughtered within a day or two of birth.

We cleaned up the workshop, sorted out the tools, and used wooden boards bolted to the walls and nails to hold the different tools in their predetermined place so that they could be readily available. The house had a large cooler room at one end of the veranda next to the kitchen. This was a double-walled brick construction. Both walls had every other brick removed, the hollow gap in the inside lined with thin wire mesh. This was filled with porous coke, which was derived from burnt coal. A water pipe which had been pierced at two-inch intervals was affixed to the top of the wall over the gap and from this water dripped continuously down the inside soaking the coke. The constant evaporation of the water ensured that the temperature within remained substantially colder than the outside ambient temperature. This was used for the hanging of slaughtered carcasses and shot game, the storage of vegetables and other semi-perishable goods. We had replaced the coke with new coke and unblocked the holes in the water pipe. We would use it to store those vegetables that perished quickly and keep them cool before being transported to the Windhoek market.

For weeks, all was quiet. No more attacks by leopards on the corralled farm animals and with no sightings made, we all assumed that they had moved off to new territories. This assumption was favoured by all, as none was keen to hunt these animals in the dense gallery forests of the river.

After a few of months, the farmhands' efforts were beginning to show results. We had completed the vegetable garden and we commenced harvesting the first of our efforts. We had renovated the homestead, repaired reservoirs, fixed corrals, and attended to a host of other items. Now the men had started the arduous task of putting up fencing to create multiple fenced off camps which would enable us to better control the movement of the sheep and cattle and to avoid over-grazing. To add to our good fortune, the farm had received better-than-usual rains, as did the catchments' area of the two rivers. They both flowed strongly for a few days, the pools on the river were again full and the overall water table was replenished.

I had settled down to the job of farm manager, no longer getting quite so involved with the manual work itself, as initially had been the case, but now took on the role of supervising and instructing.

Yes, I have to admit that as matters began to take on a routine I experienced my first feelings of loneliness, my thoughts dwelling on Wiebke and Klara, but I would then erase these thoughts from my mind.

The baboons remained a constant menace. A large troupe roamed the riverbanks in both directions from the house, but lately they had tried a foray into the vegetable gardens. The maize and watermelons seemed to hold a particular fascination for them. The flapping plastic on the fences no longer worried them. They'd realised that all these did was make a noise and held no danger. Another woman had to be added to the daily guard, but still the baboons were not deterred. The watermelons and cobs of corn were ripe, ready for the picking. We had no alternative. It was time to shoot a few. We found this to be a good deterrent.

I decided to do this alone. I believed baboons could count and when confronted by more than one were inclined to keep their distance, in fact, a substantial distance.

The two women were told to stay home. Before sunrise I made my way to the gardens armed with a Mauser 7 x 57mm rifle, this with telescopic sights. The sights were supported by looped rings of steel, enabling the use of the open sights below. By the time I got to the gardens, dawn was already a growing mauve streak on the horizon. Using a machete, I cut a few branches and constructed a hide in the corner of the gardens next to the watermelons and then concealed myself in it and waited.

Other than a duiker, which on seeing me had fled and wormed its way through a hole on the fence, I saw no other animals. I made a mental note to have the hole repaired.

It took two hours before the troupe arrived, actually hearing their barks before I saw them. I knew the troupe well, having often seen them in the river, the dominant male a huge fellow who commanded respect from all. Of course to the baboons the fence was no barrier at all and they scaled this with impunity.

Finally, their leader came in sight, walking on all fours. As he neared the fence, he jumped up into one of the trees and slowly surveyed the garden. For five minutes, he watched. I didn't make a move and during this time a few of the other males began to appear.

I could have shot the leader from where I was but I thought I'd wait until he was in the garden proper. I believed that killing him there ensured that the baboons would associate it with death and that they would never again venture over the fence.

Finally, the leader seemed to decide that the coast was clear. He clambered over the fence followed by the other males. Still, I decided to wait. They made straight for the watermelons, some of which were already ripe. The troupe leader was the first to pick up a watermelon and smash it to the ground, breaking it open and sticking both hands into the pink pulp. Others followed suit, each with their own melon. I realised that they would destroy the crop within hours.

I flicked off the rifle's safety catch, slowly rose from my haunches, and took aim at the troupe leader. He was never still, always moving as he busied himself with another melon. I took a bead on the centre of his body and squeezed the trigger. The single blast was loud in the garden. The large baboon jumped into the air doing a complete somersault. With loud barks of danger, the troupe scattered and fled, most in the direction from which they'd come.

The troupe leader also ran, with one arm dangling. I could see the blood glistening on his shoulder. He was badly wounded. He had difficulty scaling the fence. I took aim and fired again but missed. My second shot seemed to give him further impetus and within a second or two he had scrambled to the top of the fence and over.

"Shit!" I'd wounded the animal and would now have to go after it. I wasn't the best tracker and hoped that it was leaving a fair blood trail. I ejected the empty shell and rammed another into the breech. I set off for the gate and walked around the perimeter to where the baboon had clambered over the fence. I saw the blood and started following, the trail heading straight for the river and away from the house which was already well over a mile away. With only one arm, I didn't think the baboon would be climbing any trees and this made it easy to follow his spoor. It seemed he was losing a fair amount of blood.

I followed it for about a half hour and was already deep within the gallery forest, the trail circumventing copses of bush and shrub, the baboon following a line of least resistance and moving up-river.

Up ahead, I heard a low bark and then a few grunts. The sound was typical of a baboon. With the rifle at the ready I crept forward, my body hunched down so as not to reveal my upper torso. From the sound, I knew I had to be near. I stopped and looked from left to right, trying to peer through the foliage. Amongst the trees and bush there were small clearings of sunburnt grass, about knee high. I espied a movement to my right and turned my head. The baboon revealed himself. He sat on his haunches, weak. He furtively looked around him. The troupe had deserted him. I couldn't risk a shot through the foliage, and ever so slowly worked my way right until where the foliage had thinned appreciably I was now able to take a shot without the bullet being deflected by a branch.

I was in the process of bringing the rifle to my shoulder when there was a blur of movement and something streaked across the small clearing colliding with the baboon and tumbling it. Everything jumped into proper focus. My blood ran cold. The leopard appeared huge. It held the baboon by the throat, it kicking its feet in its final death throes.

Transfixed, I crouched. Everything had happened so fast. I jerked the rifle up. In one fluid movement, the leopard dropped the baboon and seemed to cover the ground between it and me in a flash. It took a split second for me to peer under the telescopic sight and catch the animal in the open sights. By then it was on top of me. I fired blindly. I didn't even know whether I had hit it. I rammed the barrel up into the soft folds of its throat trying to keep its jaws off me. I smelled its rancid breath, saw its jaws open, revealing enormous fangs as it snarled. It then tried to bite the rifle. I felt its hind paws rake down my lower body as it tried to claw me.

Suddenly it was gone. I was in a state of absolute shock, but instinct made me crawl to the base of the nearest tree. I rested my back against it with the rifle at the ready across my knees. Seconds had passed since the attack. I was out of breath, my heart hammered in my chest, and I felt woozy. I was suffering a degree of shock. I looked down at my legs. Blood seeped from deep gouges in my upper thighs and legs. Thank God, it didn't have its claws into my stomach, it would have disembowelled me.

For a few minutes I sat there terrified, not knowing where the leopard was. The baboon was dead and lying in the clearing where the leopard had dropped it. I recollected my wits. My breathing slowed and I again began to think rationally. Where was the leopard? Was it coming back for the baboon?

The fore stock of the rifle was chewed where the animal had sunk its teeth into the wood when I tried warding it off. The deep gouges on my legs began to burn but I seemed to have no blood on my upper body except for a few big spots on my shirt, but I didn't know from where these came. Was it my blood or the leopard's? Had I wounded it?

I sat there for a while looking furtively around me, the rifle ever at the ready. I then heard voices and Joseph came into view followed by one of the hands.

I breathed a sigh of relief. Companionship was what I needed right now.

"Baas, we heard the shots in the garden and then later another shot in the river. We thought we better come and look." His eyes rounded in surprise as he saw my scratched legs and the dead baboon. "You're bleeding, what happened? Did the baboon attack you?" he asked. "No, the baboon was wounded and ran towards the river. I followed. In the river the leopard attacked the baboon and then me." The two men were horrified.

"Where's the leopard?"

"It got away," I said.

He saw the chewed rifle fore stock and realised what had happened. His expression changed to one of veneration.

"Ooow boss," he exclaimed, "You fought him off. You're lucky to be still live!"

I nodded. I didn't need reminding.

They helped me to my feet. I could walk and we made our way back to the homestead leaving the dead baboon where it lay.

At the house, I cleaned my wounds with disinfectant. When still bleeding they had looked worse than what they were. A stitch or two would have helped. I had a course of penicillin tablets in the first-aid box and I took the first of these to ward off any infection.

*

I made up my mind. I was going to get the leopard. But to try to do this on my own without backup was probably insane. Of course, South African law forbade any black man the right to carry a gun. If I gave a weapon to Joseph, I'd be in serious trouble if caught, as would he. Well, fuck the police, I thought. They weren't hunting leopard single-handed.

Disregarding the law, I set out to teach Joseph how to use a shotgun, full choke and half-choke barrels, two triggers, two hammers, left barrel first and then second barrel. Initially the poor man was confused, his brow wrinkled in concentration as he tried to absorb the mechanics of the weapon. The gun's recoil when he fired the first shot left him amazed at its power. I told him that once he was able to shoot a guinea fowl on the wing, only then would I believe him sufficiently proficient with the gun.

For days in the early morning and with the grass still wet with dew, the river would resound to the blast of the shotgun as he tried to master the intricacies of shooting fowl while in flight, leading the bird with the gun sight before pulling the trigger. Invariably the bird would continue flying. This left him frustrated and dejected, especially when I said to let me show him again, and brought a bird down with my first shot.

One morning, the transformation was miraculous. His first shot brought the bird down. He swung to another, flying a few yards from the first, and pulled the second trigger. Down came the second. Foxie ran forward, grasped each in his jaws, and gave it a few good chews to make sure it was dead. He would then look at me with his feather-rimmed jaw looking for approval.

Joseph did this again a quarter of an hour later. The man was ecstatic, his attitude one of 'just look at me!' I realised that I now had backup.

I smiled at him. "Now, you and I can hunt that leopard," I said.

For a moment, his face clouded with doubt. "You can use the shotgun," I said.

He beamed from ear to ear. "When are we going to do this?" he asked.

"Soon."

CHAPTER TWENTY-FOUR

The word was out. We were looking for the leopard and I promised a small bonus to any of the farmhands who came forward with news of its whereabouts.

Years back and for some inexplicable reason, the Lever River had split, this close to the farmstead, creating a long and narrow island about two miles or so in length. At any point in its length, it's never more than two hundred yards wide. From the air, this looked like a sliver of land in the riverbed, it surrounded by pools of water, spaced out at intermittent intervals around the island. Similar to the gallery forests, the island was densely forested, this probably because years ago it had been part of the riverbank before the river decided to branch out.

A farmhand had seen the leopard during the day in a particularly large thorn tree on the upper end of the island on the riverbank farthest away from the homestead. He had walked a wide berth around it. I parted with a pound in payment of his reward but insisted that he guide us to it, telling him that he did not have to take part in the hunt. Once he had pointed it out, he could withdraw. He wanted to stay with us. I said that we would set out the next morning at first light.

The next day, while it was still dark with only the first signs of dawn on the eastern sky, we set out. We were three, the farmhand, Joseph with the shotgun, and I with the rifle. I had locked a protesting and dejected Foxie in a storeroom. He howled a couple of times and then was silent.

The previous day it had threatened to rain and the thunderclouds that had gathered in the evening and which had remained until early morning had helped retain the ground's heat. The air still warm, there an absence of any dew. We had crossed the soft river sand to the island, its banks steep and nearly sheer where the river had gouged away at its sides. In single file with the farmhand in the lead, we followed a faint cattle trail through the grass, our approach occasionally scattering a flock of guinea fowl and once even a few Franklin partridges, the cocks' staccato cackle of warning piercing the air.

We didn't know whether the leopard was still around but I believed that the island was part of its territory and it was here where it was last seen. I needed no convincing that it would be wary. It had been hunted just once too often.

The farmhand had also taken precautions. He carried a medium-length stabbing spear and a cowhide shield. He had discarded his Whiteman's attire. He now wore only a soft leather loincloth and homemade sandals. The man's courage had to be admired.

The only advantage we had were the guns. The leopard had all the other advantages: stealth, deep undergrowth, camouflage, and an innate killing instinct.

The island was flat, our all-round vision restricted by the trees and the dense undergrowth. We'd be nearly atop the animal before we saw it. I began to doubt the wisdom of my decision. Maybe it would have been wiser simply to leave the animal alone and rather strengthen the watch on the corrals. That would've have been sufficient to keep the predator away, but we all saw the leopard as a challenge. It started when it went after our livestock. Joseph's goats grazed with our own and he sought revenge.

Forty-five minutes later, we neared the upper end of the island. Our pace had slowed. We now proceeded with caution and stealth.

I trod on a stick, which snapped. We all froze. Joseph lifted his finger to his pursed lips and shushed. The forest seemed a lot quieter. I started to perspire, my eyebrows managing to stop the sweat from my brow trickling into my eyes. My clammy hands held the rifle and I was aware of the faint beat of my heart. I turned to Joseph and saw that he, too, perspired, the moisture glistening on his black skin, his eyes round with fear. He tried to give me an encouraging smile.

The farmhand stopped and raised his hand. He stepped off the path allowing me to come alongside. Joseph took up position on his other side. It was so dense we could not see more than ten yards. Using his hands the farmhand gestured to Joseph that he should watch the ground and bush while he would keep his eyes in the trees. The farmhand knew that it required a trained eye to distinguish animals in the wild, an ability that very few White men had. He ignored me.

The three of us proceeded in a line abreast. Either the farmhand or Joseph forced us to drop back for a second or so as we passed some obstruction in our path. I raised a hand to wipe the sweat from my eyes with the back of my wrist. I thought I heard a faint scrabbling movement but had no idea from where this came. Out of the corner of my eye, I saw the farmhand turn, he drawing his arm back that held the assegai. I turned but was too late. The leopard flashed along the ground in a half-crouch. Still turning and in one movement, I brought the rifle up but the farmhand had already flung his spear. I saw this glance off the leopard's side and deflect into the bush. Its speed was incredibly fast. It bounded again and then launched itself through the air at the farmhand. The black man stepped forward with his shield raised to meet the animal, they colliding in midair with a loud thump. The shield absorbed most of the leopard's forward momentum, but it still got a foreleg past the shield. Its claws raked the man's forearm. Parallel stripes of blood appeared.

I staggered, tripping over something on the ground and falling down on my back. My hands still clutched the rifle. Before I could recover, the leopard was on me with jaw agape trying to bite my face or neck. I ventured to ward it off with the rifle across my chest. I hoped that Joseph would have sufficient common sense as not to fire the shotgun with the leopard on top of me.

The leopard was about to get its jaws into me when I was saved by the farmhand who swung his shield at the animal's head, the sharp side connecting with it just below the ear. It swung round to face him, emitting a loud snarl, and hurled itself at the man. The man was fortunate enough to get the shield into a position between the animal and himself, trying to hold it off while I scrambled to my feet. During this time, Joseph had been dancing around us trying to get into a position where he could fire. The farmhand had fallen onto his back, his arms extended, holding the leopard off. I brought the rifle up the leopard's side no more than two feet from me and as I was about to pull the trigger when in my peripheral vision I saw Joseph directly behind the animal still looking for a shot. Seeing him there, my finger froze on the trigger.

Somebody shouted, "Shoot, shoot."

The next moment something struck my forearm, ripping my fingers from their grasp on the rifle's fore stock. There was a tremendous blast and a flash of yellow flame before my eyes. The leopard disappeared from my vision. Christ, I realised that it was the shotgun that had fired. Joseph loomed over me leaning towards my left with the shotgun extended forward in his hands. Again, a blast rent the air. I got to my feet. The leopard lay on the ground, its side a red pulp where it had taken the full force of the shot. It was dying, hardly moving. I staggered to my feet, my ears still ringing. The farmhand was also on his feet standing next the leopard, his eyes like large marbles displaying their white outline, his lips flecked with spittle as he drove a long knife into the leopard, time and time, again.

"Stop," I shouted, grabbing him by the shoulder.

He turned and looked at me with an expression of bewilderment, as if he had just emerged from a trance. The vacant look in his eyes disappeared and his face broke into a faint smile.

"Sorry, Baas," he said. For a while, the three of us stood there, our chests heaving, we all infused with adrenalin.

"I'll bring a couple of the other men to fetch the animal," Joseph breaking the silence.

I wanted to tell him to leave it. The coat was worthless. It had been shot and stabbed so many times, but I nodded. I needed to fully recover from the ordeal. I realised that we'd been lucky. Any of us could have been badly mauled or killed. Leopards were protected game although if considered a marauder you were allowed to hunt it to protect your livestock. I was sure that Sergeant de Vries would understand. I would report the incident on my next trip to Asab.

CHAPTER TWENTY-FIVE

My neighbour to the west was an ex-Wehrmacht soldier with a gammy leg who'd also been conscripted into the Germany Army but, unlike me, did not have to endure a lengthy period of imprisonment as a guest of the victors after the war. Shortly after his release, he married an attractive dark-haired woman whom he met during the war. As soon as they were able, they had left Germany for South West Africa, where he bought the 23,000-acre farm. The farm was still virgin bush and devoid of any improvement or even a house.

It was customary to visit your neighbours. Invariably Sunday afternoons were devoted to this activity, but I was free to decide which of my neighbours I proposed to visit. Such visits were usually not pre-arranged. You just arrived and if your host happened to already have guests, that was a bonus giving real meaning to the adage, 'The more the merrier.' Of course, my Afrikaans neighbour Dirk Kotze on Falgras was excluded. We never visited each other. Most of the community had ostracised him.

The Sunday following the killing of the rogue leopard, I dressed in decent clothes and took Foxie with me. I drove west to the mountain range, the Schwarzrand, on the horizon, crossing the two wide, dry riverbeds, not daring to stop in case the pickup bogged down in the soft sand. Once in the foothills, the road deteriorated, the pickup bumping over rock and granite rock shelves. Hans Froehlich's farmhouse had only recently been built and stood forlorn amongst the rust-impregnated slate rocks. The house was still without a garden or trees except for a few short saplings, which had recently been planted around the house. There was a large outer building and a garage, which could accommodate one car.

The couple had a three-year-old son. His wife's name was Heidi. She was attractive with a head of naturally curly black hair which always seemed in a slight state of disarray. She wore a white blouse with a light green skirt with a wide silver belt. Her legs were bare, her feet in a pair of open-toed, silver sandals. The skirt was short, and knee-length, revealing a pair of shapely legs. She was considerably younger than he was. It was rumoured that she was finding it difficult to settle down in this desolate part of the country, placing considerable strain on their marriage.

Living alone without a woman in my life was not difficult but I would be lying if I said that I took this in my stride. Certainly, I was lonely and did have those moments were I was acutely aware of my loneliness. After returning from Germany, my stay in Windhoek had been far too short-lived to expect any relationship to develop. At the time, it just seemed that the farm was more important and that I get down to the job of manager as soon as possible. Besides, my mental and physical condition still needed time to recover from the effects of my long imprisonment.

I arrived at the Froehlichs unannounced. There were no telephones, although the authorities had undertaken to have party lines installed within a year. These are to be controlled by a small exchange housed in a soon-to-be built post office in Asab.

Those in the small village, as well as my neighbours, seemed to see me as an enigma, a loner, a single man living alone on a huge farm. To them, he was marked by some terribly inhuman and unlawful ordeal suffered under the Communists. They were wary of me, some in awe of a man who had survived Communist incarceration. They also associated me with money, my father being considered one of the wealthiest men in the country. Yet it soon became apparent that some women in our circle of family friends, which was extensive, saw me as shy and withdrawn but still a good catch, or so my sister-in-law had whispered to me one evening.

I drew up in front of the house. Foxie scrambled out of the cab and ran towards Froehlich's dogs, who appeared the moment they heard the pickup arrive. These were all fox terriers, obtained from Klaus-Peter Herbst. The hair rose on their backs as they slowly, stiff-leggedly approached each other, and then proceeded to sniff each other's rear-ends. No fights broke out, probably because they were all related.

The couple appeared from the direction of the kitchen, both with smiles of welcome, and shook my hand. He was a large man, his build bordering on obese, and his head bald except for a slight fringe above his ears and the back of his head. He was older than I. It being Sunday, he wore dark trousers with dark green braces, which contrasted with his white shirt which was buttoned at the neck and wrists. His black shoes were polished. I noticed that one shoe was slightly elevated.

The front of the house had a small veranda which had to be crossed to get to the front door. This also had a fly-screen door and faced east, protected from the afternoon sun. We sat down on the garden furniture on the veranda while Heidi busied herself in the kitchen preparing the coffee and home-baked Torte, which would be served with whipped cream. This was baked every Saturday for these occasions.

The opening topics of our discussions were the karakul pelt prices and the lack of rain, these being certainly the most important topics.

Every time I visited this man, I was reminded that my life was little different from his. Each day similar or the same as the day before. The two monthly, forty-five-mile incursions to Asab were its highlight. Yes, we lived well and lacked for nothing in terms of our biological needs and comforts but, intellectually, our lives were barren, a mundane existence. The day's entertainment was the eight o'clock news we listened to on the shortwave radio, and the magazines to which we subscribed. This life was nothing like in the suburbs where you emerged from the house to pick up your daily morning newspaper and saw your neighbour doing the same, exchanging a casual wave of greeting. Here, in the middle of this desolate land, meeting your neighbour was a drawn-out ritual, a special occasion.

The months I'd spent on the farm, the good food I ate, and the ever-present desert sun, had transformed me from an emaciated returning prisoner of war with a sickly white pallor, sunken eyes, and a skeletal frame, into a bronzed, lean, hard-muscled individual with pale laugh lines around my eyes which enhanced my light blue eyes and sun-bleached hair. As my sister-in-law said that I, backed my family's supposed immense wealth, was now truly an eligible bachelor. Added to that, I had regained my confidence and had found the ability and courage to again assert myself. This had been a gradual process and I was still left with feelings of inadequacy and vacillation.

Heidi arrived with the coffee and cake. Conversation then centred on what we, as farmers, still needed to acquire to improve our farms and livestock. I mentioned to Hans that I was leaving for Windhoek in a week's time in order to spend a few days with my father and bring back a few much-needed items.

"I'd like to go with you," Heidi said.

I saw Hans jerk his head up in surprise.

"But Liebling, we were planning to go in six weeks' time," he said.

"I know, but Hans, this is an opportunity for me. There's so much I need to do and get. And, as you know, the farm is beginning to bore me. I just need to get away to the city for a few days." From his expression, I saw that he was hesitant and unhappy. A married woman travelling alone with a man even if this were during the day and with a definite destination in mind, would not be a good idea. In our circles, it was not done, or so I believed. I knew that after the war people had become more enlightened but I doubted that we'd progressed to this stage yet.

"With the greatest of respect to Matthias, I don't think it such a good idea. Goodness, what will people think?" he said addressing his wife.

For a moment her eyes flashed. I realised that this woman had a temper.

"What nonsense. It's not like we're going to overnight anywhere," she retorted. It was evident that she was ready to oppose him. She then turned to me. "Do you have any objections?" I was beginning to feel uncomfortable, as was Hans. This was a delicate situation. Christ, what was I supposed to say?

I didn't want to offend anybody. "I'm sure it will be all right. I want to leave in the morning. I'll fill the tank at Mariental and we'd be in Windhoek by two in the afternoon," I said. "It's entirely up to you." By the time the late afternoon was on us and I was due to return to Gelwater, it had finally been agreed that she would travel with me to Windhoek. Hans would drop her off at the farm early on the morning of the following Monday.

*

Although she would only be gone for a few days, Heidi arrived with a large suitcase, certainly bigger than I thought necessary. This was placed on the rear of the pickup with my case and covered with a small tarpaulin. By six-thirty, we had already reached the main road and were speeding towards Windhoek. Hans had returned to his farm with his son.

The trip was uneventful. We stopped for gasoline in Mariental and I dropped her off just before two at family of Hans's in Windhoek with a promise that I'd fetch her at around ten on the coming Thursday.

I was disappointed to learn that my brother and his wife had left for another farm in the north of the country, so it was just my father and I at our Windhoek family home. My father insisted on taking me to dinner, which we enjoyed in the dining room of the Kaiserkrone Hotel. For the next two days, he accompanied me on my rounds as I bought provisions, farming implements, and other necessities for the farm.

The Froehlichs relied on kerosene lamps to light their house. I knew that Heidi had continuously pressured her husband to upgrade to electricity and apparently he relented. He asked that I please also load a generating plant which he had purchased from my father's general dealers store. I'd promised to bring this back with me.

The Thursday dawned with an overcast sky, the air heavy with moisture and a lot cooler. The evening weather report indicated that the central regions could expect an eighty percent possibility of rain and with heavy rains in certain areas, this in excess of two inches. The weather bureau was known to be conservative in their predictions when it came to rain and if they mentioned heavy rain, then we knew we were definitely in for a near-flood. At least this would make for a cool drive back to the farm, and hopefully the farm would receive its fair share.

We were no more than a half hour out of Windhoek when the sky darkened, the clouds becoming heavy with rain. The wind rose, blowing across the road, buffeting the pickup and enveloping the countryside in dust. I was forced to reduce speed. Then the first heavy drops splattered on the windscreen. At first, they resembled dust-rimmed stars and then as the rain increased became muddy tracks on the glass. I activated the window-washer and turned on the wipers. Minutes later the heavens opened and released a torrential downpour, the wipers hardly able to cope, and I was forced to reduce our speed to a crawl. The gravel road rapidly filled with water, the clay dust creating a thin coating of slippery mud, the pickup's wheels occasionally loosing traction.

We continued at about twenty mph, the pickup ploughing through the occasional large pools of muddy water which had collected on the road. Previously dry streambeds now gushed with muddy water, these streams breaking through the parallel mounds of earth created by the road graders along both sides of the road.

Ahead of us lay the town of Rehoboth, the administrative centre of the Baster community. The Basters were South West Africans of mixed blood, their origins dating way back to well before the turn of the century when the first German colonists and the Afrikaner pioneers had arrived. White women were scarce, the men choosing to cohabit with the local black women. Not until the First World War did this become unusual, their numbers had grown exponentially. The Imperial Germans had decided that they should have their own district and community centres and afforded them self-rule where it involved local matters.

The town was bisected by the Rehoboth River which was wide, stretching at least 200 yards across. If it flooded, which it occasionally did during heavy rains in its catchment's area, we would be forced to wait until it subsided. There was no practical detour. Unfortunately, the town did not cater for whites. There was no hotel, which left us with little option but to return to Windhoek or spend our day in the vehicle.

It was as I expected. When we arrived at the river, the cemented causeway had disappeared into a torrent of muddy water, a good few feet deep and with the occasional uprooted thorn tree gliding past as this was swept down-river. Any vehicle attempting to cross would be swept away.

Heidi and I discussed our predicament and realised that returning to Windhoek was not possible. Roads to the north were now also blocked by raging streams and rivers. We deduced this from the fact that except for one or two other vehicles, no other cars had arrived to cross, indicating that other rivers between Rehoboth and Windhoek had to be flooded. We were stranded, at least until the next morning.

We decided that we'd make the best of a bad situation. We drove into the small town to the local general dealer store where the appearance of white customers was sure to be a surprise. Whites did not reside in this district. The other customers stared silently at us, particularly the children, they hardly ever seeing any whites in the shop. We bought a few tins of baked beans and sweetcorn and then at the neighbouring butchery two large thick steaks. I insisted that I wanted to watch these being cut and was not prepared to accept those that were pre-cut and displayed behind the counter. Of course, this provoked a less than friendly response from the butcher.

"Meneer, that will make them more expensive," he said. "I can live with that. Please just do it." He disappeared into the fridge and returned with a large piece of rump, gave me a dirty look and then proceeded to cut the steaks with a large butcher's knife.

"My God, you're treating him like shit," Heidi whispered.

"I'm not," I retorted.

"Christ, of course you are. You people have no respect for your fellow human beings," she said. For a second I looked up at the ceiling in despair. It dawned upon me that she was one of the damn do-gooders, usually those who had recently arrived in the country and who found the strict segregation laws unacceptable. You had to have been born here to understand local custom and politics. One excuse was that they did not understand us.

"You don't understand," I said with a sigh.

She was now quite angry, her eyes narrowed and her lips drew into a thin line. There were two white blotches on her cheeks. Again, I saw she had trouble controlling her temper.

She brought her face close to mine so that she would not be overheard.

"Both you and Hans are Armleuchter. God knows why I ever came to this country. You're a throwback to the Nazis. You would've thought we'd had enough of them. Christ! I can't stand it when you people are like this." She spun round and walked out of the butchery.

The coloured butcher wrapped the steaks. What had just occurred was not lost on him. He looked at me and then with a sneer whispered in surprisingly good German, "My sentiments entirely."

Now, that was a surprise. God, I thought, I wasn't exactly having a good day. Ignoring the man, I slapped a pound note on the counter, didn't wait for any change, grabbed my package, and made a hasty exit. I didn't need a confrontation with the man. He was big and nobody here was about to come and help me! This was their part of the world, whites weren't exactly welcome.

It was still raining. I made a dash for the pickup and slid behind the wheel. Heidi was already in the passenger seat. She shook her head to get the rain out of her hair.

"I'm sorry," she said, "I couldn't help it saying what I said. Hans hates the blacks and so it seems so do you."

"That's bullshit, it's not true.""Then why that shit attitude in that butcher's shop?"

"The only reason was that I did not think the place all that hygienic. I mean, did you look at the place?""Are you sure that was your only reason?"

"Sure. I've nothing against the blacks or coloureds. This is as much their land as it is ours," I replied, aware of my first feelings of annoyance.

The rain drummed on the pickup's bonnet and roof.

"Can't we find some shelter? I need to get a few things out of my case," she said.

I recalled that there was a gas station next to the main road. This had a canopy over the pumps. I drove there and found it deserted, the petrol jockey sitting in his cabin. I drove under the canopy but waved the fuel jockey back as he started to approach. I opened the tarpaulin and Heidi removed a few cosmetics, comb, brush and towel from her suitcase. She proceeded to dry her hair and then brushed it. Afterwards, she saw to her face. She once smiled at me as I watched her peering into the mirror attached to the inside of the sun visor. "You're going to have to go back to the general dealer," she said. "We need a few very basic toiletry items, if you know what I mean."

I smiled and leaned over to open the cubby-hole in front of her, my arm accidentally brushing against her breasts, to reveal a bar of soap, a small packet of paper napkins and a roll of toilet paper. These were all piled on top of a 9mm automatic pistol and a few small silver wrappers which contained condoms, their contents confirmed by a graphic picture of a near naked woman and man.

She looked at the contents and then glanced sideways at me from under her lowered brow.

"Impressive. Do you honestly need all that?" she asked.

I wasn't sure what she was referring to, was it the pistol or the prophylactics? I was sure I turned crimson. I gave a slight shrug of my shoulders.

She took the roll of toilet paper, stuffed it into her purse, and headed for the sign that said 'Toilets'.

The country was in the grips of a legislatively enforced segregation policy, a cornerstone of the ruling Nationalist government's policy. The government had also promulgated an Immorality Act, which forbade any sex between members of different colour. Other promulgations ensured that whites had separate toilets from the rest, but unfortunately this was not the case here. This was the Rehoboth district. This was coloured territory and, as I said, only coloureds lived here.

She had disappeared for seconds before she reappeared, walking towards the car and then sliding in next to me.

"Good God, just drive. Find somewhere else. I can't be expected to use that disgustingly dirty toilet." I guffawed. "Welcome to the real world. So much for you and the other do-good types who are forever trying to kiss their arses. Now you're finding out what they're really like!" I said, and then in a more sombre tone added: "We're not going to find anything else. Let's back track and maybe I can find something under a big tree, a place somewhere with some bush you can hide behind."

I did find a big tree that provided some shelter from the rain and she disappeared behind it.

*

We returned to the river and saw that it was now even higher although the rain had slackened off to just a drizzle. We drove along a track that followed the river and found a tree with a dense canopy, this part of large copse of trees. I collected some firewood. It was all damp but at least I found a scattering of dry brush under a fallen tree trunk. I gathered this and used it to start a fire which loudly crackled and hissed as the other wood dried in the flames. Finally, I had a good fire going. I found two large round stones and placed these in the fire to heat up.

The rain stopped. I collected a few more smooth stones to make a seat around the fire, which we both shared sitting next to each other. For a half hour, we made small talk. I brushed the ash off the stones and placed two of the steaks on them. They sizzled, grilling in their own fat. The still air was soon permeated with the delicious smell of grilling meat. We both were so hungry we could barely wait until the steaks were done. Using a pocketknife, I opened a tin of baked beans. I cut off squares of steak which we had to stick into in our months with our fingers. We had no other utensils and had to pour the baked beans from the tin into our mouths.

"Primitive but delicious," she said. "Maybe a bit more salt would have helped." She laughed, dropping her head and, for a second or two, placing her hand on my leg.

The river rose further forcing us to abandon our campsite. I drove a little farther where I found another track that led to higher ground. This woman's close proximity with no others around was beginning to have an effect on me. During the last few hours I'd become acutely aware of this attractive woman. If I was reading the situation correctly, her demeanour was such that she wanted me to notice her. Did she not know that hiking her dress above her knees revealing her long smooth legs forced me to look at them? Or that when she bent over, I could peer down her blouse and see the tantalising roundness of her breasts?

We spent a good part of the day next to the river. By now we were both bored, sitting in the cab waiting for the weather to improve and the river to subside. Nothing passed between us for a long while. We with little to discuss and both getting tired of polite small talk, just staring through the windscreen, lost in our own thoughts.

Realising that weather conditions would not allow us to cross the river before the next day, we had no alternative but to stay over for the night. I decided that we should at least do so in a degree of comfort, there being no hotel for whites in the district. We chose to return to the general dealer store and the liquor shop.

I thought it prudent to let Heidi do our purchases from the butcher. She looked at me, wanting to comment.

"Don't say it," I said shaking a finger at her.

She laughed. "You're afraid of him."

"Don't be ridiculous." Still, I didn't volunteer to go.

While she purchased the meat, I entered the general dealer store. I bought cheap blankets, the one and only blow-up mattress, a groundsheet, disposable plates and utensils. I also found a small grid on which to grill the meat.

In the liquor store, I found a cheap, polystyrene-foam cool box. I bought beers and ice cold wine for Heidi. I added two cheap wineglasses.

We had to drive a mile or two before I found a large camel thorn tree. Its canopy was reasonably dense with one particular section near-waterproof where the tree has been invaded by a creeping alien plant, adding its dense foliage. I spread the groundsheet on the damp sand. Walking through the river forest, I looked for wood, which was surprisingly scarce, most of it already collected daily by the local inhabitants. It took me a while to accumulate sufficient wood but, fortunately, camel thorn wood is incredibly hard and burns slowly, producing the best embers over which to barbecue meat.

On returning to our new site with my large bundle of wood, I found that Heidi had already opened a bottle of wine and was sitting on a blanket with her legs drawn up, sipping from a wine glass.

She smiled when she saw me and then opened the cooler box and extracted an ice-cold beer which she handed to me. Using the pocketknife next to her, I removed the cap, clinked her glass with the bottle, and took two generous swallows.

"Terrific," I said, smacking my lips.

It had stopped raining although the sky was still overcast as the river still raged. It had already subsided somewhat, though still at flood-height.

The first signs of twilight appeared and I realised the overcast day would darken earlier than usual. I got the fire going, knowing that it would take at least an hour or more before I could start to grill the steaks.

"Come on," I said, holding out my hand to assist to her feet, "let's take a short walk along the water's edge."

She took my hand and I pulled her to her feet. She stood next to me holding my hand and seeming reluctant to release it. Did this show of intimacy have any significance? Now that the rain had stopped, the birds again flitted in the trees as they readied to roost for the night. The forest resonated with their cries, shrills, and whistles. Swallows swooped and whirred over our heads as they attacked the flying ants that emerged from their nests. The walk along the bank took on an atmosphere of tranquillity and peace. The reserve we had displayed had disappeared as did our guard. We were both relaxing in each other's company. We had become friends and now allowed a feeling of familiarity to creep into what had previously been an enforced, circumstantial relationship.

We saw a few guinea fowl and partridge, they also preparing to take to the trees for the night. She pointed out the various birds by name, which surprised me.

"How do you know so much about the birds?""I study them. I've bought a few books on South African birds."

I thought that out of character. She did not strike me to be the type and I had always looked on her as somebody who had married Froehlich simply because he was seen as a way out of a Germany, a country in ruin, with food shortages, a lack of accommodation and no future. Also, in terms of appearances, I didn't believe many women would consider him a catch. I knew that women are capable of the strangest things, a man's appearance was not necessarily a strong factor of attraction. This had to have been the case in this instance Was he a means to an end?

We returned to our campsite, the fire now reduced to glowing embers which were visible in the approaching darkness. I placed a few stones around the fire and put the grid over it. We placed the steaks on this. It would be better than frying these on a hot stone as we had done before. At least now we would have that added taste of charred meat that you only get from meat grilled over an open fire.

We ate the steaks and finished off the box of crackers, washing this down with beer and wine. I had a good few beers and Heidi had more than a bottle of wine. She was now tipsy and prone to the odd giggle.

It was past eight when we finally ate. After another drink, we decided we should try to get some sleep. I asked her whether she'd prefer to sleep in the pickup. She insisted on sleeping in the open on the groundsheet or on the blow-up mattress near to the fire, to which I had added more wood. She said that this was nothing new to her. We both lay down, she on the mattress and I on the groundsheet. She covered herself with the single blanket while I used my blanket as a pillow. Minutes later, I was fast asleep.

I awoke. I heard that the river was still flowing. It was dark. The fire had died down. I realised that Heidi was standing next to me, her blanket clutched in one hand.

She saw that I was awake.

"God, its freezing," she said.

She was right. I was cold, uncomfortably cold.

"You're right." I stood up and unfolded the blanket that I'd used as a pillow. "If it's okay with you, we can lie down next to each other and use both blankets. That should keep us warm."

"This is not the time to think of propriety. Just as long as you don't smell," she said.

"Probably no more than you," I retorted.

She chuckled and then pulled me towards the blow-up mattress.

"Let's lie on the mattress, it's more comfortable," she said.

We lay down next to each other. I then pulled the double blankets over us and, within minutes, we warmed up. I had turned away from her but she snuggled up against my back, her knees stuck in behind me. I thought of her nearness, wanting to turn round and hold her, but drifted back to sleep.

When I awoke it was already light, the air filled with the sound of birds. Heidi was still asleep next to me, her one arm over my side, her hand resting on the side of my stomach. I extracted myself from the blankets, stretched, and threw out my arms to rid my body of the stiffness I felt as I looked at the river. It still flowed, but barely. It had subsided during the night. Maybe we could get over the concreted causeway near the town.

Heidi stirred, opened her eyes and looked blankly at me. She realised where she was. She smiled.

"I see that you behaved like a proper gentleman," she said.

"What else was there to do?"

"Well," she just let her response hang in the air.

Had she expected me to make a move on her? I didn't think so.

We loaded the groundsheet, blankets, and cooler-box on to the pickup and drove back to the main road. Following the river, I saw that it had subsided considerably. When we got to the main road, we saw that a small crowd had gathered, these mostly young people, the first cars attempting to ford the river using the causeway. A car had stalled and was surrounded by young men who were slowly pushing it across. The water was still high, the vehicle's wheels submerged.

"The water is still deep but if we wait a half hour I reckon we can chance it. I'm getting tired of this place," I said.

Heidi nodded her head. When I saw two other pickups make it across I decided it was time for an attempt. We entered the water which was swirling around the wheels, getting deeper with every yard. The pickup held its ground and we inched across. At one stage the water threatened to submerge the tyres but we continued, the engine never missing a beat. Finally we started climbing from the river, the pickup streaming water. I breathed a sigh of relief.

We made good progress, only stopping in Mariental for a few minutes to take on fuel and to visit the toilets.

We arrived on the farm that afternoon at three. We saw that the rain had been widespread. Gelwater, our farm, was also rain-drenched. Huge pools of water resembling saltpans had collected on the flats, but fortunately without the high concentration of salt enabling grass to take a hold.

When we halted at the back of the farmhouse we found Froehlich's pickup already parked there and he emerged from the back door. He waved.

The Froehlichs hugged each other, Hans pleased to see his wife again. I envied him.

We told him about the river in Rehoboth. He mentioned that both his and my farm had received over an inch of rain in places.

When he heard we had to sleep over in Rehoboth, he enquired where we had found lodgings. Before I could say anything, Heidi spoke and I knew that she wanted to get her bit in before me.

"We got to the river yesterday morning and couldn't cross. We realised that it would take until the next morning before it dropped. Fortunately the rain stopped. Herr Aschenborn bought a few things from the general dealer store and we were fortunate to find shelter for the pickup. I, being small, slept in the cab. He slept on the back making a small place amongst all the stuff we'd bought," she said.

I thought it time to interject.

"For God's sake, please call me Matthias," I said.

The explanation seemed to satisfy Hans.

"I arrived yesterday around lunch time. I just managed to get across the river. You won't believe it, minutes after me Kotze's pickup appeared and passed the house. It came from across the river. The man had three springbuck and a gemsbok on the back. He must've known you were not here," he said.

"You're sure?" I asked.

"Absolutely. He didn't even return my greeting. He and his black helper just stared ahead, not even looking at us."

"Fuckin' bastard. Where the hell were my people?" I turned round. "Joseph," I shouted.

"Forget it. He and his two other men are stone drunk and have been so since I arrived."

These bloody people are all the same, I thought. You just couldn't rely on them and Kotze knew this. Having shot all the game on his farm, he was now poaching ours. I was furious.

"If I catch that bastard on this farm with a rifle, I'll shoot him," I said, hardly able to contain my temper. I wanted to jump into the pickup, drive over to Falgras and sort him out right there and them.

Hans Froehlich seemed to read my thoughts and laid a hand on my arm as if trying to restrain me.

"Don't even think about it. Even if you find the shot animals you'll never prove that these were from Gelwater. He'd just say these were shot on his property. You have to catch him red-handed on your property, with the shot buck, and the rifle. That's the only way. Christ, shooting him would not be a good idea. Catch him and take him to Asab. Our good police sergeant will see to him," Hans tried to assure me.

"What about Ehrenreich? Is Kotze also shooting on his place as well?"

Ehrenreich was our neighbour to the south. He was also single and said to have been an ex-SS officer. Rumour had it that the war had left him somewhat deranged and was eccentric, having taken a black woman as a companion. Nobody had ever seen this and this was not necessarily a sign of abnormality. Nonetheless, some of the white population probably thought so, although the Germans recently from Germany who had settled here seemed to consider the laws against this as something the nationalistic Afrikaner had inherited from Hitler. The man was also rumoured to walk around on his property in the buff. He did little farming although he never seemed to be short of money. He painted landscapes of the surrounding area, good paintings it was said. I'd purchased two of these a while back, not because I thought they were particularly good but rather because these were landscapes depicting the local surroundings. This had happened during my first visit to his home, which was intended to introduce myself, he being my immediate neighbour. Believe it, I found him about a mile from his farmhouse standing under a tree with his easel and paints. At first, I didn't believe my eyes, He didn't have a stitch of clothing on except for a large cowboy-like hat and a pair of sandals. His body was deeply tanned, except for the soles of his feet and the palms of his hands. The fact that his rather rotund body, his thinning hair, and his alcohol-puffed, pink face was not particularly attractive did not seem to bother him. When I stopped, he appeared unflustered and suggested that I carry on to the house and wait for him there. He would follow shortly. I'd never made mention to any other about my strange encounter with the man.

Of course, Hans was right. If I killed Kotze and the police proved that this was premeditated, that is that I went out with a gun to find him, I'd face the noose irrespective of the fact that the man was hunting illegally on my property.

I made up my mind. The farm foreman of mine, that damned Joseph, and those of his assistants employed around the farmhouse, had to go. I'd had enough. They'd continued to ignore my warnings; they continued drinking their home-brewed skokiaan, getting hopelessly drunk, beating their women and neglecting their duties. I realised that it was pointless speaking to them in their current state.

At six the next morning, as the sky streaked with the first light of dawn, I walked out onto the back porch sipping a scalding hot cup of coffee to find Joseph and the two assistants standing below the steps in the dust, Joseph stood with his hat in his hand and his head down, he trying to avoid looking at me. Of course, he was now trying to appear abjectly submissive and, no doubt, had impressed the importance of this on his two colleagues who also appeared just as dejected. I was not about to be swayed.

"Joseph, I've had enough. You must finish up here. I want you and your two men off the farm by the end of the month. I'll pay you all until the end of next month,that's a lot more than you should get," I said, trying to create the impression that it would be pointless trying to speak to me.

There were wails of protestation and sorrow. The wives were listening from a distance and now joined in. It sounded like a funeral just as the coffin was being lowered into the ground, all overcome with sorrow at the loss of their livelihood.

"For Christ's sake, shut up," I shouted.

This only aggravated the situation, their wives' shrill only getting higher accompanied by the wringing of hands, kowtowing, and tears miraculously streaming down their faces.

This was just simply too much.

"For fuck's sake. Just stop. I'll give you all one more chance. One only. Look in my eyes. I mean it. You bastards, do you understand?" I said trying to maintain the sternest of expressions on my face. "Now, just get to work."

There was more kowtowing as they backed off, not turning their backs on me, backing off and continuously bowing to me as if I were some deity.

I knew what was wrong. The place needed a woman. The black wives worked in the kitchen and house and if I had a wife or woman sharing the house, she'd soon establish that type of rapport with them that only women seem to be able to create. There'd be secrets shared, things like the mysteries of pregnancy and childbirth, errant husbands and sons, alcoholic husbands and other family problems, the women continuously scheming together to help each other. Well, I didn't have one, yet, but I certainly needed one in more ways than one.

The workers went about their day with a will, which must have been difficult considering their hangovers. None ventured near me.

The next day I took the pickup and with Joseph drove to the furthest outpost on the farm. I noticed that the game was skittish and gun-shy. They fled at the sound or appearance of the pickup. This could only be Kotze's work. I turned to Joseph next to me.

"I suppose you were so drunk while I was away you can't remember a damn thing?"

He presented me with a short pantomime of submission, lowering his head and rolling his buttocks on the seat with mock embarrassment, the movement releasing a waft of air so rancid with sweat that it assailed and caught in my nostrils like hot English mustard. He took on the look of one who has been betrayed.

"Jesus," I whispered as I tried to ignore the BO mixed with the sour smell of the skokiaan which permeated the cab with his every breath.

"Nee Baas, it's not like that. We did hear his shots." He shrugged his shoulders and spread his hands. "But I was too drunk to drive." For days, the relationship between us remained cold and distant, and then something happened.

*

I awoke. Somebody was calling me from the veranda. I looked at the alarm clock with its fluorescent face. It was four in the morning.

I swung my feet out of bed and padded through to the kitchen on bare feet. I turned on the light to find Joseph at the door, similarly clad as I.

"Baas," he said excitedly, "Kotze just drove past."

That was a surprise at this hour. "Are you sure?"

The track that passed the farmhouse also served as a route to other farms in the Schwarzrand. In fact, these were public roads, their existence registered as servitudes on the farms title deeds. However, seldom did we see more than one vehicle per week, so a vehicle passing was not a surprise, but at four in the morning, it was.

"I'm sure. He's after the springbuck," Joseph said.

I realised that the man could be right. We had two large herds of springbuck which grazed on the plains just west of the River. Could it be? They were never hunted and, although ever alert, did not see humans or vehicles as a threat. We always confined our hunting to the east side of the river.

I decided it was pointless to pursue him in the dark and returned to my bed.

I couldn't sleep and decided to get up. It was still dark, the proper dawn still a half hour away. I knew that if any hunting took place on the other side of the river I would not hear the gunshots as they would be muffled by the huge gallery forests along the banks of the river.

After a quick cup of coffee I took a 30.06 Vore Kufstein rifle fitted with a Leipoldt scope together with a pair of Carl Zeiss night binoculars from the gun cabinet and went outside to rouse Joseph, but was surprised to find him waiting for me.

"Morning, Baas. I knew you would want to go and look. I'm sure Kotze is hunting our springbuck."

I found his reference to 'our springbuck' rather appurtenant. We were one, nobody shot our game without permission.

We climbed into the Jeep and I drove towards the riverbed to cross to the other side. There was a slight morning chill and with the Jeep's windscreen down, the wind cut through my thin clothing. A jacket would've been a good idea.

It was not a road we drove on but rather a rough track which rounded every small obstacle, our speed no more than twenty miles an hour. The terrain was flat except for row upon row of dunes, they overgrown with desert grass and interspersed with copses of scrub no higher than shoulder height. These dune ridges had to be about 200-300 yards apart, they singular rows invariably parallel to one another. It was only when we crested a dune were we able to see some distance and this no further than the next crest or down the valley between these.

We were no more than a mile from the river when Joseph asked me to stop. Sand spurted as I slammed on the brakes.

He pointed. "Kyk daar." *Look there.*

I looked and saw the indentations of the tyres where a vehicle had veered off the track, the wheels cutting deep into the sand revealing the damp ground beneath. This could only have happened very recently. This could only mean one thing.

"The bastard!" I said. This had to be Kotze's work.

We followed the track which then crested to a particularly high spot on the dune ridge. We stopped and saw where the other vehicle had also stopped, the occupants alighting, the indentations of their boots in the smooth sand. They'd stopped to look from this high point. I climbed to stand on the driver's seat to get a better look from the highest elevation. At that moment, we both heard a rifle shot in the distance. Somebody was shooting on our land.

We both took our seats and I drove off in the direction from where I thought I heard the shot.

"He was not alone. Jonas told me that Kotze had another man with him, a black man," Joseph shouted over the din of the engine as this strained up the incline of the next row of dunes.

Four or five rows further on, as we crested the ridge, I could see a pickup in the distance. Again, I slammed on the brakes and looked through the binoculars. It was Kotze's pickup all right. He and his passenger were loading a springbuck carcass onto the back of the vehicle. They must have heard or seen us because they'd both stopped what they were doing. Surprised, they just stood there holding the dead springbuck between them, and stared in our direction. They threw the shot springbuck on the rear of the pickup and quickly climbed into the vehicle and drove off, obviously in a hurry, the rear wheels throwing up sand as they fought for traction.

The pickup was a great deal more powerful with its V8 engine than the Jeep with its four-cylinder engine, although the Jeep was more agile, but this wouldn't help in these open plains of small bush and no trees. Besides, the pickup had to be at least a mile or more from us.

Joseph and I clambered back into the Jeep and set off in pursuit. I floored the accelerator trying to catch up with them. If I were to be able to charge Kotze for illegal hunting I'd have to catch him on our property, and he'd still have to be in possession of the springbuck as well as the rifle. The man had no intention of being caught as I saw that he was heading back to past our farmhouse and then to his farm's boundary.

I soon realised that we were not fast enough to gain on him as the powerful pickup drew away.

The road ahead entered the gallery forest. Kotze would have to slow down, the road no longer straight but winding round every large tree and there were many of those. The sand was also softer being river sand, actually a two-foot layer of fine silt deposited by the river over eons. The track consisted of two-foot-deep wheel ruts made by vehicles that continuously passing over it.

The pickup disappeared into the tress but its passage was discernible by the large cloud of dust which it trailed.

We came hurtling around a sharp bend in the track when ahead I saw Kotze's pickup stationary where it had slewed off the rutted track. He approached the bend too fast and had lost control. They were desperately trying to extract the vehicle from the soft sand, the rear wheel throwing a rooster-tail of sand. It appeared to have some traction, the pickup inching its way forward.

I slammed on the brakes, the Jeep skidding to halt no more than forty-or-so yards from them.

The pickup's driver door flew open and Kotze appeared on the other side of the engine bonnet, his rifle in his hands. Quickly, and before I could do anything or shout a warning, he brought the rifle to his shoulder and a shot rang out. I heard the slug hit the front of the Jeep and realised he wasn't trying to shoot us but rather to cripple the Jeep. Another shot rang out, the right front tyre deflating with a loud pop and hiss. Joseph and I had taken cover behind the Jeep. I never had a chance to grab the rifle which was still cradled in the gun-rack.

"Fuckin' hell," I shouted, unable to conceal the terror in my voice.

"Die man is mal," Joseph added, just as terrified. *The man is mad.*

We both crouched behind the Jeep. We heard Kotze's pickup engine scream as he again tried to extract the vehicle from the loose sand. I peered over the Jeep. The wheels again spurted sand and suddenly gripped, the pickup lurching forward. The vehicle then fish-tailed back onto the track and drove away from us, disappearing as the road wound its way round the trees.

On inspection, I realised that the Jeep needed repairs before it would move again. A bullet had blown a hole through the radiator. When I raised the Jeep's engine bonnet, I saw that it had also destroyed the generator bracket. We were going to have to tow the Jeep back to the homestead with the pickup or tractor.

I took the rifle, and both Joseph and I set off for the farmhouse, which was a mile or two away. Of course, Kotze and his evidence were long gone. However, I wondered what Sergeant de Vries' reactions would be when he heard the story. I could barely control myself. As soon as I had arranged for the salvage of the Jeep, I'd be heading for Kotze's farm. I needed to confront the bastard. I already knew what game he'd play. He'd deny the lot.

*

Rescuing the Jeep had taken longer than I'd thought. The sun was already setting by the time we returned to the farmhouse from towing the Jeep. I wasn't going anywhere near Kotze in the dark. The man was too unpredictable. Also, serious as the matter was, Sergeant de Vries would be off-duty now and I didn't want to disturb the man in the evening. He'd have had a good few brandies by now and would just tell me to wait until tomorrow.

If I thought this was the end of the day's tribulations, I was wrong. I had barely sat down to a dinner of a few slices of near-stale rye bread and cold meats when I heard a vehicle approach and come to a halt outside the kitchen. For a second I had a vision of it being Kotze, but immediately dismissed this as impossible. The man would avoid me. As I stepped out on to the kitchen veranda, I saw it was Froehlich's International pickup, and was then further surprised when Heidi emerged from the cab. She was distraught, her cheeks wet with tears.

I got a fright and thought something bad must have happened. Was somebody hurt?

Heidi ran towards and fell against me, sobbing.

After a few seconds, I prised her away from me with a hand on each shoulder and then straightened my arms. I shook her gently and stared into her face.

"For God's sake, tell me was has happened." She sniffled and then wiped her nose with the back of her hand. "We had an argument. A stupid argument and then suddenly he accused me of sleeping with you when we returned from Windhoek. He said he could feel it, he said he could see the guilt in my eyes. I told him it was absurd, but he was convinced he was right. Of course, I again denied it and pleaded with him. He just wasn't interested and then he slapped me. That was the end for me. That's when I ran. I took the keys and drove straight here with the International. I didn't know where else to go. What else was I to do?"

Christ, I thought. This was an impossible situation. Nothing had happened between us. What had happened to make Hans think otherwise? I wondered whether she had said anything that could've made him jealous. I remembered her quick temper.

"You've got to go back to him and convince him that what he thinks is not true."

"Never. He hit me. I won't forgive him for that."

I knew that given time she probably would. She was just too distraught now.

"Look, Kotze took a few shots at me today. I've got troubles of my own. You can't stay here. It would create a scandal and just make matter worse."

"No," she was adamant.

"God, woman, you've no bloody choice. Drive to Asab, book into the hotel. You can buy toiletries and clothes tomorrow. I'm sure Hans will calm down and come after you, although I don't know how, seeing that you've taken the pickup. I'll talk to you tomorrow. I'll also be in Asab tomorrow to see the police," I persisted.

"Is that because of the shooting?"

"Yes."

CHAPTER TWENTY-SIX

The pickup bounced and bucked over the rock ledges in the road as I pushed it too fast to Hans Froehlich's farmhouse. The sun still hid below the horizon but dawn was well advanced. I'd left Gelwater in the early hours of the morning convinced that I had to help resolve the situation between Hans and his wife.

I hoped the Hans was approachable. Surely, he must realise that he was wrong. There was no evidence. On what did he base his attitude?

I stopped in front of the house and found Hans already standing in the yard, waiting for me to climb out of the cab. He must have heard my vehicle approaching.

"What the fuck do you want here?" he asked. There had been no greeting, his look sullen and aggressive.

"Hans, there's no need to get bloody shirty. I swear, nothing happened between us. Christ, we didn't even touch each other.""I don't fuckin' believe you. When she got back, she'd changed. I couldn't miss it."

"Well, if she did, I didn't have anything to do with it. Even if I did desire your wife do you think I'd be fool enough to shit on my own doorstep, what with this community the way it is?""Why must I believe you? Others have done it before. I mean, messed around with her."

"What do you mean, others have done it before?"

He paused, staring at the ground and then looked up, fixing his eyes on me. I saw they were bloodshot. He'd been drinking.

"She's fucked around before," he said quietly.

That certainly took me by surprise.

"Well, whatever, but certainly not with me. She stopped by last night on her way to Asab and told me what happened. She said she'd stay at the hotel," I said, not wanting to tell him that I persuaded her to go onto Asab. "Look, I'm going to Asab from here. You've no vehicle. Please, come with me and patch up this stupid bloody misunderstanding," I said and stepped closer with my hand outstretched. "Christ man, You're my neighbour."

He ignored my attempt at a handshake.

"Okay, but this is not over yet. Let me get a few things from the house."

Minutes later he reappeared. I saw that he'd changed although he hadn't shaved.

Two hours later, we stopped in front of the Asab Hotel. Hans's International pickup was parked in front of us. At least she'd listened and booked in. He'd also seen it but made no comment other than a harrumph next to me.

"Look," I said, "go and talk to your wife. I'm going across to the police. I'll see you later."

I didn't wait for a reply and crossed the road to the police station.

Sergeant de Vries did not seem surprised at what I told him. I left nothing out, giving him all the details and said that Joseph could back my story.

"I've known all along that it would come to something like this. Not that it would involve the Aschenborns, but any one of his many neighbours. I'm not surprised. Do you wish to press charges, although I suppose you've little or no evidence?" he said, leading me from the small charge office to his even smaller private office.

He sat down behind his desk and extracted the Kommando brandy bottle from a drawer, lifting the bottle, and raising his eyebrows at me. It was not yet ten in the morning. I politely declined.

"Your loss, my gain," he said and pulled a shot glass out of drawer and poured himself a tot which he threw back in his throat and returned the glass and bottle to the drawer.

"No, I won't lay a charge, it would be his word against mine, and nobody would listen to a black's evidence, certainly not against that of a white man. But I tell you, I will confront him and if he ever again threatens me, there'll be a reckoning. Of that, you can be sure," I said.

"Listen, Aschenborn, I respect you and your family but don't even think of taking the law into your own hands, okay? I hate to say this, but some around here would like to see the Aschenborns take a tumble. They think your family considers themselves above the others in the district. They're jealous," he said, making it clear that he was not to be taken lightly. I'd never heard this before. My mind reeled. God, we've never behaved in that manner.

I said nothing, but looked at him expressionlessly.

When I returned to the pickup, I saw that Hans was not there so I entered the hotel and enquired as to his whereabouts. I was told that he had gone to Heidi's room. I wasn't about to interfere. Anyway, they had the International pickup and did not need me to get them home. I was confident that they'd leave together having settled their differences.

As I was about to leave the hotel I bumped into the owner, Kraft Senior, in the pub. He insisted that I try the draught beer, proudly displaying the equipment which had just been installed. Draught beer. Hell, I couldn't resist.

Sitting at the bar, I told Kraft Senior about my run-in with Kotze.

"Nothing new, you know." He pushed the tall glass of draught across to me. "Your neighbour Ehrenreich has also had a run-in with him. He's the scourge of the area. Apparently, he chased Kotze across his farm and emptied a rifle magazine in his direction. Kotze didn't even go to the police. Watch out, Matthias, shit happens. The man's dangerous."

"I'm going to catch him," I said.

"Just watch out, that's all. The guy's an incredible shot. We had a get-together with the local farmers a while back. The bastard won every shooting prize."

"I'll remember that," I replied.

I got into the pickup and headed back to the farm. As I crossed the river, I saw the sign that pointed to the dirt track that led to Ehrenreich's homestead. On impulse, I turned to follow. I decided I needed to speak to the naked artist.

I pulled up in front of the house to see Ehrenreich open the fly-screen door and step out on his veranda. At least, this time he had a pair of shorts on.

"Christ, Peter, I'm glad you've at least got pants on," I said.

"What if I didn't? Who's here to see?" he said, looking around at the empty landscape. He then shook my hand.

"The fucking workforce, that's who," I said, exasperated. At least he appeared to be sober.

He waved his hand in dismissal. "They've seen it all before. What brings you here?" he asked.

I told him about Kotze.

"God, I'd like to get the bastard," he said after I finished my story.

"After what's just happened, he's not about to try something soon again," I said.

"Don't you believe it? That's just when the fucker will try something. That's just his way. Probably knows you've buggered off to Asab for the day to tell de Vries and is probably on your farm already."

I didn't believe it. The man had to be insane if he tried that, I thought.

"Come on, I'll get a shirt and a rifle. I'm going with you. Let's see what we find," he said, smiling.

We sped back to the main track where we turned left towards Gelwater. When we passed the Falgras homestead, we saw that Kotze's pickup wasn't there.

"What did I tell you?" Ehrenreich remarked. I ignored him.

I couldn't believe it. What was wrong with Kotze? Surely, hunting couldn't be all that important to him, knowing that he was now under close observation.

As we crossed the pans, which still showed pools of water after the rains, I saw Kotze's pickup in the distance, on our land.

"What did I tell you?" Ehrenreich said, working the bolt action of his rifle sliding a cartridge in the breech.

Christ! I looked at Ehrenreich. The idiot really meant it! "Listen, don't get any funny ideas."

"Don't worry. The bastard will shoot first if he's really got any of your venison on the pickup. I know him," he said. The pickup was stationary and, as we neared, I saw Kotze standing next to the front wheel, watching our approach. He had no weapon in his hand except for a wheel spanner. I then saw the flat tyre.

As we approached, I slowed the pickup and then stopped next to him, no more than five yards from his pickup. I noticed that the loading area of the vehicle was empty.

The atmosphere was electric, the man just staring at us.

"Kotze, what the fuck are you doing here?" Ehrenreich asked in Afrikaans, his voice sharp. He clutched the rifle between his legs, the top of the barrel surely visible to Kotze.

Oh, the man was arrogant, his stance and demeanour clearly indicating that he was not to be trifled with. I saw that we didn't frighten him.

"Fuck you, Ehrenreich, why've you got clothes on?" he said.

Ehrenreich opened the door..

"Careful," I whispered, "don't start anything. There's nothing to incriminate him on his truck."

Ehrenreich stopped, sort of half-in and half-out of the vehicle with one foot resting on the ground.

"What are you doing on my land?" I shouted.

"This is a fucking public road." Of course, he was right. This was a public road.

I saw Ehrenreich start to shake with rage, clutching the rifle tightly, his knuckles white. The man couldn't control himself any longer. He slid out of the pickup and started towards Kotze, coming to stand inches from his face. Kotze showed no emotion, those grey eyes never leaving Ehrenreich, there the slightest hint of a smile on his face.

Ehrenreich's face was white with rage. He then said with unconcealed hatred, "If I ever find you on this ground or my ground with a shot animal or an un-booted rifle I'll shove my rifle up your ass and blow you away. Do you hear me?"

The man never even flinched, nor did he draw back.

"Fuck you, Ehrenreich. Go back to your farm. We all know what you do there." Kotze hissed, his reference to his neighbour's perverted behaviour not missed, and then stepped away from Ehrenreich and turned to me.

"Mr Aschenborn, you don't happen to have a car-jack, do you?" he asked me politely as if nothing had happened, an expression of slight amusement on his face.

"Jesus Christ," I said, but then got hold of myself. I had nothing on him, nothing. Anyway, I never wanted him on my land again.

"Yes," I replied and climbed out of the truck and removed the jack from behind the rear seat.

I handed him the car-jack. "You can drop it of at the house sometime. Make it soon, I may need it. Also, I never want to see you on my land again, except on this road. Don't forget that."

Ehrenreich grabbed my arm but before he could say anything, I said, "Hans, just leave it alone, okay? Let's go."

Ignoring both of us, Kotze turned his back and squatted down, then proceeded to push the car-jack under the pickup's chassis.

I drove back to Ehrenreich's farmhouse. The poor man was confused, he not able to understand why, as he put it, I backed down to Kotze. I took a while to convince him that had we done anything to the man, assaulted or shot at him, we would've been breaking the law and would've given him an advantage.

When I returned to the farm from Ehrenreich's, Kotze's vehicle was gone.

*

Weeks went by. The rain had disappeared and except for the occasional late afternoon when a few white puffs of cloud would appear on the eastern horizon, the sky remained cloudless. The ground soon dried and new desert grass appeared, the horizon an enormous expanse of pale yellow dotted with green scrub and low thorn trees. The new grass undulated in the wind.

The vegetable garden thrived and began to make a noticeable contribution to the farm's income, this to my father's surprise. He finally, but reluctantly, admitted that it had been a good idea to resurrect it.

I had made a point of not visiting my neighbours, letting weekends go by without me leaving the farm. I often thought of Heidi, usually when my thoughts turned to women, but I knew that Hans Froehlich was now wary of me and would not welcome me although he would try not to reveal this. The couple had once visited me but I was sure that this was because of Heidi's insistence, they arriving one Sunday and she clearly glad to see me. Although cordial and friendly enough, I did perceive some reservation, he not quite sharing her joy of seeing me again. I was also visited by Klaus-Peter Herbst and his wife.

Every year, a jamboree was held in the small town. Its main purpose being to serve as a venue where farmers could buy and sell cattle and sheep. While many private deals were still concluded, quite a few animals were also auctioned, particularly prize bulls and rams which were usually brought to the show by breeders from other parts of the country as well as professional stock breeders around Windhoek. Kraft acted as the auctioneer and took a small percentage as commission.

The auction sales were usually concluded before midday. After that, the festivities commenced with races and other competitions for the children, Of course, there was a cake-baking competition for the wives, an equestrian gala, and the two highlights of the day: a horserace and a shooting competition. The shooting competition was restricted to the district's farmers and their children who were eighteen and older. All the district farmers were expected to enter this. It was restricted to high-powered rifles with a calibre of .300 or less, and the shooting was over a range of 200–400 yards. There were stationary and moving targets, these resembling wild animals, with a small target depicting the position where the best shot should be.

The Krafts were the main organisers of the festivities, making a fair financial contribution to the costs of the jamboree. They also owned the corrals and the showground, but then they invariably did well out of it, particularly from the sale of liquor as they owned the bars which did a roaring trade. A dance concluded the festivities and was held in the community hall. This usually continued well into the morning hours. This was really a barn-dance affair complete with a local band, the music primarily sakie-sakie, the Afrikaas version of Country & Western music. Casual attire was permitted. The young saw this as an opportunity to meet new faces and kindle new romances.

I left the farm early in the morning taking Joseph with me. He saw this outing as an annual highlight, knowing that I'd part with some spending money. He wore his best, a hand-me-down suit which I'd given him, a white shirt with tie, and a pair of shoes that he inherited from my father. My father had also given him a fedora. I had no doubt that when we finally returned, he'd again be near-paralytic drunk and staggering around like a floppy rag-doll.

Joseph was unable to leave any celebration without having consumed more than his fair share of liquor. Also, he was not concerned with taste or origin, as long as it packed the required punch. The only problem was when drunk he became over-familiar, as if we were parties to a conspiracy which we alone shared. I was now his best buddy, the master-servant relationship non-existent. Rest assured, when in this state it was best to keep a good distance from him. His breath and body odour enough to fell a rhinoceros. I'd made up my mind. When we were to leave in the evening, he could take a place on the back of the pickup. I wasn't sharing the cab with him.

I wore beige chino slacks over a pair of tan, calf-high boots, a checked shirt open at the throat, a wide tan belt, and a beige Stetson. Any other colour just showed up the dust, the ground in Asab a dirty chalk powder over hard rock.

At the fair, I bought a few karakul rams, which in time would introduce a softer curl and wave to the pelts I sold, this the latest vogue in the industry. I left the animals in the corral intending to load them in the evening.

The agricultural industry had a few stands displaying their latest wares. The windmill and pump manufacturers were represented as were the pharmaceutical industry with their assortment of medicines to combat sheep parasites and infections. Of course, the local agricultural cooperative was represented, they there to persuade farmers to sell their product through the co-op and make use of the advances the co-op made against payment of future production.

I was at a disadvantage in that I had not been in the district for long and only knew a few of the farmers and their families. However, I soon ran into the Froehlichs. When I first saw Heidi I had trouble dragging my eyes away. She was stunning and had dressed for the occasion, the jeans tight and revealing her curves, the blouse designed to reveal some midriff and a slight hint of cleavage. She now wore make-up, only a touch it seemed, but this was enough to transform her, accentuating her eyes, eyebrows and mouth. Her black hair glistened in the sun. She received covert glances from most men that passed and I saw that this was not lost on Hans. She enjoyed the attention she was getting. There was no doubt that most considered her the belle of the ball.

I saw Kotze with one of his daughters. We gave each other a nod in greeting. Since he had arrived at the house to return the car-jack, I had not seen him on the farm again.

Ehrenreich was there, this time appropriately dressed. I soon encountered Klaus-Peter Herbst, my neighbour on Kabias, and the pelt-buyer Steinmetz. The three of us took a table beneath an awning at one of Kraft's outdoor bars. We ordered large steins of draught beer, brought to us by high school girls dressed in Bavarian dirndls and red-flared skirts. We tipped them handsomely, this being an occasion for them to earn decent pocket money.

"Christ, Aschenborn, haven't you found yourself a woman yet?" Steinmetz asked.

Ehrenreich chuckled. "No, he spends his time looking for Kotze."

I didn't think the remark amusing.

Steinmetz looked at me and then laughed.

"Yeah, I heard about that, but I don't want to get involved. Kotze sells all his pelts to me. I can't afford to lose him as a client," the pelt-buyer said. "If he comes past I'd be obliged to ask him to sit with us, and don't you dudes get bloody rude, okay?"

Ehrenreich and I just looked at each other.

"The bastard. He's shooting in the competition this afternoon. I've also entered and I see so have you." He looked at me. "I'm going to show him what happens when you come up against an ex-German sniper," Ehrenreich said.

"Well, Peter, you're going to have to beat me first," I said.

"Who wants to take me on? I've ten pounds on myself," Ehrenreich interjected.

"Okay, ten pounds on Aschenborn," Steinmetz replied looking at me.

"I never bet on myself," I said.

*

I bumped into Heidi at the tombola, a German version of a lucky dip, where I bought a few tickets for the draw.

"What are doing here alone? Where's Hans?" I asked.

"He's upset. So. If you don't mind, I'll latch onto you. That should stop some of these lecherous men trying to make conversation."

"Well, I don't blame him. It's impossible not to look at you. You certainly look stunning today."

She smiled. "Thank you. Would you believe you said that. I actually wore this outfit to draw your attention," she said without any shame at all and laid a hand on my arm. I realised she was dead serious.

Her unbridled forwardness awakened a feeling of apprehension in me again. I'd had a few beers and probably was feeling a little more forward than usual myself.

"That it has," I conceded and then asked, "Where's your child?"

"I left him with a couple of nannies at the crèche the mothers have got going here. He's in capable hands," she replied, her hand still on my arm.

I was uncomfortable. I didn't want Hans to suddenly turn up. That could only open old wounds.

I've got to go," I said.

"I've got five pounds on you for the shooting competition," she said. "Your odds are at 8-1. That's because nobody knows you. Kotze's at 2-1.

286

Don't you let me down. If you win for me, I've something special for you," she said smiling. I thought the promise provocative.

"I'm looking forward to that," I said. Christ, what on earth made me say that? That was the last thing I should've of done. She raised her eyebrows and pursed her lips.

"Then make sure you win but, if you don't, I may just have a consolation prize," she replied.

I saw Hans approaching.

"Here comes Hans. I'm off."

He hadn't seen me yet. I made a discreet but quick withdrawal.

*

The small village boasted a shooting range, this merely a flat piece of ground with a large, ten-foot-high berm at one end with a deep trench dug before it. The target operators took cover in the trench and it was from there that they operated the moveable targets and radioed the results to the judges using walkie-talkies.

It was four o clock, the sun already beginning to cast shadows. Fortunately the shooters had the sun behind them.

The final was down to three of us: Kotze, Mr Daniel Visser, a farmer from up on the plateau to the east, and myself. I had chosen a 7x57mm Mauser hunting rifle from the gun-cabinet on the farm and had spent a morning lying behind a sandbag, prone on my stomach, sighting in the rifle. I'd bought Swedish ammunition, which was considered the best. It was expensive but I was not ready to trust the local stuff. The Swedish make was known to be consistent.

"Mr Matthias Aschenborn. Three hundred yards at a moving target," the loudhailer announced.

I stepped forward and lay down prone on the mat, the rifle cradled in my hands. A hush had descended on the crowd. I worked the bolt action slowly and slid a cartridge into the breech, and pulled the butt against my shoulder. I had also worked on the trigger. This now only required a slight touch to fire the rifle.

"Ready," the hailer blared.

This was followed three seconds later, "Now."

A cut-out board depicting a life-sized kudu bull about to leap over some imaginary obstacle emerged from behind a screen, this moving from right to left at the speed of a kudu in full flight.

287

"Lead, man. Lead the target," I whispered to myself, taking a bead in front of the cut-out just in front of the buck's nose and at a height in line with where a heart-shot was considered to be. I led the target for a few more yards and then squeezed the trigger. The recoil thumped me in the shoulder. A few seconds later a disk on a stick rose from the trench. I'd hit the small target. There was an exchange on the walkie-talkie and then the hailer announced, "Fourth ring on the target." This was followed by a cheer from the crowd.

I fired twice more, once missing the target entirely and the other in the fifth ring. Only the best shot out of the three would count.

I then had to do the same from a standing position, difficult at that range, but I put one shot in the target and that into the third ring. I thought I'd been lucky.

It was then Kotze's turn. He was using a Weatherby .275 Magnum. He had all three shots from a prone position in the target, but all these were in the outer ring, mine beating his. Imagine my surprise when he walked over and shook my hand.

"Well done," he said. "I'll have to be careful if I venture on your farm again," he said in Afrikaans and laughed.

I smiled. I couldn't help thinking he was trying to say that what was past was past and should be forgotten.

Well, Visser's shooting made the rest of us feel like amateurs. The man was incredible. All his shots were in the target, irrespective from what position he'd fired, with two of these in the inner circle. He did his shooting with a .222 Remington. I then heard that he had taken the trophy for last three years, the man a near-legend in the area.

After the shooting competition, my neighbours and I, joined by Steinmetz, took a table at the bar and settled down to some serious drinking, the beers followed by scotches and then brandy liqueur. Imagine our surprise when we were approached by Kotze, who asked to join us. Before Ehrenreich could even pass a remark, I gave him a hefty kick under the table.

"Certainly, sit down," I said.

At first, the atmosphere was infused with tension and silence but this soon lifted, Steinmetz forcing the conversation, no doubt so as not to offend his client. Even Ehrenreich mellowed, taking up conversation with the man.

Kotze rose from the table. "Got to go and have a piss."

Once he disappeared in the crowd, I turned to Ehrenreich. "So much for SS snipers. Christ, you even got beaten by the Luftwaffe," I said.

"Fuck you, Aschenborn. I just had a bad day, all right?" he mumbled, staring at his glass.

"It was the sunburn on his dick that was bothering him when he lay down on his stomach," Steinmetz said. We all broke out in loud laughter.

Even Ehrenreich had to smile. At that moment, Kotze returned to the table.

"What this all about?" he asked. Steinmetz told him.

Kotze looked at Ehrenreich and started laughing.

"That's nothing," he said, "let me tell you about his best performance. Once, this a while back during the week, I arrived unexpectedly at his place with my wife. Guess what, the bugger had no clothes on. My wife was dumbfounded. Sure, she'd heard about him but never believed the stories, and now she was seeing this for the first time, real-life stuff. God, you won't believe what she said." He then chuckled. "She was flabbergasted. God, can you imagine how embarrassed I was." Kotze then added, "You know what she had the audacity to say to me? If there'd been a competition I had no hope of winning."

We all roared with laughter, Ehrenreich giving the table a resounding thump with the palm of his hand, he pleased with the joke. It seemed he now saw Kotze in a new light and Steinmetz beamed because his client had been accepted in our circle again. Or so it all seemed.

Addressing Kotze for the first time by his Christian name, Ehrenreich said to him: "Hennie, at least your wife's observant, she knows what counts." This resulted in more laughter.

We were in jovial spirits and more drinks were ordered.

An enormous fire had been started, required to produce coals over which a large barbecue was planned. Music could be heard coming through the large, wide-open double doors of the community hall. We could see the first couples on the dance floor.

The four of us were slightly drunk by then. We rose from the table. The three married men were off to find their wives while I ambled over to the community hall where I propped myself up against the bar and ordered another scotch. There were quite a few men strung out along the bar conversing loudly, a good few already well inebriated. I was one of them.

A while later, I saw the Froehlichs on the dance floor, I could see that for Hans dancing held not pleasurebut torment, his gammy leg a hindrance. In my sloshed state, I had to give Heidi a wink, which she returned over Hans's shoulder, accompanied by a flash of teeth as she grinned at me.

About half-an-hour later while I was talking to another farmer's wife at the bar, Heidi arrived and squeezed in between us. I saw that this annoyed the other woman who gave Heidi a dirty look and then sauntered away. She gave the departing woman a dismissive look.

"That was rude, Heidi. Where's Hans?" I asked.

She turned to me. "He's had a lot to drink. He wanted to go outside and get some air." She was standing right up next to me, her hip pressing against me. She already had a hand on my arm, which she now gave a slight squeeze.

"Come on, dance with me," she said.

"No, I don't want to piss Hans off again," I murmured in her ear.

She slid her hand in my trouser pocket laying her fingers on the top of my thigh. "Who cares?" she whispered."Jesus, Heidi," I exclaimed, acutely aware of her fingers which I hastily removed from my pocket. My arousal even in my half-drunk state had been immediate. I was terrified that Hans would arrive.

Leading the way, she pulled me to the dance floor.

Sakie-sakie is not the right music for slow dancers. It's a combination of guitar, drums, and concertina or accordion or piano, and has a rather vibrant tempo It needs time to grow on you if you're hearing it for the first time. I certainly hadn't yet assimilated to it but I could at least follow the tempo.

Soon we were gliding across the floor, one of the few couples who weren't pumping their outstretched arms up and down. The gyrations of some of the couples was comical, their bodies swaying in unison from side to side with every step, their clutched hands pumping up and down like an indecisive train signal. This was no nightclub shuffle, the steps were too long. She had her pelvis hard against me, our inner thighs literally rubbing together. I mean, she had to be aware of my arousal.

God, I thought, this woman had total power over me. I could've taken her right there and then given the right circumstances. She knew it.

"Where's Hans?" I asked.

"I told you, he's outside. Wait at the bar. I'm going outside, I'll check on him," she said, her eyes darting around the dance floor. The woman made me feel like a teenager trying to arrange a groping session in some dark corner.

I sidled through the couples towards the bar and slid in next to Steinmetz.

"Good God, man, what were you two doing on the floor? Old Froehlich will shoot you," the pelt-buyer said, sliding a scotch he'd ordered towards me, an amused look on his face. "Fuck, friend, you are a randy bastard, but so it seems is she. Hey, just be careful. You don't want to be seen as a sort of Don Juan around here," he added.

"That's bullshit," I said.

"Well, I don't know. You should have seen yourself as I'm sure a few others saw it too. You can be glad Hans didn't see you. Want some advice? If you must, take her outside," he whispered from the side of his mouth, but I hardly heard him above the noise.

Heidi returned and stood next to me. Steinmetz looked at her and then said, "I'm off to find my wife." He smiled and left.

"He knows," she said.

What was she implying? He knows? Did she mean that the man knew that we were hardly able to keep our hands off one another? I was so damn aroused I could hardly think straight. Or, did she mean he believes we were having an affair?

"Hans is fast asleep in our pickup. I think he's passed out. Follow me," she said, again taking me by my hand and leading me through the people towards the entrance. Fortunately, there was so many around none could have realised what was happening.

I had no idea where she was taking me, I just followed as if in a stupor. The next thing I knew we were inside the small cemetery of the village, which had a few large peppercorn trees interspersed between the tombs and around its perimeter. Most of the graves were covered by slabs of flat marble with a headstone.

She led me to between two burial plots under a tree and then pulled me towards her, put her arms around my neck, and covered my mouth with hers, her tongue probing mine and grinding her pelvis into my hardness. My last coherent thought before I gave myself over to this seduction was that Hans, in his present drunken state, wouldn't wake up soon and start looking for his wife.

I pulled away. "I can't do this, Heidi. Stop. You're married to Hans. This can only be bad for all of us," I exclaimed softly in protest, frightened that I could be overheard.

At first, she seemed to listen without attention, ignoring my protestations, trying to draw me towards her again.

"No," I again exclaimed and drew away, taking her hands off me and moving two steps backwards.

"But I'm going to divorce him," she said..

That came as a shock.

At first, I didn't know what to say. "Fine, that's your business, but I don't want to be mentioned as a respondent, okay? I don't deny that I've feelings for you but it's better that we not see each other. Don't come and visit me on the farm. I don't want anything to do with your divorce and I don't want to hurt a friend. Your husband is a good man," I said.

I heard a laugh behind me and froze. I recognized it. I turned slowly round and saw Hans Froehlich leaning on the fence smoking a cigarette.

"I heard it all. I was following her. You can have her, she's no more than a whore. I told you she'd done it before. Yes, she can have her divorce, but I'm keeping the child," he said, not disguising the malice in his voice.

He flicked his cigarette into the road behind him. "Come on, Heidi, let's go home. I'm not going to fight with you. It's over."

She hesitated at first and then followed him. There were no farewells, she never turned round as she slowly walked away towards their pickup. Hans's sudden appearance was not what I had expected. The full implication of what had just occurred hit me.

"Fuck," I said. This is awful, I thought. Thank God, nobody else saw this. I certainly didn't want to be mixed up in their domestic tiffs. I didn't quite believe Hans's remarks, implying that his wife was a hussy. It was probably just as I had thought. Hans had never been more than a means to an end. She never loved him and she just used him to get out of Germany. The child now seemed to have been an accident.

I didn't think I was up to driving to the farm in the dark in my state. Besides, Joseph was nowhere to be seen. I climbed into my Ford truck, leaned back with my head propped up in the corner of the cab, and fell asleep.

CHAPTER TWENTY-SEVEN

For three weeks, I never moved from the farm and tried not to let my thoughts dwell on Heidi. This was difficult at night. I heard from Joseph that Heidi had packed her things and left the farm, taking her child with her. He must have relented. I wondered what she'd do. Not once did I hear my name mentioned. Maybe I had not been blamed for the break-up. I hoped it would remain so.

At the end of the third week, I was forced to drive to Asab as the household was running out of essential supplies.

Although the new post office was being built, we still had to use the post office counter within the general dealer store. I approached the counter and saw that we had a new postmistress. I thought that this had to be the woman who'd also operate the new switchboard that would control the party lines.

I greeted her in Afrikaans and asked whether there was any mail for me. She handed me a stack of envelopes.

"Hello, Matthias," I heard.

I looked up from the envelopes, turned and saw Kraft Sr, the owner of the store, looking at me.

I returned the greeting.

"I take it you've heard about the Froehlichs?" he asked, the corners of his mouth turned down, his eyebrows raised.

I walked over and shook his hand. "Yes, I have, if rumour is anything to go by."

"It's true. She passed through here about a fortnight ago. I have something for you. She left letters for the neighbours, you know, thank you letters for the friendship and courtesy that all had extended her, the usual thing. I liked her. I didn't think Hans's comments about her were justified. There's one for you. Come to my office, let's have a cup of coffee."

A clerk brought the coffee on a tray, having to clear a space amongst all the papers on his desk to set it down. He slid open a drawer and extracted an envelope that he slid over the desk to me.

I took it and put it into my shirt pocket. I wasn't going to read it in his office.

"I'll read it later," I said. He looked at me for a few seconds, but I was unable to read his expression. I wondered whether he had an inkling of what had happened.

We finished our coffee while making small talk, he telling me that he proposed to expand the business. We discussed the Odendaal Commission's findings. The commission had been set up by the government to make a feasibility study as to whether the government should not buy us a few adjoining farms and create a reserve for the blacks in this area. It was said that this would be a few hundred thousand hectares in extent. It was rumoured that promulgation was soon to follow, which would then empower the government to expropriate the surrounding farms but with compensation to the previous landowners. It was to be called the Bersheba Reserve. He asked whether I would join the other farmers and resist the government in court.

"No," I said, shaking my head, "I've discussed this with my father. It's pointless, like farting against thunder. Anyway, the amount they're offering isn't all that bad. You'll all lose. This government isn't going to listen to us. Dammit man, they already consider us a fifth province of their South Africa."

He was disappointed, but I was not to be persuaded.

I bought the groceries and other items I needed and left.

As soon as I was a few miles from the village, I pulled over, opened the envelope, and read the letter.

'My dearest Matthias

When you read this, I will already be long gone. Hans was always good to me and never treated me badly. It was just that I never really loved him, although at one stage, I did believe I did. That was only for a short while and it was then when my son was conceived. We talked it over. He said he knew that I did not love him, but had always hoped that this would change.

I'll be divorced within six weeks – he said he won't contest the divorce action and even granted me custody of my son provided I give him access at all reasonable times. Of course, I agreed – he has always treated me well.

Surprisingly, he never made issue of our short interlude in the cemetery and does not appear to hold any grudges. I must tell you that he did say that he thought you an honourable man.'

Maybe he had seen me trying to resist her advances when we were in the cemetery. I had no idea how long he could have been standing at the fence watching us.

I continued reading:

'You probably are not aware but ever since the rains forced us to stay over that night in Rehoboth, I've had you constantly on my mind. Normally, I'm not a schemer but must confess that I've been ready to do anything to get together with you.

What Hans said was in a moment of anger. He did not mean it. I'm NOT a hussy!

I'm going to live in Windhoek and will find myself a job. I'll put my son into pre-school. Hans was kind enough to give me some money, enough to get started, and promised a monthly sum for our son's schooling.

When you next come to Windhoek, I would very much like to see you. You can drop me a note at Box 26, Windhoek. It belongs to a friend of mine.

I miss you.

Love

Heidi.'

It was near midday. It was hot in the pickup's cab but I didn't notice. I sat there with the windows open and the letter on my lap, staring, my mind in turmoil, realising that this woman was in love with me. Was I in love with her? I thought so, otherwise why did I have these feelings for her? I knew that if I pursued her this would start a scandal that would probably embarrass my family. A dalliance was one thing, but to be the cause of a divorce was another, and that was what all would believe. I returned the letter to its envelope and placed it in the cubby-hole. Right there and then I resolved not to go after her.

CHAPTER TWENTY-EIGHT

Six months passed and we were emerging from a bitter cold winter. In the semi-desert, the cold at night was intense. Often we experienced black frost, the pipes in the house occasionally freezing. Invariably by midday, the temperature would rise to near 20°C, but the moment the sun disappeared behind the horizon, the temperature would plummet, the cloudless sky rapidly allowing the accumulated heat to radiate from the ground.

I kept to myself, my visits to my neighbours few, barely sufficient as not to be seen to be bad mannered. Of course, I avoided visiting Froehlich. Actually, we avoided each other. This suited me. The same applied to my trips to Asab. I kept these to a minimum and I made no trips to Windhoek. My nights were lonely and every evening I sat in the lounge next to the radio, a kerosene heater next to me, and listened to a shortwave transmission of the eight o'clock news. After that, I would usually page through some magazine, aware of my loneliness and my thoughts without fail drifting towards Heidi. I would conjure thoughts of wanton passion with the woman until my whole being ached for her. At times, I wondered what kind of existence I was leading, but then I had spent years in the gulag which had accustomed me to coping with isolation of the heart and had taught me to suppress my emotions. I was able to cope with this better than most.

After about three months Hans Froehlich had unexpectedly arrived and thereafter his visits became frequent, often during the week and without forewarning. Mostly he was looking to borrow something. Our workshop on the farm was well equipped with tools and farming utensils. He avoided discussing Heidi other than once, in passing, mentioning that his son was well. The loneliness got to him and he once confessed that he was looking at getting himself a mail-order bride from Germany again. A few of the single farmers, those with German backgrounds, resorted to this in order to find themselves a life's partner. When he raised it, I didn't believe it a good subject to dwell on.

It was during the winter that the new post office was completed in Asab and the party lines to the farms erected. Initially, the new telephone rang constantly, the farmers talking to one another. Every time it rung, I was forced to listen carefully to the number and sequence of short and long rings to hear for whom the call was intended – two short and three long, that was for me. Fortunately, the novelty soon wore off and the ringing of the phone became less frequent.

Of course, my father was one of the first to phone me; he was not pleased because the open party line forced him to tone down the verbal barrage he clearly wished to release at me, but still he made it obvious that my absence from Windhoek displeased him immensely and that I should ensure that I visited soon. He ended the conversation emphasising that it was business that demanded my presence. I had to go.

A week later, I left for Windhoek. By now the cubbyhole in the pickup contained a number of letters from Heidi, all along the same vein, all with the dominant question of when was I planning to visit her. I had never written to her and the last letter from her had arrived six weeks ago.

My father was pleased to see me and if his true intention was to discuss business, he never raised it specifically. My brother George and his family were also staying at the family home in the Bismarckstraße while he and his wife looked for a house of their own. My father had brought him back to the city and had appointed him manager of the two engineering businesses the family there.

Imagine my surprise when one evening after dinner when we sat down in the sitting room with the women still in the kitchen, he suddenly turned to me and asked.

"What happened to Froehlich's wife?"

For a moment, I was stunned. He noticed this and before I could recollect my wits, he continued, "Yes, don't look surprised, I heard all about it. Apparently, she was rather keen on you. Whether this was reciprocal I don't know, but I'm asking."

Where on earth had he heard this? I was sure that it had to be either Steinmetz or Kraft who had told him. I made a mental note to confront them when I next saw them.

"Jesus Father, that's private," I retorted without thinking.

He walked over to the fold-down liquor cabinet, poured two of what I thought to be overly large cognacs, and handed me one.

"You may think so. I don't. Taking up with a married woman whose husband happens to be our neighbour makes it my business." He frowned, his look intense, showing his disapproval.

"That's crap. Nothing ever happened. Whatever you heard is exaggerated. We never touched each other. I respect Hans Froehlich. We're friends."

He chortled, "I'm glad to hear that, but then why the divorce and these rumours?"

"I don't know, maybe they didn't get on. As for the rumours well, you know what people are. Besides, I hear the divorce was amicable."

"So I hear." He paused and then added, "Do you know she lives near here? Actually, just four houses away. She's stays in a cottage on the Rüdiger property. She's got a job. she assists Reimann behind his dispensing counter at the Reimann's Apotheke."

I sipped my cognac and didn't respond, indicating that I did not wish to discuss the subject. This didn't deter my father, he pressed on.

"Well, aren't you going to visit her?" he asked.

"For fuck's sake, Father. Leave it alone!" Again he chortled softly. "My, listen to the man's language. I just wanted to let you know where she's to be found," he said.

My brother had now joined us and poured himself a single malt whiskey to which he added some ice.

"I'm bringing you back to town," my father then said to me.

I looked at my brother. He just gave me a slight nod. Don't get riled, it said

"Why's that?"

"I'm getting old and tired of running around the countryside, trying to manage our interests. I want George to stand by my side and you to assist him."

"What about Gelwater?"

"I've fixed a price with the government. They've accepted it. Everything is done. The deed of sale only needs to be signed. You'll appreciate that to try and hang onto it would be pointless. They'd eventually take it anyway," he said.

For a moment I felt we'd been cheated but then realised that my father was right. At least he had negotiated a price and he seemed to be satisfied with it.

"The animals and equipment?" I asked.

My brother took a cigar from the humidor and lit it. He sprawled in a lounge chair, his head back, and blew a cloud of smoke towards the ceiling, "I'm going to distribute Gelwater's livestock and it's other paraphernalia amongst our other farms," he said.

"What about the workforce?" I asked.

"Well, what about them? The usual two month's salary, that's all and then they're on their own. Easy, we just terminate the labourers' SWANLA contract," George said matter-of-factly.

"Good workers. I'll vouch for that. Rather callous, wouldn't you say?""Who cares."

"Fuck you, George," I said, taken aback by his response.

"Hey.! Both of you, shut up. If they're any good we'll take them to the other farms, okay?" my father responded with more fierceness than I expected.

George gave me a dirty look.

"I'm off to bed. Good night," I said. I didn't need my brother's company at that moment.

I lay on my bed reading and then decided I needed a glass of water before sleeping. As I descended the stairs, I heard raised voices. My father and my brother were in the throes of what seemed a serious argument. I could not help hearing my father belabouring the point that he was the father figure in the house and that all the farms and businesses were his, and that his say was final. It was evident that he was furious.

The moment I sat down to breakfast, I realised that my father was in a foul mood. His greeting was abrupt, an unintelligent mumble, and he did not look up.

It was normal for the three of us to breakfast together. George's wife was a late riser.

No word had passed between my father and me. We had nearly finished breakfast when I asked, "Where's George?"

My father threw down his napkin in clear disgust. "You won't believe it. Your brother has decided to leave the family, resign his position, and, as he put it, seek his fortunes in South Africa. I told him that if that's how he felt then he should do so," he said, but it was evident that he felt betrayed and was disappointed.

"It'll blow over," I said.

"No, it won't – tensions have been simmering for quite a while. You arriving and your remarks about the workers and my apparent support, as he put it, seemed to have been the final straw. Well, if that's his feeling, then so be it, my father retorted rising from the table, unhappy. He left the house for his office in town.

The moment my father's car disappeared down the road, George made his appearance and sat down at the table opposite me. Even Moses picked up the tension, his greeting to George subdued and without the usual banter between them.

"Brother, what the fuck's going on?" I asked.

"Listen Matt, don't you stick your nose in my bloody business."

"Hold it there. Christ, man, I'm only asking. Father said you're leaving the family. I mean that's bloody ridiculous." I could see that he was trying to keep a grip on his emotions. He was looking down at his cup as he slowly stirred the coffee. He then let out a long sigh.

"God, I'm just tired. Every day he lectures me on umpteen issues, what I've done wrong and how I should have done it. Then, what you said last night was the last straw. He berated me because of my shit attitude, as he put it, towards the blacks. I just snapped," he said quietly.

"What about me?"

He took a slurp of his coffee. "You set it off with your 'be good to the kaffirs' philosophy," he said.

"That's madness! After spending fuckin' five years in the gulag, I thought I'm pretty well qualified to stand up and say what I think when it comes to treating people. Your 'who cares?' statement is exactly how they treated us in case you weren't aware of it. For a German who remained supportive of the Jews, your attitude towards the blacks is despicable. Anyway, where the hell did that suddenly come from?""God, another kaffir-boetie. I'm sick and tired of hearing about what you had to go through in Russia," my brother said under his breath, rolling his eyes at the ceiling.

I jumped up and so did he.

I had my fists balled at my side as a near uncontrollable rage overcame me.

"You fuckin' inhumane bastard," I said through clenched teeth. My brother swung at me, his fist connecting with my temple and sending me sprawling. I fell against the round breakfast table, sending crockery and cutlery scattering with an enormous crash. I was dazed and hurt. I extracted myself from the mess and got to my feet, my body still hunched over, my brother standing six feet from me, a look of disdain on his face.

Moses burst into the breakfast room from the kitchen, his face greying at the spectacle before him and skidding to a halt, not knowing what to do. I also heard someone descending the stairs in a rush. This had to be Ruth, my sister-in-law.

I straightened in a flash and aimed a punch with my left at his jaw. He tried to avoid it but my fist connected and he went down on his knees, shaking his head. I heard my sister-in-law scream which snapped Moses into action and he stepped between us.

"Hör auf! Hör auf!" Moses shouted, *Stop it! Stop it!* keeping between us to ward us off from one another.

By then Ruth got to her husband and, stepping in front of George, she shouted his name trying to pin his arms at his side, in a panic. I stepped a few paces back, my chest heaving and the adrenalin pumping. I left the house in the pickup resolved not to return until he had left. Permanently. It was either him or me. I phoned my father from the Kaiserkrone Hotel and told him that I wouldn't return until George had left. My father attempted to persuade me to reconsider, but his heart was not in it. He'd heard from Moses what had occurred. I told him that I planned to stay the night in the hotel.

"That is so stupid," he said, disappointed at my attitude, but then cut the connection.

*

I was a long day. I didn't really have anywhere to go and besides, I was still overwhelmed by the morning's events.

I walked the entire length of the Kaiserstraße, Windhoek's main street, looking into the windows, admiring the new cars in the dealers' showrooms, the salesmen trying to persuade me to buy a car. I also browsed the bookshops and bought the odd item.

At around four that afternoon, I found myself walking past the Reimann's Apotheke. I stopped outside the shop window and looked at the display. The display had no backdrop and I could see past them right into the shop. In any event, to see what was inside was my intention. I saw Heidi. She was side-on to me in earnest conversation with a customer. She was dressed in a white starched uniform with white low-heeled, slip-on shoes. Her black hair was piled on top of her head. She was beautiful. I wanted to go in but thought I'd wait until she had finished with the customer.

The customer left and Heidi busied herself with some papers on the counter. I entered the pharmacy. There were two counters, the other minded by another attractive woman. The dispensary was behind Heidi and I could see Reimann, the pharmacist, amongst the shelves of medicines. Everything was white: walls, ceilings, shelves and racks, even Reimann's pharmacist's uniform was white.

She wished me good day before she'd lifted her eyes, but when she recognised me she broke into a beautiful smile. Her eyes told me all. I realised that she was happy to see me.

"Hello, Matthias," she whispered.

I didn't know whether I should shake hands with her or not and just stood there, my expression surely one of indecision, and feeling rather foolish.

Hello," I said and then added, "My God, you're beautiful."

She giggled. "Thank you, it's nice of you to say so," she replied.

I looked up and saw Reimann behind her looking at us with a frown.

"I see you close at five. I'll be back right after you close."

She nodded and I walked out of the shop.

I crossed the road to the Hansa Hotel on the opposite side of the road and ordered a draught beer at the bar, which I drank slowly to kill time. I kept one eye on the pharmacy. At five, I left the bar and returned to the pharmacy. A few minutes later Heidi emerged. She pecked me on the cheek and looped her arm into my own.

"God, it took you long enough to look me up," she commented, "but I'm not complaining, I'm just happy to see you."

"I'm sorry, but—"

She interrupted me. "Don't say it. I think I understand."

"Where's your car?"

"I usually walk. I need the exercise."

"Well, mine's way down the road. I've been window-shopping. Walk down with me and I'll take you home, unless of course you want to go for a drink?""I'd love to but I can't. I've a sitter looking after my child. She's waiting to go home."

We arrived at her cottage and I insisted on parking in the driveway, not wanting my pickup to be seen from my father's house but not telling her.

"Your father lives just a few houses from here?" she remarked as I brought the truck to a stop.

"That's right."

"Well, come inside," she said, leading the way.

The cottage was small but pleasant. We entered through the kitchen. The kitchen was small: a Formica table with three chairs surrounded by a stove, a refrigerator, sink and cupboards. A washing machine hid under a counter and a window above the sink gave the room light. A black woman in traditional Herero costume, her attire a throwback to how women colonists dressed at the turn of the century in tight bodice dresses with high necklines and long flared skirts, warmly greeted Heidi. Heidi's son sat on the floor with a few toys scattered around him, but on seeing her mother she rose and ran to her, grabbing her hand and then looking at me with large eyes.

The black woman had already collected her personal things and, with a goodbye, left.

From the refrigerator Heidi took a bottle of cold beer and a half bottle of wine. She handed me the beer with a glass and then led me through to a small lounge, indicating that I should take a seat on the settee.

She poured wine into a glass and took a sip.

"If you don't mind, I just need to get out of this uniform. It's not the most comfortable dress," she said and disappeared into an adjoining room, leaving the door slightly ajar. I poured the beer from the bottle into the glass. Already the bottle was frosted with beads of condensation, the beer being ice cold.

"I presume you'll be staying for supper?" she asked loudly from the bedroom.

Well I—"

She interrupted me. "You can't say no. We haven't seen each other for ages. We can't go out, I don't have a babysitter."

"Oh, all right, that's fine," I replied. I did not want to see George again and Heidi's offer was actually a blessing in disguise.

Heidi emerged from the bedroom, her son following her, still not quite sure of this intruder, his eyes following my every movement.

She had changed into a light cotton dress. Gone were the stockings. Her legs were now bare and her feet shod in open-toed sandals. She'd undone her hair and this now cascaded down one side of her face. She had brushed it. It shimmered in the sunlight that filtered through the net curtains. She let herself drop onto the sofa and then squeezed into a corner with her legs neatly tucked under, she facing me. Her son sat down on the floor next to her. I let my eyes glide over her and took in every detail. She returned my look, the slight, sagacious smile on her lips indicating that she controlled the situation. A shiver passed through me as part of me reacted to the signals of expectancy that seemed to materialise.

I cleared my throat and reached for my glass on the coffee table.

"My, my," she said, "you haven't changed. You've still got that young boy's demeanour when it comes to matters of the heart, or should I rather say, arousal."

I recalled how embarrassingly direct this woman could be.

Arousal? God, I thought that was probably a very apt description of my current state of mind. I'm sure I must have had a look of bewilderment on my face.

She slid across the sofa and kissed me briefly on the lips. "I have to prepare supper now," she said. "You can join me in the kitchen. Bring your glass."

She made me sit down at the kitchen table.

"I've one large steak, a rump steak, which we can share with a salad and a bread roll. How does that sound?""Perfect," I replied.

While the griddle heated up on the stove, she soon had chopped tomatoes, cucumber, onions, peppers, and lettuce in a large glass bowl to which she added a salad dressing and black olives. The salad was ready. Soon the steak sizzled in the pan, smoke rising from it. The backdoor was opened, the draught sucking the smoke out of the kitchen.

The three of us ate in the kitchen at the small table, her knee touching mine, neither of us trying to move away. The steak was delicious, as was the salad. This I washed down with another bottle of beer.

After supper and still at the table, I smoked a cigarette while Heidi busied herself with her son in the bathroom. The sun had sunk below the horizon, the short-lived tropical twilight upon us. In half-an-hour, it would be dark. Already the streetlights were illuminated.

305

I realised that my father would be waiting for me to join him for supper. I had seen the Bakelite phone in the lounge. I shouted down the passage and asked whether I could use the phone. She said it was okay. I dialled the house. My father answered.

"Father, I won't be home for supper," I said.

"Well, if you're trying to avoid your brother, he's not here."

"I'm not trying to avoid him," I lied. I didn't want to see him.

"When will you be home?"

"I don't know."

He harrumphed. He was not happy. He'd have the huge house to himself, something he detested. "Okay, bye." He put the phone down. I heard the click and then the dialling tone.

Heidi returned to the kitchen, her son in tow.

The child seemed disappointed. "Bath too quick," the young boy said.

Heidi blushed. "I usually let him play in the water for a while. I didn't this time. He's not happy," she said with a rueful smile. I knew she'd rushed the task for my benefit.

The sun had set. The room darkened. She switched on two shaded table lamps that cast a soft warm glow and then took her son off to bed, returning in a while.

"The young woman sleeps at last," she said smiling and sat down on the sofa but now next to me.

She was a woman without restraint. She leaned across and briefly kissed me on the lips again. I caught the faint taste of wine. She laid her head on my chest, her body against mine.

"God, you've have no idea how I've missed you. Yet somehow, I just knew that you'd eventually turn up. Now, how's that for intuition?" she asked, snuggling even closer to me. I now had my arms around her and stroked her hair. I was now aroused.

"Don't keep me in suspense too long," she stammered so quietly I hardly could hear her. "I know that we've both been aching for the touch of each other since the jamboree at Asab. You cannot imagine the scenes I've visualised at night while lying in my bed just thinking about you." She took my hand and placed it on her breast.

Again we kissed, her tongue caressing mine. I felt her hand nestle in my groin, it pressing against my arousal. I desperately wanted this woman. I turned and drew her hard against me. I felt the tempo of her breathing quicken as her own arousal began to manifest itself. I slid the shoulders of her dress off her body, which now gathered around her waist revealing her breasts still cupped in her brassière, the smooth roundness seeming to demand release from their confinement. With one hand, she reached behind her and unclasped the brassière and let it slide down her arms. The now aroused nipples pointed slightly upwards. My hand found her breast and I let my fingers slide over its silky smoothness. I lowered my head and kissed her neck, my lips then sliding over her breasts and down her belly. She drew in her breath and shivered.

I felt her hand on my outer thighs. Then it slid round towards my crotch, she rubbing my erection with her fingers.

Our mouths came together again, kissing passionately, her hand not letting go of me, she firmly holding onto to me. I pulled her skirt up until my hands rested on her buttocks, the thin silk of her panties under my fingers. A feeling of heightened intensity manifested itself, the eroticism of the moment taking hold. I slid my hand over her pubes, she again giving jerk as I gently probed her with my fingers.

"Oh my God," she hissed in my ear. "I'm sure Klaus is already asleep. Let's go to the bedroom," she whispered *sotto voce*.

I swept her up in my arms and carried her towards the bedroom, where I lay her down on the bed, her arms still clinging to my neck.

She kicked off her shoes while I unzipped the rear of her dress and stripped this off her; she was now only clad in her panties, these so sheer, I able to see the dark shadow of her sex triangle. I pulled my clothes off dropping them where I stood and then slid onto the bed to lie on top of her, propped up on my arms. I removed her panties and slid my hand up her thigh until I touched her wetness. She gave a low growl that seemed to reach into my soul.

"Oh, Jesus," I whispered.

This woman enkindled my most hidden emotions. It was as if every previous inhibited emotion, including those that I'd so successfully kept concealed during the war and the years in the gulags, and my last year, had been set free.

In anticipation, she raised her pelvis as I entered her. Our coupling was hard and fierce and it seemed that it was only a moment when she uttered a subdued shriek, both of us succumbing to orgasmic bliss.

Later, as we lay in each other's arms, she said: "You probably never knew it, but ever since I first laid eyes on you, this emaciated man, pale, gaunt and with that somewhat fearful and mournful look in your eyes, I was drawn to you. All your emotions and trials were written on your face. You seemed fearful of all, not that you were afraid, but rather that you trusted none."

"I'm sure it couldn't have been that obvious," I replied, brushing my lips over hers.

"It was. I remember watching you slowly emerge from I knew not what, as the months passed. Whatever it was, I was sure it was your own little hell. I watched your confidence return. I watched as you gained weight, not fat but muscle. I saw the change in your features as they took on an appearance of inner strength, and your body fill out and you gradually turning a caramel brown in the sun. The wives in the community started to talk about you. Of course, over and above that, the Aschenborns had money, they would say."

I chuckled. "Me? A topic of conversation amongst those wives? Never!" I blurted in mock disbelief.

"It's true. I fell in love with you," she said.

"I love you too," I said.

*

Heidi had to get to work. The baby sitter arrived just after seven-thirty. I drove her to the pharmacy and then drove home.

When I walked onto the enclosed porch, my father was already seated at the breakfast table. He gave me a perfunctory greeting. Clearly he was unhappy. I slid onto my chair and Moses arrived with a cup of coffee. I looked at my father's plate.–He was having a Continental breakfast.

"Moses, I'll have the same."

"I've a nice piece of rump?" he said.

"Okay, I'll take that as well."

He smiled, pleased.

"I see you slept out. Was she nice?" he jokingly enquired without looking up.

"If you must know, I met up with Heidi Froehlich," I volunteered.

I had caught him by surprise but he again assumed his somewhat nonchalant attitude.

"How is she?" he asked.

"Well, very well in fact. She's divorced now," I replied.

"Are you and she are now an item?"

"Christ, Dad," I said. I hardly ever called him 'Dad' although I know he liked it.

"What's so strange about that. You've only just come from her, or so I must assume. It goes without saying that you must've ... how do I put it ... well, you know, I suppose. Have we a serious relationship in the making here?" he retorted, smiling as if he had just come to a brilliant deduction.

"Jesus. That's rich coming from a father," I exclaimed and threw my napkin onto the table sliding my chair back.

He reached out a hand and grabbed me by the arm. "Sit. Don't be such an asshole. I'm merely pulling your leg and, besides, if you must know, I think she'd be good for you. Furthermore, I don't like it that you don't have a woman in your life. Well,I think it's unhealthy. So, stay and eat your bloody breakfast and talk to me."

We sat in silence for a while.

The silence was too heavy. I had to say something.

"Have you heard from George?" I asked.

"Yes, I was still going to talk you about that. It would seem that he's having second thoughts about deserting the country and us. I'm sure Ruth has had a lot to do with it. She's let him have it with both barrels. That's a strong woman, you know. She brooks no nonsense from him," he chuckled. "Your brother is scared of her. Well, maybe not scared, but he certainly harbours a deep respect," he said and then added, "Probably one of the few good things he did, marrying her."

He'd finished his breakfast and Moses brought him a last cup of coffee which he drank while smoking a cigarette.

"Well, I'm going to avoid him," I said.

"Don't be bloody ridiculous. He regrets every damn word he said and now don't you go and be stupid and hold it against him. I can remember you losing your temper and besides, I must admit, I've been riding him. Listen, Matthias, he'll never admit it but he needs you. Go and talk to him sometime today."

I didn't think I'd do that but did not want to say that to my father. I did not reply and left his suggestion hanging in the air.

As he prepared to leave for the office, he made a point of again reminding me to speak to my brother. I realised that he was concerned. He didn't think the latest run-in with my brother was to be ignored.

*

I waited an hour before I phoned him at the Aschenborn Engineering Works. The receptionist put me through.

"Morning, it's me," I said.

"Yes, what do you want?" he replied without a greeting.

"Look George, I think things got badly out of hand yesterday. May be we should talk?" He harrumphed and then said, "Maybe."

"Let's meet for lunch. How about the Kaiserkrone Hotel at one?"

He agreed.

I got to the hotel a few minutes before the appointment and asked the maître d' to give me a secluded table for two. I didn't want anybody overhearing us if we got into an argument again. George could be quite volatile at times, but I couldn't see my brother taking a swing at me in public.

Promptly at one, he entered the dining room dressed in slacks, white shirt, and tie. He saw me and walked over. He didn't greet me. He just sat down, signalled to the waiter, and ordered a draught beer.

"George, I'm glad you came."

"Well, okay, what's it you want?"

"Don't be so bloody aggressive. I think you took my remarks out of context the night before last."

"May be I did, but between my father and now you, I just don't think it worth it. First off, I'm a qualified mechanical engineer but he pays me a salary you'd pay a bloody boilermaker. He doesn't even have a clue as to how much pressure I take daily in this. And finally, he never says thank you."

I could see he was getting annoyed again.

"Easy George, I know what Dad's like. But what I'm primarily here for is to make peace. I don't think you and I should get at each other. Besides what my personal ideology concerning the locals is, shouldn't be an issue. I—"

George raised his hand interrupting me. "It's not an issue, our father's the damn issue. He needs to get off my back," he said.

"Let me make a suggestion," I said. "Let us both confront him, please, on an amicable basis. No bloody shouting. We tell him that he's not paying us enough and tell him that this is a bone of serious contention, both of us agreeing on this. I'll live in the house with him, but he must ensure that your income is sufficient for you to buy a decent house and he must appreciate that you're married and you and Ruth want a home that's entirely your own."

"So far so good," he said.

The waiter brought the Telleressen we'd ordered. This was a plate heaped with boiled potatoes, red cabbage, and an enormous schnitzel. We also asked for draught refills. We both started eating.

"As I said, we'll talk to father and I'll make it quite clear that I'll work for you and not question your judgement as to how it relates to the business, and I'll basically do what's expected of me provided it's within reason," I said.

"Where would you live?""In the family house, of course. Where else? I tell you what, we'll press him for a week's special leave so that you can find a new accommodation. I hear you're staying in a hotel. The sooner you get your family out of there the better. But still I would, for the time being, keep away from the house," I said to him.

"I agree. When do we do this?" he asked, pushing his half-finished plate aside and lighting a cigarette.

"Let's do it after two this afternoon."

He smiled for the first time and held is hand out, "Sorry that I lost it, but I agree, let's fix it. I've got to go but I'll see you at father's office at two-thirty.

*

The seat of our father's business was situated in a four-storey building situated on the corner of a side street and the main city thoroughfare. The executive offices took up the top floor. I stepped out of the lift into the reception area. My father considered this a place of work and had never thought opulence a necessity. Everything was functional, the carpeting durable and in a drab colour designed not to show dirt. There was a three-place sofa and two easy chairs for guests. A receptionist sat behind a counter. A passageway, accessed through two glass-panelled doors, led to the offices which were situated at intervals along the passageway. My father's office was the last on the end. It was twice the size of the other offices and Venetian blinds covered all the windows. His desk took up a corner, the rest of the room being dominated by a large conference table with eight chairs. There was an aperture in the wall permitting him to converse with his secretary in the adjoining office through a sliding glass panel.

His secretary was not at her desk. Without having myself announced, I stepped into the office. My father looked up from his papers and gave me a welcoming smile.

"George is behind me. He'll be here in a few minutes," I said, sitting down in one of the chairs facing him. I added, "We're talking to each other again."

He didn't comment but pursed his lips and frowned. Just then, George walked into the office and took a seat.

"Good afternoon, son. I take it you've had a good day?" my father said brightly. Did I detect a hint of sarcasm? In a situation like this, my father was inclined to resort to this tactic if for no other reason but to indicate that he was above the dissensions of his minions.

My brother detected it. "Good afternoon. No need to be supercilious."

Me ... supercilious? Never!"

My brother just sniffed, stretched out his legs, and lit a cigarette.

"Dad," I said wanting to start the discussion before he passed another of his imperious remarks, "George and I had lunch and discussed a number of items, particularly those that we think need to be addressed."

"And what may they be?" my father asked, arching his eyebrows. What I had thought at lunch was a good idea did not seem to have that attraction any more. His demeanour was indicative of what I'd seen before, he could be downright difficult at time and the consequences be damned, a dangerous situation for the recipients.

"Look, Father, we've all got to work together. George is married and can't live with us in the house. He needs to get his own house but, on his salary, that's rather difficult. He has to be able to meet the mortgage payments. He needs an increase and now that I'm living in the city, so do I," I said, hoping that this was with strong conviction.

"What do you guys want? Life handed to you on a plate?" I looked at George. He rolled his eyes.

"Don't you fuckin' rolls your eyes at me," my father said, raising his voice.

Christ, I thought. It was already getting out of hand.

I kicked my brother's foot.

"Sorry," George said quietly.

"God, what a bunch of whippersnappers." My father sat upright in his chair. "Okay, here's what I'll do. George, find a house, not a bloody castle. Whatever the payments, plus, plus, plus that relate to the electricity and upkeep, I'll give to you in the form of an increase. I have to admit, you have done a fair job, but don't think I'm entirely satisfied," he said. The bastard, I thought. Stab your son and then give the knife a twist.

"He needs more than that," I interjected.

He looked crossly at me for interfering. "Let me be the judge of that. As for you, whom I need to remind is still a bachelor, I'll add another third of your current salary to it. That should more than compensate for your move to the city, or should I rather say, to the fleshpots. You live in our house, eat there, drink my liquor and use any vehicle of your choice. What do the English say, you're on a good wicket. Don't knock it."

"That's sounds fair. George, what do you think?"

"It is. But, Dad, what about cars? I need a car for Ruth."

My father didn't hesitate.

"Give your car to Ruth and buy a pickup through the company."

"Thanks."

My father rose and extended his hand. I could see that he thought he'd still won the round. He shook our hands.

"Oh, by the way. No more fistfights. I'll throw you both out. Okay?"

George and I left and when we got out of earshot, we both broke down with laughter.

"God, is he arrogant," my brother said.

I had to agree. This had to have been my father's attitude at his magnanimous best.

"But you'll agree, we got more than we expected," I laughed. I was pleased with what we'd achieved.

"I wouldn't be so happy. You might just turn out to be the new whipping boy."

I harrumphed. "Not bloody likely."

CHAPTER TWENTY-NINE

A degree of normality returned to the Aschenborn household. George's wife Ruth was overjoyed at the news and spent her days house-hunting and driving us to distraction with her endless descriptions of the houses she had seen and their features, be they good or bad.

George and his family were back in the house, dinner a family affair again. Probably Moses most appreciated this turn for the better. He seemed to suffer the most whenever conflict broke out in the house. My father once mentioned that whenever he and my mother had a serious run-in, poor Moses would develop some mysterious ailment which would inexplicably confine him to his room in the servants' quarters for the duration of the no-speaks period between them.

Fortunately, the house was built in such a manner that my brother and his wife had two bedrooms and their own bathroom on the one side of the top floor to themselves. My father had his own bathroom en suite and I used the general bathroom that led off from the passage. The house was of typical German design with large, high-ceilinged rooms and concrete floors which my father had tiled some years before. Prior to that, they were polished concrete.

Heidi was a strong woman with what I can only describe as a ravenous sexual appetite. She seemed to delight in removing her clothing and taunting me, not that it took much to pry a reaction out of me. I would respond to the occasion with a degree of alacrity that even alarmed me at times.

One morning at breakfast when I had arrived home a little earlier to merely shower and change clothes, my father and I the only ones sharing the breakfast table, he blurted, "Matthias, for God's sake, you've got to do something about these nightly escapades of yours. Not that I care, but our neighbouring gentry has deemed it appropriate to make some comment."

My father said jokingly, "I ran into Hans Wirtz yesterday who mentioned that he had seen you on a number of occasions exit the Rudigers' and walk the short distance to here. He immediately followed this statement with a question querying whether it was true that Mrs Heidi Froehlich was renting a cottage from them."

"Inquisitive bastard," I laughed.

"It's not funny, you know how these people love a scandal, and dirt involving the Aschenborns is not what I'd like to hear. I suggest you discuss this with your ... whatever ..." he seemed at loss for words for a second "... and make sure you go about your business more discreetly. Need I say more?"

"Your friend Wirtz spends his day watching the bloody street," I said crossly.

"Well, he's old. He hasn't got much else to do," my father said.

My brother walked in. "I heard that. I was on the back porch. Can I say something?" he asked.

"Sure," I said.

"We've got our own cottage on our property. It's nicer than the Rudiger's. It only needs dolling up. Why don't you do it and offer it to her?" he asked smiling, and looking around to make sure there were no others who could overhear him, added, "You can then have your poontang on your doorstep at your beck and call."

An appalled look crossed my father's face.

"Don't be so crude. I don't have to listen to this. But if you want to give, hire out, or whatever the cottage, you're free to do so." my father said, getting up from the table. "And you, George, can least of all afford to make such comments. If Ruth only knew."

Our father disappeared, leaving us alone. I thought it a hasty retreat, not waiting to find out what could happen next. My father's words at the breakfast table had left us in no doubt that the subject was not to be broached again.

"Christ, you're such an asshole. Poontang. Fuck you, George," I snarled.

So typical of my brother, he thought this hilarious. We both rose to leave for work.

I visited Heidi that evening and during dinner put my father's proposal to her. I gave no hint that this had originated from my brother and father.

"No, why would I want to move from here?" she asked. I could see that my proposal surprised her. "The rent is fair and I can afford it. Besides, I'm happy here," she said.

I realised that this was getting delicate.

"Well, it would be easier for us to be together and we wouldn't be a topic of conversation," I said.

She seemed surprised at my response. "Are you insinuating that we are a topic?"

Careful, I thought to myself, don't say the wrong thing.

"I'm sure a number of people are wondering what's going on," I replied.

"What you're saying is that they know that you spend your nights with me, isn't it? Is that so bad? Quite frankly, I don't give a damn what they think."

This wasn't going as I would have it. I could see that she was taking affront.

"Look Heidi, this is the Bismarckstraße. An address here still indicates some social standing. Every damn house is occupied by an ex-German colonialist family who has attained a degree of success in business. God, they could not be more straight-laced. I've heard a couple of remarks. I have to confess, we are already a topic of conversation," I said with an obvious degree of exasperation.

"So, that's why the suggestion. You want to keep out of the public's eye but still you want to bed me, isn't it? It would be more convenient if I lived in a cottage in the Aschenborn's property." she hesitated for a second, "How should I put it? That's it, a kept woman," she said quietly and then picked up a sofa cushion and hugged it to her chest. She was upset.

I felt my cheeks flare red and I opened my mouth to reply, still not quite sure what I was about to say. Before I could speak, she continued.

"Don't bother. You just want everything a marriage has to offer but without the marriage," she muttered.

"That's not true," I said.

"Then why not marry me? You've said you love me, but no, you want to treat me like a concubine."

Oh, she was right. I'd told her often enough, usually during or immediately after one of our euphoric sexual encounters, realising that it was probably the only times I may have said that. Christ. It dawned on me that I'd probably said it while in an expansive mood brought on out of self-gratification. I had that distinct feeling that I was on the spot.

"I'm not ready to marry anybody," I managed to say.

"That's bullshit. Your problem is that you'll never be ready."

"Not true."

"Do you love me?"

I knew I did. "Yes.""Then marry me," she said, fighting back the tears that threatened.

I held her look, my eyes never leaving hers. I realised it was decision time, this wasn't going to go away. Yes, I did love her. Then why not?

"Will you marry me?" I asked, almost choking on my words and then forced to clear my throat.

"Yes!" she shrieked, her expression jubilant. She rushed into my arms.

All this had a profound effect on me. It was as if something that had niggled at my conscious had disappeared. It was as if I'd been set free again. I know that many other men may have thought otherwise. It was not so in my case.

"Come on, let's walk across to my father," I said, pulling her towards the door.

"I can't go like this," she said.

"Of course you can. We'll only be away for ten minutes. Klaus won't even know we've gone."

We entered the house through the back door and, pulling her by the hand, I led her to the lounge to where my father sat with a brandy snifter in hand, his glasses perched on his nose, studying the weekly newspaper that had been delivered that day.

He lifted his eyes at the click of her heels on the tiles.

"Mrs Froehlich," he said. "What a surprise." He rose from the chair, taking her right hand, as the other was still held by me. This was not lost on him and I saw him surreptitiously look at me, a question on his face.

She smiled. "Herr Aschenborn, it's good to see you again. This is rather embarrassing. I'd rather you called me Heidi as opposed to Mrs Froehlich." She turned to look at me. "Matthias, I believe you need to tell Mr Aschenborn why."

"We're getting married," I said.

My father's face broke into a large smile and, so unlike him, he grabbed me by the shoulders and hugged me patting me on the back. "Thank God," he said. He then released me, took Heidi in his arms and kissed her once on each cheek. "Heidi, I'm so happy, especially because it's you."

Heidi couldn't restrain her feelings. She blushed and then tears of happiness rolled down her cheeks.

For a few minutes, there was no stopping her as she smiled and sniffled. We sat on the sofa next to each other, holding hands, my father opposite us. We had to leave, Heidi not wanting to leave her son asleep in the house alone for too long. My brother and his wife were out, but my father said he'd tell them the moment they got home.

CHAPTER THIRTY

Heidi and I were married within the month. We didn't believe that a grandiose wedding was the way to go. She was recently divorced so we settled for a civil wedding and held the reception at the house. Only the closest of friends and our senior employees with long service were invited.

Meanwhile, it was decided that we'd stay in the Bismarckstraße in my father's house, the cottage now renovated and waiting for us to take occupation. We tried to keep the wedding low-key but somehow it leaked out, a reporter taking station outside the magistrate's court where we were actually married and he then following us to the house.

On our return from our weekend-long honeymoon, I found that the issue of the *Allgemeine Zeitung* that followed the wedding contained an article with two photographs splashed on the second page. It contained a brief description of the proceedings and also mentioned my war record and the fact that I'd spent time as a POW in Russian captivity. I could've done without the publicity especially because I was marrying a recently divorced woman and many would believe I had been the cause of the alienation of her affections for her previous husband, Hans Froehlich, whose name, to my chagrin, was also mentioned in the article.

Months before and soon after my return from Germany I had applied to the Director of Civil Aviation in Pretoria for a pilot's licence. From the house on Niemannsweg in Kiel, my old flight logbooks were produced as well as most of those from the period during the war, these indicating the types of aircraft and the hours I had flown. So were my original German licences acquired at Husum produced. The authorities accepted these records, and after undergoing a medical examination by a recognised Flight Surgeon in Windhoek and undergoing a flight test in a twin Piper Comanche, I was issued with a Private Pilot's Licence as well a Radio Communications Licence. According to the licence, I was allowed to fly both single and multi-engine aircraft with a weight not to exceed 10,000 pounds.

Heidi and I secretly discussed where we proposed to spend our proper honeymoon. The weekend away we'd spent at the coast was not really a honeymoon, we having taken her son with. We did not intend to let anyone know where we intended on going. What we both agreed was that we wanted to be far from civilization, somewhere remote would be ideal. Between us, we decided that we'd hire an aircraft and fly to some place inaccessible, except by air. We'd load the aircraft with everything we needed: tent, sleeping bags, food and drink.

Finding a suitable aircraft in South West Africa proved to be rather difficult but eventually I was able to hire a De Havilland Beaver, a high-wing tail-dragger fitted with a 450hp radial engine and capable of carrying six passengers with a spectacularly short take-off and landing performance. The hire rate was exorbitant but my father insisted that I hire the aircraft. After all, he said, it was only for ten days. George and Ruth also volunteered to take care of Klaus in our absence. I was pleased to see that the two women had soon established a rapport and it was obvious that here was a close friendship in the making. At least the two children could play together.

The neighbouring territory to the east was Bechuanaland, a protectorate governed by the British Crown. The population of the vast country totalled fewer than a million. The Kalahari Desert took up most of the country. It was only in the north that water was abundant, particularly in the Okavango Delta, a vast swampland created by the Okavango River which flowed out of the Angolan highlands and meandered southeast into the centre of the country. It never made it to the sea, it just disappeared into an enormous wetland of two thousand or more square miles situated in the middle of the Kalahari Desert. The country possessed little or no industrialisation or commercial farming.

The Kalahari was a dangerous place, a place of wild animals: lions, leopards, elephant, rhinoceros, deadly snakes and buck of every description. The locals lived off the land, the Bushmen hunting as they had done for thousands of years with bow and poison arrows, nomads of the desert. The country was said to be a poachers' paradise. The British tried to control the illegal hunting, specifically of elephant, but this was difficult in a country with very few roads and mere tracks through deep sand, the police relying on camels to move from place to place. Illegal hunters were seldom caught. Some had disappeared, victims of a harsh and unforgiving land, never to be seen again. However, the British South Africa Police, BSAP, did own a few Piper Super Cubs and a good pilot was capable of landing them anywhere, provided the area was clear of bush and scrub. They were used to keep a general eye over the country and to periodically check on the various police outposts.

For the white poachers, the conditions were just as tough as those encountered by the police. They remained a near-insuperable deterrent. It took guts and determination to live in this land. The advent of the aircraft created better mobility, but a lack of cleared airstrips and the restricted loading capacity of aircraft did not really help the poacher. Nonetheless, some still believed poaching to be a means to rapid wealth.

*

A few weeks after our short stay at the cottage saw us at first light on our way to the airfield. The sun had yet to peek over the horizon when we were already airborne, the rear section of the aircraft loaded with our camping equipment.We brought a large nylon tent, gas cooker, folding table and chairs and everything else we thought we would need.

In the sub-zero temperature of the early winter's morning, we climbed to 8,500 feet and cleared the Aus Mountains, flying west towards the border with Bechuanaland. From a friend of my father, I obtained the coordinates, these only an approximation, of an airstrip on the edge of the swampland. This was said to be near a large, deep pool of drinkable water and that some enterprising visitor had actually erected a thatched open hut, a large lapa as it were.

Once we cleared the mountains, I descended to about five hundred feet, the Beaver skimming the terrain below. It is only then that I become aware of the remoteness of this land. It is flat from horizon to horizon with only the parallel ripples of the dune ridges interrupting its plains. There are no rivers, no roads, and no settlements. It is bleak and desolate, flat savannah interspersed with bush and thorn trees.

Heidi stared out of the side of the aircraft at the ground that passed below.

"This looks like one of the best places for a honeymoon," I said.

She turned to me and smiled, "That it is, but then we don't have to share this with anybody. It's truly ours alone. That's the way I would've wanted it. Just you and me for a while."

The cold morning air was so quiet the aircraft flew itself, only requiring minute corrections from time to time.

321

"Listen, sweetheart, I don't want to repeat myself, but this is no paradise down there, although it may look like it from up here, we will have to watch ourselves, what with lions, hippo and crocodiles. We have to be careful where we swim. No walking from camp on your own and always have your rifle near you," I said.

"I'll remember."

"Good."

I'd taken two rifles from the house: an 11.7mm Mauser and an 8 x 60 Steyr with telescopic sights. I'd also brought a 12-bore shotgun for birds. I had no permission to take these into Botswana but even if we ran into the police, they probably wouldn't even ask. No sane white man would venture to where we were going without a rifle. Passports were not required.

*

Three-and-a-half hours later, we saw the start of the swamp and a few minutes thereafter, the makeshift airstrip came into sight. First, I did a low fly-by to scatter any animals that may be on the strip. Satisfied that all was clear, I brought the plane round onto final and soon the wheels kissed the ground, the aircraft rolling out. I parked the aircraft just off the strip. After the final 'tick-tick' of the propeller as it windmilled to a stop, we became aware of the silence of the bush. Only the call of the birds and waterfowl could be heard. Although it was winter and but eleven in the morning, I could feel the heat.

I saw the lapa about a hundred yards away, situated on the shore of a deep pool surrounded by reeds. only the side bordered the lapa and airstrip, which allowed unrestricted passage to the water's edge.

Heidi and I started moving our equipment to the lapa and, as we neared the water, we saw a few large crocodiles slither from where they had sunned themselves on the mud bank's edge and disappear below the surface.

"God, I don't think a swim's a good idea," Heidi said, concerned by what she'd just witnessed.

"Just be careful. Rather, let me do the water collections from the pool," I said.

It took a few trips to get our gear stowed under the lapa. Once close up, I realised that whoever had built the lapa had done so hastily. It was crude and makeshift, but still it would provide cover against sun and rain.

The table was erected and the chairs unfolded. I went off to find wood. I thought a fire a good idea but we'd only light this just before evening. Anything else that required warming or cooking could be done on a small gas stove we'd brought. The heaviest piece of equipment was the miniature kerosene fridge. It took two hours before everything was shipshape and ready, even the fridge was now stocked with wine, beer, and bottles of tonic water and ginger ale.

I took two beers, these still cold from a crate, and handed Heidi one. We both collapsed into our chairs with audible sighs.

She smiled at me. "Cheers," she said, holding up her bottle.

We touched glasses.

*

The forest had long forgotten the loud, foreign, and intrusive snarl of the aircraft's engine and the natural sounds of the wild had returned.

From below the lapa, we had a view of the water and its edges as well as the area that led to the water. A large number of animals of various species could be seen in the vicinity of the water. We saw springbok, kudu, and wildebeest. We saw a solitary hyena and an elephant in the distance. I knew there had to be lion around but we saw none. Of course, I was concerned. The lapa was not protected by a boma of cut down branches from thorn trees stacked together to form a wall around the camp. This meant that I'd have to ensure that we had a decent fire going throughout the night. I spent most of the early afternoon collecting wood which, fortunately, was in abundance.

At around five, with the sun moving towards the western horizon, we took our rifles, merely for protection, and decided on walk along the tributary that fed our pool with water. The water hardly moved, the summer rains in the Angolan Highlands long past. Animal movement had created a path along the water's edge and the going was easy provided we stuck to it. As we walked, we would disturb small buck and the occasional flock of guinea fowl. We had gone no more than a half-mile when we stumbled on a clearing, and it soon became evident that this had been somebody's campsite. The few empty cans and beer and liquor bottles strewn on one side told me that this had to be a white man's camp. This wasn't the work of locals. I could see where their fire had burnt and this didn't seem to have been too long ago.

One of the amazing things about the Kalahari Desert is the absence of rock or stone. Other than a few isolated areas separated by hundreds of miles, it's all sand. Any movement leaves a hoof, boot, or foot imprint, the sand similar to fine beach sand. The area of the clearing still bore the marks of those who had camped here before, and it was obvious that the group that had camped here was large.

"Look Matt, there's a boma." Heidi pointed into the bush where I saw an adjoining clearing taken up by a high boma in its centre, the branches piled nearly six feet high and designed to keep the largest of animals at bay.

We walked over to look at our find. The boma was completely enclosed but we soon found where the entrance had been closed with branches. I also noticed that the branches had not yet lost their leaves, meaning that this had to be a recent construction.

We pulled the branches from the concealed entrance and then squeezed past into the boma. This was no more than thirty feet in diameter. For a moment, we contemplated our bizarre find. I whistled softly. The first thing we saw was the stack of ivory tusks. I thought there had to be at least 30–40 tusks, all leaning against each other forming a curved pyramid. They gave off a carrion smell where the bits of flesh that still stuck to the root-end of the tusks had rotted. There were other stores in wooden crates and strong khaki canvas bags. This was somebody's base camp as it were.

The number of tusks indicated quite a number of killed elephants. I was appalled. Elephants were protected here. Yes, licences to hunt elephant were issued, but certainly not to kill fifteen or more. This was an illegal hunting camp and that it was why it was concealed far away from the airstrip.

When we landed, the airstrip had shown no trace that it had been recently used. In fact, I had made a point of remembering to take a hatchet and cut down those of the small bushes that had re-emerged, some of which had already reached knee height. It was unlikely that an aircraft would leave any trace and if it did, this would soon disappear in the desert winds. Previously I had thought that nobody had been here for a year or so.

"Somebody's shooting elephant for the ivory. It's got to be poachers," I said.

'Are we in danger?"

"Well, I'm not sure, but I don't think that whoever it is plans to get caught. They probably fly the ivory out. That's why it's hidden so near to the airstrip. There's got to be more than a ton of ivory here. You'd need a large aircraft to fly this lot out," I replied.

"Don't you think they've left a guard?"

I looked around. "I don't think so. What would be the point?"

"What are we going to do?" she asked, her concern evident on her face.

"We just ignore it. We'll go back to the camp and forget about it. It's not our concern."

She did not appear to be satisfied with my reply, her concern still evident, but she said no more.

We replaced the thorn tree branches closing the boma and then retraced our steps. I swept our tracks in the sand away with a branch thick with leaves which I broke from a tree. We made our way back to the camp, the desert twilight already fast approaching.

That evening we dined around the camp table, drinking beer and wine and eating steak and lamb chops which I had barbecued over the fire.

Our sleeping arrangements were a great deal more complicated. I had scoured Windhoek's shops looking for a double camp bed. This was not to be found. It seemed that when camping, enforced celibacy was the rule unless some ingenuity was applied. Rest assured I persevered and settled for two camp beds which I would place together with two boards cut to size crosswise over the beds, and on top of this, we'd have one of those new-fangled mattresses, a double one of course. This was packed with some new miracle fibre guaranteed to ensure comfort. Even Heidi was impressed with my resourcefulness.

Of course, there was still the worry of wild animals, but I believed that a big enough fire would be sufficient to deter any inquisitive predators. With the camp bed erected near the fire under the open sky, we retired after a few drinks at about ten. We made love. Only once was the quiet of the night interrupted by the roar of a male lion reverberating through the bush, making us jump, even the crickets interrupting their usual nocturnal sounds.

An uneventful night passed even though my fire had burnt itself nearly out during the night, only a heap of ash and glowing coals visible in the morning. No animal had attempted to near our fire.

After breakfast, we set out again but in the opposite direction. We took only the Mauser and the Bergstutzen Drillinge shotgun, this an over-and-under design with two 12-bore shotgun barrels on the top with a 7 x 57mm rifle barrel beneath. It was a fairly common shotgun used in Germany for hunting and as we needed to shoot something for the pot, the shotgun was an ideal weapon.

Quite close to the camp, we came upon a herd of elephant who soon had our scent. They were alert and stationary and with their trunks up-raised testing the wind, they turned to face us. Within a moment, the matriarch moved off, taking the herd with her. I knew that they do this when hunted frequently, associating the scent of humans with death.

To shoot anything large would have been a waste so when we came across a duiker I didn't hesitate and shot it.

We carried the carcass back to the camp where I hung it from its hind legs and skinned it, dividing it in pieces which I stowed in the refrigerator for our evening meal. I took the hide and entrails and buried them a good distance from the camp in order to keep the scavengers away, particularly hyenas.

CHAPTER-THIRTY-ONE

I opened my eyes. Something had wakened me. A slight mist hung over the ground and the sky was still grey. I lay on my side with Heidi cuddled in front of me, both of us facing the same side. I turned over.

I was shocked rigid. Two men stood by the fire just watching us, the one a white man with a rifle which he had cradled in his arm, it pointing at the ground, the other a black in a loincloth, a small blanket over his shoulders, and clutching a short assegai.

It took a moment before I recollected myself. We looked at each other, not saying a word. He had seen that I had wakened and that I was looking at him, but he said nothing. He was tall, maybe six feet, two inches, dressed in khaki trousers which were stuffed into calf-high hiking boots laced to the top. He wore a short-sleeved bush jacket, this also khaki, and a felt hat with what looked like a hatband made from a strip of furred animal hide. His face was covered by a short growth of whiskers, it not having seen a razor for a few weeks, they black but mottled with flecks of grey. The lines from his eyes were white against the deeply tanned skin of his face. He obviously spent a good deal of time in the tropical sun. He said something to the black who then walked to my pile of wood near the burnt-out fire and threw a few pieces on it. Heidi stirred next to me and mumbled.

I was in a rather embarrassing situation, I was stark naked as was Heidi under the lightweight quilt.

"Get up," he said to me in English.

"Do you mind?" I said lifting the quilt slightly showing that I was naked.

A slight smile of amusement appeared on his lips.

"That's not going to bother me. Get up," he said louder. He spoke in English.

Again, Heidi stirred. What could I do? I slipped from beneath the quilt, careful not to allow them to get a glimpse of Heidi. I turned my back to them as I sidled over to my clothes where these were draped over a camp chair and proceeded to dress.

"What's going on?" I heard Heidi say in German and turned round to see her sitting up in the bed with the quilt gathered at her neck.

"Nothing, just stay there," I said to her.

"You are German?" he asked.

"Yes."

"So am I," he said in the same language.

She must have realised that something was afoot from the tone of my voice. She just stared at the two intruders.

Once I was dressed, I faced him. "What do you want?" I stared at the man. Had I see him before? I didn't think so. I should have known him to be German, his English had a faint but distinct accent.

Again the man said something to his companion who then came forward and collected our two rifles and shotgun.

"Why are you doing that?" I asked, referring to the collection of our weapons.

He ignored my question.

"What are you doing here?" he asked.

I briefly smiled. "Actually, we're on honeymoon," I said.

He barked a short guffaw and then composed himself.

"You're kidding," he said.

"It's true. We choose this place because we wanted to be alone," I said.

"How did you know about my camp?" he asked.

I realised that this was what it was about.

"What camp?"

He snorted. "Don't take me for stupid. We found your tracks, although you did your best to conceal them. They led us here. We saw that you were even in my boma," he said.

I realised that it was futile to deny this.

"Yes, we found your camp. We took nothing and left it as we found it. That's normal etiquette in the bush, isn't it?" "You realise that you've become a problem," he said.

"Mister, please just listen to me. What you do here is your business as much as what we do here is ours. Let's leave it at that and just both go our own way. There is very little possibility of any other arriving. I don't think you'd see any authority here for at least another year. Who's to know what?" I replied hoping that I had convinced the man.

I heard him suck air through his teeth as he just stared at me.

"I don't think so, anyway, let's move away, and give the lady some privacy so that she can dress." He motioned me to move with a wave of his rifle, we walking towards where the Beaver was parked next to the strip.

I didn't want to pry or say too much. I was hoping that the man would see reason and just walk away leaving us alone, but I had a feeling that it was not going to be quite that simple. He knew that I knew he was a poacher. I could fly out of here and have the BSAP here within a day or two. They'd be hot on his trail.

"I'd like to go to your aircraft," he said, again motioning with his rifle in that direction. "Please lead the way. I need to immobilise the plane until such time when I've left. That'll be a day or two," he said. He'd spoken German to me, this with a hint of a Bavarian accent.

So, he intended leaving in a day or two. That could only mean by aircraft. Any other way would require a number of vehicles and therefore was bound to run into a police patrol.

The man must have been reading my thoughts.

"I will fly out of here with my ivory. I've ten of the locals working for me, so I suggest you don't try anything. Just remember that if anything should happen to you, everything you possess that's here will be theirs. I'm sure they'd find the idea attractive," he said, walking slightly behind me and to the side and I just able to see him out of the corner of my eye if I turned slightly.

"Were you in the war?" he asked.

"In the Luftwaffe," I replied after first hesitating, but then I saw no harm in telling him.

"In Russia?"

"For a while, both during and after, as a guest of Stalin. And you?" I replied.

"I had to flee for my life. I was a lieutenant in the Waffen-SS. After the war, the Russians were rounding up all the SS. I had to go underground. Others in the Party aided my escape and got me to Holland. From there I came to Africa."

"And your English?" I asked.

"Oh that. Well, I made a point of learning to speak it as soon as I got here. After all, most of this belongs to the English one way or another. It helps when you can speak their language," he replied.

329

We hadn't exchanged names and I had the distinct feeling he did not propose to do so. He never asked for mine. Nonetheless, I was intrigued.

We got to the De Havilland Beaver. I wondered how he proposed to immobilise the aircraft. Instead of a key, the Beaver had a large four-way switch: Off, Both Magnetos, Left Mag, and Right Mag. De Havilland probably never imagined people stealing an aircraft.

"Got a spark plug spanner?" he asked.

I produced it. He then proceeded to remove four spark plugs.

"I'll keep these and the spanner," he said, holding them up. "You can have them when we leave. In the meantime, you're free to walk around as you wish, but without a rifle, I'd suggest you be careful. I'll leave my right-hand man with you, with a rifle just in case a lion or something decides to visit your camp."

Well, that was pretty conclusive, I thought. We weren't going to fly out of here with a few spark plugs missing from the engine. At least, he seemed to be accommodating and was not planning our sudden demise.

Back at the camp, I filled Heidi in and assured her that he meant us no harm.

"But won't he think we'll tell the authorities," she asked.

"Tell them what. I don't know his name, I don't know to where he'll fly to from here, in fact, I know nothing and he knows that," I said but was not entirely convinced that I was right.

The poacher disappeared with his men leaving us with the one guard. A short while later they reappeared, the men each carried an elephant tusk over a shoulder. They dumped them next to the airstrip, pulling thorn tree branches over them to keep them hidden. They made a few trips and by midday, it seemed that all the tusks had been moved. By now, I was sure they were waiting for an aircraft. We slept another night under guard and on the third day at about ten in the morning, I heard the drone of a multi-engine aircraft.

The sound grew louder and louder, I recognised the unmistakable rasp of radial engines. The aircraft flashed overhead, I recognising a Lockheed Lodestar, a commercial version of the military aircraft, a Lockheed Ventura. The aircraft then banked, lowered its undercarriage and approached to land.

I realised that our captor must be part of a far larger organisation. Aircraft such as the Lockheed Lodestar required money and these aircraft were not easy to come by. I saw that the plane showed no registration or identification numbers.

The hunter's men started loading the piled tusks into the aircraft followed by the loose stores which had also been brought from his camp. Once they had completed the job, he paid his men. From their behaviour it was evident that they were being paid handsomely, they kowtowing and raising their hands, the flat of their palms together in appreciation. Hopefully, this would dissuade them from stripping our camp after the Lockheed Lodestar left.

He came across to me carrying our three guns and handed these to me. I saw that the two bolt-actions had been removed from the rifles. He took two linen bags from his right-hand man and handed me one.

"The bolt-actions are in this. There are not cartridges. I'll drop these at the end of the runway when we about to take off. That's the best I can do. I'm sorry to have been inconvenienced a fellow German officer, but I'm sure you understand," he said.

Just then, a man appeared in the aircraft's cargo hatch in the side of the aircraft.

"Dietmar, in Gottes Namen, macht schnell!" the man shouted.

In a flash, everything fell into place. I recognised the man. I'd seen him in the flesh in Russia and then his photograph dozens of times thereafter. It was in the gulag. The Russians were forever cross-questioning the German prisoners, looking for Germans whom they maintained had murdered civilians and Russian prisoners of war or had starved them to death.

The Russian NKVD had harassed prisoners in the various gulags, producing photographs when looking for German, Estonian, and Ukrainian war criminals. He had featured prominently in their records. He was certainly no small fish. He had been high up on the NKVD's list. I clearly remembered the commanding officer of the Sonderkommando detachment in German-occupied Russia when I was shot down.

"Sturmbannführer Fassbinder," I whispered to myself.

My captor stopped in mid-stride and swept round to look at me. "What did you say?" he said.

Of course, all Germans knew that some organisation had been created by the Nazis, its task to create an underground movement to spirit members of the German Gestapo and SS out of Germany. Apparently,

331

they were supplied with false documents and money and secreted out of the country under the noses of the Allies. It was believed they'd mostly gone to South America, to countries who were not concerned with their past and where no extradition was applied. To see them here in Africa was a surprise, although a few Germans, my father included, believed that a good few had sought refuge in South Africa and South West Africa. Using assumed names, they felt relatively safe. the ruling Nationalist Party in South Africa, the government now ruling South West Africa, was supportive of the Nazi cause during the war and made no effort to apprehend war criminals.

I didn't doubt that the pilot who'd looked out of the open cockpit side window was also either German or Afrikaans.

The poacher looked at me through narrowed eyes. He jerked his head towards the man in the hatchway.

"Do you know him?" he asked.

I'd said his name and I had always known that it was not sound policy to stray from the truth. This tends to catch up rather rapidly and this situation was changing by the second.

"For a moment I thought he looked remarkably similar to a high-ranking German political figure that'd once inspected our squadron near Smolensk in Russia during the War. I must be wrong. It would be remarkable if I were right," I said with what I thought was the required degree of nonchalance.

The poacher just stared at me, his dark eyes fathomless.

"Was ist los?" The man in the hatchway called. *What's happening?*

"Garnichts," the poacher shouted, not taking his eyes off me. *Nothing.* Inwardly I breathed a sigh of relief, maybe this was not about to become an issue.

" Be careful you don't grab the devil by the tail. I'm going to drop the ammunition for your rifles from the aircraft just before we take off," he said and then swung round and clambered into the hatch it shutting it behind him.

The port engine propeller began to swing. The Pratt and Whitney radial coughed, sputtered, and then settled down to a roar, this soon followed by the other engine. The aircraft turned to face down the runway and then, with a crescendo, it trailed an enormous cloud of dust as it accelerated down the strip and then climbed into the sky swinging northeast.

As the aircraft disappeared, I shook my head. I was obvious that I had a problem. They had my name and knew from where I came. I had volunteered this information a day or so ago while in conversation with the poacher.

"Fuckin' hell," I said to myself.

"What's wrong?" Heidi asked. I told her, leaving nothing out. I could see her pale as the significance of what I said hit her.

"Come, let's find the ammunition," I said. I turned round to see where the locals the poacher had left behind were. They'd disappeared.

We found the ammunition and cleaned the dust of the cartridges. We then loaded the rifles and the shotgun.

"Heidi, I think we should get out of here. Let's go home," I said taking her hand.

"I agree. If there's enough of the day left, let's leave now. I heard what he said, that bit about not grabbing the devil by the tail. What did he mean?" she said, it now clear that she was unhappy.

I sighed. "He was telling me in no uncertain terms that I should forget what I saw and heard and, of course, the same would apply to you. I can promise you the Israelis are looking for these people. You know, Wiesenthal the Nazi-hunter and his people, as well as the American War Crimes Commission and everybody else. I can assure you that Fassbinder was bad news indeed. He has to be on their list and probably the other ex-SS officer as well. They must know each from the war."

CHAPTER THIRTY-TWO

We were both in a sombre mood when I drove the pickup into the backyard driveway of my father's house. He was not expected in before seven that evening. Heidi and I, with the assistance of Moses, unloaded the camping equipment from the pickup and I returned the firearms to the gun cabinet.

When my father arrived, we were in the lounge waiting for him. None would sit down to supper until he arrived. Heidi and I were famished. He was surprised to see us, not expecting us for another few days.

My father took a seat in the lounge to have his usual pre-dinner drink, this either beer or whiskey depending on the heat of the day.

"Well," he asked taking a sip from his glass of whiskey, "what was the problem? You didn't get on each other's nerves so early in the marriage, did you?" he enquired amused. "You're not going to believe this," I said, "but we ran into a couple of poachers."

"Hang on, a moment. I don't even know where you were. Tell me all," he asked, looking at us attentively.

I proceeded to give him a detailed account, with Heidi chipping in to add her comments from time to time.

"From what you are telling me, they sound like a bunch of SS who have settled in Africa, God knows where. You're lucky they didn't kill you. Grabbing the devil's tail, you say. Aircraft displaying no registration? Be careful, they're serious. What I can tell you is that our good friend Alex Stern will be very interested in what you've to tell. He's never said it in so many words but I think he works for the Israelis. Goes there once a year for two weeks. It's common knowledge that the Wiesenthal Institute has contacts in every country where it is thought the Nazis would be able to find undercover refuge." He finished his drink and put down his glass. "Anyway, I'll not say anything. You can decide what you propose to do. But please, you've had enough grief for one life. Don't do anything stupid." He turned to look at Heidi, "Don't let him do anything stupid, will you?" he said and rose from his table. "Come, let's eat."

The next day my father phoned me at home and asked that I come round to the office. He said that Alex Stern would be meeting with me in the next hour. My father mentioned no reasons but I could well guess.

When I got to the office, Alex was already there. After some small talk, my father left the office leaving the two of us alone.

Once the door closed behind my father Alex began. "I didn't want to discuss this in front of any other. Your father told me about your honeymoon – not what you expected, I suppose," he said humorously and extracted two large files from a large black briefcase. "I don't know whether this was mentioned to you but I'm a minor cog in the Wiesenthal Institute – the Nazi-hunters, if you like." He grinned at me: "Don't be surprised – I'm Jewish!"

"My father had guessed it," I said.

He placed the first file in front of me and opened its hard cardboard cover, the first page revealing photographs, most in German military uniforms.

"Your father mentioned that you thought one of those you saw on your trip was Sturmbannführer Fassbinder. Can that be possible? That would truly be incredible!" he asked.

"Look, Herr Stern, I've seen the man before. In fact, right in front of me. He was a SS Sonderkommando officer in occupied Russia," I said.

I could see that he was taken aback by what I'd just volunteered.

"How do you know about this?" he asked, becoming wary.

"Please, I never had anything to do with them, but when I was shot down I had to spend a while in the extermination camps while I waited for my squadron to collect me. Believe me, I saw enough."

Alex asked, "Did you view any war crimes while there?"

"No I didn't, except for one particular atrocity. I saw the bodies stacked between the logs which they then burned," I said.

Alex paged through the file and then stopped and turned it so that I could get a proper view. He pointed at a photograph. "Is that him?" he asked.

I studied the black and white picture. It was Fassbinder all right, dressed in a normal SS-uniform. He was younger then. It was a very good picture, taken in a studio with proper studio lighting. There was no mistaking him.

"That's him," I said without hesitation.

Alex leaned back in his chair and gave a low whistle.

"I suppose you don't know where they took off to, do you?"

"No, I don't. The aircraft's registration numbers were removed."

I understand it was a Lockheed Lodestar, is that correct?" he asked.

"I believe that's what the commercial version of the Lockheed Ventura is called," I replied.

"Well, other than the South African Airways there are very few of these that are privately owned in Africa and these usually belong to airlines, not private individuals. I'll have to do some digging. You don't have any objection to me passing on your name to the Wiesenthal lot as the man who found Fassbinder?"

"No, why not as long as this is kept under wraps and I certainly wouldn't want my wife mentioned."

He smiled. "Top secret. You need not worry."

He closed the file and stowed this in his briefcase. He rose from the chair.

"Matthias, you've rendered the Jewish people a tremendous service. Thank you very much," he said. That evening Heidi wanted to know what had happened and what had Alex had said. Strangely, my father said little, but I did not doubt that Alex would keep him informed. My father only asked that we not mention the honeymoon incident and Alex's visit to any other.

*

I settled down into my new position rather well and surprisingly my brother and I made a good team. Our relationship was amicable and we accommodated each other and our personal quirks rather well.

George accompanied me to Gelwater to wrap up the handover of the farm to the government. We were one of the first farmers to do so. We also ran into Hans Froehlich who also was disposing of his farm. He had bought another in the Aranos district which was about a hundred miles away to the east situated on the plateau, far from the main highway that ran south towards Cape Town. He was about to start a cattle and sheep drive to his new home. He smiled when he first saw me, sticking out his hand to congratulate me and to wish Heidi and me the best. I was bowled over. The man revealed no hostility whatsoever towards us.

More than three months had passed when one morning I arrived at the office to find Alex Stern with his son, Ginger, and two others waiting to see me. This was a surprise. We all took seats in the boardroom. My father had joined us. It was only once the coffee had been served and we were alone that Alex addressed us.

He pointed to the two strangers at the table and chuckled, "I've introduced them as Mutt and Jeff, but I'm sure you realise that these are just pseudonyms. They are here to find, or rather deal with, Fassbinder and his consorts. Matthias, because of you we've made extraordinary progress. We traced the aircraft. it's Rwandan registered and stationed at Kigali, the capital. It belongs to some large business consortium heavily involved in the coffee industry and mining. Most of the consortium is German."

"Christ. What are they doing way down here?""There are quite a number of Germans in Rwanda. They are mostly involved in the coffee-growing industry on the slopes of the mountains. Many of these families originally came from the old Tanganyika German colony. They grow quite a bit of coffee there and before the war the Germans were big importers. Some of these plantations are owned by Germans. Rwanda belonged to the Germans at one stage until Belgium took it over. Anyway, we've established that a selected few of those Nazis that we seek are to be found there, including our Mr Fassbinder, the others are small fry, ex-SS soldiers and the like, maybe two or three on the wanted listed for minor stuff. Of course, Fassbinder now goes by another name, he's Albert Karl Klemm, born in Dar es Salaam in German Tanganyika on a coffee plantation, believe it or not. Your poacher has stayed with his proper name. He was Waffen-SS. We're actually not after him provided he doesn't get in the way."

Doesn't get in the way? I thought that sounded ominous. I looked at Alex, raised my eyebrows, and then looked at his companions.

Alex saw the look I gave them.

"Let's just say they are visiting from Israel. But they've told me that a few of the Germans in Rwanda have a business going, with fingers in Mozambique, Belgian Congo, Rwanda and, of course, down here in Angola and Bechuanaland. They illegally hunt elephant, taking the tusks to Rwanda where there is no control whatsoever and then disposing of them on the international market, usually the Far East. Apparently, this is quite a large money-making business."

"Why haven't they been caught? I've never heard of anything like that," my father asked.

One of the Israelis spoke up, his English tainted with a rather peculiar accent. "They use aircraft, private airstrips and only hunt in the remotest of areas, no more than ten to twenty elephant at a time so that the ivory can be flown out on one aircraft, usually the aircraft that you saw."

I looked at them. They both had the features and complexion that is associated with those who were Sabras, native-born Israelis.

"That's all rather interesting and I appreciate you filling me in, but what can I do for you?" I asked.

"We have a few questions," the one who had been named Mutt said.

I nodded. He then proceeded to take me through the time I had spent with Fassbinder, wanting to know everything down to the finest detail, all of which I willingly provided. I knew what these criminals had done The mere fact that they were fellow Germans weighed heavily on my conscience, something akin to a nation's shared guilt for atrocities done by small fraction of the population.

We finished. "That's all I can tell you," I said.

There followed a long silence. I felt forced to ask, "Is there anything else?"

Alex looked at my father, something passed between them. He turned to me.

"We have just learnt that Fassbinder's man was dropped off in the Okavango swamps a few days ago and is on a hunting trip again. He'll be in the bush for a couple of weeks, regularly sending his men back to his base camp with the ivory," he said.

"How do you know this?"

"That we cannot tell you, but we can say that it is confirmed," he replied.

The base camp, that would be the boma in the bush that we'd found.

Alex looked directly at me. "The Israeli government wants us to capture Fassbinder. They then want to smuggle him out of the country to Israel—"

Before I could stop myself, I guffawed loudly. "Sorry," I said, "but that's illegal and insane."

Alex ignored my comment and continued: "… and we want you to help us."

This was no joke. They were deadly serious. I looked at my father. His face revealed nothing, not a muscle twitched. I realised I wasn't going to get anything from him. I was on my own with this.

I fished a cigarette from a packet and lit it. "That's not fair," I finally said, blowing smoke through my nostrils.

"You know the place, you know where the boma is, and you know his people, well, at least some by sight. You're the obvious choice," Alex said. "Where these people come from, 'fair' is not a word in their vocabulary when dealing with these murderers. You've got to understand that."

"No," I said loudly. Not ever. I'd be part of a kidnapping. That's what it'll be."

"It can't be a kidnapping, they're in Bechuanaland illegally. You'd be there legally, you're from South Africa. You've free access to the country," Ginger retorted. I could see that he was quite taken up with the idea. "I'd come with you. Dammit man, I served in North Africa and Italy against the Nazi's. I know enough about fighting a war and the fuckin' Germans. Of course, present company excluded," he added.

Sure, he had a point but that didn't help me.

My father intervened and quietly said, "Matthias, you don't have a choice."

He looked at me and I at him and saw how disappointed he would be if I refused. Alex was his best friend. I wanted to say I did have a choice but then thought better of it. I'd only hurt my father if I did.

"Christ. All right," I said. My father's face broke into a smile, as did the others.

"Good man, I knew you would," Alex said, smiling triumphantly. "I've hired a Beechcraft Traveler from United Air for a week. I gave you as the pilot. They know you. They were satisfied, but you must show your licence before we leave. I want us to leave in two days."

"What about these two?" I said, looking at the Israelis. "They're not South African."

Jeff smirked and produced two passports. From the coat-of-arms on the front, I saw that these were South African. They had to be forgeries.

"Jesus," I quietly said.

Alex smacked the table. "So, it's all legal!" He then laughed loudly, happy with the developments. "And we won't be there illegally. I got permission from the British High Commissioner in Gaberones. It cost twenty quid a piece and each can shoot three animals but not elephant, rhino, or giraffe. We're a hunting party." He withdrew a telegram from his pocket and waved it at us.

Alex's gung-ho attitude did nothing for me. I believed he had underestimated the seriousness of the risks involved.

Needless to say, Heidi was appalled at the idea when she heard of it. I had a problem restraining her from trying to discuss the proposed trip with my father and Alex. I eventually got her to understand that she was not supposed to know.

I joined Alex, Ginger, and the two Israelis at Alex's home that evening. Heidi knew why I was there. We formulated a plan and it was decided that we would take two of our own trackers with us. They would be fetched from a farm of the family's which was nearby. I was to retrieve them in the morning. We would be armed with civilian guns, hunting rifles, shotguns and pistols. No military weapons were to be taken.

Although I didn't say so, I knew that Fassbinder would never allow himself to be taken alive if he knew that we represented an Israeli hit squad after Nazi war criminals. I didn't think it would take Fassbinder long to realise this.

CHAPTER THIRTY-THREE

The growl of the aircraft's two radial engines rose in intensity as I pushed the throttle levers forward to the stop on the centre control pedestal. It was still so dark that I could barely make out the runaway ahead of me, and used the aircraft's gyrocompass to maintain a straight take-off track. The dawn was still a faint grey brush stroke on the eastern horizon. The temperature gauge, which the outside sensor protruded through the cockpit's Plexiglas front screen, read -2°C and we all were bundled up in padded jackets except for the two trackers who had blankets draped over their shoulders. Ginger was in the seat next to me. Once airborne and flying by instruments, I turned right to avoid the mountains ahead of us and climbed until I had sufficient altitude to turn east and clear them.

Fortunately, dawn comes swiftly in the tropics and within fifteen minutes, everything below us was visible.

We had planned thoroughly and decided that to land on the airstrip would advertise our presence, alerting our former Waffen-SS poacher if he happened to be in the vicinity. We could do no more than hope not. We assumed that Fassbinder was not there but hoped that he'd arrive when the ivory and the poacher were collected by aircraft.

Fortunately, it was winter and the dry season, the water in the swamps having receded to leave large flat areas of baked mud, the firmness of which could be gauged by the depth of the trails made by the large animals, elephants, rhino, and buffalo, as they criss-crossed the baked ground.

The flight was uneventful and, a few hours later, the faint airstrip next to the swamp came into sight. I brought the aircraft down close to the surface and extended the undercarriage and flaps to slow the aircraft. We soon found an area to our liking and to make doubly sure that the surface was suitable for landing, I first let the wheels kiss the ground a few times and then took it up again. We circled around to see what marks the impact of the wheels had left. There were none. The ground was rock hard. We landed. I taxied the aircraft as close to the nearest trees as I could. We then manhandled it into position so that it was at least partially obscured by the canopies of the large trees. Branches were cut to add to the camouflage.

We setup a makeshift camp under the trees. No fire was permitted and we used two paraffin stoves we had brought to cook and heat water. Fetching water was a real chore but could not be avoided. The trackers were sent to keep an eye on the boma and to watch for the return of the poacher and his men with whatever ivory they had. We believed that when the ivory tusk tally reached about thirty we could expect Fassbinder to arrive with their aircraft, this being about as much as the aircraft could load.

We soon realised that we seemed to have arrived unobserved. We espied no movement from around the lapa and no animals came to investigate, so we thought that they all had to be miles away.

The next day one of the trackers returned and told us that there were already twenty-four tusks in the boma. We would not have long to wait until the aircraft returned. We thought that the poacher could be expected back at the camp in the next day or two.

We were correct. Two days later, the poacher returned, his squad of porters carrying the ivory into the boma. This was watched by our trackers.

We had already found ourselves a spot on one side of the airstrip at the threshold furthest from the camp where we concealed ourselves. We pushed the aircraft way back in the trees so that it was now completely camouflaged. It could only be found if somebody stumbled on it, which was highly unlikely.

I remembered that they had loaded the tusks in record time. This meant we'd have to act fast once the aircraft arrived.

We were fortunate that it was winter. Had it been summer I think we probably would've come to blows. We waited four days before the aircraft arrived. We had also moved position closer to where their aircraft would park, this being no more than a couple of hundred yards from us. We hardly dare move, afraid that we would give our position away. By then feelings and tensions were running high. We had to keep hidden, were uncomfortable, and bored out of our skulls. After days of not washing or shaving we had all lost our scrubbed-clean city looks and now appeared the worst for wear, sprouting stubble, some sunburn, and slightly cracked lips, not to forget our clothing which was no longer clean and began to take on a distinct smell.

The distant drone of its engines heralded the aircraft's arrival. It was the same Lockheed Lodestar. We watched it land and then taxi to the same spot it had before, swinging round to face towards the runway before the pilot shut the engines down. When the hatch opened, I recognised Fassbinder as he stepped to the ground. The poacher, our Waffen-SS officer, walked to greet him and they shook hands.

I already cradled my rifle in my hands. It was the Steyr 8 x 60mm. With the rifle propped up on my elbows, I took careful aim through the telescope at the main landing gear tyre and squeezed. I saw the dust spurt from the tyre as the slug tore through the rubber. The aircraft settled, tilting to one side. The reaction of those around the aircraft was immediate, the men throwing themselves to the ground. I took aim at the other tyre and shot a hole in it too, the wheel also deflating. Part of the plan was that they'd be unable to escape with the aircraft's tyres shot out, and walking was not an option. They were marooned.

Seconds later, a bullet whistled over our heads, followed by the loud report of the rifle. The air was so dry that my rifle's muzzle blast had raised a small cloud of dust, which must have been seen. Although we were well-hidden, this must have accounted for the answering fire. Fassbinder had scrambled back into the Lodestar but immediately re-appeared with a weapon, which I saw from the long magazine that protruded from below was an automatic rifle of sorts.

"Watch out. That's an automatic rifle he's got," I said to Ginger who was prone next to me.

"Hang on. Let me give them something to think about," he said and took careful aim at those lying on the ground. His shot impacted right in front of them. I was able to see sand burst into the air and this was sufficient to make both men scramble to take cover behind the aircraft's wheels.

The Israeli called Mutt crawled to alongside me. "Well, that'll stop the aircraft. What do you suggest now? Do we wave a white flag and ask for a pow-wow?" he asked, it clear that we now faced a Mexican stand-off.

"Don't be ridiculous. We'll have our asses shot off," I said. "We wait. If anybody arrives who is carrying ivory, we shoot, but shoot to miss. Let's not kill or wound any of the locals."

"Unlikely. They don't know how many we are and I don't think they even know who we are. But no doubt, they're bound to make a shrewd guess," I said.

"May be they think we're police?"

"I don't think so. The police wouldn't just fire without announcing themselves."

Just then, fountains of sand stitched across the ground in front of us accompanied by the loud chatter of the automatic rifle in the distance. Instinctively, we all pressed our faces into the dirt.

"They must've seen us, probably got binoculars. They certainly know where we are," Ginger muttered.

"Christ. We actually have ourselves in a spot here. Okay, I admit we have the upper hand in terms of armed individuals. I doubt whether Fassbinder has weapons for his blacks and besides, they probably have never fired a rifle before. However, come night things could be different. Stealth will be the name of the game and we won't and don't have a thing on the blacks when it comes to creeping around," I said.

"They'll know we've got an aircraft," Ginger said.

I pulled a face and nodded in agreement.

"I suppose it's a pointless exercise asking them to surrender?" Jeff said.

I gave a chuckle.

"You're damn right. They're never going to surrender to us, especially not Fassbinder. He knows what awaits him," I replied.

For half-an-hour, nothing happened. We each took a few shots at them, and they returned fire and sometimes and even initiated a short exchange, probably more to remind us of their presence.

We couldn't just keep lying here merely taking an occasional pot-shot.

"Come on, start crawling backwards until we're back into the trees and bush and are completely concealed. Leave everything except weapons, ammunition, and water. If we don't move, they'll be onto us by tonight. They're probably thinking we're going to try the same," I said.

We crawled a good hundred yards on our stomachs. If we thought we did this unobserved, we were mistaken. A couple of bullets ploughed into the sand and over our heads, some too damn close. This was alarming. I was terrified that a bullet would find one of us. But once deep in the trees and bush we were able to stand upright.

Now that we were out of danger, at least for a while, Ginger and the two Israelis had a short discussion and then approached me.

"Look Matthias," Ginger said who was clearly the nominated spokesman, "we've been discussing the situation. This is not your fight. They probably don't know where our aircraft precisely is but must know that it's near the runway somewhere and camouflaged."

"They're going to try and find it," Jeff interjected.

"Yes, they are. We are suggesting that you stay and guard the aircraft, keep one of the trackers with you. We'll go after them," Ginger said.

"Damn it, man, there are three of them," I said. "They are not going to send just one man if they're after the aircraft. And, don't forget their trackers."

"Hmm, point taken." He paused for a moment. "Fuck it, what are we going to do?" he exclaimed with a grimace..

"I can tell you this, without outside assistance they're fucked, and that aircraft is stuck here. Both their tyres have to be bust. They'll need to replace them. I doubt whether they're carrying a spare," I said and chuckled.

"Just listen up for a moment," Ginger said. We all turned to face him and looked at him expectantly. "Okay, we may have come here to grab them, but I think we've kind of got ourselves into a bind here." There was no mistaking the irony in his voice. "Their aircraft's not going to fly out of here, so what are they going to do? They'll try to grab ours. That's what I'd do. We don't have an alternative. We've got to return to the Beechcraft and protect it. They'll come to us, rest assured," he said.

"You're right. They'll probably come tonight." Mutt said.

"Well, it's decided then. Let's go," Ginger said.

Taking a wide detour and making sure that we remained deep in the trees, we made our way back to the aircraft. I was sure that they would approach from the runway. Although the moon was three-quarters and its light would be sufficient to see quite a distance, it was insufficient to approach the bush. Any torch would be an immediate giveaway. The poacher, the former Waffen-SS soldier, really worried me. They'd been formidable troops in their heyday, definitely not those you wanted to mess with. They used to relish close combat, especially at night, usually using their trenching tools as a weapon. The German army used to issue what was termed a Nahkampfspange, a close combat award for every

345

hand-to-hand combat fight with the enemy. I didn't need reminding that many of the SS soldiers were said to have accumulated over thirty of these while in Russia during the war.

I took stock of the weapons we had. There were the two rifles that Ginger and I had. The Israelis each had some new-fangled Israeli lightweight machine-pistols with a removable stock and firing 9mm bullets, a weapon I'd never heard of or seen before. This had a long magazine that protruded from it. It really was small, but probably very effective. Of course, we all had automatics, these all 9mm as well. Our two trackers had only their spears and machetes.

When we got back to the aircraft I realised how well-camouflaged it was. I never saw it until we were nearly upon it. I was famished and the first thing I did was open a tin of pilchards which I ate with two slices of stale rye bread. Everybody else seemed to be hungry as well.

We all lay down beneath the wings, there still being a good part of the day left. Our two trackers would keep watch. Their eyes were attuned to the bush and they would see suspicious movement well before we did.

*

I woke up. Ginger was shaking me by the shoulder. I saw that it was nearly dark.

"Come on, Matthias, it's time to play soldier again."

I joined the others beneath the wing. Ginger seemed to have taken charge. "Listen, I think we should break up into pairs, one watching for a frontal approach with the others on each side. They're not going to come from the bush, too noisy with twigs, branches, et cetera." He indicated the two trackers. "They stay together and watch the side nearest to Fassbinder. Matthias and I will watch the front and you two watch the other side. We're not going to be more than twenty to thuirty yards away from each other," Ginger said looking at us.. Nobody objected. "Okay, let's do it."

If they approached along the runway and kept low so as not be silhouetted we'd never hear or see them, there being no stones or twigs, just soft sand and thin grass. They'd be on us before we were aware of them. I hoped all the others realised this.

I also knew that Fassbinder would rope in some of his own trackers and this was their country. They had to be a formidable foe as they were on home ground. I could picture one of them looming out of the darkness with a spear raised to stab me. I shivered.

"Jesus," I said softly to myself.

Ginger seemed to realise what I was imagining. "Don't worry, I'm just as worried. This wasn't a good idea. It's not Fassbinder I'm worried about, it's those fuckin' blacks of his," he whispered.

*

It was about two in the morning. Ginger was asleep next to me. The slightest of breezes had arisen, this blowing softly in my face. I was tired with a slight headache, probably from straining to see in the dark. The moon had crossed over and was now behind us. It even seemed quieter now. The insects appeared to have tired as well. The mosquitoes were a plague, notwithstanding the insect repellent we had applied. The worst was that I couldn't swat those that came too close. That would just give our position away.

I caught a strange smell, barely perceptible but definitely there. I'd smelt this before but for a moment was unable to place it. With a jolt I realised what it was, the smell of somebody who'd spent too much time around an open wood fire, the smell of wood smoke mixed with the rancid smell of sweat and stale tobacco smoke. An icy shiver passed over me.

I placed a hand over Ginger's mouth and shook him. He opened his eyes, which were wide and showing white in the moonlight. I had a finger to my lips.

Within seconds he perceived what was going on and nodded his head. I withdrew my hand. I went through the motions of smelling, which he then did. Again, he nodded, withdrawing his automatic and flicking off the safety. I already had my pistol in my hand.

At least the smell of the man that was carried on the breeze gave us an indication as to where we could expect an attack from.

My mind was being bombarded by a myriad of thoughts. If we shot first would this constitute murder? Did we have to wait until they had initiated the attack by firing a shot or throwing a spear? We couldn't turn round and say they were war criminals. We'd have been expected to take this to the authorities and not carry out a unilateral action against them. Any way I looked at it, it seemed we were in serious trouble.

I could have spared myself the agony of indecision. From my right a fusillade of shots erupted. I distinguished pistol and rapid automatic gunfire, the muzzle flashes bright in the dark.

"Watch out," Ginger screamed in my ear.

My head snapped around to see the poacher charging from the front, an automatic in one hand while in the other he brandished a huge machete. He was followed closely by three blacks with spears.

My reaction was instantaneous. I brought the automatic up and fired, but as I squeezed the trigger, the piece bucking in my hand, he ducked. The bullet passed harmlessly over him but hit a Black tracker directly behind him. The man flung his arms out, the spear falling from his grasp, and he sprawled backwards onto his back. I could hear shots next to me as Ginger fired.

As I lowered the automatic to aim at the mass now slightly to my right, which had to be the poacher on the ground, a pistol spat flame and I felt something tug at my shoulder. I knew I'd been hit. I returned fire, my shot followed by a grunt of pain. I'd hit him.

"Du Schwein!" he shouted followed by another few shots, these seemingly right in my face. Again I was hit somewhere in the right thigh. Ginger's automatic barked again.

This had all taken place in the space of thirty seconds. There was no more shooting. Nothing moved.

"Don't get up," somebody shouted. I remained prone on the ground. I felt light-headed and realised that this had to be shock.

"Are you all right?" Ginger asked in a quite whisper.

"I'm hit. I think twice," I replied, trying to feel my shoulder. My fingers came away with blood on them, the wetness glinting in the moonlight. "Shit. I'm hit in the shoulder and the leg," I whispered, feeling the first pain.

There was a loud wail, a death scream, this about fifty yards in front of us. I wondered what had happened. Ginger crawled away from me, disappearing in the sparse grass. I presumed he wanted to find out what had happened. The shock now really got to me and I was close to blacking out. I fumbled for my water bottle and took a few swigs of water. This seemed to help. I wondered how much blood I was losing.

A shadow passed in front of the moon. It was Ginger, who now walked upright. The danger was over.

"Oh, they're gone," he said. "Okay, let's attend to you. Thank God, we brought a decent first-aid kit. One of our trackers killed one of theirs, stuck a spear into his back. That was the loud scream you heard. The poor man's lying out there. He's dead. A black man who died because of what his bosses told him to do or paid him a pittance to do." He was appalled by what had happened.

I had to be the luckiest man alive. Both wounds were superficial, no bone or vital organs had been struck. I was going to hurt for a while and would be immobile. A bullet had passed through the main muscle above my collarbone. That impeded a lot of my shoulder movement and hurt like hell. I had a groove, this quite deep, along my thigh muscle. Initially, this had bled profusely but had now stopped. In the faint light of the moon, and with a surprising degree of professionalism, Ginger applied dressings and strapped my wounds. He also gave me two tablets, these powerful painkillers.

"Try not to sleep, although the pills are bound to kick you in the ass," he said in an attempt at humour as I washed them down with a swallow of water from my water bottle. "Can't let anything happen you. You've got to fly us out of this hole."

I wondered how he proposed I do that considering how I was shot up.

"How are the rest of them?" I asked.

"Fortunately, nobody else was hit. It seems our attackers have withdrawn," he replied.

I sighed. I felt both relief and frustration. "Christ. This has turned out to be a real cock-up," I said through clenched teeth. I was in pain.

We all gathered under the wing. I had to hobble there assisted by Ginger. We all settled on the ground in a rough circle.

"Firstly, I'd just like to say this. We're not giving up. That bastard Fassbinder can't be allowed to get away. He'll disappear again and God knows if we'll ever find him," Ginger said.

There were murmurs of support from the two Israelis.

"There is no way out of this other than by air. They'll try to get our aircraft," he continued.

"I think you're forgetting something. That plane's definitely fitted with an HF radio. They could call for help," I said.

"Who would they call?" Ginger asked.

"Your guess is as good as mine. I don't know but that's what I'd do. I think we need reinforcements," I said.

"That would involve more people. We don't want this operation to leak out," Mutt said.

"Well, I don't think we have a choice. Better we call and get help before they do. They may have done so already," I said.

It wasn't going to be as simple as that. HF communication was primarily reserved for aircraft and air traffic controllers. Any message would have to be routed through a government agency. There would be no privacy unless they had their own HF channel. Was that possible? I doubted it. Then, something struck me. I had an idea.

"I've an idea. The Eros Airport tower opens at seven. Hopefully, young Pfeiffer is the controller on duty, he usually is, and I know him rather well. I'll get him to phone my father." I told the others hoping that I'd be able to contact Eros direct and not have to have my message relayed by some other.

*

Just after seven, I clambered into the cockpit and switched on the radios. I was fortunate. Eros picked up my transmission immediately and it was Pfeiffer in the tower. The problem was that Windhoek International Airport control tower would also pick up and monitor my transmission.

Using the aircraft's call sign, I asked Pfeiffer to inform my father that we required assistance and that we needed more hands to overcome the problem we had which was not related to flying at all. That shouldn't arouse any suspicion. The worst would be that the authorities would frown on their communication channels being used for anything but flying. I hoped that my father would realise what I was getting at.

Then came the bombshell, we'd never logged our departure.

"India, India, Juliet, this is Windhoek Control, we have no log of your departure from Eros. Advise current position, number of paxs, status and intentions. Over."

"Christ, we're in the shit," I said to Ginger.

I didn't know what to say.

"India, India, Juliet. Do you read me?" the overhead loudspeaker blared.

I realised I had to take a chance.

"Windhoek, current position Gobabis. Three paxs, over."

Gobabis was an unmanned airstrip close to the border with Bechuanaland.

"India, India, Juliet. Next time remember to log your flight plan. We will relay your message. Over and out," Pfeiffer replied.

I exhaled. Christ we'd been lucky. Pfeiffer had probably saved my bacon. He had reprimanded us, Windhoek happy with his actions.

I knew my father would immediately react but wondered whether he'd manage the arrangement and be able to depart Windhoek and be here within the day, bearing in mind that the flying time was two-and-a-half hours.

By nightfall, no aircraft had arrived and we knew we would have to fight off Fassbinder and his crowd come darkness. They were bound to again attempt to take our aircraft from us, this being their only viable means of escape unless they too had radioed for assistance.

Now that Fassbinder knew exactly where our aircraft was positioned, I realised that if he'd had any sense, he'd position his people in the trees where they could conceal themselves during the day with the intention of launching a night attack. We had to get the aircraft into the open to ensure we received warning of our back-up's approach. Fassbinder would not want to damage the aircraft. He needed it. At least that was a consolation. Nobody wanted to be marooned here. I mentioned this to the others. We all agreed and frantically started stripping the camouflage from the aircraft. There was little daylight left.

As soon as it was free of branches, I started the engines and taxied to the centre of the dried mud plain. By then it was dark and I wondered what our adversaries had seen. Armed with our weapons, water bottles, and something to chew on, we took up position around the aircraft and nervously awaited the attack, which we knew had to come.

It was a brilliantly clear, cold night and the sky a myriad of stars as there was no light reflected from nearby cities to diffuse the night sky. The pale brown mud plain reflected the moonlight, bright enough to give us background against which we'd be able to detect any movement. We stood around the aircraft with one of the trackers sitting on the wing to give him an elevated position from which to keep watch. This was not going to be the case during the entire night. The moon was due to set at about four in the morning.

At the first sign of dawn, we realised that they weren't going to attack. We pondered the situation.

"Hey, I'll tell you what. The bastards didn't attack because they've got help coming," Ginger said.

I realised he had to be right, but we too had help on its way, or so I hoped.

The constant threat of attack and the fact that we'd been here for a while began to work on everybody's nerves. Tempers were short and moods were ugly. No doubt, the same was happening in the enemy's camp. Every now and then, a few shots were exchanged. I noticed that Fassbinder's people were careful not to hit our aircraft. What was the reason? Did they believe they could still overwhelm us?

It was near eleven when one of the trackers pointed skywards. I listened intently and then heard the faint drone of aircraft engines that approached. The aircraft had to be low. I couldn't see it. The drone became a roar and a De Havilland Dragon Rapide appeared, low over the bush and trees, and flashed overhead. I saw the South African registration number under its wing. God, it had to be our help. Would Fassbinder's assistance arrive in a South African aircraft? I doubted it. Shots broke out from Fassbinder's camp and I realised they were shooting at the Rapide. They knew it was here to help us.

We all pushed the Beechcraft off the strip to allow the Rapide to pass high over Fassbinder's camp and land on that piece of runway next to where we were parked. The Rapide didn't need a great deal of runway. It is a two-engine biplane capable of landing within a few hundred yards.

As the Rapide approached, we all opened fire on their camp, forcing them to keep their heads down as the aircraft flew over it on its final approach. The wheels settled and the aircraft trundled towards us and then swung round to face down the runway. As soon as the engines ticked to a stop, my father, Alex Stern, Otto Ewald, and my brother jumped from the aircraft's hatch, all armed with an assortment of weapons. They were dressed in boots and khakis. Otto Ewald was about the same age as my father. He was a huge man with a round face, his jowls sagging, but his forearms were the size of hams, indicative of the man's strength. His was nearly bald. I realised he must have piloted the aircraft as he had a licence. He knew my brother and I from when we were still children when he was already in my father's employ. I also knew that he played a part in my brother's infamous swimming pool saga, the secrets of which I still was to learn.

After a hurried greeting, I told my father briefly what had occurred and mentioned that I thought Fassbinder was also waiting for assistance to arrive.

He interrupted me. "Hurry, hurry up. Put these two aircraft on the runway to block any other landing," he said, a cruel smile breaking out on his face. "Maybe the pilot can get the plane down, possibly on the dirt next to the runway, this clear area is so large, but we'll have a reception committee waiting. He'll endeavour to land over our heads in the direction of Fassbinder. Just make sure everybody is ready."

My father wasn't finished yet. "Listen, use anything you've got, but we've got to dig a trench in which to take shelter, even if it's only shallow. The moment their aircraft arrives, they're going to force us to keep our heads down. We'll need something to protect us. Heap the sand out of the trench as a barrier against their gunfire but dig this away from the strip. We've got to keep the runway open."

I realised he was right and soon everybody was doing what they could, digging into the sand with pieces of wood and pushing the sand out with their hands. We had a shallow depression in which to lie, with a berm of sand on one side to protect us. In my wounded condition, I couldn't assist and just watched the others toil in the sun.

As soon as the trench was complete, my brother beckoned that I should take place next to him behind the berm.

"Christ, little brother, you're a bloody warmonger. How did you get involved in this shit? Now, you've even got me got me risking my ass. I mean your SS friends seem serious about killing us. To crown it all, I was forced to be a passenger in an aircraft with Otto Ewald flying. I don't know what could be worse. Do you know what a lousy pilot he is? God, I was terrified. I nearly shat myself."

"You didn't have to come," I said, not that I felt for him. Our father would have left him little choice. As for Otto Ewald, well, he had to be the worst pilot. His idea of flying was to yank the aircraft's controls around without any feeling, his huge hands gripping the yoke in a death grip with white knuckles protruding. Some of his flying escapades had become folklore in the flying community. I could imagine the consternation in the cockpit, with my father continuously berating him.

That would've been enough to make any passenger nervous. I was glad I had missed that. I believed my father regretted the day he insisted that Otto Ewald get a pilot's licence.

My brother just harrumphed and then let loose a number of expletives, none of which was complimentary. Still, I had to chide my brother one more time.

"Was Otto's flying really that bad?" I asked straight-faced.

My brother glared at me. "Fuck you, Matthias. We couldn't find another pilot, not that we didn't try hard enough." At least I had the last laugh, but I was truly glad to see them all.

My father had been right. The occasional bullet was fired at us, these either embedding in the berm that protected us or whizzing overhead. Alex was with the two Israelis. My father crawled to join us.

"Dad," I said, "aren't we going to find ourselves in a shitload of trouble when we get back? Shooting at people, no flight plan, misleading the authorities, et cetera. God, they can't ignore that. They'd have to do something."

He didn't appear to be quite so concerned.

"Well, not really. Sure, there's going to be trouble. You'll probably be arrested while this mess is sorted out, but Fassbinder is wanted internationally. If we do bring him in and this gets to be known, we should be all right. After all, he's an international criminal. Good God, man. Alex tells me he was directly instrumental in the murder of thousands, or so he says. The man had direct command over the actions of the SS-Einsatzkommandos in his district somewhere in Russia. His capture will justify any action we may take short of outright murder. Secondly, who started shooting first? However, if the Brits catch us here, it could get rough. This is their sovereign territory and they're not going to take kindly to us breaking all their laws. As you know, the BSAP does it by the book."

I could only hope that he was right.

CHAPTER THIRTY-FOUR

We had barely settled down to an uncomfortably long wait, lying behind the berm and wondering what our next course of action should be when again I heard the drone of aircraft engines. This had to be Fassbinder' friends. I was not surprised, with shot-up tyres he'd no alternative but to have called for assistance.

The sheer size of the aircraft as it passed overhead shocked me. It was a Douglas DC-3, a powerful twin-engine American-built transport aircraft, a real workhorse. I wondered how many people it had aboard, no doubt all armed to the teeth.

Our two aircraft blocked the open strip we used as a runway and there was no way that the DC-3's pilot was going to get the plane down on that section. However, the floodplain was wide and with this now the dry season he had other alternatives.

The large aircraft banked, its undercarriage slowly appearing as they dropped from the wheel wells. This was followed by the flaps being extended. I realised that the pilot was going to land and as he straightened out onto a final approach, I could see where he proposed to put the aircraft down. The moment the pilot's intentions became obvious, Fassbinder' men laid down a barrage of gunfire and we were all forced to take shelter behind the berm. A fusillade of shots thumped into the mounds of sand, and it would have been suicide to attempt to stick your head above it.

The Dakota, still at speed, passed over us with a thunderous roar. Its wheels then touched and, with its tail still high, it rolled towards Fassbinder' position. As it passed Fassbinder's Lodestar, it swivelled round in a cloud of dust as the pilot gunned one engine. The hatch opened and five men jumped to the ground, all armed with an assortment of weapons. The men threw themselves onto the ground.

"Hold your fire. Let's not waste ammunition," Alex shouted.

We stopped returning any fire and soon all shooting stopped. Alex peered over the berm, propped up on his elbows with the binoculars glued to his eyes.

"I don't see any blacks. It looks like they've left," Alex said.

"Hell, with all the damn shooting that's going on, I don't blame them. I'd run for my bloody life. Just look at our trackers, they're terrified," Ginger said. He was right, our two trackers cowered behind the berm. They knew what a bullet could do, having seen enough shot animals on the farm.

"If I were them, I'd abandon the ivory, climb into the Dakota, and fly out of here. If the pilot could land, he certainly can take-off again. Of course, that's providing we let them," Alex said.

I had to agree. The only way to stop a take-off was to park our aircraft in the Dakota's take-off path. I said so.

"Well, maybe we should do just that," my brother said dryly.

"That could be expensive. I don't think the aircrafts' insurance covers that sort of application," my father interjected with a sardonic smile indicating that doing so would see our aircraft destroyed at some time.

"Matthias, how far is it to Maun? Isn't there an airstrip and a police outpost there?" my brother asked.

"I'm not sure. The map indicates an airstrip. It's about fifty miles from us. We're actually on the western side of the swamp, Maun's on the eastern side. I believe there's a village with one or two trading posts. Not all that small, probably bigger than a village," I replied.

"Are you telling me there is no road or track to here?" He turned onto his side to look at me.

"There is none. Fly in or use a camel, take your pick, that's the only option you have unless you have a small convoy of four-wheel-drive vehicles," I countered. By midday, the heat became unbearable under the burning sun. Most of us retreated into the bush and trees on the edge of the mud-plain to find shade, being hastened on by a few shots from Fassbinder's crowd. Still, we kept a close watch on the open area between our aircraft and theirs.

It was near three in the afternoon and I had dozed off while lying below a thorn tree, the heat oppressive.

One of the trackers shook me awake. "Baas, listen," he said pointing to the sky.

At first, all I heard was the buzz and singing sound of insects, but then I perceived the drone of an aircraft engine. I jumped up.

"Christ. There's an aircraft coming, single engine, I'm sure," I shouted.

All rose looking in the direction from where the sound emanated. It was from the west. I took the binoculars from Ginger and looked in the direction of Fassbinder. They too all stood staring up into the sky in the direction of the approaching aircraft.

"There," the tracker pointed.

I swept the sky with the binoculars and picked up the plane. It was a high wing monoplane. I recognised it, a Piper Super Cub.

"Shit. It's the police. They're going to wonder what the hell is going on down here. They're sure to want to land. This must look like a bloody poachers' gathering," I said and could not but notice the surprised and comical reaction of my friends.

"British Police," Alex exclaimed in dismay.

I turned to Otto Ewald. "Let's clear the runway. They're sure to land," I said. I could see that the aircraft was already turning to final, the pilot probably trying to carry out the same landing as did the Dakota, on the rough mud-bed.

The pilot saw our intentions and did a single go-a-round to give us time to get our aircraft out of the way.

The airstrip was clear and the Super Cub landed. It could only accommodate two, seated in tandem, one behind each other. It taxied to a stop and two men climbed out. They were dressed in khaki uniforms, short pants, and cotton tunics.

Alex stepped forward with my father at his side to greet them, they all shaking hands. They were Chief Inspector Masters, who was also the pilot, and Superintendent Johnson.

The Superintendent let his eyes take in the number of people, the numerous aircraft, and the various rifles we carried. Fassbinder and his crowd stood at the bottom of the airstrip looking at the proceedings. They were sure to see the BSAP insignia emblazoned on the aircraft's rudder and had to know who our unexpected visitors were.

"Goodness, either you're having an air show or this is the biggest illegal hunting party I've ever come across," the Superintendent said, his eyes closed to slits and highly suspicious of what he saw. The amazing thing was that they had climbed from the aircraft unarmed.

I wondered how Alex proposed to handle the situation. Alex stepped forward as if he didn't want anybody saying anything before he had a chance to speak.

"It's a rather lengthy and complicated story, Superintendent. If you will join us in the shade I'll tell you all, and the reason we are here armed as we are," Alex said, his face showing little emotion.

The Superintendent stared at him and then said, "Lead the way."

The Piper Cub now straddled the airstrip with the Beechcraft and Rapide on each side of it. Fassbinder could not take off. The long finger of the mud plain that jutted out from the swamp was now completely blocked.

The four men, who now included my father, sat on the ground to one side of us, their voices a murmur. The Superintendent repeatedly interrupted Alex to ask questions. After twenty minutes they rose.

"Just gather around. For your benefit I need to fill you in," the Superintendent said. "I've heard your version and it would seem it's just too far-fetched not to be true. I can't arrest Fassbinder as much as I cannot permit you to kidnap him. Assuming he has papers or permission to be here, there is not a thing I can do. I'm told that you're all from South West Africa and therefore do not require papers to be here." He gave the two Israelis a meaningful glance. I wondered whether he had guessed that they were not South Africans, but then the Israeli Intelligence was master forgers. They held his look. I had no idea what Alex might have said about their origins.

The superintendent continued, "Please instruct your tracker to accompany us. They know where the ivory cache is. None of you is permitted to leave. This may entail staying the night, so prepare for that possibility."

With that, he beckoned the tracker whom my father had indicated, and strode off with the pilot down the strip towards Fassbinder and his men.

We kept a watchful eye on the proceeding with Fassbinder. They seemed to converse for half-an-hour and then the two police officers walked off towards the boma with our tracker leading the way.

The three men reappeared an hour later. From the gesticulations and the occasional shout, it was clear that an argument had broken out. Finally, the Chief Inspector and the pilot left the group and started to make their way back to us.

A shot rang out. The Superintendent staggered and fell to the ground. The Chief Inspector started running towards us.

"Open fire. Give them covering fire," Alex screamed.

Without thinking, I pulled out my automatic and started firing blinding even though Fassbinder was out of pistol range, but I did hear a few rifles start firing. The next thing I saw Otto Ewald running towards the enemy, seemingly oblivious of the gunfire. We continued to fire, forcing the poachers to keep their heads down. I had found my rifle and worked the bolt action shot after shot, ramming cartridge after cartridge into the breech. Otto Ewald seemed to effortlessly scoop the Superintendent into his arms and then flung him over his shoulder. He spun round and, hunched, retraced his steps towards us, jinking from side to side. Meanwhile the poachers had organised themselves and now lay down withering return fire, they far out-numbering us. Jeff, the Israeli, was hit and with a cry crumpled to the ground. One of the trackers helped the man to his feet and assisted him towards the trees.

I looked round. I couldn't see the Chief Inspector, but finally saw him crouched over next to the Piper Cub talking into a microphone and I realised that he must be calling for help.

"How is he?" I asked Otto Ewald who had opened the Superintendent's bush jacket and had undone his belt buckle.

"Shot through the side. He's bleeding badly, but I think I can stop it. I believe the bullet may have nicked a kidney," he said. "The murderous bastards. We can't let them get away with this."

I wanted to ask him how he proposed that we stop them but then thought better of it.

The shooting of a police officer would have serious consequences and Fassbinder must realise this, I thought. His action had ratcheted the intensity of the conflict up a few more notches. This was now a fight to the end. The ivory was no longer important. All Fassbinder would want to do is escape. There was only one way and that was by air.

Bent over, the Chief Inspector bolted from the plane to where we were hidden in the trees. No gunshots followed.

Still gasping for breath he said, "I spoke to Gaborone and told them what happened. They're sending help. I'm just wondering what help they can send." He looked at his superior and Jeff lying on the ground. "We've got to get him to a hospital as well as that wounded chap of yours."

Have you any weapons?" Ginger asked him.

He nodded: "Two .303 rifles on the aircraft."

"Better you fetch them. I think we're going to need them. I believe this lot is going to rush us. Just overwhelm us by sheer numbers. They must realise that this is now out of control. Christ. They've shot a policeman. That's a hanging offence," Ginger said but sounding sure of himself.

I was watching the Dakota. I saw no movement. I was sure Fassbinder and his men had backed into the trees and were now hidden. They could even be working their way round through the bush towards us, I thought.

Alex chewed his fingernail as he too gave thought to what we should do next.

"Don't you think we should cripple the Dakota as well?" my father ventured.

"Why? They can't take off. Our aircraft are completely blocking the strip. They'd have to move them first. A small plane could fly out, but never the Dakota," I said.

Alex turned to the Chief Inspector who had sat down with his back to a tree trunk and had lit a cigarette.

"Chief Inspector, I think you should listen to this. They outnumber us. It is better we surprise them before they do the same to us. You have to understand where I'm coming from. This man Fassbinder is responsible for the murder of hundreds of people. I, my son, and these two men," he indicated Jeff lying on the ground and Mutt next to him, "would never be forgiven if we let him get away. If he makes it back to Rwanda, he'll disappear, God knows where to. Brazil, Argentina, Paraguay, you name it. He'll just be gone like the others. That can't be allowed to happen," he said, his voice firm and resolute.

"We wait for help," the Chief Inspector said. He believed that now that they had arrived they were the authority.

Alex looked towards the Dakota and then pointed with an outstretched arm. "What help? Two men in another small plane? God, they'd make little difference. No, sir, we have to do what we have to do."

"Sir, I must warn you of the—"

"Quite frankly, I can't permit the consequences you've warned us of, but I do accept that we've been warned," Alex interjected and then turned to George and me. "Are you with us?" he asked.

"Of course." I said. I knew we had no alternative. Fassbinder was up to something. There was no sign of them. All the others including my father sided with Alex.

"Okay, we leave Jeff and the Superintendent. The Inspector can stay here if he so wishes. We make our way towards the Dakota but keep deep within the bush and trees, and spread out not presenting a single target with our trackers in front. Hopefully, we'll see them before they see us," Alex said.

We collected our weapons and moved deeper into the trees. What a motley and raddled band of men, I thought. We were dirty and unkempt, a band of six men, two of whom were in the early sixties. I was frightened and apprehensive but had to agree that this was our only option. We had no fight with the rest of Fassbinder's crew, only him. Did his men know this? Okay, there was the matter of poaching and the shooting, but I believed that if we caught Fassbinder, the others would realise that it would be pointless to continue the fight.

The trackers moved well-ahead of us and it was agreed that if they saw anything suspicious they would use a specific birdcall to warn us.

The bush was dense and it was hot. I started to perspire as I moved through the bush, careful not to tread on sticks or branches. To my left and right, I had my brother and father next to me but they were so far away that I would only occasionally catch a glimpse of them through the branches and leaves. My Steyr already had a cartridge in the breech. The safety was off and my finger lay against the side of the trigger guard.

There was a crashing sound as something moved in the bush. I dropped to the ground. Just yards from me, a waterbuck broke though branches and flashed past, it seeming not to notice me. It took a while before I'd recollected my composure. The animal had given me a fright.

As I rose to my feet, I heard a distinct warble. The bird sound we'd agreed upon with the trackers. Slowly I returned to my prone position. A silence seemed to have descended on the bush. I squeezed my eyes shut for a second to get rid of the perspiration that threatened to blur my vision. I'd made up my mind. If I saw anything that remotely looked like the enemy, I'd shoot first. By the time we would see each other the range would probably be down to a few dozen yards and it was difficult to miss at that distance. The thought was terrifying.

The loud staccato of an automatic weapon rent the silence. This was followed by a scream. There followed the shrill cry of birds as they took off from the tress in alarm. I thought this had to be about fifty yards away. I remained motionless.

"Phsst." I swung round. It was George crawling towards me.

Once he was alongside me, he whispered fiercely: "I wish I knew what the fuck going on."

I shared his sentiments entirely. The scheme we had devised to take on the enemy no longer seemed such a good idea. We and the enemy stumbling towards each other till we confronted one another in the bush, it then coming down to who could shoot first.

I felt a slight coolness on my face. A breeze had sprung up. I looked up. It was more than a breeze. Up above, the top of the trees swayed slightly in the breeze.

"Everybody move back," I heard Alex shout. He repeated this a few times.

I retraced my steps but still keeping a sharp lookout around me.

A while later we had all returned to the where our injured lay.

"That wasn't a good idea," Alex said.

"Who shot whom?" I asked.

"I saw movement ahead of me and let off a short burst," Mutt said. "It seems I hit somebody. Of course, the way we went about this it could so easily have been one of you."

"Come on, people, we need a better plan," Alex said, his impatience evident.

The strength of the wind had increased considerably, it beginning to pick up dust from the dried mud plain and creating a haze, the sun poking through as a bright orange ball. This was unusual. The wind usually makes its appearance in the afternoon in the desert and invariably blowing from the northeast, the direction we would have to take-off in.

A sudden flash of inspiration hit me like a jolt. The wind. That was the answer. Excitedly I turned to Alex.

"Alex, we've got to flush them out into the open. We've got to set fire to the bush. The wind is blowing away from us."

"God, that's crazy. We'd all die. There're no firebreaks here. The aircraft will go up in flames," he replied, looking at me as if I'd gone crazy.

"No, they won't. They're parked in a clearing.Tt's free of anything that could burn. A few blades of grass we surely can manage to douse. Fassbinder and his crowd would have no choice but to run for the open ground and they'd have to be damned quick about it. A fire here would

362

take hold like wildfire. It's winter. The place is a tinderbox. This is the only open ground. If they wanted to make it safely to the water they'd still have to cross here."

The Inspector was aghast. "You can't set the swamp alight," he shouted.

"It would burn itself out once it got to the edge of the swamp. That's the way the wind is blowing," I said.

The police officer seemed dubious but I saw that he'd caught on to what I was saying.

"God, what am I letting myself in for? But it seems we've no choice. We've got to get these two chaps to hospital. All right, do it." I told the trackers what to do. Their faces broke out into wide grins. That had to be a good sign, I thought. They wouldn't be happy about it if they thought we could burn the aircraft or ourselves.

Soon, the wind pulled smoke from the bush directly in front of us. This was quickly followed by a loud crackling and the first signs of yellow flame as the fire took hold in a number of places, the flames soon higher than the bush. Driven by the wind, the fire rushed from our position at a seemingly inordinate pace and for a moment I reflected on the poor animals that could be caught in this inferno.

It was evident that any who intended on escaping the flames would have to make for open ground. A minute or two later the first of Fassbinder's men hurriedly emerged from the bush as predicted.

"Don't shoot. Wait until they're all in the open," Alex said

By now, the raging fire had taken on the sound of a dull roar interspersed with incessant crackling. Clouds of dark grey smoke billowed upwards, driven off by the wind.

"Open fire, but just over their heads," Alex said.

Immediately there followed a volley of shots. Fassbinder's men were no more than 100–150 yards from us. They dropped to the ground at the first sound of gunfire, immediately starting to return fire.

We were concealed, or at least to a degree. They weren't.

"Return fire, shoot to kill," Alex shouted, rising to his knees and opening up with his rifle. Mutt's machine-pistol began to bark, stitching a line of sand geysers in the ground. Screams broke out amongst the poachers. We'd obviously found a few targets.

Suddenly a figure rose, his hands in the air followed by one other.

"Stop firing," Alex ordered.

The fire had moved so rapidly that it was almost on the shores of the swamp, leaving behind a blackened wasteland which smouldered with the odd fire burning and smoke spiralling upwards to be wiped away by the wind.

It seemed that they had all surrendered. There were fewer than I thought, but then I saw those lying on the ground. We had our weapons trained on them as we approached in a line abreast.

Some of the thin grass on the mud plain had started to burn. I sent our trackers out with green branches to beat out the fires lest they got to the aircraft.

The Inspector stepped forward, his Lee Enfield rifle in his hand and at the ready, pointed at the men.

"You're all under arrest for murder and poaching. Don't move. Keep your hands in the air. We'll not hesitate to shoot," he loudly said but with a quiver in his voice.

Fassbinder, the Waffen-SS poacher, and another stood together, conversing in German.

"Bleibt still!" I shouted. *No talking!* I was sure that they were concocting some plan and pointed my rifle menacingly at them, hoping I looked ruthless.

While we kept our rifles and automatics trained on them Mutt approached and relieved them of their weapons, always staying out of the line of fire. These he piled in front of us. automatics, rifles, a machine pistol and shotguns.

Alex and Ginger had gone to see to those who lay on the ground where they'd been shot. They soon returned.

"There are three dead. The last one died a minute ago from blood loss. There was nothing we could do. One seems to be their pilot," he said.

"You won't fly our aircraft out. Both pilots are dead," Fassbinder said.

We all knew that the Superintendent was in a bad way as he had lost what I thought to be a copious amount of blood. He was weak, slipping in and out of consciousness.

"Inspector, the first thing we need to do is get the Superintendent to hospital," I said, realising that the nearest hospital was in Gaberones. We only had three hours of daylight left. "Take the Rapide. It's faster than your Cub."

"I can't leave these men as prisoners in your care," he retorted, but it was clear he faced a quandary: his commanding officer's need for medical assistance was still foremost in his mind.

"Here's an alternative," Ginger piped up. "Why don't we load the whole damn lot of us into the Dakota and Matthias can fly it to Gaberones? We can collect the other aircraft later."

"Out of the question. That's too dangerous," he said. I wondered whether he was hesitant about giving command of the large aircraft to me.

He then spoke again. "Okay, you stay here for the night and guard these men. I'll fly out in the Rapide and return tomorrow. I'll take both wounded with me." He lifted a finger in warning. "Just make damn sure nothing happens." It was only for the Superintendent's sake that he was doing this and clear that he had agreed to this against his own better judgement.

We soon had cleared the strip. The Superintendent and Jeff were loaded into the Rapide, lying on the floor as we had removed a set of rear seats. After familiarising the Inspector with the aircraft controls, he started up the engines and soon after they were airborne.

We had two sets of handcuffs which we reserved for Fassbinder and the Waffen-SS officer. They refused the handcuffs and finally we had to force these on them, Fassbinder persuaded to do so after Mutt whacked him on the head with his automatic's barrel, a thin trickle of blood appearing from beneath his hairline.

"You swine. You'll regret this," Fassbinder said in near perfect English, a hateful snarl on his face. Mutt raised his pistol as if to strike the man again.

"Stop that," Alex screamed at Mutt. "Get away from the men. Matthias, you do the other man."

In disgust, Mutt threw the cuffs to me. I quickly handcuffed the Nazi officer. We constantly had to have guns trained on the other prisoners. We had no means of securing them.

Alex sent Otto Ewald and Mutt to the poacher's camp to search through the aircraft for whatever food and drink they could find. Our trackers searched the opposite side of the mud plain for firewood. The two returned from the aircraft with very little. It was obvious that those who'd arrived in the aircraft had not planned on staying for long, but still we found a bottle of brandy and whiskey and a few bottles of soda water, albeit all warm. There was also a large packet of biscuits, cookies, coffee and sugar, and a few cans of Vienna sausages.

An argument broke out between Mutt and Alex. I had no idea what it was about. The exchange was in Hebrew.

Ginger came across to me. "They arguing because Mutt is insisting they be handcuffed with their hands behind them for the night as they are now. They're asking to have their wrists manacled in front." He chuckled, "How did Fassbinder put it? 'How do I piss?' is what I think he said. I need not tell you what Mutt's reply was. God, these Nazi-hunters, you don't want to get on the wrong side of them. My father says that we should not be inhumane. What a fuckin' laugh," he said.

I watched. It seemed Mutt finally relented. The two men were re-cuffed, their hands in front.

Nobody enjoyed the supper. The coffee was fair although without milk. The whiskey with warm. Soda, I did without. The biscuits were awful.

Fassbinder started to complain about the fare.

"Shut the fuck up. Technically speaking you already have been sentenced to death. Your hanging is a mere formality," Mutt shouted.

Again, Alex had to tell the Israeli to shut up.

We were arranged in shifts to guard the prisoners. Mutt, Alex, and Ginger would take the first shift while Otto Ewald, my father, and I would take the second.

The current situation did nothing to improve our spirits. All were in a foul mood and most were utterly exhausted, none having slept well for a number of days. They had but one desire and that was to go home.

I had curled up alongside the fire and by nine I was fast asleep with the Steyr alongside me.

CHAPTER THIRTY-FIVE

The pain woke me. It was excruciating. It was as if somebody was trying to bore a steel rod into my temple. Also, I couldn't breathe. I tried to move my head from side to side but couldn't. It was as if it was clamped in a vice.

Suddenly my mouth was free. It was with immense relief that I sucked air into my lungs.

If you don't want to die right now, be still and absolutely quiet," a voice hissed in my ear. Fear nearly paralysed me. I knew the voice, it was Fassbinder. He had an automatic against my temple. That's what had been hurting me.

I lay still, trying to let my eyes roam over the camp. The fire still burned but it was low. I saw four local blacks in loincloths standing within the circle of the firelight, they with machetes and spears in their hands. A feeling of fear and dismay jolted through me when I saw a spear protruding from Mutt's chest. He lay on his side, his arms akimbo and the white of his still open eyes reflected in the fire light. He appeared to be dead. Ginger's head lay at a grotesque angle, the ground round his neck soaked with blood. Alex also lay sprawled on his back, not moving, but I could see no sign of injury. Like myself, my father, my brother and Otto Ewald were awake, each with one of Fassbinder's men standing over them with a weapon.

"If you're looking for your trackers, don't. They're dead. They're lying beyond the fire in the dark," Fassbinder said matter-of-factly, his voice a soft rasp in his throat and a cruel grin on his face. "Get up. Don't try anything stupid," he added. Only then did I see that he was still handcuffed, the automatic held in a two-handed grip. Restricted as he was, it must have been some feat to keep the automatic against my temple and nearly suffocate me.

A feeling of sadness, dismay, and fear numbed my senses. My friends were dead and I was sure we'd all be next.

One of Fassbinder' trackers added wood to the fire, which soon caught, the area around the fire lighting up, enabling me to see properly what was going on. Also, I saw the first signs of the approaching dawn, the

367

sky above the canopies of the trees on the east already slightly tinged with grey.

Alex groaned. With relief, I realised that he was still alive. He propped himself up on an elbow and with a grimace opened his eyes. I saw the expression of profound shock and disbelief that crossed his face as he realised what had happened.

Fassbinder had noticed the movement and swung the automatic to point at Alex. "Stay where you are and don't move," he barked.

Fassbinder sat down on the sand to face me. "You are going to fly us out of here in the Dakota," he said and then waited a few seconds to let the implications of what he just said sink in. "At first light, I'm going to load you and those who are still alive into the aircraft and we'll leave before any others can arrive. Are you familiar with the Dakota?" he asked.

"No."

"But it's like any other large aircraft, isn't it?" he asked, but I did not miss the flicker of concern which crossed his face.

"Yes, I suppose it is," I replied. I knew that whatever I said wouldn't matter. He had no one else who could pilot the plane. To resist at this stage would be futile. I also dismissed the thought of sitting in a Dakota with Otto Ewald at the controls. In relation to anything else he'd flown before, the DC-3 was a complex piece of machinery, radial engines, variable pitch props, and retractable undercarriage. It was very different from the Dragon Rapide.

We were all herded towards the Dakota, but another hour was lost as Fassbinder and one of his men attempted to remove a part his handcuffs. They proved that firing a bullet at the steel flexible joint of the cuffs was no more than a myth. After a few shots, the handcuffs were still intact and Fassbinder's hand peppered with lead splinters. It took the best part of half an hour of hammering before these parted, but he found himself with a cuff on each wrist.

With all the aircraft on the mud plain, it gave the impression of a small country airfield. The Cub and Beechcraft were pushed to one side and we were all bundled into the Dakota. Most of the interior was given over to cargo space, leaving only seats for eight which faced forward, these diagonally across the fuselage in rows of two. The trackers had manhandled the aircraft into position and it now faced down the strip.

368

My father, Alex, and Otto Ewald were made to sit in the forward seats, belted-in with instructions not to attempt to loosen their safety belts and to keep their hands on the armrests where they could be seen. Behind them sat Fassbinder's men, their weapons ever ready. Two of them stood with the machine-pistols that previously belonged to the Israelis clasped in their hands. One of them was my Waffen-SS officer, the poacher.

With Fassbinder behind me and an automatic trained on my back, I stepped through the bulkhead door into the cockpit and slid into the left hand-seat, he taking the seat next to me.

I looked through the cockpit screen down the length of the strip. The first signs of the actual sun were now visible, shafts of orange light streaking near horizontal across the top of the trees. As is usual in the morning, there was no wind. The strip was not particularly long and the DC-3 would require most of it to build up sufficient airspeed to get airborne but I foresaw no problem. Fassbinder was agitated and impatient and obviously concerned by the early return of the BSAP with reinforcements. He forced me to dispense with an exterior pre-flight check, which I thought foolhardy considering the fact that the aircraft already displayed a number of bullet holes. Fortunately, I had seen no fuel or oil leaks and assumed that nothing vital had been hit.

I had no doubt that my fate and that of my family and friends was a foregone conclusion. Fassbinder would kill us. Why he had not already done so was a mystery. Maybe he thought that had he killed them, I may have been uncooperative, choosing to rather die with them than help him escape.

I went through the cockpit check, my thoughts, and actions mechanical, one part of my brain desperately trying to find a way out of this predicament. I believed it imperative that I do something before we left Bechuanaland, but what?

With the pre-flight check complete, it was time to start the engines. I worked the port engine throttle-lever, lifted the switch guard, and toggled the three-way switch to start the left engine. With a loud whine the port propeller started to spin, the exhaust belched a cloud of blue smoke and the engine took and settled down to a steady roar. Similarly, I started the starboard engine. The aircraft's cockpit layout was standard and I easily familiarised myself with the essential controls. When I made to switch on the radios, Fassbinder stopped me. We were to maintain radio silence.

Nobody would have any idea of this flight and its destination. I allowed the engines to warm up and then went through the run-up to check the magnetos. The port engine ran slightly rough. I thought maybe it had a slight oil build-up on the spark plugs and assumed this would clear once full power was applied.

I realised my only hope was to crash the plane, but to do so without it seeming to have been done purposely would be difficult.

I turned to Fassbinder. "Your port engine is not happy, it's somewhat rough," I said.

"I know, the pilot had mentioned this to me but said it was okay. It shouldn't be a problem. It'll settle down as it has always done before," he replied.

"Well, if it decides to cough on take-off, we may not clear the trees at the end of the strip. I thought I'd just let you know," I retorted.

"Don't get flippant. Just fly the plane. Do anything wrong and your dead," he said. God, I hoped we would survive what I had in mind. The moment of reckoning approached for all of us. I prayed that my family and friends had the common sense to have strapped themselves into their seats well. I had strapped myself in without a thought through sheer habit after years of flying. Fassbinder had not done so, probably to allow himself some movement if I attempted to do anything truly stupid. Did he really think I would attempt to overpower him with all the guns around?

With the brakes on, I advanced the throttles, the snarl of the engines rising to a thunderous crescendo, the aircraft beginning to vibrate and strain. I released the brakes and the plane surged ahead. I pushed the yoke forward, rapidly bringing up the tail. The aircraft threatened to yaw to the left, which I corrected with the rudder pedals. The end of the strip approached, she was ready to fly but with the slight down-trim I had selected as opposed to the normal take-off trim, she wasn't going to lift without assistance from me, her main gear remaining firmly on the ground. To get her unstuck, I would have to purposely fly her off the deck with more than the usual back-pressure on the stick.

"Fly you bitch," I said aloud, more for Fassbinder's benefit than my own. I saw the first sign of concern on his face as the trees began to loom ahead. He must have realised he wasn't strapped in and began to fumble with his safety belt. The moment his eyes were off me, I yanked the starboard engines mixture control right back and pulled back on the stick. By this time, we had more than the necessary flying speed. The engine spluttered and died, starved of fuel and windmilling in the slipstream. I also yanked back the pitch to feather the propeller to stop the drag imposed by the stopped engine.

"Fuckin' hell! Dead engine," I screamed more for effect than anything else.

We had just managed to clear the trees, the crowns of which were surely nearly touching the aircraft's belly.

I saw Fassbinder lean back and grip the seat, the automatic now in his lap, his eyes wide and his face pale, all in anticipation of a crash that he must have thought inevitable. He did not seem to realise that this engine failure was self-induced. I took this all in within the space of a split second.

I neutralised the yoke and stomped my foot on the left rudder pedal to stop the aircraft yawing into the dead engine. We had more than the necessary flying speed. She still flew beautifully, quite capable of climbing if necessary. I pulled up the undercarriage but kept the aircraft just above the trees. It would seem to any other that she battled to maintain altitude and was barely airborne. This wasn't lost on Fassbinder. He was still staring ahead, frozen in his seat.

"Shit," I screamed and at the same time allowed the plane to sink and touch the top of the trees. I switched off the magnetos, the fuel cocks, and the master switches. She grazed the top branches, the bottom arc of her one spinning propeller spewing shredded foliage as it razed through the tree canopies. She slowly settled, flying into the top branches, they level with the cockpit. The slapping of the branches against the fuselage reached a crescendo. She began to buck and then crashed into larger branches, but her forward momentum had hardly decreased. Thereafter, everything was a blur accompanied by a cacophony of sound, explosive bangs, crashes and thumps. I threw my arms up to protect myself and then ducked down below the instrumental panel as I saw a particularly large tree loom ahead. I was flung violently forward in the seat restrained only by the safety harness around my waist and over my shoulders. I thought every bone in my body was breaking. I then blacked out.

*

I opened my eyes. Pieces of thin broken tree branches complete with green leaves filled the cockpit area. The aircraft's nose pointed steeply downwards at an angle. The Plexiglas windscreen had disappeared, there now being open gaping holes to the outside. My harness retained me. My shoulders were on fire where the straps had bit into them.

I turned to look at Fassbinder but could not see him. A figure had hurtled through the open bulkhead door and collided with the instrument panel and throttle pedestal blocking my sideways view. There was blood everywhere. The body was in a fœtal position. I tried to push it away but could not. I moved my limbs to see if anything was broken. They all seemed to work. Blood dripped from my forehead where it had hit the yoke. The floor under my left foot had buckled inwards, shoving my leg upwards and jamming my foot against the underside of the panel. I unsnapped the harness and extracted myself, virtually having to stand on the panel. I was then able to see Fassbinder.

It was clear that he had never managed to fasten his safety belt. He'd been flung forward against the Plexiglas and now hung half outside the windscreen panel, his torso jammed up against the small opening which previously had held the windscreen pane, his girth not allowing him to slip through. He had to be dead. Nobody could have survived that.

I started to panic. What had happened to the others? Clambering upwards, I managed to squeeze through the bulkhead door. The fuselage had broken in half, the tail section separated from the forward section. This had broken behind the wing root. The four in the forward seats, my father, brother, Alex, and Otto Ewald, were still sat lying chest-down on their knees, held by their safety belts. Otto Ewald was conscious. He too had a long gash on his forehead which streamed blood. My next thought was Fassbinder's men. Of those that had stood, one had gone through the bulkhead door and the other had collided with the bulkhead edge. Both were dead, I did not need a second glance to verify that. Two of the men had been flung from their seats, sailing over the heads of the forward passengers and had collided with the bulkhead. They too had died instantaneously. Two others were still seated, both concussed and bleeding. One of them was the Waffen-SS officer.

The first to come round was my father.

"Dear God, are we still alive," he whispered in German.

"Dad, you're alive. Just try to get out of the seat and help me with the others. Can you do that? Are you hurt?" I asked with my heart in my mouth.

"I'm all right."

My brother was already groaning and fumbling to loosen the belt. It snapped open and he fell forward against the body plastered against the bulkhead.

"George, are you okay?"

He groaned again. When he saw the blood on his hands and body from the dead man in front of him, he issued a loud expletive and hurled himself away.

"I think I'll live."

Alex was already out of his seat as was Otto Ewald. Except for a few cuts and gashes they seemed okay. The two remaining associates of Fassbinder had also come round, one of whom was scrabbling for his weapon. Otto Ewald grabbed him by the hair and then socked him in the face with fist the size of a boar's hog. The man collapsed as if pole-axed.

"George, Alex, get hold of all the weapons, especially those machine-pistols," I shouted.

"Fassbinder?" my father asked.

I shook my head.

"Dank Gott," he said. "Otto warned us that you were going to crash the plane," he added.

I turned to Otto Ewald.

"How did you know?" I asked.

He grinned. I saw that his lip was badly split. "I realised that you were holding the plane on the ground well after when she should've been flying. You had to be up to something. They were going to shoot us. Did you know?" he said licking at the blood that flowed from his lip.

My father snorted, "Christ Otto, tell us something we don't know."

It was a tricky business exiting the plane. We had to help each other. The thorns tore at us, scratching our arms and faces and tearing our clothes.

Otto Ewald unceremoniously pushed the two prisoners from the aircraft, they falling twelve to fifteen feet through the branches to the ground where they collapsed.

We were no more than a mile or so from the airstrip. After a few minutes to recover from the exertions of exiting the crashed plane we started the slow trek back to the airfield. The two prisoners led the way followed by Otto Ewald and Alex, each armed with an automatic pistol. We moved slowly and often rested. All complained but were glad to be alive. The fight had gone from the prisoners, they realizing that it was over.

We broke out into the open at the end of the strip and as we approached the other aircraft. We saw a few of Fassbinder's poachers searching through everything that had been left behind. Otto Ewald opened fire, the poachers scattering and running hell for leather into the bush.

Everybody needed water. We found a few bottles from which we all thirstily drank and then collapsed on the ground next to the still-smouldering campfire. The only thing to do was await the return of the Chief Inspector.

CHAPTER THIRTY-SIX

It was past midday when we heard the approach of an aircraft. This increased and then, with a roar, a DC-3 passed overhead, the roundels of the Royal Air Force clearly visible.

The aircraft landed and disgorged a squad of BSAP police and a few ranking officers including the Chief Inspector who walked towards me.

"Bloody hell. What's happened here? Where's the Dakota? Is that it lying in the bush?" he demanded."Sit down. Fassbinder is dead."

"Dead? What the hell happened?"

"It's a long story. They overpowered us and tried to fly us out. We crashed the plane a mile from here. Some died. Some of them were our own," I said.

We spent an hour under the trees being questioned. Meanwhile, a detachment of black BSAP were sent out to find Fassbinder's trackers, if they could be found. Most of the remainder led by Alex returned to the crashed aircraft to recover the dead. The two prisoners were handcuffed. First-aid kits were collected from the aircraft and rudimentary first-aid was applied to those that required it.

The Chief Inspector and I continued talking. I learnt that the Dakota had been borrowed together with some of the police force from the Southern Rhodesian Air Force and that this was the reason for their late return. Jeff was in hospital under police guard but was out of danger, as was the Superintendent.

"Mr Aschenborn, of course you realise that you're under arrest," he said.

I nodded.

"But don't be too concerned. Fassbinder ... well, you should know that isn't the name he usually went by. We knew him as Behrens and we've been after him for a while for numerous crimes, all related to poaching and fraud. Of course, in Rwanda, he was safe. We have no jurisdiction there. The man had amassed a fortune, most of this from illegal activities. So, you and your friends should soon be released. No mention will be made that you pursued a Nazi war criminal. I mean what's the point, the man's dead."

We flew a week later into Eros Airport in Windhoek in the Beechcraft and the De Havilland Dragon Rapide. The BSAP had never incarcerated us and they assisted us with a change of clothing and medical care, putting us up in a decent hotel. I heard from the Chief Inspector that the DC-3 had returned to the delta and collected the cache of ivory. They destroyed Fassbinder's camp and the boma, leaving no trace of it.

Heidi was overjoyed at my safe return. Ginger's death dampened any attempt at jubilation.

My father had arranged a sumptuous dinner for the whole family and we retired to the sitting room while Heidi and Ruth were busy with whatever women do after dinner. Cognacs were poured and the cigars selected from the humidor. It was only my father, George, Otto Ewald, and I.

"Okay, father. Now that we have all emerged safely from a deathly experience and before we have another re-occurrence, I believe that being the only one who does not know, I should be told of the so-called swimming pool incident. I believe I've earned the right to know. Otto Ewald made mention of it on the plane back from Gaberones and expressed surprise that I did not know," I said.

There were roars of laughter all round.

My father blew smoke at the ceiling. "Do you think we should tell him?" he asked, looking at Otto Ewald.

"Tell him, as long as he is sworn to secrecy. Wait, let me tell him," Otto Ewald replied, taking a generous swallow of his snifter.

My father nodded.

"As you know, in the old days all the water used in Windhoek was obtained from hot springs, the water near-boiling. When you wished to bathe, you simply opened the cold-water tap. The water was so hot that at times you were forced to allow it to cool down before entering.

"Well, the municipality built a near-Olympic-sized swimming pool which was filled every few weeks from the springs. The swimming pool and the springs were near the Lüderitz and Garten streets, the swimming pool just below the water works."

I said I knew where that was.

"In the winter, what with morning temperatures near, or sometimes below, freezing the swimming was closed and the pool left empty."

I looked at my brother. His expression was blank. He drew on his cigar.

"Your brother, in his wisdom, had come to the conclusion that it was wrong to close the swimming pool. Whenever it was filled in summer all had to wait a few days before they could enter. The water was simply too hot and it first had to cool down. Obviously, the same would've applied in the winter. So, why not fill it? Unfortunately, their requests to your father's good friend Grabouw, the then illustrious Chief Engineer, fell on deaf ears. The boys decided on some unilateral action."

The three men chuckled. Otto Ewald then continued.

"Your brother arrived one afternoon in the engineering works with an enormous block of hard wood, about a foot in height and width and double that in length. I remember that the boys could hardly carry it. There followed a truly complex explanation of what they wanted and why. It had something to do with some school project. Anyway, I still remember that your brother produced a rather impressive diagram of what he required, complete with measurements down to fractions of an inch."

My father looked at George. "You know, you were a dubious little shit. Did you know that?" he said somewhat jokingly.

George didn't comment.

"Well, in the old days there was a lot emphasis on the fact that he was the boss's son, if you know what I mean, so I immediately got an apprentice fitter and turner onto the job. This massive piece of wood was inserted in a lathe and an exact replica of what the diagram showed was produced."

He took another swallow of cognac and made himself more comfortable.

"The swimming pool was built on a slope. To empty it they merely opened a gate valve and the water poured out into the drainage system on the down-slope side. The bottom of the pool had a further recess in the floor of about two-by-three feet and a foot deep where the pool water entered the outlet pipe. As you can expect, the outside gate valve on the slope was chained and locked and to break it would have constituted a criminal offence."

My father guffawed. "Otto," he said, "you've put that so elegantly, criminal offence, but let me not interrupt you."

"Of course, it was winter, the pool was empty and the gate valve was chained and locked but left open." he snickered. "Your ingenious brother then proceeded to ram this specially engineered wooden plug into the outlet pipe using a four pound hammer. Once this was done, he proceeded to the water works—"

"Fuck proceeded. He broke into the bloody place," my father interrupted.

"Never mind. Anyway, he got into the works, opened valves, and dug a trench diverting some of the hot spring down the slope and voilà … into the swimming pool. By the next day, the pool was near-full and all the boys had to do was let it cool down. Of course, word spread and days later, every child in town was having a winter swim. It took a few days before the local municipality realised what was going on and stopped their fun. You must not forget, your father was an honorary member of the town council."

A glance at my brother told me nothing. His expression was impassive.

"You realise that the wooden plug, actually the terminology then in use was 'the fuckin' cork', was submerged in fifteen feet of water. The gate valve was open but, to release the water, the 'fuckin' cork' had to be removed. So what did they do? They hired a diver at some horrendous expense. His assessment of the situation was soon forthcoming."

Otto Ewald was no longer able to carry on and collapsed in laughter, the tears streaming down his face. My brother's stone-faced expression began to crack, the slightest of smiles on his face.

"Come, come, Otto. It wasn't funny," my father said, but I saw that he too was having difficulty in containing his laughter.

Otto Ewald recollected himself. "Matthias, by now the dilemma had reached the council and all knew that it was Aschenborn's eldest who'd rammed the 'fuckin cork' into the outlet. The diver's assessment was a shock. It was not humanly possible to remove the plug because the wood had swelled. To cut a long story short, after long debate in the council in which your father tried to say as little as possible, the chief engineer decided that the only way to remove the plug was to dynamite it." He turned to my father, "Johannes, I think you should take it from here."

My father's expression took on a solemn look.

"Well, this was rapidly developing into a crisis. At the mention of dynamite, as you can well imagine, I was horrified. The diver was to drill a one-inch or one-and-a-half inch hole into the plug, this under water, mind, insert a stick of dynamite with a long fuse leading out of the water. I objected but was ignored. By now, the magnitude of the problem had intensified to such a degree that most of the council was present when the plug was to be destroyed, merely out of curiosity. There was much debate as to how much damage the dynamite might create. Those idiots expected a low rumble under the water with some disturbance on the surface. Fortunately, I'd persuaded my colleagues to put a fair distance between them and the pool."

Otto Ewald broke down in hysterical laughter again and then still giggling said, "You should have seen that bunch of arseholes in their three-piece suits, pocket watch chains, and homburgs standing defiantly in a row, watching the proceedings." He laughed again.

My father continued, "The fuse was lit. Christ. We didn't know that the idiot, Grabouw, our illustrious city engineer, had decided to increase the charge. He still denies it, maybe he'll admit to it on his deathbed. Anyway, the explosion was nothing short of truly spectacular. You'd swear that a U-boat had been depth-charged in the pool. The total contents of the pool seemed to shoot a hundred feet or more into the air." My father started laughing. "The council was literally overwhelmed, they were swamped by hundreds of gallons of water and knocked to the ground, yours truly included. We were a ragged, drenched mob when we picked ourselves up."

By now, we were all laughing, tears streaming down our faces. Even George now laughed. Otto Ewald sat on the carpet doubled-up in laughter.

"The atmosphere of absolute shock was indescribable. Grabouw got such fright he was catatonic. The dramatic results of his plan were well beyond his wildest expectations. You've never seen a swimming pool empty so fast in your life. There was a six-foot crater in the bottom, the sides were cracked. Christ! It was a fuckin' disaster and, believe it or not, my bloody son was the cause of it." My father could no longer contain himself and merely whimpered, he so weak from laughter. "They'll never forget him," he managed to say softly.

I took a while before we could speak again.

"That's not all," my father said. "After the mayor got up he sort of sidled over to me, I still can hear the squelch of his shoes and his drenched look, you just cannot imagine what he looked like. Normally, he was such a pompous ass, but now he was just a caricature. He looked at me and said, 'Your son, wasn't it? I think we need to talk'"

Again there followed howls of laughter.

"Needless to say, the council meeting that followed a few days later was truly interesting and spirited. It was unanimously agreed that Grabouw didn't have a clue when it came to the power of dynamite. Then followed compensation and conditions, these all directed at me. The compensation wasn't the worst. We arrived at an amicable figure, the municipality absorbing most of the cost.

"The conditions were another matter. In truth, George was banned from the district. I undertook to send him to school in Germany. I chose a naval academy in Kiel run by naval officers where the degree of discipline befitted that of a warship. Most of the cadets were sons from German Junker families, almost all with prefixes in front of their names. It was agreed that he would not return before his schooling was complete. In turn, the council undertook to hush things up to the best of their ability. George's name never really became public. You can now understand the secrecy. That wasn't easy. The bloody explosion had been heard all over town."

I looked at my brother. He smiled. My assessment of him had gained a notch or two.

Printed in Great Britain
by Amazon